Tangled Promises

PROMISED DESTINY
BOOK ONE

LYNN U. WATSON

Lynn U. Watson
Stepping through time
Stitching stories of faith

Scripture quotations are from the King James Version of the Bible.

Tangled Promises is a work of fiction. All incidents and dialogue, and all characters with the exception of some well-known historical figures, are products of the author's imagination and are not to be construed as real. Where real-life historical figures appear, the situations, incidents, and dialogues concerning those persons are entirely fictional and are not intended to depict actual events or to change the entirely fictional nature of the work. In all other respects, any resemblance to actual persons, living or dead, events, or locales is entirely coincidental.

Second Edition

ISBN: 978-1-7329281-4-5 (print)

ISBN: 978-1-7329281-3-8 (ebook)

Dedication

We will not hide them from their children, shewing to the generation to come the praises of the Lord, and his strength, and his wonderful works that he hath done. For he established a testimony in Jacob, and appointed a law in Israel, which he commanded our fathers, that they should make them known to their children: That the generation to come might know them, even the children which should be born; who should arise and declare them to their children… ~Psalm 78:4-6

Imagining this story and its sequels, I paused often to ponder family legacies, especially those of faith from my great-grandmother passed through the generations to my own grandchildren.

Mikah Beth

Eighteen years ago, you were the first to call me Gramma. This story's for you, Sweet Pea. Continue to boldly proclaim God's love and shout His praise wherever you go, and declare even to your children yet unborn what He has done.

The rich and poor meet together; the Lord is the maker of them all.
~Proverbs 2:22

German Word List

GERMAN NOUNS ARE ALWAYS CAPITALIZED

Apfel – apple

Backhaus – bakery (often with a coffee shop)

Bleigessen – a traditional New Year's game, involving dropping hot lead in water and interpreting the shape it changed into indicated the future.

Danube – 2nd longest river in Europe; it begins in southwest Germany

Danke – thank you

Dinkel – spelt

Dinkel schneiden – cut spelt

Doktor – doctor

Erntedank – Thanksgiving

Federbetten – feather bed

Frau – Missus / woman

Fraulein – Miss / young lady(ies)

Gasthaus – guest house, inn

Grossvater -- grandfather

Gut Apfelhof – fine Apple Home – community (Gut commonly used with the community's name – residents under the protection of the Gut Herr of their home village / town)

Gut Dinkellhof – fine Spelt home or community

Gut Herr – Nobleman of the Gut, Good Sir, or Good Lord

Gut Herrin – Nobelman's wife

Guten Morgen – good morning

Herr – Mister / Mr. / man

Herren – Misters / men

Ja – yes

Kartoffel – potato

Kartoffelsuppe mit Krabben – potato soup with crab

Kirschkuchen – cherry cake

Kind – child

Kinder – children

Lehrer – teacher

Mach schnell – hurry up

Mädchen – girl

Mamsell – servant who runs the Gut Herr's household

Medizin -- medicine

Meine junge Dame – my young lady

Meine Kind – my child

Meine Kinder – my children

Meine kleine Kinder – my little child / children

Mutter – mother

Mütter – mothers

Mutti – mom / mommy

Nein – no

Oma – grandma

Onkel – uncle

Opa – grandpa

Sehr gut – very good

Sohn – son

Streuselkuchen – crumble cake

Tante – aunt

Vater – father

Väter – fathers

Vati – dad / daddy

Wein – wine

Wiener Schnitzel – traditional meat dish

Zeitung – newspaper (Illinois Staats Zeitung – Illinois State Newspaper)

Zimf-Streuselkuchen – cinnamon crumble cake

Tangled Promises: The Two Families

REINHOLD FAMILY & STAFF

- Gut Herr Kraig Reinhold – Baron of Gut Apfelhof
- Gut Herrin Lydia Reinhold – Kraig's wife
- Clara Reinhold – oldest Reinhold daughter, twin to Curt
- Curt Reinhold – oldest Reinhold son, twin to Clara
- Hannah Reinhold – 17-year-old daughter
- Emmaline Reinhold – 13-year-old daughter
- Wilhelm Reinhold – 11-year-old-son
- Oma Dorthea Reinhold – Kraig's mother, the children's grandmother
- Tante Adeline – Lydia Reinhold's sister
- Onkel Martin – Adeline's husband
- Tante Caroline – Kraig Reinhold's great aunt, sister to Kraig's father
- Onkel Knut—Caroline's husband
- Mamsell Lotti
- Fritz – doorman
- Dora – cook

- Alice – Clara's personal maid
- Daniel Becker – carriage driver, Clara's true love
- Rosa Becker – seamstress, Daniel's mother
- Jost – coachman
- Hans – coachman
- Willy – coachman

WOLFF FAMILY

- Gut Herr Gerwig Wolff – Baron of Gut Dinkelhof
- Gut Herrin Margaret Wolff – Gerwig's wife
- Georg Wolff – son, courting Clara
- Megs Wolff Schmitz – daughter, living in America
- Gus Schmitz – Megs' husband
- Harold – a driver for the Wolff family

Note: Barons are the lowest of the nobility classes. A mayoral title. The community's Baron or Gut Herr often owned much land and was a businessman. The welfare of his resident's was his responsibility. Gut Apfelhof is a fictitious rural community. The Reinhold's treated their staff like family. There is often more familiarity between them and their servants than might be expected of nobility.

Gut Dinkelhof is also rural and fictitious, but the Wolff's do not have the same kind attitude as the Reinholds.

Chapter One

GUT APFELHOF, *Württemberg, Germany, Sunday, 21 August 1881*

VATI'S STRONG, warm hand clutched hers and anchored Clara to his side. Despite the tumbling kaleidoscope of butterflies creating an unpleasant stir in her tummy, she manufactured a smile for their thirty dinner guests.

"Family and friends, it is my pleasure to announce Georg Wolff, heir to Gut Dinkelhof, will court our daughter, Clara." Vati placed her hand in Georg's plump, sweaty palm.

Thunderous applause extinguished her dream and ignited Clara Reinhold's worst nightmare. A cacophony of congratulations echoed in her ears while the larger-than-life jumble of blurry faces spun around her. She covered one ear with her free hand, stifling the din. They wove their way through the room, handshakes and good wishes bolstering Georg's vainglory. Clara hoped her forced smile filtered her dismay and held back the acid burning to escape.

Georg bowed to the crowd. "Excuse us a moment, please." He waltzed Clara into an alcove behind a leather screen separating them from onlookers. He tipped her chin up and stared into her eyes. "You are mine now, my sweets." His smug tone betrayed Georg's one and only pleasing feature, his dimples.

The endearment infuriated her every time.

Georg tightened his grip, pulling her against his chest. She jerked back. A duo of Romeo y Julieta cigars poked from his vest pocket, a pungent reminder of her star-crossed love.

"Courting doesn't make me yours." She removed one tobacco stick from his pocket and twisted it slowly. "My Romeo promised to protect and rescue me from you, and he will."

Georg reached to take back his expensive Cuban cigar, but she flicked it, sending it flying over the screen.

"You humiliate me before our guests because of a servant's promise during a silly charades game ten years ago, a promise your lowly carriage driver cannot keep. Forget him. You're mine." As if his reprimand fixed it all, he raised her hand and planted a kiss on the back.

"I'll never be yours, Herr Wolff." Tears welled, stinging her eyes and blurring her vision, but she welcomed the unmistakable sight of her twin.

"Caught this sailing over the screen. I believe it belongs to you." Curt dangled the cigar just out of Georg's reach. "You ruined the day. As if Vati's announcement was not poison enough to send my sister reeling, I heard your added venom."

"If truth is poison, then so be it. She's mine."

Curt cut his eyes at Georg and shoved him away from Clara. Guests milled about them, murmuring and snickering. Strength and a moment's reprieve surrounded her when Curt led her out of the room. A trusted family servant awaited.

Drawing in a deep breath, Rosa crossed her hands over her mouth like a gate, holding back the thoughts obviously fighting to escape.

With a finger to his closed lips, Curt silenced her. "Take care of Clara, please. I will keep Vati distracted while you help her regain her composure."

Rosa rubbed Clara's back. "Let's take the back stairs to your room and freshen you up."

They reached Clara's room. When they entered, Rosa guided her to sit on the edge of her bed. She pressed a wet cloth to Clara's eyelids.

"Danke. The coolness of the cloth is soothing." Clara peered down at her rumpled attire. I would rather not return to the party. I don't care what Georg thinks, but Mutti and Vati will be displeased."

"Would you allow me to rearrange your hair? Smooth the wrinkles from your gown? This sapphire one is so becoming on you."

Clara nodded and moved to the seat by her mahogany dressing table. While Rosa tended to her needs, Clara lifted the small carved sunflower from the table. A treasured gift that Daniel, her Romeo, had created for her. She hoped caressing its smooth edges would relieve the knot in her chest, but tender thoughts of Daniel did little to soothe the melancholy in her heart today. Her and Daniel's dreams were crushed.

Rosa cradled Clara's cheeks between her palms. "I will talk to God about it tonight and ask Him to help you."

"You're too kind to me. There's no help this time." Clara forced one foot in front of the other and trudged from her room.

"Romans eight, twenty-eight," Rosa whispered after her.

Rosa imparted perfectly timed Bible verses as easily as taking her next breath—always worth paying attention to. Clara stepped back into the room and picked up her well-worn Bible from a shelf beside her bed. She traced the cover's familiar gold-embossed cross and intricate borders and opened to the passage.

"'And we know that all things work together for good to them that love God, to them who are called according to his purpose.'

"And His purpose for me? To be courted by Georg? Married to the Big Bad Wolff?" She swallowed hard, struggling to will deep disappointment into resignation. "I can always count on you, Rosa, when I need a friend. Thank you for whisking me away from the guests for a few minutes. And for drying my tears."

With a warm smile and a gentle hand, Rosa encouraged her. "Go and rejoin your family."

She dallied in the hallway leading from her bedroom to the grand staircase, a showcase for Mutti's paintings of special family moments. At the New Year's Ball, when she was thirteen years old. Georg had already taunted her with his unwanted suggestions. He had claimed her then as *my sweets*. A shiver crawled up her spine. She still shuddered at the memory of Georg's behavior toward her that night. Clara turned away and crept back into her nightmare, the tell-tale creaks and pops from the stairs giving away her approach.

Curt took her hand. Her brother's turquoise eyes looked sympathetically into hers. Many guests have gone home. Georg left the room and stomped off toward the pump house. Perfect spot for puffing up his bruised ego."

"The crowd has dwindled? Is dinner over? Did the guests leave because of me?"

"More likely, the vicious Wolff scared them away."

A giggle slipped from Clara's throat.

"Made you smile at least. Besides, only the dessert course remained to be served after Vati's announcement. Let's join Tante Adeline and Onkel Martin in the parlor."

Spicy scents wafted from the chrysanthemum bouquets in the foyer as the twins wandered toward the parlor.

Clara stopped Curt on their way. "But what about Vati? I ruined his proud moment. I fear he'll not forgive my unlady-like behavior tangling with his plans."

"He accompanied a few departing guests to their coaches."

"But he'll be back, and what punishment awaits me?"

"Worry about that later. Tante and Onkel are waiting for you."

Two servants and her Tante and Onkel remained when they entered the room.

Tante Adeline patted the empty seat next to hers on the soft white sofa. Clara accepted the vacant spot.

"Somehow God will work it out for good, Clara."

That verse again. Cocooned childlike against her Tante's side, her nerves stilled. The tender call of a single violin and the sweet aroma of Adeline's lavender perfume enveloped her.

"I'd love to be a cricket in the corner tomorrow morning. I'd cease my chirping long enough to hear the words when Curt speaks to your Vati about this arrangement. Curt will fight for you, Clara."

THE COCOON FILLED with soft melodies and lavender's aroma had seeped away. Hours had elapsed since the family's dinner guests left, and sleep eluded Clara. She stared at the half-moon shining through her double window, making lace shadows dance on the walls. An image of Daniel driving the carriage to a spot on the lawn, of his arriving to escort her into their happy future, danced before her. The handsome man's expression was filled with love for her. A love she freely returned—a preposterous dream.

"God, I love You. Are You out there somewhere beyond the moonlit sky? Tell me, please, what Your purpose is in this and how it will work out for my good. I love my family and Gut Apfelhof, but the expectations stifle me. You know I detest this arrangement with Georg. Fill my mind with Your thoughts. Make a way for Daniel and me to share our love."

A gentle knock. "May we come in?" Hannah's soft words greeted Clara through the keyhole. "We brought chamomile tea and lemon drops."

"Please?" Emmaline's worried voice joined Hannah's.

The welcome response to her whispered prayer lightened her throbbing pulse. Clara opened the door for her younger sisters. Brigitte, the family's salt and pepper schnauzer, bolted through the doorway. Clara averted disaster by snatching the tray from seventeen-year-old Hannah's trembling hands.

The candle thirteen-year-old Emmaline carried illuminated the terror etched on the sisters' faces.

"Did you two encounter a ghastly monster? Please. No more bad news."

Hannah checked behind them. "Nein, no monsters, but we have questions."

"Are you leaving us, Clara?" Emmaline's words quivered along with her limbs.

"What does Vati's announcement mean, anyway?" Hannah twisted her fingers this way and that.

"Life will be so different at Gut Apfelhof without you." Emmaline began sobbing.

"Do you mind setting the candle on the tray? All the shaking your body is doing frightens me."

"Goodness, I should have thought about the danger." Emmaline placed the candle safely on the tray.

"We don't care for Georg either." Hannah curled her lips and shook her head.

Clara set the tray on a side table and poured each of them a cup of tea. She smoothed the bedcovers. "Come on up here with me."

Sitting on the bed, crossed-legged and in their nightgowns, Brigitte squirmed between them. "I've always loved our times together like this, especially reading stories to you both when you were little Mädchen. I hate why you're here now."

She sipped her tea and rolled a lemon drop on her tongue, then reached to rub the dog's head. "We're courting. I'm not leaving you now. Not for a long time. Not with Georg if I can convince Vati."

Hannah and Emmaline each released a dramatic sigh of relief. The schnauzer arffed her gratefulness, too.

"Georg will escort me to parties and special events. He'll call on me at home."

Hannah gasped. "That's awful news. He stinks of those horrid cigars. We'll all be pinching our noses when he's around. Probably for a day or two after he leaves." The younger girls covered their mouths, stifling their laughter.

Except it wasn't funny at all. Clara closed her eyes and shook her head. Fears clawed at her heart. She'd never desire to be alone in life, but she would choose it over the agony of marriage to the Wolff.

Emmaline broke the silence. "We could ask Daniel to spirit you away to a castle in the forest—an ideal hiding place."

Heat rose in Clara's cheeks. "Emmaline, always dreaming and planning. I'd do anything to be with Daniel. I'm enticed by your schemes, but I'd miss you both. Besides, leaving alone with Daniel is improper. He's our carriage driver—a servant. The rules are important to Vati. What punishment when we are caught?" Clara's raised hands dropped lifelessly to her lap. "Your plan sounds perfectly wonderful, but I put the kibosh on it."

"These rules!" Emmaline forced her hands to her hips. "Then why not a plot to banish the snobbish noble expectations? Society ladies in France are choosing their own husbands now. They stand up to convention. They're attending college and working in important positions, like Oma's sister. I'd love a similar opportunity."

"I'd welcome an opportunity to marry the man I love. If we would like a husband, we would each set our hearts on the one man we truly care about. The one who returns our affection. For me, Daniel. The one so opposite of Georg in every way." Clara's chin quivered. "Oh, how little noble breeding guarantees fine character."

"Old Georg is a sloppy braggart. Who needs him?" Hannah balled her fingers into a fist and pummeled the covers. Tea splattered as Mutti poked her head in the door.

"Good evening, meine Kinder." Mutti held a hand to her forehead and let out a sigh. "Clean up this mess, and everyone go back to your rooms." The sisters moaned but scurried to do as Mutti asked.

When only the two of them remained in the room, Mutti's expression softened. She stroked Clara's hair. "I'm not sure why your Vati chose this man for you, but I'm sure he has important reasons. We'll respect his decision. For now, we could all use a good night's sleep. Pray for fresh perspectives tomorrow."

A few deep breaths calmed Clara's soul. She lay across her four-poster mahogany bed, covered by her lavender Federbetten embroidered with sunny daisies and delicate pink roses. Mutti sang her favorite childhood lullaby.

Lullaby and goodnight!

With roses bedight!

With down over spread in baby's wee bed,

Lay thee down now and rest –

May thy slumbers be blest.

Lay thee down now and rest –

May thy slumbers be blest.

LULLABY AND GOOD NIGHT!

Thy mother's delight

Sweet visions untold

Thy soul shall unfold

God will keep thee from harm,

Thou shalt wake in my arms.

God will keep thee from harm,

Thou shalt wake in my arms.

BEFORE THE SECOND VERSE ENDED, Clara had drifted to sleep, dreaming of security in Daniel's arms. He twirled her in circles around their lovely garden. A thunderous commotion on the floor above her room interrupted the delightful visions and aroused Clara from her slumber.

Chapter Two

KRAIG REINHOLD'S STUDY, *Gut Apfelhof, Monday, 23 August 1881*

VATI STOMPED HIS FOOT AGAIN. Items rattled on his roll-top desk. "It's the only arrangement that makes sense."

"I disagree." Though Vati's words invited no argument, Curt defended his sister's honor. "How does this arrangement make sense? You expect me to trust Georg? With Gut Apfelhof? With my sister?"

"I do." Vati poked his long finger toward Curt's face. "Imagine how large Gut Apfelhof will become when we add the Wolff property to ours."

"What? I don't understand."

"We provide a dowry, of course, but my agreement with the Wolffs when Georg and Clara marry combines our land holdings."

Curt loosened his shoulders, ready to pounce. "You jumped from courting to marriage quickly. Clara deserves far better."

"It's an excellent decision."

"Excellent? Why does it matter how large the estate grows, especially if we add a man of such low integrity to our family by choice?"

"I care. You should, too. It's your inheritance one day."

"I care that Gut Apfelhof has long maintained its reputation as a friendly community known for its Baron, who treats residents well and with fairness. Integrity is important."

Vati pursed his lips. His eyes widened. "Well, finally, a point we agree upon."

"Do you hear the contradiction in your argument? The last thing Georg has is integrity, and you'll force me to share the inheritance with him!"

"He's a fine man, Curt."

Curt strolled to the third-floor wall of windows and rested his fingers on a crosspiece of the multi-paned glass. He scanned the Reinhold estate, the center of their beloved Gut Apfelhof. Raking his hands through his hair, he took a deep breath and faced Vati.

"Residents trust you as their nobleman. They love you and our family. You and our ancestors built the kind of trust fellow noble families envy."

Joining him at the windows, Vati made a sweeping gesture across the acres. "They do trust me, as should you and your sister."

Curt clenched his jaw, sucking in a breath between his teeth. "Many realize Georg's reputation with women, but few speak of it. Who knows what activities take him to Monte Carlo so often? An arrangement with a man of such poor character will tarnish your reputation."

"Doesn't matter. I am the Baron of Gut Apfelhof—the Gut Herr. They'll respect my decision." Vati walked back to his desk.

Curt stared at Vati. Sweat gathered beneath his collar. "Respect for respect's sake. You'll sacrifice a measure of their trust."

"Your comments dishonor me, son."

It took every ounce of self-control Curt mustered to keep from shaking his white-knuckled fist in Vati's face. He calmed his fiery thoughts and gentled his voice to a more courteous tone. "Everyone cares deeply about their neighbors here. I always believed you cared deeply about your own family, too. I say no."

"And I didn't ask."

"Of course." Curt clipped his words. "The rules."

With one hand, Vati rubbed his brow. The fingertips of the other tapped incessantly on the desktop. "And if this involves a certain other man's interest in Clara, I'm capable of handling the matter."

"Daniel serves us well. Clara treasures your love and approval. She values your traditions. Don't you believe her future happiness is more important than your sacred customs?"

"We follow the rules of nobility here. Must I remind you again that marriages between servants and nobility are forbidden? We serve the state. The state entrusts the church with collecting taxes and ensuring compliance with rules for the privileged class. Our titles and the future of Gut Apfelhof depend on our obedience. Georg is my choice for Clara."

"Daniel, Clara, and I grew up together in our rural Gut Apfelhof. We attended Lehrer's classes together and became best childhood friends. Why do the rules change in adulthood?"

While twisting one fist in the palm of the other, Vati took a deep breath and exhaled hard. "Nothing's changed. It's our way, Curt. Simply how things are done. And there's more. If you knew, you and your sister would understand."

Curt dropped his arms to his side. He cocked his head toward Vati. "Help me understand then."

As Vati whisked his arm across the top of his Grossvater's ornate rolltop desk, his prized beer stein shattered into smithereens. Pens, journals, and chess pieces flew about the room. Black ink spilled onto the gold and ivory Persian carpet.

Gazing toward the floor, Vati glowered over the mess. "Do not challenge my authority!"

"I will find you proof of Georg's rancorous activities. The future of Gut Apfelhof may not be as bright as you picture it. I promise to follow his every move, especially with Clara."

Curt exited the room as Vati sank into his well-worn leather chair. Vati spoke to himself, but his words reached Curt's ears.

"Yesterday, my decision and the announcement hurt Clara badly. Now this argument with Curt. A few days ago, I complimented him on his keen business insights. *Oh Lord, when did this room full of my dreams for my children become a place of nightmares?*" Vati groaned. "But this arrangement is necessary."

Curt quietly pushed the door closed and left Vati wallowing in his storm. He made a vow as he left the room. Curt would learn the truth of the *more.* He would fight for the desires of Clara's heart.

COMING FROM VATI'S STUDY, Curt spotted Clara peeking from her bedroom door and slowed his step. The lump in his throat silenced his words. "I don't have any thoughts worth sharing at the moment anyway," he whispered under his breath.

He reached out, rubbing her arm and calming his shakiness. His eyes burned, but his love and sympathy for Clara far outweighed his worry about unmanly tears. Fear gripped him—fear of what would lie ahead for his sister. "Vati and I spoke, Kirsche."

"'Kirsche—Cherry. Funny, the name you called me since we were small children."

"Silly, but it fits your red hair and your normally cheery disposition."

"And you call me Kirsche today? My mood falls far short of bright and cheerful. Danke. I'm sorry I interrupted you. I'm anxious to hear about your conversation with Vati. Since your shoulders twitch nervously, I assume your arguments failed to thaw him?"

Curt furrowed his brow. "He made his decision. Something I said incited a vigorous maelstrom, and he crumbled in his chair—a side of him I had never witnessed before today. His words clearly conveyed the message that his decision was final, but his actions and the tenseness in his tone argued a different point. There's more to this story, and secrets lurk in his past. I'm certain of it."

"Secrets? What secrets?"

"He wouldn't tell me, but he said there is more. If you and I knew we would understand. It's as if something haunts him. I can't say why I think this, but perhaps he's even being blackmailed."

"Vati loves us. He's always there to listen when we need him and wrap his strong arms around us. Stories we read with him transported us to magnificent places and inspired a treasury of real and imaginary adventures. Never would I have suspected angst from his past haunts him."

Curt rubbed his head. "I wish I understood."

After passing them hurriedly on the stairs, Vati dashed out the front door, slamming it behind him.

"You know he will head to the stables to confide in Artax. He and his horse share a tight bond, and Artax keeps his secrets. If only the horse talked."

"I admire he talks to his stallion. Brigitte hears plenty of my woes. I learned well from his example."

"What an understatement. Let's head out through the kitchen and spy on his conversation with his four-legged friend."

As they descended the stairs, Mutti's and Rosa's voices carried from the kitchen.

"One bright spot for Clara today. A letter arrived from Megs. Clara misses her terribly." Mutti paused for a moment. "A year already since Megs, the one sensible member of the Wolff family, left for America. I pray the young couple fares well in Chicago. But I digress. Back to this arrangement Kraig made. More heartbreak for Clara."

Mutti continued in a cautious tone. "Rosa, everyone around Gut Apfelhof talks to you. Enlighten me, please."

With a tug on her hand, Curt signaled to Clara. They ducked around a corner and under the stairs. Their favorite hiding place when they were children still provided a perfect vantage point for eavesdropping.

Rosa cleared her throat. "I believe the Gut Herr desires his daughters to marry within your prestigious circles. I see no argument with following the rules for nobility, do you?"

"Hmm. Nein. No argument there. Go on."

"Frau Lydia, our German laws require young men to be twenty-five and young ladies to be twenty-two to apply for permission to marry. Clara's twenty-six. Even though she's celebrated enough birthdays, do you think the Gut Herr waited a little longer until he found a suitable nobleman for her?"

"Perhaps I could believe that if he'd found a good nobleman. There must be another reason."

"After my Vater and husband died when our inn burned to the ground, I've never forgotten how your fine husband insisted baby Daniel and I live here at Gut Apfelhof."

"Nor have I. One thing I especially love about him is his care for others, but go back to our conversation about Clara's situation. You have more to add?"

"At the time when Daniel and I came to live here, things happened that affected both of us. I never understood why. The incident wasn't spoken of again. Could Gut Herr Reinhold's choice be driven by some bit of that long-ago rumor?"

Feet shuffled, and skirts rustled across the kitchen floor. "Sounds like their chat is over," Curt whispered.

"At least we learned Mutti's opinion differs from Vati's. But what does Rosa know?"

"Vati may have returned to his study, but in case he hasn't, you disappear to the garden. I'll check on the orchards. We'll stay out of his way. Later, I'll assure him we are keeping the wild creatures out."

"More like big bad Wolffs."

Curt snickered. "You're always attempting humor in your sketches and in your words."

"And what is so funny about the truth? Mutti's right, by the way. I do miss Megs. Where is the letter she mentioned?" Clara scanned their current location. "The front door is the quickest way out."

On their way to the door, Curt snatched an envelope from the sideboard. "Here's Megs' letter."

"Danke!" She slipped it into her pocket. They walked down the hill of their family's spacious farm and estate. While enjoying the intoxicatingly sweet aromas of the ripening apples and inhaling the crisp autumn air, they forgot the challenges of the moment until a man stepped in front of them.

DANIEL INTERCEPTED them on the path. He took Clara's hand, spun her toward himself, and whispered in her ear. "My lovely lady." Warm color flooded her cheeks.

Bouncing up to the trio, Brigette begged attention. Curt grabbed a stick to play fetch. "Come on, girl. We'll give these two some privacy."

She pressed her face against his chest. If only he could have held it there forever.

"I regret your Vati's choice for you, but it was no jack-in-the-box moment. His announcement held no surprise, since the rules and traditions of the centuries remain in place, unaltered by any dreams and desires owning our hearts."

"These traditions? The Bible teaches that God created us all equal in His eyes. Some people, however, do display higher morals and more impeccable integrity than others."

"And you count Georg among the lackluster group?"

She nodded. "If only Vati understood. To be your *Lovely Lady* or Georg's *My Sweets?* I detest his smooth-tongued endearment. Life with him promises bitterness beyond measure. I desire to honor Vati, and I choose to be your Lovely Lady." Her laugh mocked her own impossible words.

"I promised to protect you always, especially from *him.* I pledged to you my heart and my love on your sixteenth birthday. My word remains steadfast today, ten years later."

"The rules foolishly contradict God's word. I long for you alone. We both love the Lord, the only prerequisite in the Bible for being equally yoked. My word and promise to you abide in my heart for all time. But how?"

"Run away with me. We'll make a new life."

"You tempt me, Daniel. Your suggestion promises a perfect answer to our dilemma."

"Then leave with me."

"How many additional problems would your plan create? We both love my family and your Mutter too much. We would risk our children never knowing their grandparents. I love your idea, and I hate it. I'm overwhelmed by a sinking feeling in my gut."

Daniel hugged her. "My Mutter prays for a solution for us."

"Precious Rosa. If anyone's prayers reach God's throne, hers do. Curt believes the Wolffs are being devious and untrustworthy. He and I just overheard a conversation between your Mutter and ours, hinting at some secret from the past. Would you ask her to pray that Curt learns the truth?"

"Something specific or a mere hunch? I harbor plenty of hunches about the Wolffs."

"You do?" Clara twisted a dangly curl, tucking it behind her ear.

"Many doubts and mistrusts, in fact. What is Curt thinking?"

"I'm uncertain what Curt suspects about the Wolffs. Vati's actions and comments this morning caused him to believe something is amiss, maybe in Vati's past. After hearing our Mütters' conversation, I predict Curt will visit Oma tomorrow, persuading her to divulge Vati's secrets. She hates gossip, but she hears plenty and hides a proverbial carpet bag of accumulated information about families in our community. I trust Curt convinces her to share a piece about the Wolffs and Vati."

"And if he uncovers unflattering truths about any of them, do the rules change?"

"If he proves the Wolffs' rancorous indiscretions, Curt believes Vati will release me from this nightmare, but the rules remain."

"I'll remind my Mutter to pray harder. I will pray for Curt's endeavor and offer my help."

"No matter the outcome of Curt's investigation or the fulfillment of our promises, much loss looms for our future." Her hands trembled, and her chin quivered. "Sometimes I'd like to admit defeat—let the ground swallow me up and bring an end to our troubles."

Daniel squeezed her hand. He had certainly been tempted to think that same way. "But when Curt succeeds, you lose Georg. A new beginning for us then? We hear America is a land of opportunities."

"I'm envisioning possibilities as wide as the sparkling sea spread beyond us. A new beginning. A beautiful picture of new experiences, new places, new friends, and life as your wife. I could swim right into that adventure."

"What an adventure it would be. We'll grow our dream and our family in America."

Moments later, Clara pushed away, tears running down her cheeks. What had Daniel said?

"If we leave Germany, we lose our families. No one here will agree to marry us. If someone performs the ceremony in secret, when Vati learns of it, he'll send us away. Worse, he enlists his friends in higher places than his to annul the marriage. I lose you. You may lose your position."

"Shh. Put the worries and troubles aside until another day." He pulled her back toward himself.

This time Clara completely melted into his chest. She rested there until he tapped the top of her head. When she looked up, he lifted her chin. Her lips met his in a kiss sweet as honey.

"Promise sealed again." Clara beamed.

"Promise sealed again."

Yips and approaching footsteps announced that Curt and Brigitte had concluded their game.

"The same promise from the birthday party?" Curt ran his hands through Brigitte's ruffled fur. "And Vati's arrangement complicates your hopes?"

"You eavesdropped on us, but ja. Same promises." Daniel raised his eyebrows. "Clara mentioned your scheme to unravel the agreement? A tough assignment you've placed on yourself."

"Agreed, but what little I know of the situation is too shady to ignore."

"My day's work awaits me." Daniel patted his back pocket, checking its contents. He gifted his lovely lady a broad smile and kissed her cheek. "Curt, I'm eager and willing to help."

~

"This garden is special, a peaceful refuge." Clara walked through the iron gate ahead of Curt.

"Has been for generations." He winked at Clara, his eyes blue-green, so like Vati's.

"Ja. Reinholds before me sketched their dreams and vented their disappointments here, too. Stories well-protected by these garden walls." Had any of them found solutions to make their dreams come to life? Had new joys covered their disappointments?

Clara wandered to her favorite corner. She doubted anything would change her situation. "How appropriate—a yellow rose bush bloomed here last week but today dropped its golden petals for the season. Despite our promises to one another, our dreams—mine and Daniel's—are all doomed, too."

Her twin was silent. A few moments later, he tapped her on the shoulder. "Are you going to read the letter, Kirsche?"

"Feeling so sorry for myself, I almost forgot." She pulled the letter from her pocket and tugged a lace handkerchief from her sleeve—a shield against tear-smudged ink."

15 July 1881

Dearest Clara,

It's summer. I miss chasing fireflies and picking flowers, wandering through the orchards wishing the apples would ripen more quickly, and riding our horses through the wide open spaces. I miss spending time with you, my cherished friend.

When are you coming to Chicago? It is a wonderful city with abundant opportunities. The city looks different from the countryside we love, but its charms grow on me daily. Gus and I made a lovely home for ourselves here.

He's employed, as I have shared with you before, by the Illinois Staats-Zeitung, the number one German-language newspaper in the United States. They also publish several English papers in Chicago, but The Illinois Staats-Zeitung's circulation ranks second only to The Chicago Daily News. Gus performs his duties well, and his boss promises he'll become a manager very soon.

You can't imagine how grateful I am for the funds Pa gifted me when Gus and I married and left Germany. A most generous gift and one so out-of-the-ordinary to bestow on a daughter. Obviously, he realized Georg would waste it on women and wild living. My brother is a contemptible man! A lesson you and I learned early.

Pa's gift allowed me to begin my business. You know how I love fashion. This city flourishes with opportunities, even for women. Gus agreed, and I opened a dressmaker's shop for the fine ladies of Chicago. I'll be traveling back across the ocean soon. The new designer fashion houses in Paris will provide perfect inspiration for my clients' gowns. I've made special arrangements with House of Worth and Maison for us to visit. From Sajou, I'll import Paris' fine fabrics for the ladies, too.

I long for a visit with you. Agree to meet me in Paris. Oh, I know this would be so inappropriate, but perhaps if Rosa traveled with you, your Vati would allow Daniel to escort the two of you. Rosa taught us excellent skills in handling needles and thread. They provide me with the ability to create exquisite ensembles. Rosa would enjoy the trip. Invite her to come, too. Her traveling with you gives you an advantage. How could your Vati say no to you about Daniel coming along if Rosa's included?

I arrive in Bremen in early September and will travel by train to Paris. I'm reserving rooms for all of us—you and me, Rosa, and

Daniel—at The Westminster, 13 Rue de la Paix, situated in the center of the designer fashion house district. A short carriage ride delivers us to the Louvre and other galleries. A leisurely stroll leads to the Sentier district, where haberdasheries and luxury shops line the streets.

When my letter reaches you in Gut Apfelhof, there is no assurance of adequate time to write your response. Please send your immediate reply by telegraph.

See you 5 September 1881 in Paris.

Fondest wishes,

Your dearest friend always,

Megs

"Oh Megs, if only you knew how my life has changed since you left." Clara's heart sank. She pulled her shawl tighter to ward off the chill traveling through her limbs.

"May I?" Curt reached out to hold her hands.

She nodded in agreement. Eventually, her quaking body stilled. "I need Rosa."

Chapter Three

RELIEF FLOODED Clara's heart when Rosa welcomed her into the sewing room.

"Goodness, poor girl." Rosa rested her hands on the sleeves of Clara's dress and held her at arm's length. "I'm peering into those chocolate eyes of yours. Where's their familiar sparkle?"

Rosa lowered herself onto the royal blue and silver brocade love seat beneath the window. She stared quietly at the ceiling as moments passed. She patted the space beside her. Clara was grateful for a plain day dress today—no worries about an awkward bustle.

"Please tell me, what do you find most troubling about your dilemma? Georg is sloppy and smokes those stinky cigars, but what else has you so upset and why?"

Clara pinched her nose. "Ugh! Those cigars are the worst." She used her sleeve to cover her nose. "How do I even begin? You remember my favorite emerald velvet ball gown? You designed it and made it for me when I was thirteen when

Mutti and Vati allowed me to attend my first New Year's Ball?"

Rosa smiled. "Ja, and I'm reminded of it each time I walk by your Mutti's works in the hallway. You look very happy in her colorful painting of the evening. I remember you delighted in wearing the gown. You spun and danced with your Vati and your friends."

"Ja, a pleasant memory or two lingers with me too." Clara shivered. "But that evening was the worst night of my life. Georg made incorrigible suggestions to me all evening. He asked me to accompany him to an area behind the house where no one would hear us talk. We both knew the impropriety of it, but he was persistent, and I went. Most of his comments were beyond my comprehension then, but they petrified me. The games were about to begin. My heart pounded in my chest. I was thankful for a few partiers who made a quick check of the grounds for stragglers."

"And they saw you?"

The door opened, and Mutti entered. "I've been standing outside the door and have heard every word. I'm concerned for you, meine Kinder. I'd like to hear the rest of your story."

"It would be wise to include your Mutti in the conversation."

Clara nodded.

At Mutti's suggestion, the three moved from the sewing room to the upstairs sitting room. "It'll be much more comfortable here. I suspect you'll share enough discomfort without us crowded in the sewing room between fabric bolts and spools of lace."

Rosa's smile and the tender-hearted look in her eyes urged Clara to continue. Clara's next words came out like gravel in a tin bucket. "The partiers did see us and called out, 'Georg, Clara, hurry. It's time for the New Year's games. Everyone's ready to begin the Bleigiessen.' Georg smirked at the interruption, then said, 'Everyone takes part in the silly tradition, dropping their hot metal into the water. If your lead casts into a mushroom, you'll be lucky in love tonight, Clara. So will I.'"

Mutti gasped. She covered her face with her hands.

"He made such a suggestion to you?" Rosa's cap fell to the ground as she pulled at her hair.

"He did, and I didn't really understand then. I do now. But dropping hot metal into cold water and interpreting the shape to predict what the evening or the coming year would hold? Even at thirteen, I found the tradition quite harebrained. Georg made it sound creepy as well."

Rosa bit her lower lip. Mutti kept her head down.

"God sent those guests to rescue me. I thank Him, He did. Georg is fifteen years older than me. Imagine a thirteen-year-old approached in such an inappropriate way by a twenty-eight-year-old man. Similar advances came with every opportunity he found. The Wolffs are neighbors, and Megs is my friend. Until now I have told no one, not even Curt or Megs, about that night. What is wrong with me? Don't I deserve a better man? Is that why Vati did this to me?"

"I don't understand the why either, but I know Georg's type. You've endured his awful behavior for thirteen years. Half your lifetime." Rosa scooted sideways to make space for a hug.

Clara's tense body fell into Rosa's extended arms, and they cried together. Their shoulders shuddered with each sob.

"You didn't tell anyone, but I have eyes everywhere. I witnessed Georg's behavior toward women. Lydia, you must have, too."

Mutti just stared.

Tapping a fist to her mouth, Rosa released the air from her puffed-out cheeks. "Nothing you say surprises me, Clara. Men use women. Men run the world, and they believe in their right to treat women like property. It's been the same way since Adam and Eve ate the forbidden fruit. You've read the Sunday school stories. This is typical of how it's been for women. That doesn't make it right, though."

"It doesn't make it right at all. If blood can boil, I'm certain mine is bubbling over right now." Despite her anger, Clara gently nudged Mutti's shoulder until she raised her head. "Vati treats you, Hannah, Emmaline, and other women respectfully. Doesn't he realize Georg isn't a pleasant person, and the man's disrespect for women is appalling? Does Vati believe I'm not a good person either?" Her hands trembled. Her nostrils flared. "Everything's contradictions to me. Georg is totally despicable. Why is this happening?"

Mutti pulled her hands from her pocket, rolling little lint fuzzes between her fingertips. "I don't have an answer to your question. Rosa, help me."

Pursing her lips, Rosa tilted her head down. *Oh, please, Lord, I need understanding. I'm unclear why her Mutti is quiet. Clara is depending on me for advice. I have none. What would you tell her?* She whispered her prayer.

"Oh, precious girl, I wish I understood." Rosa clasped her hands together. "The most God-fearing of people sometimes abandon excellent sense and make poor decisions. I'm reminded of Hagar's predicament. Abram and Sarai's lamentable choice for producing an heir left Hagar feeling alone and abandoned. But God saw her. He blessed her and her child, too. And Hagar came to know Him as El Roi, The God who Sees. Do you believe God sees you and the difficulty you face?"

"I remember the story, and I want to believe He sees me too, but does He see any of us?" Clara hesitated. "Another question. Georg's first wife passed the previous winter before the New Year's Eve party. Are either of you aware of what happened to her? How she died? Did God see her and even care? Mutti, do you care if God sees me?"

Mutti dropped the lint fuzz into a porcelain dish on the side table and picked at the seams on her dress. She lifted her eyes to Rosa.

Instead of rubbing the cameo at her neck, Rosa massaged her temples. "My knowledge is more opinion than facts, and I'd rather not spread a rumor."

"Megs and I were young, but she told me how Georg forced Sarah to drink mugs of steaming tea several cold winter nights in a row. She complained of stomach pains, became very weak, and died. Was she expecting a baby?"

"Your questions make knots form in my stomach." Rosa pressed a hand on her middle. "What makes you ask them?"

"I've heard about the pennyroyal tea. Ladies drink it to make their monthly time come back, but it doesn't always work. They give birth to a baby a few months later, one unable to live on its own. Other times ladies die. Or both."

Rosa shifted position on the loveseat again. Her forehead wrinkled.

Shaky waves jolted through Clara's body as she persisted with her questions. "Did Georg not want children and insist on the tea? Or was Sarah's delicate condition an excuse to eliminate her from his life? I'm so scared."

"Only Georg and Dr. Pfeiffer have the answers to your questions, and neither will talk. You and Megs were very young. Looking back, it's easy to see how you came to this conclusion, and I understand your fears." Rosa squeezed Clara's hand.

Tears stung Clara's eyes. She plucked a pig figurine from the side table and crushed it until her knuckles turned white. She needed help.

"You've hardly said a word, Mutti. You defer to Rosa to answer my questions. Last night, you made it clear we'll respect Vati's wishes. What about the word respect have you heard in any of this? Please help me understand and change Vati's mind."

"It's the rules for women, to accept and honor the decisions of our husbands and Väters, and it is even more important for nobility. I must agree to his plan."

"I've heard the rules since childhood and memorized them, but I consider them a poor excuse for placing me in this predicament. I love Vati. He's always ready for an adventure with me, and his lap and his arms have soothed many childhood fears and disappointments. Right now, I find respecting his choice impossible." She found it as difficult to swallow the painful lump in her throat as accepting Vati's plan.

"But you must."

"Really! Because of Georg's past behavior, I trust few men. With all my heart, I believed Vati to be trustworthy."

"He's a loving and good man, very reasonable in most all of his decisions. Look around at how he's loved by the residents of Gut Apfelhof."

"They do love him, but you continue to avoid my questions, Mutti. Why this out-of-character decision he's made? Would you want to be married to a man like Georg?" Bile from her raging anger rose in Clara's throat.

Mutti shook her head. "Nein, I wouldn't choose him or any man like him either, but I argued with your Vati once when you and Curt were babies."

Clara's eyes widened as she chomped down on her lower lip. "About what? You and Vati never argue."

With her elbows propped on her knees, Mutti leaned her chin into her hands. She lowered her eyelids like she searched some deep reserves of the past. Lifting her head at last, the story unfolded. "When I questioned another of your Vati's decisions, he picked up a crystal vase and threatened to pitch it across the room. I attempted to wrestle it away. He grabbed my hand and twisted hard. My crooked and paralyzed fingers are the result."

Clara clenched her fists and stiffened her gaze. "Nein! Why?"

"The why doesn't matter. It happened. I forgave him long ago. Nothing like it has happened since. I prefer to preserve our peace."

Sucking in a breath, every muscle tightened in Clara's body. "It does matter. The why matters very much. You lied to me."

"I'm sorry, Clara. I only meant to respect my husband. You didn't need to know."

"All these years, I believed the story you told me. You had an accident with a horse when you were a child. Curt and I hid under the stairs this morning while the two of you spoke in the kitchen. What's the big secret lurking around here, and what does it have to do with Georg and me?" Clara rubbed her pounding head. The tears she had held back washed over her cheeks.

"Again, I'm sorry. You are your Vati's precious daughter. It scared me to think you would fear him if you realized the truth. I protected you. Your brothers and sisters, too."

Rosa pushed her handkerchief into Clara's hand. Clara blotted her eyes and stifled her sobs.

"Thank you for your honesty and your apology, Mutti, but my question remains. Will you speak to Vati for me?"

Mutti held her breath and bit her lower lip as she released the air. "No matter my opinion, I'll not risk another battle. I paint instead and deal with my feelings in my artwork. Several pieces remain unseen."

"But Mutti. I'll never feel safe with Georg. I could never trust him. He has already hurt me. How could I ever respect him?" Her toes curled inside her shoes. Her voice rose with the ever-increasing pounding of her heart.

Mutti held Clara's hands in hers. "We expect the Wolffs for dinner Saturday evening. Maybe Vati recognizes strengths in him we haven't seen. Their family traveled much of the past year and was unable to attend social events here in Gut Apfelhof or at our friends' homes around the state. Perhaps the arrangement isn't so hopeless as you believe. Please give him a chance."

From the grimace on her face, Mutti didn't believe her own words. Still holding the little pig, Clara considered hurling it across the room. Oh, no. Like Vati throwing the vase. Any hope of luck from that little porker was nonexistent anyway. *Like my prayers, God. Hopeless too. You are not helping me either.*

Clara brushed her fingers over the letter in her pocket. Megs' invitation had not included Mutti or her little sisters, but why not?

"I'm returning to my studio now. I love you so much, Clara, but I can't help you with this. I'm sorry."

"Me, too, Mutti." She hugged Mutti tight. "Before you leave, may I ask a different favor?"

"A favor that doesn't involve Vati's decision about Georg, I hope?"

"Not about Georg, but it does involve asking Vati's permission."

Mutti tilted her head toward her daughter. "What would that be?"

"Megs' letter. She's invited me to meet her in Paris. She included Rosa and Daniel, too. I recognize the folly of asking permission for Daniel to go, but it would be great fun if all the ladies went. You, me, Rosa, Emmaline, and Hannah. Megs loves all of you."

"Slow down, please." Mutti smiled. "First, danke for not proposing that Daniel travel with you. And now what is the occasion for Megs' visit to Paris? When is this trip?"

"She asked for me to meet her on September 5th. She is staying for the week, and as soon as she hears from me, she will reserve rooms at The Westminster on Rue de la Paix."

"She's traveling alone?"

"She didn't mention anyone traveling with her. She's arranged to visit fashion houses and haberdasheries. Megs opened a dressmaker's shop in Chicago. She's quite successful and will be looking for new ideas and exquisite fabrics and trims to please her clients."

"Vati would never approve of you traveling alone." Mutti rubbed her forehead, but the corners of her mouth twitched up just a bit.

"I don't expect that at all. Megs thought Rosa would enjoy exploring the fashion scene too. And I am inviting you and my sisters. Will you help me ask Vati?"

"It'd be a lovely chance for all of us to get away for a few days, but it'll not change anything when we return."

"The situation here has been quite upsetting. Being away from Gut Apfelhof for a few days will allow me to think about all that happened to me all too quickly. Will you help me convince him? Please?"

Hands clasped as in prayer and eyes squeezed shut, Rosa rocked back and forth on the sofa.

Mutti's eyebrows knit together, and she toyed with a button on her cuff. A smile inched up her cheeks. "Paris with my daughters and Rosa will be delightful."

"Just like Breuninger in the spring. You'll help me convince him?"

"Ja, I will. Dora prepared his favorite midday meal. We'll ask him at lunch."

Rosa released a long-held breath and clapped her hands. "I'll pray while you talk to him. And, Clara, Proverbs 3:5-6."

A verse she'd memorized long ago. *Trust in the Lord with all thine heart; and lean not unto thine own understanding. In all thy ways acknowledge him, and he shall direct thy paths. Oh Lord, if only You would, direct my path to Paris, please.*

"AHH." Vati rubbed his tummy. "Kartoffel pancakes with Apfelsauce and Bratwurst. No finer lunch anywhere. Especially tasty when I enjoy it with my favorite Frau and Fraulein."

Clara was pleased to see the twinkle in Vati's eyes. Cords of tension around her heart loosened. Clara dared to believe Vati's answer would exceed all she hoped for.

"While we have you to ourselves, Clara and I would like to ask you for a special favor."

"Your smiles are large, and your cheeks are extra-pink—both of you. Lydia, you've not stopped flipping your coffee spoon over and over in its saucer. I've given you no reason to fear me. What is it you two are so excited about, but you're afraid to ask? Do I look like a monster?"

"You don't resemble any monster I've encountered, but you could show your hero side." Her charming smile preceded Mutti's request. "Clara received a letter from Megs today. It included a special invitation. I'll let her explain."

Almost before Clara finished her plea, Vati declared, "What a grand idea. We'll send two of the coachmen to keep you safe. Have Lottie make plans. The Westminster is a lovely hotel. A wonderful time awaits you."

"Really? You mean it?"

"Exactly the kind of diversion you could use, correct?"

Clara smiled widely, jumped up, and pulled Vati to his feet. "Danke."

He swung her around, then reached for his wife to join their jubilation.

"Danke, Kraig. I'm looking forward to seeing Paris again. It's a perfect season for it, and we'll be back before Erntedank."

"Georg asked to see me." He gave his wife a quick kiss.

Clara's stomach sank. But she refused to allow the mere mention of his name to dampen her spirits. "The doorbell chimed a few minutes ago."

"I'm headed to the orchard. I instructed Fritz to have him meet me out there." The kitchen door banged behind him.

Before Clara could skip off to share the news with her sisters, Mutti caught Mamsell Lottie's attention and began making plans for Paris. But even if Mutti convinced Vati to allow Daniel to accompany them to Paris, he wouldn't be able to stay. Another impossible daydream.

Catching her on her way, Georg grabbed Clara from behind. Both hands on her shoulders, he spun her around to face him. "I've been standing here a while."

She cringed at his touch. "How long a while? Didn't Fritz instruct you to meet Vati in the orchard?"

"Long enough to hear your plans to escape me. I'll be waiting for you wherever you go. Don't think for a minute you can get away from me so easily, my sweets."

Chapter Four

MONDAY AFTERNOON, *23 August 1881*

THE CUCKOO CLOCK in the foyer chirped twice, marking the time for her sisters' afternoon lessons. Clara climbed the stairs leading to their classroom. Eager to share the good news with her sisters, she whispered a prayer on her way.

I didn't trust You at all for a good outcome when we asked Vati, but You answered better than I hoped. I haven't honored You or Vati well and need forgiveness. Thank You for putting it on Vati's heart to say yes despite me.

Brushing off the sobering thought and Georg's threats, she whirled her way into the lesson room with thanksgiving on her lips. The familiar smell of old books and Lehrer's peppermint candies greeted her. Her sisters spun a globe, using their fingers to discover new locations. With fifteen minutes until Lehrer Frederick arrived, Clara had plenty of time to share the news. "Emmaline, Hannah, have you kept up your

French? Megs invited me to join her in Paris, and you're coming too!"

Hannah pointed to Paris on the globe.

After three big twirls of her own, Emmaline grabbed her sisters and spun again. "Do you think they have a merry-go-round in Paris? I'll inquire when we arrive. I'm fluent in my French. Clara, Lehrer Frederick will help you brush up on yours, too."

"Not hiding a drop of your enthusiasm!" Clara kissed Emmaline on the cheek.

"And Vati has agreed to this?" Hannah raised an eyebrow.

Clara nodded.

"With the happy transformation from your dull expression over the last several days, I already knew he gave permission." Hannah's eyes sparkled.

"Observant of you. I admit heaviness and unhappiness climbed atop the throne of my heart this week. Ja. Vati agreed. We're visiting Paris. Mutti and Lottie will arrange a respectable travel plan for the five of us."

"Five?" Hannah counted on her fingers. "Three of us plus Mutti equals four."

"Rosa's coming, too. And two coachmen will accompany us because five women traveling together provides ample opportunity for trouble."

"Speak for yourself about staying out of trouble." Emmaline's mouth rounded into a perfect O.

"And what do you know of trouble, and what trouble would

I be in, little sister?" Clara twisted her lips and squinted her eyes at Emmaline.

Emmaline shrugged and suppressed a giggle between clamped lips.

"As for the plans, I believe Mamsell will enlist Daniel to drive us to Crailsheim."

"Daniel? Ja, could be trouble for you right there." Emmaline fluttered her eyelashes in Clara's direction. "More opportunities for you and Daniel to share romantic looks. Like when we left for Breuninger's, maybe he'll kiss more than your hand."

"Whatever are you speaking about, Emmaline? Vati must never learn about Daniel's kiss." That would be kisses. Lots of kisses.

"You try to hide them, but everyone knows about the two of you." Emmmaline giggled.

While her sisters chattered about Paris, Clara escaped into her memories of the trip Emmaline had mentioned. Traveling to Stuttgart for the grand opening of Breuninger's department store—a day well before the Georg arrangement.

A late February morning. Sunshine glistened off the frosty branches and streamed into my second-floor window of our three-story half-timber home. Daniel drove our bright yellow Landau carriage.

The emblazoned red Gut Apfelhof crest displayed on its side touched a warm spot in my heart—not as warm, though, as the mark left by the dashing driver, the love of my life. Dressed in his fancy suit and top hat, he pulled the carriage around the circular cobbled drive to our front door.

The twinkle in his deep blue eyes mimicked the morning rays as he gave me an affectionate and tender look. Despite Mutti's and the sisters' presence, he kissed my hand and then my neck as he helped me into my seat. The wintry morning filled with warmth and promise.

Emmaline tugged at Clara's stray curl. "Are you still present in our conversation, or are your thoughts miles away?"

Her sister's question jolted her back to the chill of her current circumstances on this sweltering summer day. "I'm so sorry. Mutti knows we're all going. She was with me when we asked Vati's permission. We'll party in Paris in less than two weeks, but I need a favor from both of you this week. Help me survive Saturday evening with Georg and the Wolffs?"

"Do you think they'll still come after you delivered that sting to his ego?" Hannah picked up a book and fanned its pages.

"Georg doesn't give up easily. Vati assured me he smoothed the repercussions of my questionable behavior. Unfortunately, we still expect the family for dinner Saturday evening." The words burned in Clara's throat.

"Most unfortunately." Emmaline scrunched her face.

"Every detail of this new arrangement makes my stomach churn. When I read Megs' letter, Curt was with me. He promised to ferret out the motives behind Vati's plan. When he learns the truth, maybe all of this will prove nothing more than a bad dream." She could hope.

"Until then, exemplary behavior and expected attention to our guests will help me please Vati. Even if I'm not happy about this arrangement, Vati agreed to the Paris trip without argument. How horrible if he changed his mind."

"We'll help you. Then we're on our way to Paris." Hannah paused and gazed at her sister. "You're always up for adventures in a book. You read *Little Red Riding Hood* to us when we were little, but you feared walking us across Gut Apfelhof to Oma's cottage afterward."

The softness in Hannah's voice carried Clara back to the moment. "Now I'm living the story with the Wolff on my tail. I'll tend my basket of fruit well when Georg's nearby. May I count on your prayers? I don't know how, but I must put my best effort forward to honor Vati and his arrangement with Georg. The Paris trip won't carry my troubles down the Danube, but it promises a pleasant diversion after Saturday's dinner party. Sunday morning at church, I predict I'll need to repent much for my thought life the previous evening." *O Lord, please keep my tongue in check.*

"We'll pray for you, Clara. We promise." Emmaline nodded her agreement to Hannah's promise.

"Hope you can pay attention to Lehrer's lessons." Clara winked at them.

The classroom door opened, and Mutti stepped inside. "It gladdens my heart to see all of you so happy. Mamsell Lottie has already commenced with our travel arrangements." Mutti tapped her fingernails on the doorframe where they stood. "Clara, there's another matter we must discuss, but here comes Lehrer now. We'll leave him and the girls to their studies."

As they exited, Lehrer Frederick bowed to Clara and Mutti.

"Is your concern about the trip?" Clara clutched a handful of her skirt.

"Has Megs asked her Ma to join you in Paris?"

"Her letter didn't mention Frau Wolff. Megs invited me, and Rosa as my chaperone. She suggested Rosa's presence would provide her an opportunity to study the new fashions for our sake." Clara twisted the fabric of her skirt. "She invited Daniel as well, but I knew that his coming would be impossible. I intend to wire Megs tomorrow, accepting her invitation."

"I'm disappointed Megs would make such a suggestion, but thank you again for realizing the impropriety of it." Mutti nudged Clara's hand free from her skirt and held it in her own. "You must advise Megs our number grew, and tell her Vati will cover our expenses."

"Of course. I imagine we must invite Margaret and do it graciously. Why, oh why, is my best friend also Georg's sister? His Ma talks about him incessantly. She'll be angry with Megs for not inviting her and angry with me for the same reason."

Mutti rubbed the digits of her permanently wounded hand. The gesture often communicated her discomfort in matters. "Perhaps she'll welcome the invite if received from you."

"A scary conversation."

Chapter Five

REINHOLD ESTATE, *Saturday evening, 27 August 1881*

"USE THE OPAL FASCINATOR, a perfect embellishment with my gown, and for anchoring these wayward curls."

Alice, Clara's personal maid, stood behind her in the long oval mirror. She nodded, then removed the hairpins jutting from her mouth. "Ja, a lovely complement to your new gown, but I am doubtful it will secure these stubbornly spiraling ringlets."

Flickers from a gas lamp reflected the gems' fire and illuminated tiny blazes in the mirror, making it easy to spot among the other pieces in Clara's collection. Alice picked up the sparkly decoration. "You wish to impress Georg?" She clamped the hairpins between her lips again and went back to work on Clara's hair.

"Nein." She lifted her chin. "But it's imperative I please Vati tonight. Please do a fairy godmother miracle for me."

"From your mood, a nearly hopeless task, but..." Alice twisted, retwisted, and twisted yet again, attempting to secure the ringlets with the clip Clara chose. She anchored the curls and the fascinator, then reached for a strand of gold braid and wove it between the pins, the Opals, a pink rose, and Clara's hair. "With a bit of luck, they'll hold until you reach the dinner table." Alice stepped back and brushed a few loose strands from Clara's shoulder.

"You're skeptical?"

"We are both all too familiar with your locks' penchant for rebellion."

"Perhaps reflecting their owner's propensity for rebellion." Clara stood, smoothed her skirts, and took a deep breath. "Danke." She silently urged her twitching fingers and tingly insides to be still. When she opened the door, her Vati met her, humming a merry tune.

"Meine junge Dame, how lovely you look tonight." He lifted her hand and pirouetted her like a ballerina. "The rich color of your gown accentuates the sparkle in your dark eyes."

"Danke, Vati."

"This evening, please play the music you acquired in the spring. I love it when you play the song."

Clara swallowed back the sour taste in her mouth. "I love the piece, too, Vati—the best thing I brought home from the Breuninger's trip, and I enjoy playing it. But tonight? Johann Strauss's Waltz, *Roses from the South?* A beautiful love song with tender words. You know my feelings. The ivories will not sing the same."

"Georg cares about you. This will please him."

Mutti joined them at the top of the winding oak staircase. Vati offered one arm to his wife and the other to Clara. Hannah and Emmaline followed behind. "Beautiful ladies, time to greet our guests."

In front of a towering vase of sunflowers in the foyer, Curt conversed with Oma and his younger brother, Wilhelm. Curt's eyes widened when the rest of the family joined them. "Promises to be an interesting evening."

Clara wrinkled her nose and cocked her head toward her twin. He winked in response. Oma laid a gloved hand over her heart and smiled demurely, then whispered to Curt.

"Nothing but your best behavior tonight, all of you." Vati's eyes pierced Clara's for several moments before he shifted toward Curt and Oma.

The doorbell chimed, and the doorman, Fritz, announced the Wolff family's arrival.

After handshakes with both Wolff men, Vati motioned toward the parlor. "We will be more comfortable here while we wait for Henry to announce dinner is served."

Mutti clasped Frau Wolff's hand in hers. Lovely embroidered cuffs embellished the sleeves of her gown. "What exquisite designs."

"Danke, Lydia."

While the men talked business, Oma followed Mutti and Frau Wolff to the opposite end of the parlor from the men. Clara scrunched in behind her sisters off to the side of the room, partially concealed by the royal blue brocade draperies.

Georg poked his head between Hannah and Emmaline. "Do you intend to hide from me this evening, Clara?"

"As if a possibility to do such exists."

"Come now, my sweets. You belong by my side."

She wrinkled her nose, but Clara kept her lips sealed.

The dinner bell tinkled, and Henry called to the group.

"Let the young couple lead us to the table." Vati motioned Clara and Georg forward. Apple-adorned place cards with each diner's name were arranged around the table. Vati and Gerwig seated their wives. Curt seated Oma at her place next to him, and he and Wilhelm made the gentlemanly gesture for their younger sisters.

Georg pulled his chair back, ready to sit. He narrowly averted the faux pas and reached over to Clara's chair. "My apologies, my sweets. I am new to this."

New to this? Hardly. Clara bristled, ignoring his dimpled attempt to gain her pleasure. She slowly released a deep breath.

Family and guests joined in singing the common table prayer. "Komm Herr Jesus, be our guest, and bless what You bestowed on us."

"Amen." Vati opened his napkin and placed it in his lap. "Time to fill our plates and our tummies."

Georg remained silent during the blessing, but he unashamedly asked for generous helpings. Clara peeked between the already wayward russet curls dangling before her eyes and witnessed Georg lick his fingers clean. *Clean?* Vati would expect them to stand together for something, and Georg would want to hold her hand again. She wished she had not forgotten her gloves.

"Gerwig and Margaret, danke for joining us tonight." Vati stood. "It delights us that Georg courts our beautiful daughter, Clara."

"Much happiness to Georg and Clara!" Herr Wolff raised his glass. Clinks sounded around the table.

"Clara, Georg, please stand with me. Erntedank is a mere eight or nine weeks away. Your parents asked all our servants to create a festive combined party. We'll have much more than an abundant harvest to give thanks for this year."

"Danke, Herr Reinhold. I'm most pleased." Georg took a bow.

Clara was not pleased at all, but she smiled, certain her expression showed as much warmth as a cold rock.

Her seat at the far end of the table between Curt and Emmaline allowed Oma a convenient position for quietly observing. She folded her delicately embroidered linen napkin into a perfect opera fan. Oma's gesture of waving the fan in front of her face was not lost on Clara. She hoped to whisk away the embarrassment for her oldest granddaughter.

Clara observed Emmaline's scrunched face and the way she rubbed her cheek. The sisters agreed upon signal when witnessing their target exhibiting atrocious manners.

A glance toward Georg proved Emmaline's cue accurate. She offered Georg her napkin. He wiped the soup he had dribbled down the front of his shirt and waistcoat. Clara peppered her disgust with giggles and did her best to hide them with her sleeve.

Georg wadded the napkin and set it next to his plate. "Kartoffelsuppe mit Krabben, simply the best soup in all of Germany. Perhaps, Clara, you and your family have not traveled to Schleswig-Holstein and experienced their shrimp and potato masterpiece."

Clara tapped her fingernails on the table. "Right now, you are making a mess with our Gut Apfelhof Apfelwein and cheese dumpling soup, a house specialty."

"Oh, but you have tasted nothing yet, my sweets. Monte Carlo serves rich, meaty lasagna with the finest of wines. And French pastries. Oo la la."

"You focus totally on food—food unavailable to us at the moment. And truly, I've tasted dishes of which you speak. While they're tasty temptations, could we enjoy the delicious fare Henry, Dora, and the staff prepared for us tonight?"

"But my future wife must have the very best the chefs of the world create." Georg bored them with his twaddle through the rest of the meal.

When Vati signaled for Dora's attention, his voice was music to Clara's ears, breaking off Georg's culinary soliloquy. "Please serve our dessert and coffee in the formal parlor. Shall we move there, my friends and family? Clara promised to entertain us. You'll be moved by the heavenly sounds her skilled fingers and our brand-new piano provide. I imagine all of us, especially you, Georg, being transported by the piece she's chosen."

"Will you be playing a frolicking party tune?" Georg sputtered.

"That depends. Which songs do you consider party tunes?" She made her way to the piano, but not before Herr Wolff stepped up to it first.

"What superb work carving and inlaying your family's crest

on the piano. A J. P. Sauer instrument—such a prestigious company, too. Their work's notable."

"Danke. I allowed Clara to choose the new instrument. I agree, the company did magnificent work on the crest. We also kept the older Bösendorfer. The girls enjoy playing together. For tonight, I've asked Clara to play solo, a special piece she's mastered."

Clara began. Had the piano faced the corner of the room instead of into it, she could have avoided seeing everyone's eyes on her. Less than ten measures into the music, she spotted Georg with his arms folded across his ample middle. His vacant eyes traveled away from this room and Clara's song.

Her fingers froze. He could at least express fake pleasure or move outside her line of sight. But she must honor her Vati. Clara found her imaginary mask, mentally positioned it, closed her eyes, and let her memory take over. The schnauzer sat at her side. "Brigette, this is for you tonight—for you and for Daniel," she whispered. Finished, she opened her eyes. Georg had vacated the room.

Family and guests regaled Clara with compliments and applause.

"Encore! Encore!" Frau Wolff cheered. "Mein Herr, we simply must look into a new piano ourselves."

"A fine idea, and it'll be available for Clara at our home."

Harsh lines fanned from Frau Wolff's squinty eyes.

Coming up behind Clara, Vati touched her arm and quietly requested another song. She perfectly executed a short piece and excused herself. Hannah followed close on her heels.

CLARA RUBBED her hand over the serpentine carving on the special settee. The thick pine-colored velvet cushions offered a little comfort. "I've had no need of one before, and I always considered courting chairs more of a snake in disguise. Tonight I'll be grateful for this one's larger sections to keep Georg from slithering too close."

"Your words paint a scary picture. Vati asked me to chaperone the two of you. I'll shorten the candle as much as possible."

"Thank you in advance for twisting it down so that it'll fizzle quickly and end my obligation to Georg early this evening. He's probably off smoking one of those grotesque cigars now."

His absence was short-lived. Georg plopped down next to Clara and squirmed to a perfect position for blowing insincere flatteries in her ear. "My sweets, at last, we spend special moments together. It's been a long wait, but you've matured into a ravishing young woman."

"I remember well my age had little to do with your inappropriate attentiveness toward me when I was much too young. How will you assure me of your honorable intentions now?" She shrank back from his caress on her cheek. Her fists clenched as tight as her chest.

"I'm a distinguished and powerful man. I'll be delighted to have you at my side when we attend the finest parties. I'll introduce you to royalty much more important than either of our families. I'll bring you gifts from around the world and dazzle you with chronicles of my adventures."

"I am certain you will regale me with incredible tales." Out of respect for her Vati, Clara hoped she had hidden the sarcasm in her voice.

"I returned from Paris last week. I walked the street where the new fashion designers and artists were setting up shop. The motto of the new cult of beauty. *Beauty for the sake of beauty.* I do not understand women's fascination with the haute couture, but I expect my lady to arrive in style."

"Rosa creates stunning ensembles. Aren't you pleased with my attire?"

"Of course, I am, my sweets. Haven't I complimented you on your fine appearance tonight? But where did you acquire those cheap beads in your hair?"

"Cheap? Obviously, the fire in these semi-precious stones ignites the worst in you. Or reminds you of my feisty personality."

"Don't wear them again. I'm pleased to escort you to Paris to discover all the lavish new styles they offer there. Something more luxurious for your hair, too."

"Look around us. We live in finely appointed homes. Our Väter each own and govern large landholdings, and our families attend regal parties. What more do you require? I'm content here at Gut Apfelhof. I love our community and our neighbors. Would you like to hear what I'll be teaching the children in Sunday school in the morning?"

"Children? Your Vati's and my courtship agreement states I'll be introducing you to new experiences and new places. You'll accompany me on my travels, allowing little time for the folly of children. I plan a return trip to Paris in September. Join me —chaperoned, of course."

Behind Georg's back, Hannah twisted the candle another half turn. Its flame fizzled before Clara accepted or declined the invitation. And before Georg rattled on any longer about fantastical intentions while ignoring her interests. Even if he hadn't meant it, Clara wished he had at least mentioned he chose her because he cared about her.

The couple rejoined their families, and the Wolffs readied themselves to leave. With everyone's faces looking on, Clara prayed he would spare her the slobber of his goodnight kiss. Even on her hand, it would take an entire bar of soap and a good spritz of cinnamon oil to cleanse the smuttiness away. She wished for the improbable.

Before the Wolffs left, Margaret cleared her throat. "Lydia, will you and Clara join me for a mid-morning tea this coming Thursday?"

"How thoughtful. Of course. My daughter and I accept your invitation."

"Danke. Half past ten o'clock at our home. We have traveled far in the months since Megs left, and I've missed the company of my lady friends."

"I'll have Mamsell include it on our calendar."

The men finished their conversation, and the Wolffs departed for home.

"You did all that I asked and more tonight. Danke." Vati wrapped Clara's shoulders in a warm embrace. "Give him a chance. He promised me he desires to make you happy more than anything. I trust his word to me."

Clara avoided eye contact with Vati while he spoke the words on his mind. "Really? I hope so. Everything with him is more difficult than you imagine."

"I know, sweet Clara, I know."

Her breathing slowed for a moment. Vati's last words reached her ears with gentleness, the way she remembered them before the Georg arrangement and before he'd said yes to the Paris trip. But with a quickness, queasiness reclaimed her tummy. Questions and concerns corkscrewed like tornado clouds, and fear rose in her mouth.

"I'm longing for a time with you like the ones before Georg."

"My door remains open to you any time."

"Promise? And you'll not yell at me like you did Curt?"

"All pleasant, ja. Vati-daughter time, like the ones before Georg, as you say. See you in church tomorrow."

"Monday morning. I'm holding you to your promise."

SUNDAY MORNING, *28 August 1881*

THE BARON'S FAMILY, always on display, faithfully occupied the first pew. Sunshine streamed through the rosette window above the altar of St. Luke's Kirche. Splintered into colorful broken shards, the bright beams spattered their hues upon the congregation.

Sharp, vivid reminders of my shattered life. Are everyone's lives like mine? Are they all burdened with their own broken-hearted stories, but no one speaks of them? Who is studying me from behind? Are my cracks visible? St. Luke, a physician in the Bible, treated broken bodies to help them heal. But it is not my body, it is my broken heart. What have I done to deserve this, Lord?

Pastor Lange stepped to the lectern and opened his Bible. "The Epistle reading for today is from Ephesians 6:1-4. *Children, obey your parents in the Lord: for this is right. Honour thy father and mother; which is the first commandment with promise; That it may be well with thee, and thou mayest live long on the earth. And, ye fathers, provoke not your children to wrath: but bring them up in the nurture and admonition of the Lord."*

She had memorized the verses as a young child. The opening lines smudged her conscience. *I'm doing my best to honor my parents' wishes. I am, right, Lord?*

A shiver prickled her arms. *It's not honor when I obey grudgingly, is it?*

But what about the other part? Vati nurtured all of us in the faith and God's word. On this Georg matter, he hasn't made obedience easy. Those words about being well with me if I'm obedient. Help me, Lord, look after my own heart.

The temporary camouflage of colorful sunbeams that surrounded her had moved on. Clara wrapped her arms across her body, a shield to hide the guilt consuming her.

During the sermon, her focus drifted to the window that depicted the little children gathered around Jesus. She found comfort in the scene. It had always reminded her of time in her Vati's lap, reading stories and letting him love her troubles away. *Will tomorrow's conversation with Vati be a happy one? Lord, let him realize how I'm striving to obey him, despite my desperate pain being in Georg's company. How do I obey in a way that honors Vati and honors You?*

A poke to her side startled her. "*Psst.* Get up." Hannah's whisper alerted her that she alone hadn't risen for the final hymn. Her heart and mind had been far from the order of service. She stood and mouthed the words to the doxology.

. . .

PRAISE GOD from Whom all blessings flow.

Praise Him all creatures here below.

Praise Him above ye heavenly host.

Praise Father, Son, and Holy Ghost.

HER THOUGHTS RETURNED to her conversation with Georg last night. *I reminded him we have much to be grateful for, Lord. Why am I having difficulty praising You for Your blessings? I want to trust You, Lord. But my heart is filled with fear.*

Chapter Six

MONDAY MORNING, *29 August 1881*

"Come in."

"Danke. I crept toward your door, but you invited me in before I reached it. How did you know?"

Clara entered Vati's study, and he drew his daughter into his arms. "When did you grow into such a beautiful woman anyway, meine Kinder?" He chuckled. "You persistently snuck up on me as a tiny Mädchen. I still hear your heart going bump and thump as you tiptoe to the door."

"It's quaking like thundering horses' hooves this moment. Do you hold my attempted stealth against me after our conversation in this room a week ago?"

"Not at all, mein kleines Mädchen. I'm happy you're here." Vati led her to their favorite seat in his study and settled beside her on the brocade loveseat with its horse motif, just like he did when she was a little girl. "You and your Mutti gave me all the details about Paris, the Cult of Beauty movement, fashion, and sidewalk artists. I'm not so sure I like the word cult, but I suppose the new style needs a name. I do expect you to have a wonderful time."

Vati rested his chin on his curled fist. "Something more is on your mind. What do you wish to discuss?"

"Danke again for granting your permission for us to travel to Paris to meet Megs. Before I lose my courage, have you and Georg schemed together about this trip?"

He released his fist, squeezed his earlobe, and squinted. Vati tilted his head toward her. "What do you mean?"

"I say this with great respect. I believe you know exactly what I mean. I'm the last to learn about many things affecting my life."

"I always choose to do what I believe is best for you."

"Then what is best for me feels miserably unfair."

"Let me judge what's fair." Vati's thumb caught the tears meandering down her cheek. "Your shoulders are quaking."

Her quivering chin caused her to stutter. "The le-letter from Megs inviting me to j-join her in Pa-Paris did not include her brother."

"Absolutely not. He's courting you, not married to you. Why would she have invited him?"

"I can't think of one good reason, but are you aware that on Saturday night, he invited me to go to Paris with him at the same time?"

"I did not. Quite a conundrum for you."

Clara lifted Vati's walnut trinket box from his desk and followed the diamond inlaid pattern on its lid with her pinkie. After a few trips around the intricate design, Clara forced a hard exhale. She stared at Vati. "It's worse than a conundrum. Did Georg already inform you of his plans, yet you kept it from Mutti and me?"

"Nein." Vati thumped his fist on the arm of the chair. "When he brought up the subject, I instructed Georg not to even think of mentioning Paris to you or inviting you to go. I'll not have immoral and unconscionable behavior tainting my family's reputation."

"Your sizzling voice matches the look on your face. You must be aware of Georg's history of exactly that kind of behavior. I do not trust him to respect your answer."

"You and your Mutti will visit Frau Wolff for tea this week. I've asked your Mutti to listen well. I know you will, too."

"What do you expect us to learn?"

"I'm expecting you to enjoy the tea, but a little extra vigilance never hurts."

"Frau Wolff has never liked me. I place little importance on titles and privilege, but I've always thought the Reinholds held a higher rank in these parts. The Wolffs only recently granted nobility status."

"True enough but not a fact our family lords over them."

"For that, I'm very grateful. The Wolffs are different. That woman's nose pokes so far out and up, it looks like a crooked branch in the clouds. Most of her conversations reveal how she considers herself better than everyone else."

"Clara Lydia Reinhold, shame on you."

"My apologies, Vati, but I'm thinking Mutti will bring much curious information back to you after we visit with her on Thursday."

"We dislike gossip in this family, but if my women are in danger, I need to know."

"I pray nothing we learn will change your mind about the Paris trip. And Vati…?"

"Ja?"

"Georg threatened to follow us."

"Could he intend revenge for you ruining his expensive cigars? Or perhaps he teases you? I trust he'll stay away as I admonished him. Besides, Willy and Hans will protect you."

CURT AMBLED down the stone path from their larger estate home to his Oma's cottage. He took care to avoid stepping on her abundance of flowers flowing over its edges. The door opened as he poised his hand to twist the door chime. The light in Oma's mist blue eyes and her deep dimples reminded him again of how loved he was.

"To what do I owe the pleasure of my grandson's visit?"

"I have a question about family history."

"Ask."

"Whenever one of your grandchildren confides in you, you keep it confidential, right?"

"Why, of course, unless…" She raised an eyebrow and twitched her lips.

"Right, unless we plan to intentionally hurt ourselves. Rest assured, I've no such plans, but I'm curious about Vati's past."

"Ask him."

"I did. He refused to answer. Then he and I argued about his arrangement with Georg and Clara. He claims it's about more than the rules and does not expect us to understand. I asked him to explain. His actions shouted that he wasn't willing to talk about it. Does guilt fester in him over some incident long ago?"

"My, but I've forgotten my manners. A neighbor stopped by with fresh juice from our apples earlier this morning. Pour us each a glass. Then have a seat here on the porch with me, and talk to your Oma."

Curt served the juice and took the seat next to hers. "Memorizing all the nobility rules serves the purpose of obedience for obedience's sake. You are the wisest woman I know. You often harbor differing points of view and share them privately with your grandchildren. I respect your opinions."

"Women's opinions hold little value."

"But you have one. And facts too. I need to know, and I need to understand Vati better, especially about this."

"Clara entertained a few men I believed were better-suited matches for her than Georg. Neither Clara nor your Vati approved of them." Oma's gaze wandered to the bumblebees buzzing her flowers, then met Curt's again.

She propped her chin on one hand. "I observe the starry look in Clara's eyes when she converses with our handsome carriage driver. But then, oh, the rules our class must follow. In the end, the decision belongs to the woman's Vater."

"But why Georg? Clara and I, Hannah, Emmaline, Wilhelm—we all respect Vati. We love him. He loves us. This arrangement with Georg? Nothing about it makes sense, and I've never witnessed him lose his temper like he did last week."

"He let anger control his actions? Why, Kraig is the mildest-mannered man I've known, and I have only known him to act out of rage once, a very long time ago. What else bothers him?"

"Exactly what I'm asking you." Curt shook his head. "The incident you mention. When? Why? What happened?"

She closed her eyes and drew a few deep breaths. "My Otto. I thank the Lord every day my Vater chose such a wonderful man to be my husband. Kraig takes after him in every way. They traveled to Stuttgart regularly on business matters."

"Like he and I do now?"

"Ja. They considered the Kruegers' Gasthaus their home away from Gut Apfelhof. Rosa's Mutter had passed away. She and her husband lived there with her Vater and helped him run the inn. Otto and Kraig received a warm welcome there. They doted on Rosa's little boy, Daniel, too. They recognized Rosa's fine needlework skills and brought your Mutti and me lovely gifts she had embroidered."

"Our Rosa and Daniel?"

"Oh, ja, the same. Your Vati and your Opa stayed at their Gasthaus when the fire broke out. They whisked Rosa and the boy to safety first. Lenard Krueger and Rosa's husband, Herman Becker, worked tirelessly rescuing guests. Flames completely engulfed the inn, but Lenard and Herman entered the inferno one more time to ensure they'd left no one behind. They never came out." Oma reached up her sleeve, retrieved a lace hanky, and blotted her eyes. She brought the hanky to her lap, twisting it with trembling fingers.

Curt steadied her hands. "I've never heard about this fire. Are you able to tell me the rest of the story?"

"Not much more to tell. Rosa's husband and Vater both lost their lives rescuing those fifteen guests still inside. You and Clara, two six-month-olds, kept your Mutti's hands full. Maids and a nurse provided much-needed help, but she had two babies to suckle and was still recovering from the difficulties of birthing twins. Otto and Kraig brought Rosa and Daniel to live at Apfelhof."

"Their presence here caused a problem?"

"Kraig and Otto offered Rosa the position of dressmaker to your mutti and me. She admired Rosa's skills and looked forward to a beautiful new after-the-babies wardrobe. But now a two-year-old resided here, too, adding to the hardships for your Mutti. She accepted, even encouraged, your Vati's decisions and the kindnesses he easily extended to those in need. This one stretched her hospitality."

"They never argue. Did they argue about this?"

"Ja, and the argument escalated. He hurt her hand during the encounter. Your Vati has carried the guilt of the moment ever since. He caused your Mutti's permanent disfigurement. She forgave him years ago. Because he lacks grace for himself, the past torments him."

Curt's jaw dropped. Words were slow to come. "With Mutti's fingers stiff and unbending, Vati sees the results of the injury every day."

"Now you know." She pushed on the floor with her toe, setting her rocker in motion.

"I'm sorry, Oma. I wearied you with my questions." He hugged her and patted her puffy white curls. "Danke for telling me. I'm not sure I'm closer to the answers I seek, but you shared a part of my parents' story I never knew."

"Lean your head toward me, Junge." Curt complied, and Oma planted a kiss on his left cheek. "Right where the angels kissed you."

"If an angel kiss is a blessing, Georg received double. Not a comforting thought."

"But you're handsome on the inside too."

He rewarded Oma with his boyish grin.

"Observe his every move with our precious Clara." She extended her pointer toward him.

"You don't have to tell me twice." Curt accepted her instructions with wide eyes and an exaggerated nod. "But please keep your prayer garden well-tended."

Curt was on his way, filled with an extra measure of confidence. He would carry out his plans.

Chapter Seven

THURSDAY, *1 September 1881*

STANDING WITH MUTTI AT THE WOLFFS' crimson red front door, Clara's knees thumped together as she rattled their Wolff-shaped door knocker. She almost lost her balance when the door immediately opened.

"The Reinhold ladies calling on Frau Wolff." Mutti's voice behind her saved her from further embarrassment.

The Wolffs' doorman announced their arrival, directing them to join Frau Wolff in the parlor. The woman's gaze darted about the room before she invited them to be seated on the white and ivy-green linen settee opposite her favorite needle-point chair.

Three Blue Willow cups, three small plates, and a footed compote filled with warm pretzels occupied the table between the seating. A servant dropped a sugar cube into each cup and then poured their tea. She took care to float the cream on top. After handing a cup to each lady, she placed a warm baked pastry on each of the small plates and excused herself.

"Enjoy ladies. I'm excited for you to share all I've missed these past months while we've been away." Frau Wolff leaned toward her guests.

"The tea smells heavenly, and the swirls of cream are so pretty." Mutti savored her first sip.

"Clara heard from Megs recently, expressing excitement that she'll be in Paris this coming week. She asked Clara to join her. I'm sure you've received word about the trip from your daughter as well."

"Nein, I had no word about her plans, but I believe it. Megs and her impulsive decisions. She sent you a letter, Clara, without an invitation for me to join her, too?"

"I'm sorry." Clara nodded and looked at Mutti.

"Margaret, I am certain there's an explanation. Perhaps a courier lost a letter to you in transit."

"I'm not convinced. She was too eager to get as far from home as possible."

"She addressed the letter only to Clara." Mutti set her cup back in the saucer. "Megs suggested she invite Rosa too, to see all the new fashions. Kraig has agreed to the trip on the condition that Hannah, Emmaline, and I accompany them. Come with us. You know Megs will be excited to see you."

"Will she?" Margaret stood and paced in circles around the parlor. "I'm grateful for your invitation, but I would have preferred my daughter had requested my presence instead. Gerwig and Georg are making a trip to Monte Carlo at the same time. They mentioned acquiring a new business there. I'll stay home and feel sorry for myself. It's obvious, Megs prefers your company to mine."

Clara looked away and nibbled on her pretzel.

Mutti turned to Clara with raised eyebrows. "Monte Carlo? Didn't you hear Paris?"

"I'll just stay here to direct your Mamsell and ours about the Erntedank festivities." Frau Wolff interrupted Clara's response. Her pouty lower lip and the daggers in her eyes stuck so far out she could've tripped on her hostility. "You'll hardly be back in time to help at all."

"Your concerns are unfounded. Our trip lasts one week, leaving three weeks until the festivities." Mutti motioned to Clara. "We'll be on our way. Your doorman will see us out, and our carriage awaits us. Thank you for your hospitality. The tea and hot pretzels were delightful."

Frau Wolff's chin edged up a centimeter or two. "I've always been grateful the Wolff ancestors brought the northern German custom of East Frisian tea to us here in Württemberg. I'm glad you enjoyed it. I suppose Daniel is driving your carriage? Clara, remember you're promised to my son."

"We're disappointed you'll not travel with us." Mutti stepped back to allow Clara to exit ahead of her.

"Humph. I doubt you are." Margaret followed them out the door.

The look of disgust Frau Wolff aimed toward her brought stinging tears to Clara's eyes. Except for her friendship with Megs, she would rather not be a part of this family at all. The woman's attitude hurt.

Frau Wolff addressed Mutti. "And your man even allowing his women, especially the woman my son is courting, to venture out without her Vati or brother on a trip like this is beyond disgraceful."

"Do you know Kraig gave Georg fair warning that he will not tolerate your son following Clara? He refused him permission to take her on any trips." Sparks flew from Mutti's eyes. "Two of our footmen will travel with us. We've endured enough of your impertinence for one day."

"Or maybe Kraig invited your driver to accompany you to Paris." She breathed deep, pulled herself perfectly upright, and rubbed her chest. "After all, he brought you here."

"Daniel is our driver, Margaret."

With nostrils flared, Frau Wolff scrunched her mouth into a knot and held up a hand as if to push the Reinhold women away. "Very well then. Good day, ladies."

Daniel assisted Clara and her Mutti into the carriage to return home. He held Clara's hand a few moments longer than necessary. His smile and his touch had melted her insides, but she dropped her gaze to her feet and sighed at the predicament that had pushed them apart. Daniel climbed to his seat and signaled the horses to move forward.

"Mutti, the Wolff family oozes discontent. They fancy themselves superior to everyone." Clara glanced toward the handsome driver and back to Mutti. "Despite my resentment, I endeavor to respect Vati's wishes. Any respect for the Wolff family, other than Megs, wanes more each day."

"The Wolffs have been our neighbors for years. Until now, our families have lived in close proximity with little contention, but your claim holds merit. First thing in the morning, we'll learn from Mamsell Lottie how the plans are coming for the trip. Traveling to Paris excites me. It delights me even more that the trip will be with my daughters.

"I'm grateful for your Vati's thoughtfulness toward us about the trip. Many men claim women unfit for more than sitting at home, stitching pretty samplers, hosting tea parties, or being the pretty baubles on their men's arms. Your Vati allows us freedom."

"Ja. The proverb about women and gouty legs is best left at home. What does it even mean? Gouty legs?"

"I think it implies all women are short and stubby."

They giggled so hard that Clara declared, "My sides are splitting. Yours too?"

"Oh, ja." Mutti wrapped her arms around her middle. "I need more than a corset to hold myself together."

Even if it were true, Clara saw no reason it should keep them home. "If chubby legs are a bad thing, why do men take notice of us at all?"

"Wise insight, meine Kinder. On to another subject. Giving Mamsell our ideas for Erntedank will assist in the planning, help keep Margaret's agitation down, and ease Lottie's burden working with the Wolffs' Mamsell."

"About Frau Wolff's agitation. She was rubbing her chest when we left and appeared to be in pain. Do you think her frequent agitation causes her troubles? She complains about it when she is flustered or perturbed."

"That wouldn't surprise me one bit. We'll all enjoy the trip more without her. Should she change her mind, I pray she leaves her cantankerous spirit at home."

"Right now, I hear Rosa's voice in my head. 'Luke 10:41-42.'"

"Ja, Margaret enjoys her role as a Martha or at least supervising her Martha. Unlike Martha in the Bible story, Margaret's attitude may be the death of her."

DANIEL DROVE the carriage to the front entrance of the Reinhold home. He pushed a folded note into Clara's hand, then waved to the two women as they entered the house.

"We'll freshen up and find Mamsell later." Mutter excused herself.

Happy to have a moment to read Daniel's note, Clara headed to her room. She secured the door. She loved how Daniel always decorated his messages with drawings. Today, it was two ducks like those in the pond by the orchards.

My lovely lady,

The ducks are insignificant to the message, but I know you enjoy them. Check behind the brick soon.

I promised you and Curt I'd be willing to help him with the puzzling secret. I won't risk writing it down, but I'm excited to say I may have stumbled upon a clue to an important piece of the mystery.

I'll apprise Curt in the morning. I trust he'll know how to proceed.

Today was my day off. I'm grateful I worked instead. I'm always thankful to have moments with you, but I wouldn't have learned this tidbit if I'd been anywhere else. How convenient, I always keep paper and pencils in the carriage.

I love you forever,

Daniel

He'd filled the note with much to ponder. She would find a private moment to visit the hidden garden spot. She tucked his message under her pillow. Did she have time for a nap before she and Mutti met with Mamsell?

A knock on her door two hours later roused her. She rose quickly, then brushed the wrinkles from her dress and met Mutti at the door.

"The cuckoo chirps three o'clock already." Mutti pointed to the stairs. "Let's have our chat with Mamsell."

They found her seated at her desk by the kitchen's sunny corner window, writing notes on her calendar. Dora removed a pan of simmering apples from the stove and set them aside to cool. She chose a large metal spoon from a rack on the wall and stirred the dinner cooking in a large copper kettle. Potatoes and carrots were piled on the stone counter ready to be cleaned and chopped.

Clara breathed in the mix of foods and spices. "The savory smells whet my appetite for dinner."

Mutti nodded. "For now, may we discuss Erntedank and Paris plans with you, Mamsell? Clara and I conceived a few ideas of our own for you."

"I've already been busy with plans for your Paris trip, ladies." Lottie removed her spectacles and looked up from her desk. "And I've consulted with the Wolff's Mamsell. We'll have Erntedank plans in place when you return, but I must inform you, Doktor Pfeiffer has been called to attend Frau Wolff at Gut Dinkelhof now."

"What happened? We visited her earlier today." Mutti's jaw gaped.

Lottie shrugged. "When he brought you and Clara home, I sent Daniel on errands near the Medizin office. He saw the Wolffs' driver parked in front of the Doktor's place and rushed inside. Daniel waited for the driver to leave Pfeiffer's office and voiced his concerns. He asked how he could help. The driver told Daniel that Frau Wolff urgently needed the Doktor's assistance. He'd been sent for help when the Gut Herrin collapsed. Doktor Pfeiffer would head that way within the hour."

Pressing a hand to her heart, Clara cocked a knowing glance toward her Mutti.

"Is there a kind gesture you'd like me to do for them in your name?" Lottie asked.

"You may tell their Mamsell whatever help she requires, please contact you to let us know." Mutti rubbed her stiff fingers. "Handle any assistance in our name, indirectly through staff. We're here for them, whatever needs arise. Be sure to share that the invitation is still open if she recovers in time and changes her mind."

"Did our visit contribute to her malady?"

Mutti's eyes widened. "I pray the good Lord I said nothing capable of coming back on us so quickly."

Clara twisted a loose curl. What would a wild animal like a wolf do when provoked?

Chapter Eight

FRIDAY MORNING, *2 September 1881*

"I THINK a surprise visit to Georg is in order." Outside the carriage house, Daniel had Landus ready as Curt had requested. Curt took his horse's reins from Daniel's hands. "I intend to catch him off guard and learn more about his upcoming plans, but I need a good excuse to be there."

"I have just the one you need, but could we step inside the carriage house?"

Curt followed him past the carriages and a pair of nickering horses.

"Pull up a hay bale and have a seat." Daniel reached into his pocket. "I found this on the ground after the Wolffs left Saturday evening. Guilt riddles me for holding on to it. Truthfully, I would've rather burned the thing. The seal was broken when I found it, but I admit I peeked at the contents. When I recognized exactly what I held, I returned the paper to the envelope without reading it. I didn't want to know the details. One would expect Georg to return looking for his courtship agreement, though."

"Definitely official, sealed with the church insignia. Vati met with Pastor Lange and Georg to make the agreement." Curt pulled the document from the sheath and perused the details. "As I suspected, this promises Clara's hand in marriage after a six-month courtship. I'm surprised, too, that Georg hasn't missed it. Thanks for bringing it to me instead of Vati."

"Go ahead and return it. By the rules, she isn't meant to be mine anyway."

"Daniel, my friend, Clara's heart is my priority in this matter. You are Clara's most important interest and her heart."

"Kind of you, Curt." Daniel bit his lower lip. "One more thing. While I waited on your Mutti and Clara at the Reinholds this morning, there was a scuffle behind their carriage house. There may have been some nasty punches thrown. All I saw was Rudi Feldt jumping on his horse and heading home. I can only assume Georg was the one cussing."

"Danke. Now I'm even more eager to confront Georg. We'll talk again later." Curt hurried to the Wolffs' estate. Intending to sneak up undetected, he looped his horse's reins to a tree at the far edge of their property and walked the remaining distance. Loud voices coming through the open windows of a stone outbuilding attracted his attention. He crouched behind a wagon stacked with cut spelt. He remained out of sight of the men but within earshot of their conversation.

"Did you run to your Ma about the new business?" Gerwig shrieked. "I specifically instructed you to keep our affairs quiet."

"Nein!" Georg shouted. "I haven't told her or anyone else."

"Not even Ma or Megs? Your Ma is extremely upset, and her health suffers. Lydia and Clara visited yesterday, and Lydia told her husband about us making a trip to Monte Carlo to gain a new business. He's asking questions—a lot of questions. Lydia learned of our private business from your Ma. What have you told her?"

"I never thought Ma would tell. Besides, we have an agreement with Herr Reinhold."

"No matter, if the Reinholds snoop into our personal affairs, I predict things will turn ugly. I expect Kraig to change his mind about you and Clara if he learns the truth. How much did you tell your Ma?"

Curt clenched his jaw. His leg muscles quivered. He itched to sneak up and choke the scoundrel. Instead, he held his breath, determined to keep his presence hidden. A better chance to hear what came after the long pause in the conversation, too.

"The truth, Georg. All of it."

"I invited Clara to Paris with me. At least I presented the invitation to her as a trip to Paris. I gave Herr Reinhold the same version when I asked his permission."

"You asked to take his daughter on a trip, hours away from home? You're courting her, not married to her."

"I assured both of them I secured chaperones to accompany us, but you and I know we're not going to Paris."

"You lied about the destination? What were you thinking?"

"Thinking it would be a great time with my sweets."

"This is hardly a humorous situation. Perhaps your attitude speaks more truth of your intentions with Clara than your words."

"I appealed to Ma to accompany us. I described all the fanciness of the place—the gold chandeliers, Corinthian columns, the beauty of the stained-glass ceilings rising tall, tempting her with the attention she would receive at the spa. She loves performances like those held at the magnificent theatre. I further impressed upon her how special it would be for her and Clara to do this together since they both miss Megs."

"This is how your Ma found out. What else?"

"Think about it. Clara asked me how I intend to prove my honorable intentions. With Ma along there would have been no question about my integrity."

"Why would Clara even question your integrity or your motives? I'm not blind. I see her hesitancy in this relationship. She shows you no admiration."

"I don't believe you. What would keep her from adoring the successful man courting her? Her whole life I've regaled her with stories of how great I am."

"What? You believe touting bragging rights gains a woman's respect?"

"Of course."

Bawdy expletives from Gerwig were followed by a loud thud. Curt imagined the man shaking a sore hand or hopping on one foot. His voice surged with growing anger. "Clara avoids eye contact with you when you speak to her. Her smile is hard and put on, and she fidgets much in your presence."

"I haven't noticed."

"Then you're blind. Her respect is for her Vati. She's doing her best to honor his decision about you in this matter."

"I don't believe you for a minute."

"Son, how will you make her care? We expect a woman to respect and obey her husband, but her love in return contributes much peace in your home. Besides, we need her on our side."

"Ja. We need Herr Reinhold to believe this alliance is to grow their landholdings, but it's really for us to take advantage of the Reinhold money. See any irony in your motives, Pa? Lack of integrity?"

"Kraig denies his beautiful daughter nothing. Do you hear the importance of my last statement? Don't give him reason to change his mind."

"I am the best man for her!"

"Not so presumptuous. Why did she decline your invitation to Paris?"

"She didn't. You and Ma gathered your coats, ready to leave the dinner party. The courting candle extinguished as I extended the invitation. She left the question hanging in the air, and I've no idea why Herr Reinhold refused.

"You have no idea? Quite a dilemma you have put us in! You drew your Ma into it as well."

"But…"

"But nothing. Antics far less reckless than yours tarnish and even destroy family names. Even if your Ma survives her current health crisis, the possibility remains we will lose the arrangement—the one bringing us much closer to the

Reinholds' fortune and your future with Clara. I should disown you."

"You wouldn't."

"Take Clara flowers. Write her poetry. Make her feel like the royalty she is. Skip your atrocious bragging, and keep your manners impeccable. Be sure Gut Herr Reinhold observes you being nothing but a perfect gentleman to his daughter. Pretend if you find the challenge is too much for you. If her Vati dissolves the courting agreement, I assure you, our new business is doomed. Do as I tell you! Now!"

"Ah, but experiencing the lavish surroundings of Monte Carlo would bedazzle her, and she would know I am the best man for her."

"Enough of that. There was another matter needing attention. You did correct the problem?"

Pounding footsteps headed away from the conversation.

Curt skedaddled to his horse.

"LANDUS, DANKE." He stroked his horse's mane. Their energetic ride around the estate after leaving the Wolffs had helped calm Curt's agitation. Until now. Curt delivered Landus back to the carriage house staff to be cooled down. The few words he had shared with Daniel earlier still upset him. He had much to consider. As he walked toward the house, Clara stood in the drive chewing her lip. Frown lines dug into her forehead. He followed his sister at a distance. She ran to her favorite escape.

He peeked through the garden gate. "May I join you?"

She motioned him in. "Did you see Georg leaving?"

"I'm glad I didn't. He's agitated me enough for one day. He visited you?"

"Georg brought sweet things, but this is far out of character for him."

"What things?" Let's walk and talk. I'm too upset to sit still."

She stepped to his side, and they ambled along the garden paths. "Flowers. Poetry. Those things that cause admiration to swell in a lady's heart." Clara rubbed her nose and shook her head.

"You don't sound impressed." Curt spat the words out from between his gritted teeth.

"He claims he wrote the poetry, but it's more like he stole it from an ancient Minnesang love song. Georg wouldn't have brought the flowers or the poems or even made a feeble attempt at exemplary behavior of his own accord. We've known him far too long and far too well. What motivated him to act so differently today?"

"Pressure from his Pa, maybe?" Curt massaged the back of his neck.

"I know Daniel's sweet notes are from his heart. He's enchanted me with them since we were children. He left me one this morning with two tiny carved swans and a message about how our love story mirrors Swan Lake. So thoughtful. He knows how much I love fairytales. Georg's attempts to impress wreak as badly as his stinky Cuban cigars."

"I know for a fact, Kirsche, Georg did not act of his own accord. Herr Wolff threatened him if he didn't do those things. He gave him all the ideas."

"That explains it, but how do you know?"

"I'm collecting pieces of the puzzle, and I won't quit until the secret behind Vati's decision is clear."

"Daniel mentioned in his note that he learned some things for you. Has he told you what? Can you tell me?"

"He has. While he waited for you and Mutti at the Wolffs, he heard a ruckus behind their carriage house, then saw Rudi Feldt galloping away. We're not sure how that connects yet, but we intend to find out."

"Another thing. Georg invited me to go to Paris with him. Then his Ma told Mutti and me that he and his Vater were going to Monte Carlo at the same time. I believe he planned a switch—that is, if he could have convinced me to go and had received Vati's approval. I can't believe that if he cares about me, he would conceive such a deceitful plan."

"I agree."

"You always protect me from troubles, listen to my dreams, and believe in them. These aren't dreams. They're a great big nightmare."

"I'm on your side, Clara."

"Danke. You're saying Vati and Gut Apfelhof's reputations will sustain substantial damage by the Wolff men if this courtship continues?"

"Sadly, your concerns are legitimate."

"Then help me, please. I love Daniel only and always." Clara collapsed against her brother's shoulder. Her tears dampened his jacket.

He patted her back. A boulder of helplessness grew in Curt's chest. "I'm doing all I can. I find no benefit for you or our beloved Gut Apfelhof in Vati's arrangement. But I need you to help me."

"How? I cannot argue with Vati."

Her twin caressed her hand, looked into her brown eyes, and missed their sparkle. "Here is the most difficult part for you. Even if it's more of a masquerade, show some care for Georg. That will please Vati. And I'm following sources close to discovering what is really behind the Wolffs' mysterious business activity."

"More mysteries? I did try to appear appreciative of his gifts, but would you have me lead him on?"

"I despise this whole setup as much as you." Curt kicked an acorn lying on the ground and set it sailing. "I need proof for Vati. He's an astute businessman. However, when he believes he knows a person or family well, he trusts easily and demonstrates kindness."

"Maybe he's too trusting and kind."

"My point precisely. Those living on our land love him. He believes everyone's intentions are honorable."

Her curls bounced like loose springs as she shook her head. "Can you believe Vati was here and witnessed Georg's antics?"

"Showing off love gestures for Vati to see? Hmm. He wouldn't have known Vati was home, but he probably hoped it would work out that way."

"And Vati hadn't missed a thing. He smiled as he talked to

me about how Georg has the makings of the perfect doting husband."

Curt huffed loudly. "Vati compliments Georg's insincere attentions. When will he acknowledge what's hiding in the Wolffs' misadventures on the French Riviera?"

"Vati refused for him to accompany me anywhere, but why did Georg lie about the destination? And why the threats he aims at our Paris trip? Trouble could lurk in either place."

"He could hardly expect a consideration from Vati about Monte Carlo. The beauty of its setting shrouds the gambling, spas, and high living there. Vati avoids it himself, but he understands the realities of the place and the depth of danger lurking behind its gilded façade."

Clara touched her temple. "Oh, but this sounds ridiculous."

"What does?"

"His expectation for me to accept his courting decision. Our usually gentle and loving Vati shows so little concern for my future happiness. The Paris trip with Megs. I cannot help it, but his permission for us to go looks a lot like tossing some table scraps to the dog. Like a distraction from bigger problems."

"There's more happening than we see. I don't know what, at least not yet. I'm poking around, and I will learn the truth."

Clara traced an embroidered flower on the cuff of her dress. "You must have an opinion about it."

His arms slackened at his side. He stepped to the garden bench and motioned for Clara to sit by him. Curt groped for the words.

"I have asked God again and again why this is happening. We're both being affected by the decision. Vati expects me to share my inheritance with Georg."

"Nein." Her entire body shook from her sobbing. "You know I'm praying, and we must accept God's answer, whatever it is. God sees far beyond what we discern, but I'm struggling with my faith. Does God even see us, Curt?"

"That's been a bitter mouthful for me to swallow, too. I want to believe God does see us. Maybe this'll help you. He answered my prayers with Ecclesiastes 12:13-14. *Let us hear the conclusion of the whole matter: Fear God, and keep his commandments: for this is the whole duty of man. For God shall bring every work into judgment, with every secret thing, whether it be good, or whether it be evil.*" With his elbows propped on his knees, Curt tapped a fist to his mouth.

She scrunched her eyebrows. "He led me to the same one. Are you puzzled over how to apply these verses, too? And it talks about a secret thing again. When we listened to Mutti and Rosa's conversation, it sounded like they shared a secret. You think Vati harbors a secret."

"And Georg hides dirty secrets, I'm certain. It's too early to know which ones will be made known to us, but we must trust God's judgment and wisdom. Sweet Kirsche, until He reveals more, we will do our part to be obedient. We have a big challenge facing us, but we both have a huge stake in this."

The garden gate creaked.

"Pardon me. I didn't mean to intrude on your conversation."

~

CLARA PERKED UP, tucking back the ever-wayward curl. A lightness filled her chest. "Daniel. What brings you to the garden?"

"I have the horses saddled for you and Curt. All ready for you two to make your regular weekly visit." Daniel winked in Clara's direction. "The sick and invalids, unable to attend church, love it when the two of you drop in to see them."

Daniel turned his attention to Clara. She leaned easily into his hug.

"Did you find the surprise?"

"O Daniel, I did. I was just reminding Curt how thoughtful you always are."

Curt cleared his throat. "Are you two going to be lovey all day, or are you ready to ride, Clara?

"Today? Will we be visiting today? It's already after lunch, and I'm not dressed for visiting. Everyone's packing for Paris."

Daniel's chin dipped in a bemused nod. "You always look radiant to me."

"It's way too easy to fluster you." Curt shook his head, laughing. "Listen to Daniel. He says you're always radiant. The others may be packing, but your bags have been ready for two days. We'll bring a little joy to others today, and tomorrow the joy's all yours. Tomorrow you will leave for Paris."

"And I have the privilege of driving the ladies to the train station." Daniel winked at Clara. "Curt, don't look."

The depth of Daniel's kiss surged through her whole being. Even her curls tingled.

Chapter Nine

SATURDAY, *3 September 1881*

Ladies rarely traveled light. Off to the side of the carriage house, luggage had been piled on the grassy area next to the cobbled drive and was ready to be loaded. The piles resembled mountains as high as the Bavarian Alps. Daniel swallowed his laughter and directed the coachmen to ready a second carriage.

Fritz glanced around at the bags he had collected. "I'll make Mamsell aware the ladies have a little more time before they leave."

When he reached for the knob, Clara bounded through the door barely averting a collision. "What a beautiful morning. And the first fall chill fills the air, too. Are we ready to go? Can you tell I'm impatient to escape this place for a few days?"

Daniel appreciated her enthusiasm! He focused his eyes on the woman he loved.

"Whoa, Clara. You ladies created a delay this morning." Fritz pointed toward the carriage house where servants scurried to prepare the extra horses and conveyance. "I'm headed inside to let Lottie know the Frauen and Frauleins have a bit more time."

Clara gawked back and forth from Fritz to Daniel. "Will this make us late for the train?"

"Nein. All the Gut Apfelhof staff know things happen when you girls make plans."

"For instance, Daniel?"

"Someone misplaces their reticule, and a search is required." He winked at Clara. "We scheduled our departure time expecting inevitable delays. No worries, my lovely lady."

When Fritz went inside, Daniel grabbed Clara's hand and swung her arm with his. I love stealing kisses when no one's looking."

"And I welcome your affection. I wish it weren't at odds with this position Vati has forced upon me." Clara's face matched her red cape.

"But this moment is ours." *Only a moment indeed.*

"Clara, are you out here?"

At the sound of Hannah's voice, Daniel released Clara and jumped back.

"We should've been more discreet." Disappointment registered in Clara's pouty lips. Hannah nearly skipped down the steps.

Little bags and packages peeked from the oversized carpetbag Emmaline carried.

Clara scurried toward her sisters. "I was out here early. You know how eager I am for us to be on our way."

"Your impatience is the only reason?" Emmaline's eyes grew wide, and the corners of her mouth twitched upward. "You're blushing."

Daniel sucked in his cheeks, muting a chuckle pushing to escape. Clara never lied well. She always changed the subject instead.

"I'm so glad you're both here now. Is Mutti far behind?"

"Mamsell whispered to Mutti and Rosa as we passed. Lines creased both their foreheads." Hannah's face bore worry lines, too. "I don't read lips, but I believe the name Frau Wolff slipped from Mamsell's tongue."

Clara gasped. "You know Frau Wolff hasn't been well, and she's jealous of our invitation from Megs."

"I don't wish to sound selfish, but I sure hope whatever happened doesn't interfere with our trip." Emmaline plopped down on one of the trunks.

"Emmaline, you sound like you are groaning all the way from your toes. This is unkind on my part, too, but I wish we hadn't invited her." Clara grasped her sister's hand. "This is a good time for us to pray. Pray for a safe journey and pray for Frau Wolff."

They all nodded. Clara joined her hands with her sisters'. Daniel stood beside them with his head bowed. He brushed Clara's elbow. It wasn't an accident. "If I may?"

Clara nodded.

Our Heavenly Vater, Daniel began, *we thank You so much for this opportunity for these women to travel to Paris to visit with Megs and to see places special to Frau Reinhold. We bring concerns to You about Frau Wolff. We hope whatever news Mamsell received doesn't affect the ladies' plans. The words of Philippians 4:6 remind us to always make our requests known to You—with thanksgiving.*

We're thanking You, Lord, and asking with gratefulness, for Your grace and mercy. Please let this situation be resolved well for everyone, and allow the outcome to bring glory to You. In Jesus' name. Amen.

For several seconds, they remained silent. Convinced God's presence had pushed everyone's worries aside, Daniel broke the stillness. "Ladies, your Mutti and mine have joined us."

"Meine Kinder, good news! Mamsell received a message from the Wolffs' home early this morning. Margaret Wolff has recovered. She asked to join us." Mutti stared down the drive. "Her carriage will arrive shortly, and we'll all travel together to Paris."

"I'm so thankful you suggested we pray about this." Hannah stretched her fingers and took a deep breath. "It's good news. Frau Wolff is well, but if we hadn't prayed, I wouldn't be content for her to accompany us."

"Danke, Daniel, for praying." Clara surveyed the loaded carriages. "Will there be room for Frau Wolff's luggage?"

"One more reason it's good we prepared the second carriage. A tight squeeze for six of you but maybe not too cramped in the Landau for only a couple of hours."

Peering directly into Clara's eyes, Daniel winked. "There's room for one of you on the driver's bench with me."

"Not funny! You know how much I'd love sitting at your side. As difficult as it is, we need to be more cautious of our attention to one another. You know Vati and Mutti would never approve. And Georg's Ma—well, we can predict her reaction. Here she comes now."

The Wolffs' carriage rolled up the drive. Georg followed on Quintus. Clara's stomach soured. Georg helped his Ma step down. He directed their driver to move her trunks to be loaded.

"Guten Morgen, Georg."

"Hello, Clara. You planned a trip on your own but refused my invitation?"

She tightened her lips and prayed that not even a hint of a smile showed. No answer slipped from her tongue.

"Pa and I have not changed our plans, and we thwarted your efforts to avoid us. I recommend you and your party keep a careful watch. You could bump into unexpected company. Is this how you intend to treat your beloved after our betrothal and marriage?"

Hope flickered in her heart. Vati had stepped out the door in time to hear the harsh words Georg had spoken to her.

"Georg, your tone of voice is most unflattering for a man of lofty standing in the community. Furthermore, you laced your comments with contempt toward my daughter, whom I allow you to court."

"I was helping Clara understand expectations. Besides, you and I signed and sealed our agreement."

"Don't believe for one minute I wouldn't retract that contract."

"But…"

"Say no more. I separated my decision to allow this trip from your request to travel with Clara. The circumstances are very different. Your Pa's plans for Paris are a lie. I suggest you leave Gut Apfelhof now."

"Ask my Ma. She'll tell you Paris was our plan all along."

"Your string of lies is growing. Please desist with them now. Leave."

Without so much as a nod to Vati, Georg spun around toward Clara once again. "Take good care of my Ma. I know she feels better, but she remains fragile and needs her rest throughout the trip. She'll be your mother-in-law soon, so you'll do whatever she asks." A condescending tone coated his words.

Clara thanked God. She was displeased with Vati's decision, but he had appeared when she needed him. He must love her despite his recent actions. How would she respond to Georg's request?

Clenching her fists at her side, she addressed him most matter-of-factly. "Georg, your Ma will be fine with us. Megs will be happy to see her, and we'll take good care of her. You're welcome to return to whatever other business you find important today."

His face morphed into a twisted knot. "So quick to be rid of me, my sweets? A proper farewell would at least include an embrace and a kiss." Georg stepped closer, taking her in his arms.

"A kiss in front of all these people? Nein." She fought against his arms until he released his hold. He tilted his head back and flashed his dimpled grin.

Fire scorched Clara's cheeks. Her entire body trembled.

"Georg climbed on Quintus and trotted away alongside the Wolff's carriage.

Vati embraced his wife and daughters, pausing a moment longer when he hugged Clara. "Enjoy your trip. Have an adventure, but don't let Paris steal your hearts." Vati delivered last-minute instructions to the coachmen and Rosa, then gazed at his wife's face and spoke in a gentle voice. "Lydia, come back to me again, my love."

Beams of sunshine sparkled in Mutti's eyes. Had Vati noticed how much Mutti loved him? Clara's eyes shined like Mutti's, but only for Daniel. Georg would never have her love.

"I hope you and my girls enjoy your visit to Paris." Vati greeted Margaret. "Please tell Megs I send my love. She's always been like another daughter to me."

The women boarded the luxury coach. Once on their way, Clara patted Margaret's hand. "I'm sorry you witnessed the scene with your son."

"Words, just words. He may have deserved your attitude, but we will agree you don't care a whit about my son's feelings or mine."

"Soon we'll board the train to Strasbourg." Clara's head sagged. "Could we leave our differences behind?"

As quickly as Margaret opened her mouth as if to answer, she closed it again and lowered her eyelids.

"It'll be best for Margaret to sleep awhile," Mutti whispered in Clara's ear. "Despite his threats, I believe Georg's travel plans will take him in a much different direction than ours. You'll enjoy our visit to Paris more when you put your worries about your big bad Wolff to rest during the trip."

It was the mother Wolff who concerned Clara now. She didn't trust whatever nightmarish plots Frau Wolff would hatch while she napped.

Chapter Ten

CRAILSHEIM STATION, *Saturday, 3 September 1881*

DANIEL BROUGHT the carriage to rest in front of the Crailsheim train station. An all too familiar figure strode in front of the carriage and planted his boot on the left front wheel. *Georg left a half hour before the rest of us and traveled by horseback, and now he's arrived ahead of us.* Daniel took several deep breaths to loosen the tightening in his chest. He'd take care of the women's needs first, then deal with this rascal.

Hans and Willy pulled the second carriage to the luggage platform. Daniel helped the women disembark.

The bright yellow carriage with its emblazoned red Gut Apfelhof crest always announced the nobility's arrival. The scene was no different today. Other travelers eyed the ladies in their finery as they congregated on the platform.

Daniel tapped his heel and scanned the men and women gathered along the walkways. The flash of her well-appointed accessories and regally styled curls flattered Clara. The blaze of her red cape covering her shiny golden gown had drawn every eye in the crowd.

Women whispered to each other. Standing a little further down the platform, the scoundrel who had kicked the carriage riveted his eyes on her, too.

Keeping a close watch on the man the entire time, Daniel purchased the women's tickets. He planned how to handle Georg and prayed Clara and the others had not noticed the Wolff's presence. Should he approach Georg or his Ma? Daniel didn't trust anyone in the Wolff family, but he owed it to Gut Herr Reinhold to watch out for the safety of his women at least until they boarded the train. He wished he were traveling with them to help Willy and Hans guard these ladies. He prayed no one meant them harm.

That the group would travel in a private coach car offered a drop of consolation. The family melded well with the community, but this trip would be long. Rest from public interaction would serve them well, allowing them to arrive in Paris ready to explore the city's glittering sites. And she would be safe from Georg for the week. *She would, wouldn't she?*

When he delivered the tickets to the women, Daniel's fingers lingered on Clara's hand a moment longer than on the others. A wind of unease swept between him and Frau Wolff. "Excuse me, ladies. One of our coachmen needs my help."

While the women huddled together chattering with excitement, Daniel set his pace toward Georg. He thanked God that the crowd hid Georg from the women because he would need to do this quickly without arousing their suspicions.

"Georg. How convenient I stumbled upon you here. And your Pa." Daniel nodded to the older man who had joined them.

"That's Herr Wolff to you. Remember, you're a servant to the Reinholds and not my peer."

"As a servant to the Reinhold family, it's my responsibility to ensure you follow the Gut Herr's wishes and that the women of his household remain safe."

"He chose me to court Clara." Georg spewed his retort.

"Regardless, Herr Reinhold specifically forbade Clara from accompanying you to Paris. His refusal of your request was firm."

"That is not your business, Daniel."

"The Reinholds' business is my business. I'm hired to see to it. Explain to me why your driver brought you and Herr Wolff here after dropping your Ma off at Gut Apfelhof."

He snickered. "Pa and I rode our horses. Much faster than your carriage. Why concern yourself about it? We may travel to Paris, if we choose. We had plans at the same time, and I'd like to see my sister."

"You and your travel plans are fickle. Seeing your sister? I don't believe you. You've spent a lifetime taunting both Clara and Megs. How will you hurt them on this trip?"

"I've never hurt either of them, not even once." Georg spat his answer.

"I have witnessed a hefty amount of your behavior toward women, these two women in particular. I grew up with them, and they're much closer to my age than yours. I conjure up ugly images about your intentions for this trip. The picture I envision, I'm certain, comes much closer to reality than the fairy tales Fraulein Reinhold loves. But never mind. Don't tell me your plans. Gut Herr Reinhold arranged for his men to keep a close eye on all the women, including your Ma—Frau Wolff. Even more so, your Ma." He gave a tentative smile.

"What if your men blink on their watch?" Georg scoffed.

Daniel returned to the Reinhold party. He pulled Hans and Willy into a three-man huddle, then gave last-minute directives to the coachmen. "I've received word of trouble brewing in Paris. Keep the ladies in sight except to sleep, please. Georg may also be traveling to Paris. If so, he'll be a threat."

With emphatic nods, firm handshakes, and brotherly hands across each other's backs, the men acknowledged the seriousness of Daniel's request. They would tend well to the safety of the Reinhold women, Daniel's own Mutter, and Georg's.

Daniel helped each of the women up the steps of the train's coach car. He longed to position himself where Clara's shoulder and his shared a warm touch. Margaret Wolff's grim expression warned him to increase the space between them instead.

"Ladies, Hans and Willy will protect you well. Listen carefully and stay mindful of all instructions they give you."

Frau Wolff's agitated expression was fixed on him. Prickles crawled up his arm. Is she plotting with Georg and Herr Wolff? *O God, please protect the women, and let this be a happy visit.*

As he pulled away from the Crailsheim station, relief washed over Daniel. Herr Wolff stood on the platform with his son. They boarded a train headed south, away from Paris. Georg would not be bothering the women, but he was obligated to apprise Curt and the Gut Herr of the situation. Oh, the lies and ill intentions consuming these Wolff men. Would the Gut Herr listen at all?

His thoughts chased him from the station to home. Daniel drove up to the Reinhold estate as Curt and Kraig saddled their horses. "Gentlemen, may I have a moment of your time?"

"What's on your mind, Daniel?" Herr Reinhold asked.

"I need to warn you of an incident at the rail station today."

Worry lines formed around the Gut Herr's eyes. "Are the women safe?"

"Ja, at least for now. You'll not want to hear this, but I trust neither of the Wolff men. They traveled to the train station ahead of us today on some fast horses. The younger Wolff informed me of their plans to follow the women, and he asked me to deliver threats to them. As I readied the coach to pull away, he and the elder Herr Wolff boarded a southbound train. Where are they headed? Monte Carlo perhaps? Hans and Willy will maintain an extra vigilant guard in case they turn back to Paris."

"Danke for the warning. You always prioritize my ladies' safety, but it sounds like all is well since the Wolffs headed the other direction." Curt and the Gut Herr rode off.

Daniel maintained much less certainty than his boss. The twisted knot in his stomach insisted he believe otherwise. Maybe he should fold his hands in prayer. Instead, he wrenched them with worry.

Chapter Eleven

GUT APFELHOF, *Saturday, 3 September 1881*

"I'M unconvinced you took Daniel's warning seriously." Curt rode his steed beside Vati. "What do you know about the Wolffs' business in Monte Carlo?"

Vati twisted Artax's reins, bringing the animal to a halt. Curt signaled Landus to stop beside them.

Narrowing his eyes, Vati cut an annoyed look toward Curt. "They sell their Dinkel grain to the bakeries and kitchens serving the appetites of the opulent clientele. It's an honest living."

Curt turned to hide his disbelieving smirk. "You're positive you have the complete story?"

"Your questions try my patience, son. The Wolffs have been peers and respectable neighbors of our family for three generations."

"Three generations? That long? Our family history here dates back much further than theirs. How did the Wolffs acquire their land? Did your Vater fill you in on the Wolffs' family history? Did previous generations of Wolffs exhibit the same questionable behaviors? Besides, they're quite recent additions to the nobility class—the Baron title conferred on Herr Gerwig Wolff a mere decade ago?"

"What're you asking? You haven't been keen on this arrangement with Clara and Georg, and you've made your opinion clear. Are you calling my judgment into question again?"

"With excellent reason. I deplored the way Georg treated Clara and Megs when we were growing up. He mistreated them continuously, and when I say mistreated, please interpret my comments about his behavior in the most inappropriate ways possible. I protected the girls as best I knew how as a youth."

"You conveniently choose to point out to me now incidents you claim happened ten or more years ago. Why didn't you come to me then?"

"Georg lorded his years over me. He made contemptuous threats toward me because he feared you'd learn of his behavior."

"Those threats should no longer be menacing to you since you're a man now. Would you be more specific with your allegations?"

"Is it necessary to expound on all manner of inappropriate and unwanted physical contact and verbal suggestions from a man to a woman? You're a married man. You aren't half-witted on the subject, are you?"

Vati shook his pointer finger in Curt's face. "You think you're a better judge of character than me? You believe me naive, but experience is an excellent professor. You claim only your twenty-six years. Mine are nearly double yours. You are unaware of my reasons to trust the Wolffs. I doubt you would understand if I told you."

Curt thrust aside the finger Vati had aimed at his face. "You've said that before. Please help me understand. I intend no ill toward you. I wish to protect your interests, my interests, and the interests of future Reinhold heirs. The Gut Apfelhof land has been in our family for centuries. How many great-grandfathers ago was the first Reinhold appointed Baron to oversee this property?"

"Our records and lineage here date back at least a few centuries."

"While barons are low royalty, our name and reputation stand tall among lords and nobles. I'm asking you to step more cautiously into this alliance with the Wolff family because of their less-proven gentility. Why not send one of our men to learn what's happening along the coast of the Mediterranean? Or while the women are off to Paris, we could make our own journey and spy on them."

Vati grinned. "You trust making such a trip to be a wise decision? If what you're seeking is proof of indiscretion and low integrity from Gerwig and Georg, how do you propose we make this trip while keeping our reputations clean?"

"A tedious chore, as you point out." If only Curt hadn't blurted out his poorly conceived plan.

"Let's wait it out. If my wisdom serves me well, one or both of them will tell on the other. Pieces of information have already leaked through Frau Wolff. I've made a firm point with Georg. I have a right to rescind my decision about him and Clara."

"We'll wait then. Remember, though, dirty wolves stink! What if the Wolffs did exit the train at the next station? Backtracked? Followed the ladies?"

Chapter Twelve

3 SEPTEMBER 1881

Clara laughed as she followed Rosa's gaze, soaking in the train's fine furnishings, the lace accents, and the velvet draperies with their spun gold trim. "Whoever designs train interiors is as amazing with fabrics and accents as you are, Rosa."

"Gut Apfelhof is magnificent, and every detail splendid, but this luxuriousness surpasses anything I've seen."

Mutti's eyes twinkled. "And we're only on the train. Amazing sites and remarkable architecture line the streets of Paris."

The women chattered on. Margaret wheezed and coughed. Her last audible gasp before she passed out caught everyone's attention.

It wasn't very sympathetic of her, but Clara wondered if Frau Wolff had planned this.

"Mutti, Rosa, do either of you know what to do?" Clara glanced from one to the other. "Is she really sick?"

Concern filled Mutti's eyes. Clara knew the answer before she heard Mutti's words. "Look at her. I've just now noticed. With her cape off, I see exactly what's causing her problems."

"*Shoo!*" Mutti sent their coachmen to the far end of the car. "And cover your eyes and ears, too. Hide behind the draperies."

Mutti undressed Frau Wolff enough to loosen the torturous contraption and fanned her neighbor's face.

"What happened? Is it my heart again, do you think?" Margaret perked up as air returned to her lungs.

"Doubtful, my friend. I hadn't taken notice before when you attracted attention with your maladies, but gracious, your royal highness. How tightly you have pulled your corset strings today. Do you do this all the time?"

"Of course. All women do. And I do want to look my best in my fancy gowns."

"Ja, most women wear them, but you seem to have set a new standard in the amount of cinching required. You know these vain inventions restrict our breathing when laced too tightly. You scared your family when you became seriously ill a few days ago. You and I will speak in private, Margaret."

"Take a lesson from this, ladies. Our figures may appear more desirable when they're all tied up, but our bodies will thank us for allowing them liberty to breathe. Does anyone else need to make adjustments before we let the men come out of hiding?"

Everyone looked up. All but Emmaline.

"You tiny young thing. Why do you find this necessary? All these ladies' magazines and their ideas make me question if the fashionable purpose of this trip is a good idea at all."

In case the men had peeked, Clara's sisters, Frau Wolff, and Rosa all hid their mortified blushes behind the latest fashion trend magazines. Mutti pulled out her sketchbook.

What will Mutti portray from this scene?

"I'm drawing a few interesting studies in ladies' attire before we arrive in Paris." Mutti answered her question as though she had read Clara's mind. "I intend for the images to rest among those which remain unseen, of course."

Clara flipped the pages of her magazine. "Rosa, do you think we'll discover less-confining styles in Paris? I look forward to a reprieve from these dastardly things."

Rosa's head bobbed, and the corners of her lips ascended into a bright smile. "Perhaps. You see the new styles from the English Cult of Beauty members on current fashion pages. Their styles are trending in Paris." In typical Rosa fashion, she added a Bible verse. "Proverbs 31:25."

"Which part of the advice of King Lemuel's mother are you suggesting applies here?" Mutti asked.

"Strength and honour are her clothing; and she shall rejoice in time to come."

"We will rejoice over a more comfortable style then?" Mutti giggled.

"Of course, God desires modesty in our dress." Rosa's bright smile turned to an impish grin. "But when we trust Him, we look to the future with confidence in His plan and some kinder undergarments."

"That seems a little far-fetched interpretation of corsets, but I'm looking forward to His plan keeping us from any further interruptions and troubles on our journey." Mutti went back to her sketching.

Rosa rubbed Clara's shoulder. "Your toes bounce, and you're covering your smile. You found humor in my suggestion, too."

Clara grinned, then turned her gaze to watch the landscapes float by. If Clara could sleep, they would arrive in Strasbourg in a blink.

Wide awake now, Clara spotted him as the train chugged to a halt at the Strasbourg station. People tumbled back from the impeccably dressed man who was elbowing his way to the edge of the platform, a pipe clamped between his teeth and a sign clenched in his oversized fists. From one coach car to the next his glare traveled the length of the train and back.

Clara grabbed Frau Wolff's shoulder. "Look over there! Whatever trouble is next? Frau Wolff, do you recognize this man?" Clara's scalp prickled. She pointed to the man holding the large wooden sign inscribed with Margaret Wolff's name.

Margaret peered from the window. "Nein. Definitely not."

With arms crossed over her chest, Clara squinted at Georg's Ma, grateful Mutti spoke before she lost control of her tongue.

"Margaret, are you being honest with us?" Mutti straightened her skirt and cleared her throat. "You're sure you don't recognize this man or know what this is about? He certainly means to get your attention."

With her eyes riveted on her Mutti's Clara gathered her thoughts. "Rosa's right about God knowing the future. But right now, I admit, God's promises don't comfort me as they should."

"Willy, please go ahead of us and learn his intentions." Mutti appealed to one coachman while firmly planting her hand on the other's forearm. "Hans, you will stay right here with us until we learn more."

"Ja, Gut Herrin," Hans replied. "It is our privilege to attend to the safety of our Gut Herr's women."

Thankful Mutti had stepped in, Clara joined her clammy hands with her sisters. "I would be most grateful for the ability to read lips right now."

Willy returned and delivered the note to Margaret's shaky hand. She opened the message from the mystery man and chewed her lips as she read. "That man is Manfred?"

"He gave me that name when I inquired."

Trains and people filled the Strasbourg station. The women moved away from the train, stepping further up the platform, eager for the next step of the journey. Frau Wolff grimaced and rubbed her forehead.

Clara poked an elbow in Hannah's side. "She's talking to herself."

The woman muttered as she rubbed her chest. Clara caught just the tail end of what she was saying. "This time the undergarment is not to blame for my pain. The mischief of these men of mine promises to bring my demise." She jerked her attention to Willy. "Is our next train ready to board?"

"Our train leaves in the morning, Frau Wolff. I've secured conveyance to the nearest inn."

"Certainly not the news I hoped to hear." The hiss of her words cut through the air.

Clara shuddered. She trusted Mutti would pull the story out of her, but did Frau Wolff have reason to fear George would follow us?

Margaret twisted and fidgeted like a floppy fish jumping from its water hole. A second later, she straightened and stiffened her body from its awkward slump. She pulled herself up to her full four feet, eleven inches of authority. "Then do something, Willy! We need to be gone from here within the hour. Ladies, follow me to the water closet." With a sweep of her skirts, she led them away.

Lord, have mercy on us. It'll take Willy some time to tend to the tickets. Please let him have a plan when we return from our business.

Mutti held her fingers over her mouth, tapping with her pointer. "This is only the first day, and Frau Wolff harbors a love affair with turmoil and trouble. I see how her son comes by it naturally."

Clara and Mutti returned ahead of the others. Willy spoke in hushed tones. "I'm wary of Frau Wolff's attitude. Combined with the commotion at Crailsheim, I anticipate a scary scene ahead. Perhaps the change in the itinerary will derail any complications ahead. I'm sending a telegram back to Gut Apfelhof informing them of our revised plans."

"Thanks, Willy." Mutti and Clara turned to find the others catching up with them.

Clara twisted a curl and tapped her feet in time to the quick pace of her heart. What would the schedule change mean?

"There is an overnight train to Paris leaving in thirty minutes." Willy held up the tickets. "You'll not see the scenery, but it leaves today. An empty car with sleeping berths is available for us. The station master wired ahead for rooms to be ready a day early and asked for a Westminster Hotel employee to meet us at the Paris station."

Margaret tossed a wadded piece of paper in the trash receptacle, then abruptly lost her scowl. A bright smile lit up her face. "Then what're we waiting for? All aboard!"

Chapter Thirteen

3 SEPTEMBER 1881

THEY BOARDED the evening train to Paris. The sleeping cars would provide privacy for a much-needed conversation. Her Mutti had invited Clara and Frau Wolff into her berth. Clara prayed silently while Mutti steered the conversation to learn what Margaret was hiding. "We're not returning home, but what are they planning to do?"

A snarl came from Frau Wolff's curled lips. She moaned and whimpered. But no answer.

"The men can make a better plan for our safety, and we'll all rest better if you'd quit keeping secrets." By the severe jut of her chin, Clara recognized Mutti was losing patience.

Frau Wolff's fingernails scratched an eerie rhythm along the paneled wall next to her. Her words came slowly and softly. "They'll kidnap Clara and me and take us to Monte Carlo."

"Why would they make a threat like that?"

"Because I didn't obey them. Gerwig and Georg asked me to spin a convincing story your husband would agree to, one that would allow Clara to make the trip Georg proposed. I wanted to see Megs."

"There are at least two stories, maybe three, in that pot you're stirring. They're all muddled up in a mealy porridge. And Clara's safety is your last concern?"

Rage pounded in Clara's ears. "Monte Carlo or Paris? Which was it? Why?" She bit her tongue until she tasted blood. She would keep quiet and let Mutti do the talking from now on.

"Willy attends to the safety of our Gut Apfelhof women well, and he has all of our best interests in mind, yours included. We're on our way now. You'll see your daughter, but please pray any threats remain just that."

"Clara, your Vati refused to allow you to travel with Georg. I understand his reasons. These two men of mine, they're fine men." She took a deep breath. "But they are hard-headed. No matter what decision I make, I'll have one or more people angry with me if I don't buckle to their plan."

Clara struggled to respond. Anything she said could cause more trouble. She concentrated on holding back any more tears. But what had they planned?

Mutti's hair fell around her face as she pulled the pins holding her bun in place. She raked her fingers through her silver-laced dark hair and sank her teeth into her lower lip. "What you're saying then is, you're having to choose to respect your husband, respect my husband's decision, placate your son, or protect Clara?"

"Ja, my friend. I hoped to protect Clara since I'm uncertain what they'll do."

Frau Wolff didn't know their plans either. Clara had hoped this trip would pull her away from Georg, but the nightmare of Vati's promise to him continued to grow.

Rumpling her long locks around her face, Mutti covered her eyes. "Danke for protecting Clara, but what happens next? They know we're traveling ahead of them. If they follow us, they'll inquire at all the hotels in Paris until they find us." Mutti rocked in her seat, closed her eyes, and lifted her hands to her mouth as in prayer. Quietness lingered between them.

"You shared things at your home when we visited for tea. Sketchy things about Georg's and Gerwig's business in Monte Carlo." Mutti's eyebrows squished together. She took Clara's hand in hers. "My daughter has devoted herself to respecting your son and the courtship agreement he and our husbands have made. She has cooperated with her Vati's choice.

"Grave concerns fatigue me about your family's questionable business ventures. I worry for my daughter regarding the courting arrangement. Like Clara, I've chosen the higher road. Until now I've respected my husband's choice and guarded my thoughts."

"I'm grateful. My son suffered much heartbreak when Sarah passed." Margaret's tiny frame shook. "I prayed for another girl to bring him happiness again and bring him back to his senses. I hoped kind, tender-hearted Clara would be the one."

Mutti released Clara's hand and rubbed Frau Wolff's shoulder. "Georg's wronged women for years, even before Sarah died. Reliable sources suggested Megs and Gus left for America partly to be far away from Georg and the ways he had hurt her, too. While I have suspected it for years, Clara confirmed your son behaved poorly toward her and Megs. I'm gracious with my choice of words. It began for Clara when she was a mere thirteen years old, maybe at a much younger age for your Megs. Is that true?"

"Whatever you accuse my son of, he's innocent." Frau Wolff's icy blue eyes grew even colder beneath her arched eyebrows. "He would never even think such things."

"You're calling my daughter a liar then? You tell us how kind she is and how you hope she'll be the one to help mend Georg's broken heart. I'm confused."

Clara shivered at the thought Georg could ever change. Mutti trembled too. She was as confused as Clara.

"Margaret, I'm sorry we invited you on this trip. Please return to your sleeper and pray we find forgiveness toward you and your family. Unless Kraig changes his mind, the courting agreement stands. It would be a shame for our friendship to be lost."

"But, Lydia…"

"I have no more words for you at the moment. We all need rest. We'll arrive in Paris soon. Who or what awaits us?"

~

4 September 1881

Early morning sunlight streamed through the glass-domed ceiling of the train station. Clara's body stiffened when the gentleman approached. He held a Westminster sign. Its message was ornately hand-lettered. Welcome Reinhold Party. Could they trust him?

Willy stepped forward. "They promised a hotel employee would meet us. Are you the one?"

"Oui! Welcome to Paris, our beautiful city, and the Hotel Westminster. Emile at your service."

"Thank you, sir, but first the code word."

"Sunflower."

A code word. Who had created that? Clara could think of several but didn't expect the one Willy had chosen. She liked it.

"Very well." Willy shook the man's hand. He released his grip and pointed to his fellow coachman. "Hans and I escort the Reinhold party. My Gut Herr trusts they'll be safe in your city."

"Oui. And they'll adore it here." Emile surveyed the group, stepped back, and slowly shook his head. "You have no luggage?" He flexed his arm muscle. "Ladies always have lots and lots of things for me to carry."

All six women leaned toward Emile. They stood perfectly still, staring at him with mouths agape, including Clara.

Willy singled out Mutti. "You ladies look silly, Frau Reinhold. You need to sketch a picture of yourselves. It'd bring us all a merry laugh."

"Willy, I don't believe there is much humor in your comment." Mutti tilted her head and wagged her pointer finger. "We have six women without even one extra gown and no toiletries spending several days in Paris."

"I am sure the ladies will find the finest of toiletries for purchase here in Paris, oui?" Willy winked at the porter.

"Oui!"

A tingly sensation traveled up Clara's arm. How much more pain and embarrassment would they face?

"Monsieur, they each have at least one trunk. When we made a hasty switch to a different train leaving Strasbourg, the station master telegraphed ahead to your hotel. Your fine establishment received the message, or you wouldn't be here. I pray you bring word about the luggage, too."

"My information shows eight of you need transportation from the train station to the hotel. We brought two coaches. We'll get you to the hotel and check on your bags."

What if their luggage had been sent to Switzerland, or worse, Monte Carlo by mistake? Would they ever see it again? Clara twisted a loose curl to avoid chewing her fingernails.

Emile helped the women into the coaches. A short time later, they came to rest before the impressive Haussmannian façade of the Hotel Westminster. The scalloped and fanned panels rising from the curved entry invited the travelers inside.

Clara recognized Megs' sweet musical voice calling to her through the hotel lobby. She tossed the front panels of her cape aside and embraced her friend. The two of them locked together in a hug for at least a full minute.

"It's six-thirty on Sunday morning, Megs. How did you know of our early arrival?"

Megs blinked several times as she surveyed the group. "My, did you bring all of Gut Apfelhof with you?"

"I'm sorry. You know my spontaneous nature." Clara tucked her chin. "I invited enough for a lively party, and I wired you with our plans."

"Emmaline, Hannah, Frau Reinhold, Rosa, Willy, Hans, you're all here. Give me hugs." She glanced around the group again. "And where's Daniel?"

"The Gut Herr needs Daniel at home." Mutti narrowed her eyes. "But look. Your Ma accompanied us."

"Hello, Ma. I hadn't expected you?"

"Was I remiss in believing you'd be happy to see me?"

"Things have changed since you moved to America." Mutti's answer came before Megs' Ma even opened her mouth. "If Clara has not written and posted them to you in a letter, I'm certain you will persuade her to fill you in about it this week. Could we move to our rooms where we make less of a curiosity of ourselves?"

"I reserved four rooms. One for Clara and me, one for Rosa, one for Daniel, and one extra for any servants accompanying you. Clara, you and I'll stay together. Willy and Hans, of course, we have the room for you."

Margaret pinched at the skin around her neck. "You reserved a regular room and not a servant's room for Rosa?"

"Ja, Ma, a regular room. Rosa is like family to Clara and me. We'll ask for one more room. Emmaline and Hannah will be together. Frau Reinhold, I believe you and Rosa would be comfortable sharing a room. Am I correct?"

Mutti nodded as she smiled in Rosa's direction.

"Frau Lydia, are you certain?" Rosa gulped. "I'm happy to have a servant's room. After all, I am a servant."

"Lydia, she is your servant." Frau Wolff tsk'd.

"Ma, you will stay in a room by yourself. No one will disturb you." Megs pulled her smile sideways, matching her shaking head.

"How may we help you, mademoiselles?" The desk attendant inquired.

"I'm Megs Schmitz. I checked in earlier today. The rest of my party arrived a day early."

"Oui, mademoiselle. We observed your reunion in the lobby."

"I have additional guests, including one unexpected one. If you please, is another room available on our hall?"

"Are the women joining you, by chance, the Reinhold ladies?"

"Ja. Oui, they are. The family of the Gut Herr of Apfelhof. Perhaps you've heard of him?"

"Only inasmuch as I received several telegrams from the stationmaster in Strasbourg today in reference to your friends. He apologized that their trunks did not travel on the train with them. Their luggage will arrive later today. He also asked us to confirm there are rooms for everyone. There are, and all is well."

The two friends faced each other. They both inhaled deeply, then released a simultaneous woosh.

The attendant acknowledged Willy and Hans with a glance. "I presume these two gentlemen took great responsibility in protecting the Reinhold women. Emile will show you to your rooms. Enjoy Paris."

As soon as they were safely away from any chance of twitching ears, Megs leaned close to Clara. "What's this your Mutti mentioned about things changing? We'll enjoy Paris but only after you explain what's happening at Gut Apfelhof."

Clara shifted from one foot to the other. Her knee jerked, and tumultuous waves tossed around her stomach again.

In the early morning hours after a long night's train ride, Megs' questions swallowed any chance of sleep. Clara was exhausted, but Megs was curious for answers.

"Can we at least sit on the bed?" Clara fluffed a pillow to lean against, climbed up, and encouraged Megs to do the same.

"It's more comfortable this way." Megs grinned. "Now, how's Daniel? Where's Daniel? Why is my Ma here?"

"Daniel's doing well, and he's as handsome as ever. We snuck a kiss early yesterday morning before he drove us to Crailsheim. Should I feel guilty?"

"Oh, I know you don't. What's happening? Fog covers your smile, leaving a haze over the eyes into your soul. Are you speaking of guilt because he's a commoner? His social status never bothered you before, except for obeying your Vati and the rules."

"Talk about Chicago first. I want to know all about your shop, about you and Gus, about America, about the city of Chicago." She propped her sagging lids open between her thumbs and fingers.

Megs pinched her lips. "You're keeping a secret from me, but you know I'm never one to hide what I'm thinking. I'm eager to tell you all about Chicago. First, promise me when I finish, you'll divulge what torments your heart."

"I promise." They snapped their fingers, crossed their arms over their hearts, then extended their hands to one another and clapped their palms together, a pledge of their promises since they were little girls.

"Chicago—what an amazing city." Megs' eyes grew soft and dreamy. "New businesses open every day. The city boasts fascinating sights everywhere you look. The lakefront with its spectacular views begins a short way from our door. We enjoy Lincoln Park Zoo. Our home is a spacious upstairs flat on a street adjacent to the streetcar line.

"Gus arrives at his job at the paper in less than thirty minutes. My little shop sits a few doors off State Street, close to the impressive Marshall Field's department store. Fine society ladies have discovered my talent and my dedication to their whims and fancies. My business grows steadily."

"You describe a beautiful and perfect life but a much busier one than the slow pace of the countryside at home. I almost envy you. Almost. I love our neighbors, and I'm not sure I could leave my family behind as you and Gus did."

"Life's very different in Mud City—cosmopolitan and glamorous but built on swamps. It's a city of new opportunities."

"Mud City?"

Megs giggled. "Just a nickname, but I knew you would twist your nose when you heard it."

"The stinky part is not impressing me, but I'm excited for you and Gus. You'll start a family soon?"

Megs' smile slipped. "I miscarried the first one. I didn't tell anyone because I didn't want anyone to feel sorry for me. Now I'm not sure I want children. What if I had one who turned out like Georg?"

"I am so sorry. My insensitive comment caused you pain. How does a woman even face the loss of a child?"

"Don't be sorry. Truly, as I said, I'm not sure I want children."

"Not sure you want children?" Clara was wide awake now… "Children come with marriage."

"Maybe a family is in God's plan, but I pray I'll not become pregnant again."

"Ja, all in God's plan. Your Ma would be a proud grandmother."

"*Pshaw*! She is interested in whatever Georg does or says, but she never has kindness or encouragement for me. I doubt she'd have any for a child of mine. She would coo all over his. Georg will never have children either. He only has interest in himself and whatever lady he fancies at the moment."

Clara lowered her gaze to her hands tightly balled in her lap. "You and your Ma have had troubles, but she would travel to Chicago every year to smother your child with love and gifts."

"Maybe. You still haven't answered my question about why Ma is here. No one mentioned she was coming."

"You're delighted to see my Mutti and sisters but not your own Ma?"

"It's as if they are my own little sisters. Sometimes I consider Emmaline more my sister than yours. She always jumps with excitement at everything. You may be spontaneous as you say but in your quiet way."

"I love her enthusiasm, too."

"Your smile and the sparkle in your eyes when everything is well in your life—it's missing, my friend."

"You're doing a fine job ignoring your stories and turning this conversation back to me."

"You promised. We did the special pact…"

Clara rose from her seat on the bed and shuffled to their window overlooking Rue de la Paix. Pedestrians filled the sidewalks. It would've been easier to direct her words to these strangers on the street.

"I'm over here."

Clara returned to her friend's side and mustered the courage to share her dilemma. "Your Ma is here, because if Vati has his way, he'll have me married to your brother very soon."

Megs squeezed her eyes shut and clasped her hands against her cheeks. "To Georg!" Her voice rose to a screech. "What? Your Vati made this arrangement? Everyone knows what Georg is like. It isn't possible. I heard wrong. Tell me it's not true!"

Rubbing her forearms, Clara grimaced. "It would mean we would be more like sisters than we've ever been before."

"Hardly a good reason to endorse such nonsense. I prefer being best friends rather than you married to my miserable brother."

"I'd be miserable, alright. And if by 'everyone knows' you mean you and me, then you're exactly right. Well, Curt always knew. Rosa knows, and Mutti does now. I imagine others have suspicions about his past but probably not about how horrid he truly is. They remain ignorant of the suggestions he made to you and me, even as children."

Megs hugged her tightly. Clara hoped she would not let go.

"You and Gus didn't marry and leave for America just because a new place lured you. You abandoned a difficult situation as much as you looked forward to the opportunities Chicago promised. I know you well. Your brother treated us both horribly."

Through her sniffles, Megs answered. "Ja. Pa paid us handsomely to leave. He feared I would be the town crier and give all his secrets away. He and Ma always took care of their big old baby. Pa needed him to carry out his sham business deals. In her defense, I don't believe Ma knows the full extent of the high-stakes games they play. Georg and Pa have lost much of our family's wealth. I'm curious what wretched scheme Georg connived for the Gut Herr Kraig Reinhold to pledge his daughter to him?"

"Curt's ever my hero, but nothing he's said or done has affected Vati's intentions. He and I believe a guilty secret pushes our Vati's determination in the matter. Curt ties it to Mutti's injured hand. We each heard a version of the story this past week." Clara explained the argument and the cause.

"I never knew that. Poor Rosa. Poor Daniel." Megs fought back tears. "Georg would have been fifteen. How would he have played a role in your Vati's guilt?"

Clara touched her finger to her forehead. "Back up a minute. You commented earlier about Georg and your Pa's gambling losses. If true, what proof do I show Vati?"

"You and I, along with Curt and Daniel, enjoyed solving mysteries when we were children, mysteries as simple as who stole the last stick of candy, but great fun. Has Curt picked the game back up to solve this mystery, too?"

Clara laughed. "I didn't connect it to our old game, but ja. Perhaps he did, and Daniel's helping him."

"I'll pray for their success. My miserable Ma is here with you. Again, why?"

"She played sick recently, and we hoped she'd remain at home. Jealousy won out. If we visited you, she was determined she would, too. At the last minute, she recovered well enough to come."

"She's always afraid she'll miss out on something, but I suspect she's fully colluding with Pa and Georg. I'm certain they tricked her into believing she was helping. She played the sick excuse recently? Should this concern me?"

"Do the fashions you design require corsets cinched to within a horsehair of the wearer's life?"

"What common thread do corsets and my Ma's illness share?"

"She claimed a heart problem ailed her. We discovered on the train that she needed to loosen her undergarment. It was a sight getting her straightened out. We sent Willy and Hans to the corner and told them to hide behind the draperies. Their laughter enlightened us. While the hanging cloths blocked their view, they understood the gist of what transpired."

Megs held her sides as laughter bubbled. "What an image fills my head."

Laughter burst from Clara. "And skinny little Emmaline had done the same thing."

When their amusement subsided, Clara added, "Want to know what's worse?"

"It gets worse?"

"Oh, ja. Daniel and I have been further hampered in our desire to be with one another. As if the pompous rules of nobility aren't enough, Vati added your deplorable brother to the list of hindrances. Now back to happier subjects. I've cried enough the last couple of weeks to last years beyond my lifetime. Please tell me more about Chicago and your fine dressmaker's shop."

"How do I share my joy when you're hurting?"

"I asked, and I want to hear about it. It'll allow me to think about someone besides myself."

"My vision for the shop was inspired by Mr. Charles Worth's couture fashions. The fine ladies of the city love the ability to choose their fabrics and trims and contribute their ideas for the designs. Their husbands willingly pay me handsome sums to create perfect original dresses, even for everyday attire. Much of this is so far beyond what we've seen, even in our noble families. My list of wealthy clients has grown steadily.

"At Gus' suggestion, I hired several girls with outstanding dressmaking skills. We send all the details, fabrics, and findings home with the ladies. They return the gowns to us for fittings and final delivery."

"You've created a grand business for yourself."

"America's a land of opportunity. Chicago overflows with new possibilities."

"We hear the stories, but they've proven themselves firsthand for you and Gus."

"It's true. Mr. Worth birthed his empire here in Paris. He uses live models to showcase his designs, and royalty flocks to him. I'm excited we'll visit his fashion house and others this week and learn more about how they work. Chicago's high society ladies follow their design trends. In the same way, when our clients come in for their fittings, it's as though we have live models. Other clients get ideas from seeing them. We serve fine teas and pastries. There's a party every day. The wealthiest love the attention we lavish on them. And Mr. Worth also sets the standard for ready-to-wear attire."

"You embraced the idea of women working outside the home, even becoming businesswomen, and you've been successful. Congratulations, Megs. Yours makes my life of teas and luncheons and lending kindness to our Gut Apfelhof community appear dull. I love teaching the children in Sunday school and leading the Bible Class for the women of the church. Della, Tilly, Minna, and Luisa attend regularly. They send their greetings and much affection."

"Are they still creating reticules and accessories?"

"When they have the supplies and a market to sell them. All orders they receive provide much-needed funds for their families." Clara clasped her hands together as if holding tightly to an elusive hope.

"Would they consider supplying my shop with their handiwork? I remember it well as some of the finest anywhere."

"Doing so would bless their families abundantly. Were you reading my mind? I'll present the idea. I'm sure the ladies will be very grateful for your offer."

"Did you say you're still teaching Sunday school? You know Georg does not share your love of children."

Megs' statement left a lingering stench.

"Sara's death still haunts me. I asked Rosa about it, but she appeared nervous to answer." Clara laid a hand over her eyes and shook her head. "She said that only Georg and Dr. Pfeiffer know the answer, but she understands my concern."

Megs asked a different question. "What about your artwork? You possess your Mutti's gift. Do you still escape to the garden with your pastels?"

"I treasured my purchase on our trip to Breuninger's late last spring—the sheet music for Strauss' new waltz, *Roses aus dem Suden*. Having heard it played, I mastered the musical piece quickly. Vati and I shopped together to purchase our new piano. I fancied dancing round and round with a special gentleman.

"I grabbed my sketchbook, charcoals, and pastels, then headed to the garden to draw the images. Characters dressed in luxurious velvets, silks, and brocades stepped and whirled across the page. I recognized all the happy partners except mine. My partner had no face. Not Daniel's, not anyone's. I've sketched very little since and recently prayed against your brother's face filling in the blank."

"What? No sketching? You always have a tablet in your hand. I have a wonderful idea. Come to Chicago. You'll be the perfect person to sketch the designs as the women share their visions for their gowns. Your renderings will provide a record for creating their custom ensembles. Those, along with your handwork embellishments and your music, will impress the ladies. You'll have escaped from Georg."

"Your plan sounds perfect, but the solution to my dilemma remains far more complicated. Coming to Chicago with you would devastate me. I'd never see Daniel again. A marriage to your brother requires an impossible loyalty to a husband I do not love. I see no solution that resolves my problems, and I need a nap before we explore Paris."

Chapter Fourteen

4 SEPTEMBER 1881

CLARA PUSHED off the hand shaking her from slumber.

"Come on. Wake up. It's noon already. The sites of Paris await us."

Megs' words reminded her that they had arrived in Paris earlier today. Or was it yesterday? Clara sat on the edge of the bed and twirled a curl around her finger.

"I sent a message to the others while you slept. We'll meet for a late lunch in the lobby in an hour."

"Without luggage, we'll be wearing the same dresses we arrived in. Not even a comb or brush for our hair."

"You may wear one of my dresses today."

"Danke, but what about the others? You brought enough garments to attire five more women?"

"Not a splendid way to start our day, is it?"

"Besides, gowns sized to your diminutive proportions won't accommodate my larger bones. I wish these broad shoulders proved a better resting place for the burdens I carry. If not for your brother's and your Pa's threats to your Ma, the trunks would have arrived with us."

"As always my brother created another problem for me." Megs gasped. "Oh, Clara, what a selfish comment. He instigates far more trouble for you than me. I fear I've wounded our friendship with my quick tongue."

"Megs, I forgive your comment. The news is fresh to you. You'll always be my best friend even an ocean away."

"It is an ocean away plus a lengthy land journey. Arriving at Castle Garden in New York City is the beginning. Eight hundred miles of rails lead from there to Chicago."

"Traveling to Chicago sounds exhausting." She thanked heaven Strasbourg was much closer. "I believe the morning train arrives by one o'clock today with our trunks on board."

"You're right! We'll eat lunch at the hotel restaurant. When we finish the hotel will have delivered the bags to everyone's rooms."

"As much as I despise having to be seen even here in the hotel with my clothes rumpled from yesterday's problems, I'll be thankful for them."

Clara and Megs joined the others already gathered around the lunch table.

"Mutti accused me of acting spoiled and lacking gratitude because I complained we'll miss a day while we wait on our trunks." Emmaline's pinky wiggled one of the finger puppets she always carried in her pocket. This one lacked its clothing. "Here we are, meters away from haute couture fashions without a single dress to wear."

"We're all disappointed." Clara stroked her sister's arm.

"Would you like to wear one of mine, Emmaline? But I don't believe I have a gown to fit your little friend." Megs squeezed Emmaline's hand.

"I would prove Mutti's point if I wore yours, Megs." Emmaline picked at her clothing and unsuccessfully attempted to hand-press wrinkles from her skirt. "Danke all the same."

"I notice you'll be the only one among us dressed well today." Frau Wolff fussed at her daughter.

"Be careful, Ma. If you smile your stony expression may crack."

"Ladies." Mutti intervened. "I spoke with the concierge before lunch. He'll help us make the best plan to see the sites outside our doors during the time we have here this week. Much more than fashion awaits us. Art museums, the opera, and cathedrals to name just a few. Our things will arrive before we return today."

"Megs, we must see the opera, but not in these clothes. Your Pa brought me here for its official inauguration in January 1875. I especially enjoyed *The William Tell Overture* and was disappointed selections from *Faust* and *Hamlet* had to be omitted because one soprano fell ill. Do you know what's being performed at the Opera Garnier this week?"

A flush spread across Megs' cheeks. "You and Georg both boast of your lifestyles, frequently speaking prominent names. The Reinholds participate in similar activities. We'll find the concierge. He'll have the answer to your question."

No luggage had arrived after their interview, but the ladies readied themselves to greet the sites of Paris.

"We have appointments to visit the fashion houses on Tuesday." Megs laid out the plans she'd already made. "We'll add extra sightseeing for Monday, but today a stroll along Rue de la Paix leads to the Tuileries Garden on the Seine. Fairytale adventures await."

Her red cape draped around her shoulder reminded Clara once again of the fairytale-gone-wrong that consumed her life.

CLARA GASPED as she beheld the beauty surrounding them.

"Catherine de Medici had a brilliant eye for the beauty in creation, designing the Tuileries gardens in the 1500s." Mutti held Clara's hand. "And three hundred years later it's all here for us to enjoy."

Clara spun around taking in the surrounding view. A statue of a horse drew Clara's attention. "I'll just be over here." She wandered from the group.

A moment later, she stopped and offered a helping hand to a little girl who had stumbled on the path ahead. Tears filled the little girl's eyes.

Clara reached into her pocket and held out a lemon drop. "Will this help?"

"Thank you, lady. I love lemon drops."

"Me too. Let's be lemony-yellow-lemon-drop friends."

"You will not!"

The child was startled at Georg's voice. Clara's heart beat so hard she was sure her chest would explode. The little girl ran to her Mutter and hid in her skirt.

The sculpture had shielded him from Clara's view until he strolled from behind the impressive statue of Renommée riding the horse, Pegasus.

Her knees wobbled, and words stuck in Clara's throat. A screech escaped her. "What are you doing here?"

"Looking for you, my sweets. You'll learn how difficult it is to run from me. Why did you engage with a street urchin? Children have little value."

She stomped the ground as hard as her heart pounded. Her ears were on fire too. "How unkind! And how did you find me? Megs had no communication with you about our plans. You may have an agreement with my Vati, but he forbids you from accompanying me here."

"Oh, Clara, I have my helpers. Everywhere. And our accommodations—the best in Paris. My sister chose well. When your luggage was unloaded with mine, I thought how convenient it was to travel on the train with you. At least your trunks arrived with mine. I recognized the Gut Apfelhof tags on yours when the Westminster staff began loading them. I informed them we were together. I had your things delivered to my room." He lifted her chin toward him. "Lucky in love tonight, my sweets."

"You did not!" Clara shuddered. Why had they done that without Willy's code word?

"I did." He shot her a tight-lipped half-smile. His eyes bore directly into hers.

She squeezed the edges of her gaping mouth.

"Shall we continue our walk through the gardens?" He showed her his dimples and offered his arm.

"Certainly not."

While Clara struggled to pull away from Georg, Megs and the others came into sight. Five pairs of eyes glared at the sight of them.

"Mutti pointed a finger at her. You're out of our sight for less than two minutes, and what has happened?"

"Georg, you fool!" Megs nearly spat her words in his face.

"I'm delighted to see you, too, my sister."

Mutti steadied Frau Wolff keeping her from collapsing in front of them.

"What? Why? Georg, I need a moment with my daughter. Margaret, I trust you have a few words for your son?" Mutti motioned Clara off to the side.

"He scared me. He frightened this little girl because he was angry I helped her get up when she fell. He's secured a room at the Westminster giving instructions for my luggage to be delivered to his room." Clara blurted it all out.

Mutti's turn to shout. "Hans! Willy!"

"We witnessed the whole pathetic scene. I hurried over here after I sent Hans to the hotel to correct the misinformation and have an authority ready to detain Herr Wolff. All of us together should be able to drag him back."

"Danke, Willy. I wish you'd sent Rosa too. She could have handled Clara's things.

"The hotel will help him handle things, Frau Reinhold."

"Willy, please pin my son to that statue."

"I'll be happy to ma'am."

Frau Wolf engaged her son in a heated argument. "You make it clear you dislike children every chance you have, but how despicable of you to scare that little girl—just a child."

"Clara needs to understand children aren't important." Georg worked one foot loose and kicked the statue.

"I hope that hurt! With Clara's love for children maybe you shouldn't be courting her!"

"Ma. I have an agreement with her Vati, and it's in your best interest, too, that I do."

"I'm not sure what that means, and please don't tell me. I don't want to know. And don't follow us!"

"Ma, I can't believe you finally confronted him." Megs bounced and clapped. "Georg, you need to leave Paris." She shook her head wildly, and blonde waves escaped from under the feathers and frills of her hat. "Get on the next train to Monte Carlo. You'll be happier there anyway."

A Paris police officer interrupted. "How can I help you handle this fellow?"

Willy thanked him for being there when he needed him. "Would you help me drag him back to the Westminster Hotel? More officers should be awaiting him there."

~

"OVER THERE!" Back at the Westminster Clara and Megs had entered ahead of the others. Clara pointed and dashed to Hans and the concierge. "Please tell me you plan to rid this city of him. What did you do, Hans? Who did you recruit to take care of things?"

"Clara, one question at a time. I've wired your Vati." Hans' steady voice calmed her nerves. "How easy Georg finds it to be disagreeable even to those he claims are important to him. Your Vati was duly informed that Georg's behavior here lacks any care, concern, or love for you. Of course, coming from a servant I'm not sure how much account he will make of it."

The other women had arrived and joined them.

Willy nodded. "I agree with Hans."

"I asked your Vati to alert the Paris police to have Georg detained. His request would carry more weight. And Georg's would prove an easier arrest than those they encounter amidst all the riotous situations here every day. I'm praying the Gut Herr agrees."

Rosa held her breath for a few long moments. "I wish you had sent word to Curt or Daniel. Georg overstepped the line Gut Herr Reinhold drew for him, but it's no secret to anyone at Gut Apfelhof the Baron has his priorities, promises, and thinking tangled on this subject." She turned to Clara. "I'm praying. You pray too."

"I started praying long before we left Gut Apfelhof."

Everyone turned to see what caused the commotion at the hotel's entrance. The doorman and the manager greeting Georg and his escorts upon his return to the hotel drew much attention.

"Herr Wolff, we moved your belongings to another establishment a few blocks down. You'll be comfortable there." The manager directed him out the door.

"No one treats Georg Wolff in this manner! Do you know who I am?"

"You claim to be with Megs Schmitz and her party." The manager closed the gap between them. "We have it on excellent authority your presence with them is most unwelcome."

The doorman covered his mouth. Clara paid attention from a distance certain the doorman suppressed a snort. She couldn't let the urge to do the same get the better of her.

"I don't see the humor. And you're mistaken," Georg retorted to all of them. "Clara Reinhold is my intended. My family is of upstanding nobility. You'll not give me orders."

"This is our hotel. We enforce a strict code of conduct. From the news we received from the men accompanying your intended, your behavior in the Tuileries today fell far short of the standards we expect of our guests—especially ones claiming noble rank. Or what a respectable young woman would expect of the man who courts her. If you don't leave on your own we can certainly provide extra motivation." The manager pointed to the club in his doorman's hand.

"Gossip! All gossip! I'm watching what happens here. When I besmirch the name of the Hotel Westminster across Europe you'll regret the way you've acted."

As Georg huffed off an officer blocked his path. "You're coming with me."

Back in their room Clara and Megs plopped onto the bed. Clara sank into the silk comforter. If only it could soothe the

storm of emotions beating on her heart. She muffled sobs with her pillow.

"I'm so thankful the arresting officer arrived before Georg got away. Despite his arrangements for you, your Vati still loves you very much. I'm so sorry about Georg's behavior today."

"You're not responsible for your dreadful brother." Clara blotted her eyes with the pillowcase.

"But he embarrassed you and all of us. I wish I understood your Vati's decision."

"No one wishes that more than I do."

"I don't believe we'll hear more from Georg tonight or tomorrow. Your things were delivered before we got back. Help me move them to a convenient spot in the room. Choose a fresh gown, and we'll dress for dinner."

"My appetite disappeared back at the Tuileries."

"The hotel serves a Julienne soup I've heard is delicious." Megs rubbed her tummy.

Using the back of her hand to wipe her eyes again, Clara managed a tiny nod.

"Put your thoughts of the rascal away. We have people and places to see. Tuesday, we visit Doucet and Worth. I doubt my brother will step foot in them. Too girlish a thing for him to do."

"But he loves ogling women wherever he finds them. He believes me dimwitted enough to miss his wandering eye. He wouldn't care if I did notice. Megs, how do I end this torture? I grieve over my miserable future."

"Move to Chicago."

Clara grimaced and shook her head. "You make it sound easy. You and Gus desired to leave for America without concern for the family you left behind. I love my family and would miss everyone. Even Vati. Especially Vati. He never acted like this toward me before."

"You're right about your Vati. He is a kind and loving man who treated me like one of your sisters. You're resourceful, Clara Reinhold. Make a plan."

"An easy suggestion for you, Megs Schmitz! Your Pa helped you leave Gut Dinkelhof prepared to succeed in America."

"When you come, my brother can no longer torment your life, but right now I'd rather think about Paris. We have an extra day. Would you prefer to visit the Louvre or Notre Dame Cathedral tomorrow? We'll begin early in the morning."

Someone slipped a note under their door addressed to Clara. Her fingers trembled as she lifted the flap and removed the note.

I will find you wherever you go, my sweets.

Chapter Fifteen

5 SEPTEMBER 1881

CLARA AND MEGS lagged behind the group hailing the horse-drawn hackneys. After the encounter at the Tuileries yesterday, apprehension rolled around Clara's stomach like marbles. She was grateful for Mutti's suggestion to hire a ride rather than walk to the Louvre. They caught up with the others as they boarded the carriages.

"Megs, you're giggling like a schoolgirl." Clara ran a hand down the back of her skirt. "Do I have a 'kick me' note on my back or stains on my dress?"

"Nein, silly girl. But did you notice the man leaning on the lamppost behind us? His eyes were on you as we stepped out the door."

"I focused my eyes on the door, watchful of Georg showing up. I fear he's just one step behind us or ahead of us every minute."

"Forget Georg. Climb in."

They settled in for the ride. "Before the driver pulls away, notice the dapper gentleman with wavy chestnut hair, sparkly turquoise eyes, and a nice physique." Megs motioned to her left.

"You noticed his eye color?"

"And his bright smile, too. You didn't notice, but he winked at you."

"Are you playing matchmaker? Perhaps you've forgotten I have more men than I need." Clara did a dramatic eye roll.

"But that handsome, well-groomed mystery man took a particular interest in you."

"Spying on me, you mean? Has Georg hired him to follow us?"

Megs tugged Clara's hand. "Let's not worry about Georg. I know you're ready to explore the Louvre. Art galleries aren't my brother's kind of entertainment. We'll be safe there."

"You read the message delivered to our door last night. How can I feel safe? I have a Wolff on my tail!"

THEIR CARRIAGES BROUGHT them to the front of the Pavillon Sully. Clara's breath froze at the massive west entry with its square dome, arched doors, and massive caryatid sculptures. She pointed for everyone to look and admire. The interior's broad expanse sprawled like the heavens around them as they entered.

Despite the trouble she encountered while wandering off for a moment yesterday, Clara separated herself from the group until she found the masterpiece. Lightness and darkness seeped through each other. She appeared lifelike. Mutti called it sfumato style. No one had ever duplicated Da Vinci's technique. Clara was mesmerized by the Mona Lisa painting until the unmistakable stench of Georg's cigar smoke crept closer and rose into her nostrils.

Georg's thick hand covered her mouth, sending shivers down her spine.

"Clara, let me show you far more interesting works than the Mona Lisa."

She dug her nails into the back of his hand, chomped a bite of his palm, and kicked his shin.

"Ouch!" He released his hold on her, hopped on one foot, and shook the pain from his hand.

His outburst sent museum patrons jerking backward. Screams filled the air.

Clara's chest pounded.

"Walk normally. Don't let anyone suspect a problem." Georg whispered.

"Too late." Clara charged for the door.

With an unexpected jolt, she face-planted into the chest of another man. Clara pushed herself back from the stranger.

The fellow took her hands in his before she could get them to her face. "Is this man bothering you?"

Clara looked up into a pair of shining turquoise eyes focused on her. Three exaggerated blinks. She prayed he would understand her quiet signal.

The man held up his hand in front of Georg. "*Whoa!*"

"I'm not a horse. And who are you?"

"Who I am hardly matters. I'm staying at the Westminster. You created quite the disturbance in the lobby yesterday, and this lady deserves better treatment."

"The lady happens to be my intended."

"This is how you treat *your* lady? I'd laugh, but your attitude lacks the humor I believe you intended. He summoned a Louvre official standing a few yards from them."

"The authorities know me," Georg countered.

"They know your identity for all the wrong reasons. You argued the same yesterday, and the tactic failed then just as it will today. Didn't the officer arrest you?"

The Louvre's guard grabbed Georg by the arm and shoved him toward an exit.

Georg displayed his dimples, his pompous attitude still strong. "Yesterday I was escorted to another hotel not far from the Westminster. I'll find you again, my sweets," he blustered as they hauled him off.

"Is this what it's going to take to get Vati to recognize the problem? To let his wrath loose on the man?" Clara muttered to herself.

"Is it true?" The man who had helped Clara stayed by her side.

"About me being his intended? Not by my choice."

"A small group has gathered behind you. Do you know these people?"

Clara turned to see those he referred to staring with mouths wide open.

"My family and friends. Ja."

"I'm pleased I'm safely returning this lady to you. I don't understand why the man followed you like that. I don't need to know, but hopefully, he chooses to respect you the next time you see him. How many days will your plans keep you in Paris?"

"Through the week. Thank you very much. Tell me your name, please, so I may thank you properly."

He gripped Clara's hand, smiled, and vanished into the crowds.

"The mystery gentleman eyeing you in the hotel lobby saved you from the goon, and you didn't learn his name." Megs giggled as her Ma seethed.

"Close your mouth, Megs, or I'll slap it shut for you."

Chapter Sixteen

GUT APFELHOF, *Tuesday, 6 September 1881*

KRAIG TWISTED the whirring doorbell of his Mutter's cottage. Would she answer his questions?

Dorthea Reinhold extended her arms to her son and grandson and invited them into her cozy home. "A visit from two of my very favorite men. To what do I owe this pleasure? I was sorry to miss Paris with the ladies, but this is better."

"Better than Paris? You make me laugh, Mutter."

Kraig and Curt took their usual seats on the purple sofa opposite her favorite oak rocker, each with a cup of Apfel cider she insisted on serving.

He lifted his cup toward his Mutter and licked his lips. "Ah. Sehr gut! May we ask you some questions?"

"I have questions of my own about the most recent excitement in our family. Is your arrangement for Clara with Georg a fitting proposal?"

Kraig rubbed his neck. "It is."

"Margaret Wolff spoke to your wife of a new business her husband and son seek in Monte Carlo? Do you know their plans?"

"Not the details, but it's connected to their Dinkel grain business in the region." Kraig squirmed. "I'm supposed to be asking the questions, but you're giving me an inquisition."

"Don't you believe there's more to their business? From what Lydia relayed to me, Margaret's words were very vague, as if she knew far more than she revealed. For such an important decision, your Vater would be embarrassed that you have not investigated the Wolffs further. They're nice enough neighbors, but Otto often questioned their motives. Ask those who work their land about the Wolffs' unfairness in taxing them—always adding unnecessary burdens for their families."

Kraig jabbed a finger toward his Mutter. "What do you imply? I render unwise decisions, especially toward my beloved daughter? Clara, Curt, all my children—I treasure them all." He rubbed sweat from his forehead and then looked back up at her. "Forgive my harsh attitude toward you, but please explain what concerns you most."

His Mutter scratched her head. "I visited with the ladies at the Backhaus today. The Frankens bake the best Streuselkuchen. We enjoyed some with our coffee and conversation."

"Ja. The best bakery in all of Württemberg." Kraig gestured with his hands to hurry her along.

"Gut Apfelhof people love Clara and are worried about her. The things I heard embarrassed me. Help me understand the truth about Georg Wolff and his Vater."

"Do you question my wisdom, too? Is Lydia the only family member showing me respect in this? I learned from my Vater to provide well for my family. What exactly have the women said?"

"Much of this is a case of he said this and she said that. I'm aware that when gossip fires are stoked, rumors flourish, but how much truth do these stories hold?" Mutter tapped her fingertips together. "A couple of women claimed Georg and Gerwig met two eccentric-looking men at the Backhaus for coffee and business last week. They heard lots of bragging about the pair's excursions along the French Riviera."

"The French Riviera is a beautiful place to visit."

"Ja, I've heard. According to my sources, Monte Carlo is the major attraction. I'm advanced in years, and I am a woman. But your Mutter is aware of the less-than-wholesome activities transpiring in the place. How regularly do the Wolffs visit the casinos and spas?"

"Gut Dinkelhof supplies spelt to highly acclaimed restaurants around the region. Their customers include the entertainment establishment you mentioned. Lucrative for the Wolffs to have them as a customer."

"True enough, but Otto told me of Gerwig's and his Vater's activities in Baden-Baden. The opulent palace in the Black Forest lured them years ago before it was forced to close its doors. I know the news. Monaco took advantage of the change in German gambling laws to grow their new and equally opulent attraction. I don't believe the Wolffs'—

Gerwig's and now his son's, too— business in Monte Carlo is honest and legal."

"A man's free to choose his entertainment, Mutter."

"Ja, but the entertainment he chooses defines him. I'm told by those overhearing the conversation at the Backhaus that the Wolffs made an unseemly offer to one of the men who accompanied them. What offers do you associate with Monte Carlo?" The question hung between them.

Kraig tugged at his collar and undid the top button of his shirt. "It's not a place Curt and I frequent."

"Your attitude overflows with condescension right now, son. You're one of the kindest, most generous, and loving men I've ever known. Your Vater, my Otto, instilled the highest values into you for faith, for life, for family, and for business. Lydia harbors much pain to support you in this, but she respects you. Cherish your wife."

Kraig nodded. "She's a beautiful woman."

"Remember that. Now help me understand what's changed within you."

"I am offended by your accusations. I am your same loving and kind-hearted son." Kraig had been torn in two by his concern for his family and the fears tugging at his heart. He would not share the conflict with his Mutter.

"And you are rattling out nonsense. I know you too well." Mutter flared her nostrils above a tightly drawn smile.

"You heard all this from gossiping women. When and if the accusations prove true, I'll reconsider. As for this arrangement, I trust Clara and all the rest of my family will thank me in time.

Georg already plans to increase the income of Gut Apfelhof. He is prepared to begin even before he and Clara marry." Kraig gazed out the multi-paned window of his Mutter's parlor.

The pointed steeple of St. Luke's Kirche rose above the tree line a stone's throw beyond her cottage. It stabbed at his conflicted heart. Would another meeting with Pastor Lange change anything? Reinholds' success provided funds for the building of St. Luke's centuries ago. The more recent dilemma reeked of Lange's veiled threats. What was the pastor hiding?

"Curt, time to leave. Give your Oma her happy home back."

After giving his Oma a peck on the cheek, Curt followed Vati out the door.

CURT SQUEEZED his eyebrows together and wiggled his toes. "This would be the wrong time to…"

"Ja, definitely the wrong time to press me on this subject again."

He buttoned his lips and listened.

Vati pointed toward the church. "I'm headed to the parsonage now. Pastor Lange requested to see me on an urgent tax matter. Walk with me."

Vati's expression vacillated between pain, embarrassment, and near giddiness.

"Has something else piqued your interest?" Curt asked.

"Plan to travel to Stuttgart tomorrow. We'll visit Schultz Gun Shop. Still a few days before Daniel and the other drivers collect the ladies from the train. We'll have time to purchase a gift for Wilhelm and arrive home to greet them."

"He broke a window in our home with a slingshot this past week, and you're ready to supply him with his own gun?"

"He's mucking stalls for a month, paying for his poor decision. Daniel commended his target skills during riding lessons, and his birthday is next month. At eleven, he's old enough to have his own."

"You're certain of that?"

"How old were you?"

"Ten."

"You can't even hide that sheepish grin. It's decided then."

"J.P. Sauer Company won an award earlier this year for its new drilling gun patent." Curt licked his lip. "Do you think Schultz will carry them in their shop yet?"

"They could be a special-order item, but we'll ask. I'd enjoy handling one of those myself, but I have a simpler piece in mind for Wilhelm."

"Simple as in a toy gun?" Curt pointed his index finger and cocked his thumb.

"He'd not be shooting a window out with one of those. We laugh, but I'm serious about this. I'd like him to have one of his own. Every Reinhold man since my Opa, or maybe even his Opa, has learned on the one Wilhelm uses now. I trust you or your sister will have a son one day soon. We'll pass it down again."

When they arrived at the parsonage, the door swung wide.

"Welcome! Join me by the fire. Autumn has arrived with an abrupt chill."

"Danke, Pastor, but our business should require but a few minutes of your time. Our walk warmed us. We can discuss matters here in the gallery."

"I discuss tax matters only in my study."

"Very well."

Pastor Lange directed the Reinhold men into the study. They stood across from the fireplace and the larger-than-life copy of van der Weyden's *Christ as Judge of the World* hanging above it.

Once seated at his desk, Pastor Lange withdrew a sheaf of papers from among the stacks of books and binders scattered there. "Now about this tax matter."

"A more urgent matter has been brought to my attention. Members of my family have become suspicious of the Wolffs and the agreement concerning Clara. What have you not told me?"

"It's your agreement. I've kept my word on our bargain, Herr Reinhold." Pastor Lange placed his folded hands on his desk and waited.

Curt clenched his jaw. His ears echoed his thudding heartbeat. What did Pastor mean about the tax matters and the bargain? What bargain?

"You keep serious information from me, Pastor." Vati tapped his fingertips together. "What motivates you in this agreement?"

"We have discussed this all before."

"Clara's miserable. I'm losing the respect of my family."

"As you should if you allow her to keep company with the hired servant. You know your noble position depends on following the rules."

"Ja, a fact I've been aware of my whole life." Vati's eyes widened. "I'm also aware it depends on my collection of the taxes from the residents of Gut Apfelhof and making an accounting to you and the state. I've done an impeccable job for you while maintaining the utmost respect in the community. Clara and Daniel both know their friendship may not become more than it is, yet you ask more of me."

"You understand the reasons, and God sees all."

"He does, and He also forgives when we repent. Do you have some things you should confess?"

Lange stood and moved toward Vati until their noses almost touched. "My conscience is clear."

Curt's fingers itched and twitched. If he weren't the Pastor, Curt would have punched the man.

"You're sure? Curt and I visited my Mutter today. Now, I know women gossip, but my Mutter doesn't share unfounded information. She heard disturbing things at the Backhaus this morning. Please remind me why you took sides with the Wolffs in this matter. You've pushed me against a jagged rock wall."

"Georg will be a fine addition to your family. It'll please the state to continue your title, and your little secret stays safe with me. I'm reminded of Walter Scott's poem, *Marmion: A Tale of Flodden Field, 'Oh, what a tangled web we weave.'*"

"And we both know the little rumor proved false years ago." The veins in Vati's neck stood at attention.

"What if the rumor resurfaces? What then?" Pastor Lange slapped his hand on his desk and flashed a mocking sneer Vati's way.

"Exactly what's this about? Is it your own web you weave, Pastor?" Curt pointed to the painting above the fireplace. "He's a much better judge than you or me or my Vati."

The pastor's face turned cold and pale like the bricks of the church. Curt angled his head toward the door.

With quick giant steps, Vati and Curt darted to the door.

Vati shot a glance backward. "Curt and I are unavailable for the next few days. We'll resume our conversation another time."

"Stale conversation. Expect nothing to change."

"We are going to see a man about a gun." Vati's bushy eyebrows rose above wide eyes.

"Is that a threat?"

Chapter Seventeen

RUE DE LA PAIX, *Paris, Tuesday, 6 September 1881*

The ladies paused at each window showcasing the designer's newest creations. Overlapping diamond patterns in stone rolled out like a welcoming carpet. The doors swung open to a veritable treasure trove of style and design. Clara pressed a hand to her bosom and gasped—another breathtaking sight.

"Bonjour, Pierre!" Megs introduced her party and confirmed her appointment with the doorman at Maison Worth.

"Oui, Madame, we have been expecting you. I'm to escort you directly to Mr. Worth's office."

"Merci! And my friends?"

"Oui, Monsieur Worth welcomes your party."

The door to Monsieur Worth's office opened into the ornate showroom it housed. No one uttered a word while they took it all in. A collection of Faience pottery lined the shelves. A lacy purple orchid found its home on the corner of Worth's desk. Sweet aromas wafted from it, and other examples of this exotic horticulture were tucked between the tin-glazed pottery pieces.

Mannequins were posed everywhere. Between the seating. Behind the desk. Looking out the windows with their backs toward visitors.

"He uses live models to display his work to his clients." Megs spun around, observing the collection. "These mannequins are almost creepy, except the figures wear the most elaborate and coveted gowns in the city of Paris."

"Ladies, have a seat. Monsieur Worth will be with you promptly."

Megs gestured toward the ones in the window. "He positioned those to accentuate the back sides of the gowns. He has so much to be proud of, but why are we in his private office? I did nothing special. I simply requested an appointment to view Worth's styles. My salon in Chicago experiences success, but it holds only a flicker to what this man's accomplished."

Mutti tapped Megs' shoulder. "Look at me. I know nothing about your shop in Chicago, but the gentleman has a reason. Wait for the Monsieur to inform us himself."

And as if on cue, a man of average height appeared in the doorway, twisting the right end of his dark handlebar mustache. "Welcome, ladies. Do you love what you see?"

"Oui!" at least three of them exclaimed.

"You have questions for me?"

"Oh oui, Monsieur." Megs smoothed her skirts. "We have indeed admired your work this whole time. Our question? To what do we owe the honor of meeting the man of your esteem in the fashion world?"

"You must be Madame Schmitz."

"I am. I wrote to you asking to view your work. I never dared dream of an opportunity to meet you in person."

Worth fingered fabric samples in the center of his desk. "There's a story I will share with all of you. Have you met Madame Sarah Bernhardt?"

"You mean of stage fame?" Megs' eyes lit up.

"Her image appears in magazines our Tante sends to us." Emmaline hummed a jaunty tune.

"Oui, the French actress who recently returned from a tour of America." Worth chuckled. "I'm uncertain if she had a performance in Chicago, but she visited your city. She mentioned a fine dressmaker's shop near State Street. A place called Megs' Designs."

Pinkish warmth rushed up Megs' neck. "I don't believe I've met the woman, but she knows of my work?"

"She keeps her identity cloaked, but she loved what your shop offered. On her brief visit to Chicago, she commissioned you and asked you to ship her finished gown to a friend at an address in London. She trusted you implicitly to produce a superb creation without additional fittings."

Megs pointed to Rosa. "This woman trained me in Württemberg years before I left for America. Megs turned toward the others. She's the dressmaker for these ladies—Gut

Herrin Lydia Reinhold and her daughters, Clara, Hannah, and Emmaline. Lydia's husband is Gut Herr Kraig Reinhold of Gut Apfelhof."

"Megs excelled as a student of the needle arts." Rosa blushed. "A delight to teach. More than once, I believed she taught me."

"The connection you made between Madame Bernhardt's recommendation and my request to visit. Tell us more, please."

"I may not have remembered. She had made her recommendation some time ago. Madame Bernhardt recently arrived at Maison Worth as my secretary received the day's postal delivery. The star recognized your mark on the envelope, and she brought the letter to me herself. She reminded me about the dressmaker in Chicago and asked me to provide whatever you needed. Who am I to refuse the request of one of my most notable and wealthy clients? One of my ladies will tend to you and your party's needs." His friendly smile spoke volumes about the genuineness of this man.

"I've invited my friend, Clara, to join me in America and be a partner in Megs' Designs." Megs joined hands with Clara. Her gaze shifted to Clara, then back to their host. "My best friend since childhood, Fraulein Reinhold, is an exceptional illustrator. May she make a few sketches from your designs?"

Deep lines had found their way across Mutti's face, and her hands fisted in her lap. How would Megs explain her plan? Mutti would be furious. Heat crawled up Clara's cheeks.

"Certainly. I'd be most flattered, but do not copy my designs in your work."

"Thank you, Monsieur." Clara nodded. "I promise I won't."

"Mademoiselle, color your designs to enhance your client's hair color and complexion." Monsieur Worth had given Clara an excellent tip.

"We'll gather inspiration only and create our unique designs." Megs motioned to the others. "Thank you for your kindness, Monsieur Worth."

"Mademoiselle Reinhold, provide an example of your sketches to my assistant before you leave Paris. Include a message of where you may be reached. Perhaps your talent would be an asset here."

"Thank you very much, Monsieur. I will."

"I do hope to persuade her to join me in America. She would be an outstanding addition to our staff, helping our clients see their ideas take shape before we make the first cuts."

"Madame Schmitz and Mademoiselle Reinhold, it's been a pleasure meeting you both, and I believe your talents will take you far. Ladies, I must conclude our meeting for today. Pierre will direct you to Mademoiselle Giselle. She oversees our seamstresses from design to the finished projects. It'll be her pleasure to show you the pride of Maison Worth. And Madame Schmitz, you may contact me any time. I look forward to hearing your business continues to prosper."

Mademoiselle Giselle's tour had intrigued and inspired the ladies. The seamstresses had been dressed in true Worth style and worked in well-appointed areas with an abundance of natural light shining through walls of large windows.

"Clara, I have the best idea. To the delight of our clients, I would love for Megs' and Clara's Designs to incorporate more of the luxury of this place in our salon."

With Clara and Megs at the rear of the group, their party moved back toward the grand entry with its ivory-cream arches. Clara slowed and thumped Megs on her back to get her attention, then spoke quietly. "Please, stop mentioning America. I'm being courted by your brother. I'm his intended. Tough as it is, I've promised Vati I'll respect his choice. Your suggestion creates greater distress for me. Can we agree, please, that I'll not be coming to America?"

"Most reluctantly, I'll agree for now. The invitation remains open—always."

"I would be most interested in sketching for Maison Worth."

"And you believe Georg will have his wife working and earning her own money? Come, come, Clara. How do you imagine that being even close to a possibility?"

"I'll send one or two of my sketches to Monsieur Worth as I promised."

They found the others gathered around the frilly palms in the lavish entryway.

"Mademoiselle Giselle's tour and answers to my queries far exceeded my expectations. Are all of your heads as dizzy with ideas as mine?" Megs sucked in air filled with possibilities and clapped a celebratory rhythm.

"My imagination runs wild with ideas for new gowns." Emmaline spun in circles, clapping with Megs. "Will we visit Maison Doucet too?"

Rosa and Mutti sighed.

Mutti took Emmaline by the hand and spun her close. "Rather than take in another designer today, why not several? We'll find a sidewalk café, order tea, and watch the parade of lovely ladies showing off the finery they've purchased here in the center of the haute couture fashion district. We'd be treated to designs from far more than one or two of the salons."

"I'd love to rest my feet." Clara seated herself at a nearby café table, took in the scene around them, and giggled at the outlandish ensembles strolling by. "How true, Mutti. There's much to see here on the streets and sidewalks, and a hot drink will chase the day's chilly temperatures away. We'll head to Maison Doucet after we watch this show."

The second fashion house offered equal inspiration. Two hours later, they came away with sketchpads and notepads lined with more splendid ideas than they could create.

"Can you believe all we've seen today?" Megs beamed. "Both houses have amazing designs, but nothing will ever equal the treatment we received at Maison Worth. Meet Clara and me in our room after dinner. We have so much to discuss."

Clara admired the matchbox decorated with a sketch of the Westminster. She removed and struck one of the thin wooden sticks. The tinder caught, and she dropped the tiny container into her pocket.

Soon flames crackled just beyond the fireplace's glossy marble mantle and surround. Soft light glowed from carefully placed gas lamps. A golden silk comforter complemented the jade and yellow floral stripes covering the walls.

The setting welcomed the others to Megs and Clara's room. A sideboard filled with tea and a variety of French pastries, along with adequate seating covered in shiny emerald brocades, beckoned them to settle in.

Mutti clutched her sketch pad in her lap. "You've designed all our favorite gowns. Maison Doucet and Worth's establishments bloomed with inspiration. What ideas percolate under your bonnet, Rosa?"

"Remember the verse I quoted on the train? Proverbs 31:25. Ladies, I believe going forward we'll rejoice over more comfortable styles. I envision the princess lines in your new ensembles with piping defining their elongated seams. Lovely bows will accentuate the back of skirts, which will easily float through doorways."

Are those sparks of excitement glittering in Rosa's eyes? Clara couldn't help but smile.

"You could add magnificent embroidery and layers of lovely silks and trims." Emmaline traced scallops around her neck and shoulders. With another gesturing motion, she added imaginary beads with an imaginary needle.

"I loved that a few of the hemlines rose above the floor." Hannah lifted her skirts and sashayed across the room.

Clara and Mutti sketched quickly. Rubbing in pastel touches, their ideas came to life.

"You've not said a word." Megs squinted hard at her Ma. "Don't the styles from the highest acclaimed designers in the world meet with your approval? Maybe too stayed in your ways? And, ja. I meant a pun by the word stayed."

"Who told you about that?"

"Told me about what?"

"The ridiculous incident on the train?"

"You admit to it then? You didn't expect your friends to keep that amusing moment a secret."

"These styles still require the defining lines of a corset, Megs."

"Some women may still prefer them, but I can tell you my wealthy American clients will be ecstatic over the new trend."

"I'd be pleased with more comfort in our clothing. Our slavery to the fashions of England's Queen Victoria has proved detrimental to our health, especially when our middles are cinched to extremes." Mutti shook her head. "Don't deny it, Margaret."

Megs shooed a hand toward her Ma. "You're always critical. You've no idea how outdated you'll soon be."

"I'll continue to place custom orders for my wardrobe at Breuninger's. Or maybe your Pa will take me to Italy to discover their styles."

Megs clapped a hand to her mouth. "Forgive me. Breuninger. A lovely new shopping concept, I've heard. But they hardly provide the custom designs you covet. This area in Paris boasts amazing haberdasheries, milliners, jewelers, and more. Ma, you are welcome to accompany us, or stay here if you prefer."

"Maybe I'll stroll through the museums instead. Purchase some fine art from real artists."

"Have Pa and Georg left any Wolff money for your indulgences?" Megs' eyes widened. "Ja, that must be it. It's why you shop for your wardrobe from the department store rather than commissioning gowns from fine dressmakers as you've insisted upon in the past."

Margaret scowled.

"I've touched on a sensitive issue, but the Reinholds deserve to be informed."

Clara furrowed her brow and tightened her jaw as she soaked in Megs' words. But as quickly as she had announced the news, her friend changed the subject.

Smiling, Megs eyed each of the ladies in turn. She pointed to the sketchbooks. "These are lovely designs, and tomorrow we visit the Sentier district. Did you save space in your trunks to take your treasures back to Gut Apfelhof? I'll be shipping several trunks of fabric and findings to Chicago. I am eager to visit Sajou. Its reputation has spread around Europe and the States. If they don't have the fabrics and trims your imaginations crave, you'll not find them anywhere."

"I'll be dreaming of possibilities tonight." Rosa beamed.

"Sweet dreams to all of us." Mutti stood. "It's my bedtime."

The ladies made their way to the door.

Mutti pulled Clara aside. "Megs' comments a few moments ago must have hurt you as deeply as they did me, but we'll abide by and respect your Vati's decisions. It's the proper way."

Chewing her lip, Clara nodded. She understood the intent of Mutti's whispered words.

~

PARIS, *Wednesday, 7 September 1881*

. . .

A DAZZLING rainbow surrounded the women. From colorful, tiny-patterned mosaic floors to the highest shelves with miles of ribbons. From shimmering selections of silks to cases of unique buttons, threads, and beads, to displays of the loveliest tools. Clara pushed her gaping jaw closed.

"Welcome to Sajou! What's your pleasure today, ladies?" With a flourish, Jacque-Simon Sajou waved them into his haberdashery.

"We've heard the rumors. At Sajou, every woman discovers fabrics and findings for the gowns she dreams about. We've just stepped in, and it's no rumor. A treasury of wonders surrounds us." Megs gripped his extended hand. "Exactly what we hoped to find. Maison Worth entertained us magnificently yesterday. Just look at the designs we envisioned and that Clara and Frau Reinhold sketched following our visit."

"Impressive, ladies. Your personal appearance reflects your love of beautiful things. Allow me to direct you to the area where you'll find all the newest trends and imports in silk and other luxurious fabrics.

"I'm searching for your most impressive offerings for clients of my dressmaker's salon in Chicago. Your fabrics will be a lovely treat for them. They easily recognize the finer things the world offers."

"It'll be my assistant Madame Wilhelmina's pleasure to help you with your selections." Monsieur Sajou excused himself to welcome other shoppers.

Wilhelmina rolled one length after another out before them. Their sketches almost chose the pieces. "So much more than the rumors and my imagination allowed me to expect and hope for." Megs purchased dress lengths of each one.

The Reinhold women selected enough for two gowns and two day dresses for each of them. Sixteen new ensembles in all.

"Oh, how exciting it will be to work with these grand fabrics." Rosa beamed from ear to ear.

"Please, Rosa, which ones do you favor for your new dresses? The Gut Herr would insist." Mutti patted Rosa's hand.

A step ahead of Mutti, Clara had a suggestion ready. "This sky-blue silk will perfectly complement your porcelain complexion, blonde tresses, and lovely blue eyes."

"Excuse me." A soft-spoken man approached them. "I've observed you ladies have an excellent eye for making wonderful selections. I'm shopping for my client. I promised to bring silks and trims for his wife from my time in Paris. Do you mind helping with the decision?"

Was this the same man from the Louvre? Clara toyed with a piece of soft velvet. "We'd be honored to help, monsieur. "What color are her hair and eyes?"

"Oh, dark hair. Very dark like yours, ma'am." He inclined his head toward Mutti. "And blue-violet eyes. Some of the most unusual I've seen."

"Does this one match her eyes?" Clara brushed her hand over a shimmering amethyst piece. "Your client is lucky to have you willing to shop for his wife. Many men would be intimidated and consider it a girlish thing to do."

"I'm happy to do it. I pretend I'm shopping for my own Mutter."

Clara pointed out a burnished silver trim. "This offers a striking complement to the amethyst and promises a stunning gown for the lady. With Rosa's knowledge and direction, there will be an ample amount for whatever design she chooses."

"Have them cut ten meters of fabric…" Rosa's eyes widened.

Someone pinched Clara's shoulder from behind. "I heard what you said about men being intimidated to be in such a place, believing it girlish."

Georg. She was certain every drop of color drained from her face. "I'll be home in a few days. Vati told you not to come."

Grabbing her brother by the arm, Megs dragged him away from the others. "Georg, I know you're courting Clara with Herr Reinhold's blessing, but her vati told you not to travel here with her."

"He didn't say I could not come on my own."

"Personal experience reminds me how disrespectful you are of women, but of another adult male? Especially one your senior? The Vati of the girl you intend to make your wife?"

"I only desire time with Clara now that she's promised to me. Is it so wrong for a man to spend time with the woman he loves?"

Moving closer to him, Megs raised her hand but stopped short of a smack to his jaw.

Georg immediately countered her move with his fist.

"Will you pull the first punch or ready your aim for retaliation in case I strike you first?" Megs shook her head.

"Maybe, or maybe I'll just slug you regardless of whether you hit me or not."

"You would hit a woman? You are pathetic." Megs flinched and turned toward Clara.

Clasping Georg's hand in hers, Clara spoke to him with gentle but pleading words. "I hoped to enjoy this week with our sisters, our Mütter, and Rosa—time with the women. We do have the rest of our lives to be together."

"This is part of the rest of our lives right now, my sweets. I prefer I not miss a moment." He twisted his hand loose from hers. He lifted her hand to his lips and landed another of his slobbery kisses.

"*Eww*!" Clara scrunched her eyes, wrinkled her nose, pulled back her shoulders, and swallowed the sour taste in her mouth.

Emmaline withdrew a tiny wolf from the finger puppet collection living in her pocket. She slid it on her finger and wiggled it into several mocking bows.

"Clara, remember your manners. I'll not have my reputation tarnished by the unladylike and childish behavior of my intended." The rage sizzling through his reprimand equaled the hue of his flaming ears.

The tall, handsome gentleman they assisted a few moments earlier stepped to Clara's side. Those turquoise eyes and chestnut waves far outshone Georg and his unkempt appearance. "Is this man causing you trouble, ladies?" What luck for her to have a protector who looks like this, but Clara would have rather had Daniel.

"What concern is that to you?" Georg retorted.

"I've seen you around. You're a troublemaker. These women have been helpful to me here at Sajou. I find it an honor to return their kindness. Max is the name. You must be Georg. We met recently, although less formally, at the Louvre."

Georg's icy glare met Max's handshake. "Remove yourself from the presence of my intended, my sister, and their party. What ill-treatment awaits them at your hands, Max?"

"I notice your words and actions provide little assurance of your intentions here. Ladies, we can wait as long as necessary to ensure your safety."

Sajou's owner rejoined them. When he returned, the Paris police accompanied him. "I won't tolerate such uncouth behavior in my salon. Ladies, Willy and Hans alerted me. They were here to protect you and might need help. The police will handle the troublemaker."

"Thank you, Max, and you too, sir," Clara curtsied to them both.

Each lady added words of appreciation.

"Jacques-Simon Sajou. Pleased to be of service." He finished wrapping Max's purchase.

Max gripped Sajou's hand before clutching his bundles. He exited the establishment, jingling a few coins in his pocket. The happy tune he whistled poured sunshine over the gloomy scene.

"Did you notice he gave his name as Max?" Megs whispered to Clara. "But the initials on his case are JPS."

"The last thing on my mind at the moment is comparing men's names and initials. I agree he's a handsome gentleman, and I was happy to assist him. But I have one more man than I need right now. Don't bother me about another." Clara cleared her throat. "And I remind you, Megs, that you are a married woman."

"We could arrange for Daniel to come to Chicago with you."

"Please. I can't bear to discuss this further."

They completed making their selections of ribbons and trims to complement the fabrics for their gowns. They added a myriad of choices for Megs' clients in Chicago. Mutti made sure Rosa had fine new sewing tools. She purchased a set for herself and each of her girls as well.

"I'm sorry my Ma missed out on this lovely place and supplies for new ensembles for herself. She also missed another outburst from Georg. I blame her for much of his attitude, and we didn't need her escalating the situation even further."

Clara held her handkerchief and her hands over her face to catch the tears begging to flow freely. "Someone, please, can we discuss any other subject?

Transaction complete, Mutti requested delivery. "Please have our packages sent to the Westminster. Our coachmen traveling with us will prepare them for our return trip. Danke. It has been delightful to work with you today, Monsieur Sajou. And you, Madame Wilhelmina."

Clara's shoulders drooped. "This isn't the trip I asked Vati to permit. Why do I even need new clothes? They're wasted in an attempt to impress Georg, and why would I choose to impress him anyway?"

Mutti dangled her reticule over her wrist. "I'm ready to visit the milliner's shop and Cartier. We have two days left to wander among the street artists and flower vendors. The sidewalk cafés have beckoned to me the last few days."

"Mutti." Clara's ears burned like fire. "I'm not going anywhere else without Hans and Willy right at our side. One more encounter with Georg and me will…"

"And what will you do?"

"I'll follow Megs to Chicago. That would get me out of this grievous situation.

"Just the news I've been waiting to hear!" Megs hugged her friend. They slapped their hands together in the pattern of their secret promise.

"That's enough, ladies. Our next stop will be the milliner's shop." Mutti looked up and sighed. "I'd love a new hat."

They returned to the hotel with new hats, shoes, and jewels to perfectly accentuate the dresses that would come from Rosa's sewing room over the next few months.

"I've enjoyed this so much, Megs," Rosa said. "Danke for including me in your invitation. I'm wondering if tomorrow, when we stroll through the flowers and paintings, could we also stop at Maison Hurel?"

"How did I forget? They sell all those magnificent embroidery supplies. You'll be able to add even more dazzle to your work. And Clara, when you come to Chicago with me, your sketching and your fine artistic embroidery skills will add a whole new dimension to Megs' Designs. We'll add your moniker to the name. Better than Megs & Clara's Designs, why not, MEGS & CLARA—FASHION & DESIGN FOR THE MOST DISCRIMINATING."

"Ladies, please desist with the talk of Chicago. Clara will return to Gut Apfelhof. Your Vati and Georg expect you."

Margaret stood just outside Sajou's. She inched up to her full height and attempted to block the doorway. "I listened from out here, and I learned your plans for tomorrow. I'll advise Georg of the details." Margaret's snarly tone caught enough attention to embarrass them all. "He'll assure you stay away from trouble. You've eyes for every man but him, Clara. No respect for your Vati or your intended.

"You will learn."

Chapter Eighteen

GUT APFELHOF, *Saturday, 10 September 1881*

The Gut Herr waved a telegram in his driver's direction. "The ladies shopped, and they'll require an extra carriage for the return trip." He and Daniel laughed together.

"They shopped. That hardly surprises you." Herr Reinhold grinned and shook his head.

It hadn't surprised Daniel at all, but preparing extra transportation would mean a delay in seeing Clara. He allowed visions of her curls and sweet face to dance through his mind. He might have entertained a few other ideas as well.

"Hook up another wagon, Jost. You'll drive it. If we work quickly, we'll spare the women the inconvenience of waiting on us."

Herr Reinhold cleared his throat. "Gentlemen, there's no rush." Mamsell anticipated the extra time you'd need. She requested rooms at the Crailsheim Inn for tonight." Their boss patted the pair of horses Jost would attach to the second carriage. "Finish hitching up the wagon. Drive to Crailsheim tonight. Complete the trip back in the morning."

"Very kind of you, Gut Herr. We'll return with the women tomorrow then."

Curt charged from behind the house. "Oma's gone!"

"What?" Kraig's arms reached toward the sky.

"I can't find Oma and Brigitte. When Clara's gone, she takes the pup to the garden every morning, and they play together before Oma frees the pup to run off her morning friskies. She's not there, and she is not answering her door."

Daniel rushed to his friend's side. "We'll find her, Curt. You may have passed each other and not realized it."

"I hope Georg's not involved." Curt shoved his hands in and out of his pockets.

"How would he be involved?" Herr Reinhold adjusted his high black hat and checked his watch. "We'll find Oma."

"I heard the commotion." Fritz joined the group.

"Never mind your watch, Vati! We're wasting time. Oma's missing. Fritz, when did you last see her?" Curt tapped his toes as if that would prompt Fritz to answer more quickly.

Worry lines threaded their way across Fritz's brow. "I've not seen your Oma or the Schnauzer since yesterday morning. She never misses giving Brigitte a frolic in the morning sunshine and taking her on an afternoon walk when the pup stays with her."

"Here comes Mamsell now." The Gut Herr directed everyone to the carriage house. Unfolding a map of Gut Apfelhof, he spread it out on the workbench. He massaged his earlobe. "We'll search the entire village until we find Oma and Brigitte."

"With men and several horses off to Crailsheim, we're short on legs. Mamsell, please summon Dora, Henry, and Alice. Fritz, find Wilhelm. We need everyone's help."

"Jost and I will stay until we find Oma and the Schnauzer."

The party assembled. The Gut Herr gave everyone an assignment, and they commenced with the search.

Mamsell hesitated. "Wait, everyone!"

"What's on your mind?" While he rocked back and forth on his heels, Fritz rubbed his forehead.

"I believe prayer would be wise. I'd like the Lord's direction to find them."

"An especially helpful idea, Mamsell." With heads bowed, the Gut Herr prayed. *Heavenly Vater, you see us all. We love Herrin Dorthea, and You love her more. Protect her, and lead us to her and Brigitte. In Jesus' name. Amen.*

Dora sniffed the air as she lifted her head. "Fire!"

Smoke rose beyond the orchards close to the pond. "Everyone, grab a bucket and run." Herr Reinhold hustled to locate enough buckets.

As the group came closer, Tilly and Herrin Dorthea hushed their conversation where they sat on a wooden bench by the pond. Brigitte bounced around a stone ring filled with dancing flames.

Locking eyes with his mutter, Kraig spoke to her with the same tone of voice she had long ago used with him. "You scared us all, Mutter. Why didn't you inform Mamsell about your plans?"

"And watch you attempt to stop me because you fear I'd be unable to handle a fire by myself? I only lit it to provide us warmth while we chatted." She laid her hand on Tilly's. "Or is there another worry on your mind?"

"Not at all."

Tilly pushed to her feet, but the older woman's grip kept her anchored. "You're safe right here with me.

"Tilly and I are fine. Brigitte, too." She stared at her son before saying any more to the group. "I'm sorry the Gut Herr alarmed all of you. Danke for your concern. I count you—loyal members of our Gut Apfelhof staff—among my friends the same way I do Tilly. She was out walking. I invited her to come with Brigitte and me. Along the way, I learned she was burdened by a personal matter. I appreciate her confidence in sharing with me. I've promised her I'll keep our talk private."

"Danke, Herrin Dorthea." Mamsell nodded to each of the servants. "I believe all of us agree the Reinhold family treats their staff and our community well, and we appreciate your kindness."

Brigitte sulked at Curt's feet. He rubbed behind her ears. "You miss Clara. She'll be home tomorrow to spoil you."

"Don't you think I spoil her when she's with me?" Oma grinned. "You folks came prepared for a bucket brigade. Two buckets would be more than enough to douse this little blaze."

"And we'll take care of those two buckets for you." Daniel helped Oma to her feet. "It's a relief I'll be going to pick up the ladies knowing Clara's favorite Oma and Brigette are safe." He hugged her tight and whispered in her ear.

"Danke, Daniel. While you tend to the flames, I'll walk Tilly home. Her Mutter is ill, and I'd like to visit and pray with her."

"Danke. My Mutter will be so pleased." Tilly helped Herrin Dorthea to her feet.

"No use arguing with you, Mutti. Be on your way. I'll pick you up later this afternoon."

Herr Reinhold turned from his Mutter to Curt. "See, my son, no need to worry about Georg."

Relief washed through Daniel.

No worries, at least not this time.

~

CRAILSHEIM STATION, *Saturday, 10 September 1881*

AS THEY NEARED the Crailsheim station, Daniel's heart beat faster. He imagined the taste of Clara's kisses and the feeling of her body snuggled to his chest. His eagerness surged as the train chugged toward the platform. When he spotted her through the window, icy fingers of accusation choked it all back. She belonged to the younger Herr Wolff.

"Jost, I don't trust myself to greet Clara as a member of the noble family I serve. Her soon-to-be mother-in-law has already sent me enough signals about her irritation whenever I'm anywhere near Clara. You greet them, but I'll stay close enough to hear everything."

Hans disembarked the train first. He and Jost assisted the women.

"Is there a mistake? We're grateful to see anyone from Gut Apfelhof welcoming us home, but where's Daniel?" Frau Reinhold's eyes searched the crowd.

Legs spread in a wide stance, Jost looked down at her. "He's here. He checked something with the horses and sent me to see you off the train, Gut Herrin."

"He's the driver for our family. He's well and has arrived with our carriage then."

"Ja, he's well, and we arrived together. There he is now." Jost motioned to where Daniel stood off to the side.

Daniel stepped toward them. "Ladies, welcome home. Plans have changed. We'll spend tonight at the Crailsheim Inn."

"This evening? We are not traveling home now?" Clara rubbed her eyes, her arm concealing the kiss she blew Daniel's way. "I'm ready to sleep in my own room."

"Your own bed tomorrow." Daniel winked. "The Baron asked Mamsell to arrange the night's stay at the inn. The horses traveled many miles this week. They need rest, and navigating the roads back to Gut Apfelhof safely after dark is challenging."

"A delay? This news falls short of my expectations and will cause my husband unnecessary concern about my delinquent arrival."

Frau Reinhold pulled a fist to her hip as she spoke. "Really, Margaret?"

Frau Wolff sneered and crossed her eyes.

"The Gut Herr notified the Wolff's staff of this change of plans, correct?" Frau Reinhold turned to Jost.

"Definitely. There'll be holes in the pews at church in the morning, but no one at either estate expects us until tomorrow."

"Then let's settle in at the inn." Clara cradled a package. "It's a short walk, and I would like to stretch my legs after the train ride."

"What's on their dinner menu? Hopefully, they have an excellent selection. I enjoyed most of the food in Paris, but the fine cuisine I enjoy on our family's travels spoils me. What an enormous disappointment if the last meal of our trip is less than grand." Frau Wolff retrieved a handkerchief from her reticule and wiped her brow.

"Margaret, you enjoy grumbling far too much."

Daniel found it impossible to miss the pointed stare Frau Reinhold directed at Frau Wolff.

"We'll eat whatever they serve and be grateful for my husband's kind considerations, or would you prefer to walk home?"

Georg's Ma was as disagreeable as her son. Poor Clara. Daniel followed behind Jost and the others, strolling to the inn located two short blocks from the Crailsheim station. Colorful riots of cascading flowers spilled from window boxes. Roses still bloomed on the wrought iron-fenced garden beside the two-story timber frame inn.

"Reminds me of home. We'll be comfortable here tonight." Hannah rubbed Clara's shoulder. "Maybe Daniel made a plan for the two of you."

Daniel overheard Hannah's comment. *Do I dare?*

"JUST AS I HOPED, I find you alone here in the garden. I sniffed those roses earlier, and I declared their fragrance and hues as beautiful as you, my lovely lady." Drawing it from behind his back, Daniel placed a red rose in Clara's hand. "For the one I love."

"Oh, Daniel, how beautiful. Hearing you say those words plays a tune in my heart." She hugged him tight, then abruptly released him. Her commitment to respect Vati's choice weighed heavily on her heart. "It's been a wonderful week, and it's been an awful week. Willy and Hans will apprise you of any incidents you haven't already heard about."

"More incidents than reported to your Vati? I know Georg made the trip despite your Vati's orders."

"Someone will catch us out here. I must freshen up and join the others for dinner. You and Jost enjoy your meal with Hans and Willy."

With a quick peck to Daniel's cheek, Clara ran toward the door of the inn and to her room. She missed Megs already. Daniel wasn't on her list of potential suitors, but she found it impossible to think of any other man but him in her life.

"You can't go to dinner looking like this." Hannah brushed the ever-wayward curls from her sister's face and offered her the lace hanky tucked up her sleeve. "Here, dry your eyes. Have you enjoyed our trip at all?"

"It is kind of you to ask. I'm thankful Vati granted us all permission to go. I loved traveling with everyone—well, everyone except the Ma to the Wolff. Seeing Megs was the highlight of the week. She chatted endlessly about the wonders of Chicago and kept offering me a position in her shop—a partnership even."

"Would you accept it?"

"Nein. We both know if I leave Gut Apfelhof, it'll be to become Frau Wolff."

"And marrying him scares you."

"The jaws and bite of a big bad Wolff are scary. Consider his behavior this week. I anticipated enjoying time with all of you before facing life with him. Vati granted my wish. Then awful Georg arrives uninvited."

Clara opened a small package she had chosen to carry with her as a reminder of the beauty surrounding her ugly situation. Fingering the silk strands and sparkling beads, she twirled a gold embroidery hoop around her fingers. "These are beautiful." Truthfully, she'd hardly enjoyed browsing the abundant displays of treasure at Maison Hurel, fearing another humiliation.

"We all breathed easier when he stayed away, and my heart breaks for you. Are you convinced Chicago wouldn't be your best choice?"

Clara sighed and shook her head. "Daniel's not there. I lose him either way. I lose him by marrying Georg, or I lose him by leaving for America, so very far away. And I lose because of the rules. The awful rules."

"A damp cloth to your face will perk you up." Hannah dipped a towel in cool water and handed it to Clara. "I'll rearrange your disheveled tresses, and we'll go to dinner.

Mutti and Emmaline joined Rosa and Frau Wolff before you arrived. I assured them we'd be along shortly."

"Danke. I'm not hungry, but I will join the rest of you."

"Did you receive any messages from Monsieur Worth about your sketches?"

Clara allowed herself a tiny smile. "The desk attendant at the Westminster handed me an envelope from Maison Worth as we were leaving. He's interested and sent contact information to pursue his offer."

"What splendid news! Have you told anyone else?"

"You're the first to know, but it's no use." Clara crumbled.

Hannah stroked her sister's hair and gently teased at her curls.

Moments later, Clara shoved her hand away. "We're nobility. Vati may be only a Baron, but our status discourages women from pursuing a position. And of course, Georg won't hear of his woman working. There is nothing more to discuss."

Chapter Nineteen

CRAILSHEIM TO GUT APFELHOF, *Sunday Morning, 11 September 1881*

THE SIGHT NEVER GREW OLD. Clara's pride swelled seeing Daniel seated high upon the driver's seat of their Gut Apfelhof-crested carriage. But her nightmare had followed them to Paris and returned ahead of them. There'd never be a way for her and Daniel.

Hannah puffed up her cheeks and exhaled. "Eggs, sausage, and Kuchen. My stomach promises to rumble and complain about our big, delicious breakfast while we jostle along the cobbled roads back to Gut Apfelhof."

"I'm thankful we stayed in Crailsheim last night and avoided Schinderhannes lurking in the shadows." Emmaline swallowed a long breath between her chattering teeth. "And we're a well-marked group. There's no protection of our Gut when we're on these roads."

"You've read too many old stories, meine Kinder." Mutti glowered.

"There must be others who find the criminal's life fascinating and would dare to copy." Emmaline raised her cloak and hid behind its folds.

"What gives you jitters about Schinderhannes today? He received his punishment a hundred years ago." Clara swatted off the girl's covering and her foolish worries.

Hannah tapped Clara on the shoulder and pulled her close. "We're safe from Schinderhannes, but pray Georg hasn't set traps for us between here and home."

Following a long pause, the awkward moment faded. Clara cupped her hand around Hannah's ear. "He acts like a foolish young boy attempting to capture a girl's attention with dimples and dumb stunts." If only his behavior were nothing more than childish mischief, her heart wouldn't be racing. She covered her chest with her hands as if she could hold the threatening explosion inside.

Hannah drew imaginary ribbons and bows on her skirt and whispered back. "True. Kind attentions create sweeter cords with which to lasso a woman's affection. A fact he needs to learn if he plans to court, or God forbid, marry my big sister."

A wheel flew from a carriage ahead of them. Clara gasped. Daniel pulled hard on the reins, bringing the Landau to an abrupt halt. Hannah's elbow stabbed into Clara's side. A jolt traveled up Clara's arm as her elbow thumped into the side of their carriage.

"That doesn't appear to be an Apfelhof carriage." With a hand to her forehead like a shield, Mutti reported. "I hope one of our neighbors isn't injured."

The horses spooked on the second carriage commanded by Hans and sent it off course. Jost's rig lagged further behind, enabling him to avert disaster.

Daniel jumped from his seat. Willy bounded from the luggage coach. Both men ran to the disabled carriage. "Michael Weiner. Minna Schultz. Are you hurt?"

"We're thankful you found us. I invited my favorite girl for a Sunday afternoon ride. When I came over the rise and spotted those stray rocks lying across the road, I attempted to steer the horses around them. It was too late, and I didn't have enough room to maneuver. My wheel took a hard hit. I'm embarrassed, but I'm also thankful our horses reacted well. Other than a few bruises and aches tomorrow, we should be fine."

"Let us help. You've three of Gut Apfelhof's coachmen and me at your service. None of us can move ahead until your carriage is moving again." Daniel suggested Minna wait with the ladies. "And Michael, Jost is already retrieving the wheel."

"I have tools under the seat. The pin holding the wheel in place must have come loose." Jost grabbed the wheel and retrieved his emergency box. "A quick repair."

"Do you hear them? They waste our time to fix a peasant's carriage?" Margaret crossed her arms. "The men should help them push their carriage off the road. When we arrive home, send word to their family that they need help. We're already arriving a day later than expected. Georg will be so disappointed he missed Clara last night. He planned a thoughtful surprise for her."

"Like another plagiarized poem? Respectfully, Frau Wolff, have compassion for Michael and Minna." By Mutti's stern expression, Clara knew she had wearied her enough with her attitude.

"Margaret, kindness to our neighbors is a hallmark of Gut Apfelhof. Clara will receive Georg's surprise as happily tomorrow as today. If it were our carriage, you'd appreciate others lending a hand."

Clara wished she could handle situations like these with as much grace as her Mutti.

"At Gut Dinkelhof, our men avoid associating with subordinates. Always been a fault of the Baron of Gut Apfelhof and his family—too friendly with residents and staff." Frau Wolff glared at Mutti. "Nobility stands by nobility. There's no other way. You should have taught you or your daughters this lesson."

"Mark 12:30-31," Rosa whispered diagonally across the coach to Mutti.

The tiniest smile crept across Mutti's face. "Clara knows the rules well. Knowing man's rules is not a guarantee that following them is always the best answer. Following God's rules must come first. He gave us the two greatest commandments.

"And thou shalt love the Lord thy God with all thy heart, and with all thy soul, and with all thy mind, and with all thy strength: this is the first commandment. And the second is like, namely this, Thou shalt love thy neighbour as thyself. There is none other commandment greater than these."

"We care about your family, Lydia. You are our neighbors. Georg courts Clara, and I pray they marry soon. But again, nobility begets nobility."

"Ja, by the rules you're correct, and you've missed the point entirely. You imply others who live in our Guts and work to ensure our families' successes aren't our neighbors? When we care for one another, we all delight in more joy in community. Do you agree?"

Margaret sucked in her gut and pinched in her cheeks. *"Pshh."*

Clara slipped down in her seat. Her opinion of Frau Wolff sank lower. Like Georg, his Ma was only concerned about who would serve her.

Hannah nudged her sister. "Clara, what do you think Georg's surprise is?"

"If you think you can jostle me from my melancholy mood, it's not working." With a huff, Clara shrugged off the question. "I'd like to get out of the carriage. Walk with me."

Hans snagged a length of rope from the carriage's boot.

Hannah called to him. "Would you mind helping Clara and me step down from the carriage?"

"Phew!" Clara adjusted her gown to exit with grace. "I am grateful the newer styles slim down these skirts even more and raise the hemlines. I'd rather not need help to get in and out of a carriage."

"It wasn't Georg offering us his hand. Be grateful."

"I would've preferred Daniel's to any of them."

"What do you suppose Georg's surprise will be?"

Clara shrugged again. "I already gave my thoughts, much to Mutti's chagrin. Another plagiarized poem, no doubt. He has volumes of them, and he'll demand a servant copy one for him instead of sending an original message. He claims to love and care about me, but nothing comes from his heart. Worse yet, if he plans to take me behind the bushes and slobber me with kisses, he'll get a surprise when I slap him."

"You're saying thank you prayers for the delay?"

"I am. But where did those stones come from?"

"We're ready to go again." Daniel winked toward Clara and climbed back in the driver's seat. "We'll arrive home in less than ten minutes."

"We walked longer distances in Paris, and we sat here or walked about the carriage for an hour while the men made the repairs. Walking, we would have arrived a half-hour ago. What irony." Hannah chuckled, then quickly wiped the humor from her face. "Those rocks didn't belong there. You don't suppose...?"

"Georg!" Clara's face paled. "He meant them for us."

BACK AT GUT Apfelhof *and the Reinhold Estate*

DANIEL DELIVERED the women to the front entrance. Mamsell awaited them outside the aqua-colored front door. She fidgeted with a pale blue envelope.

Daniel took Clara's hand as she stepped from the carriage. He always marveled at how perfectly his larger work-worn hand cocooned her soft, feminine one. When Brigitte jumped up demanding Clara's attention, he smiled wider. Dazzling white stars danced in his heart.

"For you, Clara. I found it on the sideboard when Georg left two hours ago." Mamsell handed her the envelope.

"Where's my son? He's not here to collect me and my trunks, and he hasn't sent our driver. It was a mistake to help those commoners."

"Frau Wolff, our Gut Herr left instructions for Daniel to drive you as soon as they unload the wagons and ready your luggage for you."

Daniel realized he had just received his instructions from Mamsell. The unwelcome news turned his dancing white stars into aggressive green spikes. He stacked the ladies' luggage. "We'll unload quickly. Fritz, please place the Reinhold women's things and my Mutter's where they belong."

"Of course. You should be able to return before dark." Fritz nodded to him. "Your caravan stopped down the road. Was the delay serious?"

"Michael Weiner had a mishap, and his lady was with him, too. He has begun courting Minna."

"How embarrassing for him."

Daniel looked at his feet to avoid eye contact with Georg's Ma. "It was. Except for one member of our party, everyone encouraged us to help get their carriage rolling again."

"Herr Georg Wolff arrived two hours ago, expecting everyone to be back. He surprised the Baron when he requested you to drive Herrin Wolff home, but the Gut Herr agreed. He believed Georg would stay to visit Clara. Instead, he left her the envelope." Fritz sorted luggage while they continued their conversation.

"I'm happy Georg left. But another hour to get his Ma back home and return to Gut Apfelhof." Another hour he'd be away from Clara. He'd help Fritz load Frau Wolff's trunks and bundles and be on his way.

"Frau Wolff. I know you're eager to return home, and I'll get you there as quickly as possible." The carriage lurched forward as Daniel took off for Gut Dinkelhof. Ignoring her groans and complaints about the bumpy ride, he sped along.

Halfway to the Wolffs' estate, Daniel spotted the graceful black Arabian horse bearing Georg back toward Gut Apfelhof. The Reinhold drivers had taxed their horses heavily this week, yet Georg expected Daniel to push them further to take his Ma home while he traipsed back to Clara. How contradictory and rude. The green spikes of jealousy ground their tentacles deeper into Daniel's heart.

"NICE PAPER AND EXCELLENT PENMANSHIP." Mutti stood by her side as Clara studied the envelope.

"But it's from him, and I would like to rip it into shreds." Instead, she carefully lifted the seal. "If my hunch is correct, the letter possesses written evidence of more crude intentions." She shielded the letter from Mutti's view and read silently.

My dear Clara, my sweets, do you realize how deep an attachment I have to you, and how sincerely and fondly I have loved you even from the very first hour of our friendship? Imagine the pain of being separated from you this week past. God knows how my heart ached for you. I'm returning shortly on my handsome horse. I've places to show you. Be certain your gown allows you to mount the steed with me.

Yours always, Georg

Agitation roiled through her head and punched at her heart. "Pain of separation?" He had done his best to intrude on all their activities while they were in Paris. "He describes a week to sound like an eternity. A lifetime with him would equal two eternities. I prefer not to ever ride on his horse. Why would Vati even allow it?"

She turned to Mutti. "Help. No matter how much I choose to honor Vati, I have no energy for Georg today. If we were a gambling family, I would place my bet that he stole these words from another's letter. His Pa's library contains an entire shelf of poetry and love letter books he copies when he has a need. Georg's body lacks even one genuine romantic bone." She handed the letter to Mutti.

Mutti's shoulders hunched as she read the letter. She gazed down at her hands before lifting her head slightly. "I'm filled with sadness for you. Your predicament fights a fierce battle with my resolve to see your Vati's wishes respected."

Prancing up the path to the Reinholds' door, Georg's puffed-out chest arrived in front of Clara at least three seconds before he did. As his eyes traveled from her crown to her toes, her stomach grew queasy.

Mutti rubbed Clara's back and slipped into the house.

"Ribbons and flowers on your hat and perfectly coordinated attire? Clothes to impress but unsuitable for riding a horse. Didn't I make myself clear?"

"Not even a hello or a welcome home?"

"Hello, my sweets. Now explain how you'll mount my stallion dressed like that. I've missed you, and I'm ready to escort you to a special place. You ignored my instructions, and you're unprepared for our ride."

"We arrived home within the past hour. Fritz moved our trunks to our rooms as you arrived. And you passed Daniel on the road."

"I passed Daniel? What good fortune for me, he headed the other way. I anticipated his unwelcome presence around you, my sweets."

"You believe I appreciated your appearances in Paris? You act as though we parted months ago, and you pined for my return for weeks and weeks."

"Change quickly, and we'll be on our way."

"Our group encountered an unexpected delay today. This afternoon, I plan to relax with my sketchbook. For Vati's sake, I'll dress in appropriate clothing and ride with you tomorrow morning. Call on me at ten."

Before she could pull her hand away, Georg bathed it with another wet kiss. Clara shook off the unwelcome gesture. "*Phew.*"

Georg mounted his Arabian.

Ever-loyal Quintus deserved a kinder owner than Georg. Pride had preceded Georg's acquisition of the beautiful animal. What price had he paid? The Wolffs appeared wealthy, but gossip had spread of their financial difficulties. And Megs' warning in Paris. At least he was on his way home for now.

An hour later, Clara spread a charm quilt on the grassy area of the garden. She enjoyed the fragrance of elderberry bushes. Chattering, skittering squirrels entertained her. Having changed into a simple day dress, she pushed her skirts smoothly under her and lay on her stomach. Propped on one arm, she sketched with the other. Images she created peered back at her with curiosity. Except for their giggles, she barely heard Emmaline and Hannah approach.

"What's so funny, you two?"

Hannah pointed to Clara's sketchbook. "Georg's horse does not appear too happy, but you captured your dreamy Daniel wearing impeccable riding attire, seated in the driver's seat of our carriage, and leading the Gut Apfelhof horses. Do you imagine him transporting you in style to a secluded spot? Will you sit under the bright blue sky and whisper love songs to one another?"

"My finger puppets imagine many stories. I'll ask them to stage one about you and your beaus." Emmaline wiggled the hand-crocheted characters occupying her pointer fingers. The blonde gent took a sweeping bow toward the lady with the red tresses.

Hannah knelt next to Clara on the quilt and pointed to an empty oval on the page. It rested atop broad shoulders. "Who is this man with no face? He's peering from the window of the well-appointed railcar pulled by the iron horse."

Clara dropped her jaw and her pastels as she stared in disbelief at the image Hannah pointed out. "Not again! I was unaware my hand traced those lines."

"Not again? What?"

"This isn't the first time I drew a man with no face without an inkling of awareness on my part."

"In the image of Daniel with you in the carriage, you obscured yourself in the drawing. Suggestions of your red curls are the telltale. But look—another man with no face." Hannah pointed to the image. "Who's this, and who's the woman outlined there? Your familiar dark brown eyes peer from the oval."

"You know his identity?" Clara posed the question to her inquisitive sister.

Hannah tugged at her lower lip. "We should return for dinner now."

Clara tucked the sketchbook under her arm. Emmaline caught the bent elbow of her other arm. The sisters skipped toward the house.

Lacking any interpretation, these images crawled through Clara's mind. She would compare the sketches of the other faceless men in the privacy of her room.

Chapter Twenty

GUT APFELHOF, *Monday Morning, 12 September 1881*

As Clara puzzled over the men with no faces, tiny bells on her maid's slippers jingled nearby. She flipped the sketchbook closed, slid it behind her dresser, and slipped into the chair facing her vanity table. Alice entered and stood beside Clara.

"You'll ride with Georg today?" Alice's face reflected behind Clara's in the mirror.

"Why the disapproving look? Do you believe this riding outfit to be unsuitable or too immodest for a ride with him?"

"Oh my lady, it's suitable and modest, but you look too good for the Wolff man."

"You agreed I'm modest. Is it the purple color?"

"No matter the hue of your outfit or if you wore rags, you're beautiful. You're too good and kind for a man like him."

"I appreciate that we agree about Georg. I wish I had the power to refuse him again today, but Vati would call it disrespect and reprimand me for it. Help me honor Vati. Which hat?"

"Wear one of your Vati's tall black top hats. Flaunt your noble birthright. I'll be back." Alice returned within moments. She placed Vati's hat atop her lady's curls. "Perfect."

The rich purple riding breeches and velvet half-skirt she donned, topped with a lavender tatting-trimmed silk bodice, emphasized the luster of her auburn locks. "For this cool September day, I'll wear my cape with the trapunto quilting, adding an extra layer of modesty." Clara smiled at the image staring back at her. Oh, but Georg was not Daniel. Oh, how she wished he were. "On second thought, would a sack-of-rags ensemble make a better choice?"

"Do you wish to change to your black riding habit?"

"Black? So dreary. It does match my mood, though—sad and disheartened by my present circumstances." She screwed her mouth at her reflection. "I'll wear the purple outfit and present myself well to Georg, mostly because it'll please Vati."

Fritz sent word her caller had arrived.

"Best of luck today, my lady." There was a touch of reassurance and a heap of sympathy in Alice's hug.

Clara lifted her Bible from her bedside table and tucked it into the pocket of her riding skirt—she would trust God's word to serve as a shield about her. She stepped into the hallway and passed Mutti's paintings. A shiver slithered up Clara's spine. That one where she wore the green velvet gown—always haunted her. She'd avoided him as long as possible. Today, whether it pleased her or not, she'd spend time with Georg. Had Vati trusted him enough to allow them an hour or two alone? Clara didn't. All these layers of clothing provided no protection for her feelings. Relief filled her as she descended the stairs. Curt spoke with Georg in the foyer. She prayed her twin would remain close by. Could she dare believe maybe Vati had planned for that? She paused and listened to her brother's conversation with Georg.

"You brought my sister a bowl of nasturtiums? What message do you hope to send? Oma taught me whoever sends those colorful little blossoms means it as a gag."

"Ladies love flowers."

"Here comes Clara now." Curt winked at his sister. "Georg has a surprise for you."

The smile she had pasted on before joining them turned upside down at the sight of Georg. "Why ,Georg, those flowers are the prettiest colors, but are you saying our plans today are nothing but a joke? Am I another source of amusement to add to your collection of braggartly tales?" Clara's eyes stung like fire.

Georg offered his handkerchief to dry them. Clara accepted, but quickly pulled it away scrunching her nose. "How long has this been in your jacket pocket? It reeks of those cigars you puff."

"Our gardener suggested I bring the blooms to you. He knows as little as I do about flowers having a language of their own—or he tricked me." Georg slapped his sides and snorted like his horse. "No wonder our Mamsell's eyebrows aimed for the ceiling when I informed her that I gathered them for you."

"I'm disgusted with the stench of your handkerchief, and you're laughing about flowers. If you continue to find me and this arrangement a comedy, you create resentment rather than goodwill."

"My regrets. Is there a book to consult before I make further botanical mistakes?"

"Wait. I believe I heard an apology."

"I'm a kind and generous man." His dimples—a sorry attempt to gain forgiveness. "Now about that book?"

"An egotistical apology. I find no amusement in your self-important attitude. You travel to exotic locations. Find a shop selling a suitable book, or perhaps one awaits you on your next trip to Paris."

"I'll inquire." He lifted her hand in his. "After you, my sweets. Quintus awaits."

Clara swiped at the sensation of insects crawling up her arms.

"Bring Lena out." Curt followed the couple and called to Daniel, who was working several yards away. "I'd like for Clara to ride her horse."

Daniel gave a friendly salute to Curt. "I'd prefer that too."

Curt engaged Georg in a conversation she couldn't hear. Clara's unease grew as Daniel delivered her chestnut mare. "You and Curt are following close behind?"

"My lovely lady, I promised you long ago I would protect you always. By your Vati's orders, ja, we are. But Curt and I protect you not because of your Vati's insistence, but because Georg's a threat to the woman we both love dearly." He held one of her hands and placed Lena's reins in the other.

She mounted, sat tall, and clicked her tongue. "Are you coming, Georg?" Clara and Lena trotted out ahead.

Georg came up beside them. "I'll lead."

"Pretty rough kick to Quintus' belly. You treat your horse like your women."

"My sweets, I bring you flowers and plan an outing for us—"

"My sweets! Who do you expect you're fooling? You disrespect your horse the same as you do me. It's the same way you treated Sarah. I was a child, but I remember, and your sister does too."

"Remember what? You don't know what happened, and you've no idea about my plans."

"I fear hearing about them. What surprise possibly awaits me on Reinhold land? I know every inch by heart."

He set the pace, leading them down the cobblestones, through the fields, and around the orchards of Gut Apfelhof. "Are you aware there's a plan to join the Reinhold land with ours when you and I wed in the spring? Ask your Vati. He has allowed me a small plot, and I'll use it to bring further success and acclaim to his Apfelhof empire."

Clara's legs grew weak. She was grateful Lena carried her without prodding. She held onto the horse's mane and stared ahead at the old cottage. Why were they headed there?

Monte Carlo travel posters lined a six-foot stretch of the wall that hid the old, abandoned cottage. Georg pointed, bowed, and exclaimed over them.

It took several deep breaths before Clara could speak. "You remind me of a circus ringmaster. Are these meant to lure me to this extravagant lifestyle you brag about?"

Clara slid from her horse while Georg bumped to the ground. He moved from one poster to the next, pointing out the luxury of the new resort destination. "A further distance than Baden-Baden or Bad Hamburg, my sweets, but only the best for my lady. François Blanc has built the most impressive casinos and spas found anywhere in the world."

Her vocabulary contained no words to adequately express her disdain.

"I went to much trouble on your behalf, and you can't even smile?"

"The Dark Forest lent beauty and eeriness to Baden-Baden's fine resorts in their heyday. The casinos, baths, and spas attracted the wealthy. With the gambling houses' principal business outlawed several years ago, perhaps the wheel still spins under the shroud of the broken house. The new house cloaks the same activity in a seaside paradise instead?"

Georg ignored her question. "Envision my pigeons right here at Gut Apfelhof. We'll build a beautiful garden around them, attracting interest and visitors to its beauty too." He whispered in her ear as he swept his hand around the area.

Even with the trapunto cape cinched securely beneath her chin, his breath sent prickly shivers down her spine. "I know nothing of pigeons except that they are messy, and I would say, worthless. And they would do their duty on our apples."

"The pigeons promise a grand addition. Perfect, like you, my sweets." His hands curved around her waist.

Tremors surged through her body as Georg's hands worked their way under her cape. Clara jerked from his grip and smacked him across the face. Lena snorted with a rattle. "You tell them, Lena." She hoped Daniel and Curt had heard and would be on their way to rescue her.

"Georg!" Curt shouted. "What just happened! I'm not asking. I'm demanding."

Her tension eased at the harsh sound of her brother's voice.

"Demanding what exactly? You can envision my pigeons here, ja?"

"Don't make a fool of my sister or me." Curt motioned for Daniel. "We witnessed your seamy behavior. Vati should never have trusted you. In truth, he didn't, and we didn't. You've made your shameful moves toward her a habit for years, and today you act no differently."

"And we're both witnesses to today's sorry scene." Daniel's penetrating look dared Georg to a staring match.

Daniel would win. Clara grinned on the inside.

"I'm not touching her. I don't know why she slapped me, but it was a girly punch. It didn't hurt at all."

Heat sizzled in her cheeks. Clara stood back, eyes wide and hands covering her gaping jaw.

"Lucky for you?" Curt ripped down one of the posters, wadded it, and threw it at Georg. I doubt Vati will believe me about your indecent actions, but I'll report your comments about the pigeons."

"Do you see pigeons?"

"I heard what you left unsaid—your extensive plans to either supply Monte Carlo with stock raised on our Reinhold property or to start a sport arena here yourself."

"I never said those words."

"I'm no fool!" Curt tore the next poster.

"I asked your Vati about the space back here, forgotten and tucked away. He agreed it would be fine if I increased profits."

"My Vati would never allow such scandalous activities to tarnish Gut Apfelhof's name. I'll drag your name through the fire with him about this!"

While her brother and Georg continued their argument, Clara crept toward Daniel until she could lean against his strong chest.

Embraced by her favorite man, the burning pain in her lungs eased.

"Your Vati will learn of this. Pray for change. I'm praying every day for your nightmare to end, and for our dream to come true, my lovely lady. No matter what happens next, you deserve so much better than him." He brushed a kiss across her cheek.

"Take your hands off my lady!"

Daniel and Clara jumped at Georg's thunderous tone.

"Not to worry, Georg. She's yours."

"By all appearances, she needs protection from the one she's promised to." Curt poked his finger into Georg's chest.

Georg countered with flailing fists and a gnarly bellow.

"I have the best idea right now. Mount Quintus and take yourself and your horse back to Gut Dinkelhof. You proved once again you can't be trusted with my sister, especially in private."

Unintelligible sounds accompanied the Wolff to his horse.

Curt mounted Landus. Daniel helped Clara join Curt in his saddle. For the first time all morning, Clara felt protected.

She leaned against Curt. There was no place she felt safer than with these two men. Securely in the saddle with her brother was a peaceful place right now. And her life needed peace. She would never trust Georg. How would she make Vati understand? *God, would You change Vati's mind for me, please? I'm poorly prepared to handle more of this man's atrocious behavior. Am I the most rebellious daughter to my parents and to You?*

Raucous laughter interrupted her prayer. She looked up in time to realize what the men had found so humorous. Georg tumbled over his saddle. A few moments ago, he was mounting Quintus. Now he had landed on his head.

She covered the smile inching up her cheeks. "Leave him here."

"What if the fall seriously harmed him?" Daniel dismounted, hastened to Georg's side, extended a hand, and helped him up. "Are you hurt?"

"Would you care if I were?"

"I care enough about you as a person to help you up."

"Leave me alone. I'll be along."

Daniel's kindness and respect for people were one thing she loved about him. He had shown much consideration for the very person Vati had allowed to steal Clara from him. She would never allow Georg to steal her love for Daniel.

"If he's hurt, his pride keeps him from telling us." Daniel and his horse stepped next to Curt's. "Should we send a wagon to collect him and Quintus?"

"I want him off Vati's property. Trouble makes a habit of arriving with him, but the neighborly thing would be to send help." Clara wrapped her arms tightly around her brother. When Curt yanked the reins, his horse sensed the urgency and wasted no time whisking them toward help, Lena right at their side all the way.

As soon as Clara's feet touched the ground, the security of her brother's strong back fled. She refused to move, but an invisible force shook her limbs, and beads of perspiration prickled her lips. She collapsed on a nearby hay bale.

Curt explained the situation to the men cleaning the carriage house and quickly instructed them to hitch up a wagon.

"The way you and those horses flew, I knew trouble followed close behind." Willy motioned to Hans, and the coachmen sprang into action.

The commotion aroused the family and staff, and they gathered at the carriage house. "Mamsell, we need blankets to line the wagon." Willy moved items to make space for the man to lie.

"How badly is he hurt?" Hans fastened the horses to the wagon.

"Not badly enough to keep him from being pompous and claiming he doesn't need help." Curt scowled.

"His shameful ego is always on display to the world. I'll send word to Gut Dinkelhof." A hint of sarcasm laced Mamsell's voice.

"Danke." Curt nodded.

Emmaline and Hannah clutched Clara's hands and led her to a nearby corner of the yard, where Mutti joined them. Mutti's smoothing her hair had always eased Clara's pain and fears. The gentle motion helped her sort her thoughts. Today her heart hurt. Oh, what she would like to do with Georg for the pain he had caused her, and for the damage he intended toward their family's home. As his Mutter had taught him, Daniel would help Georg. Regardless of his feelings, Georg needed help if he had injuries from the fall. Rosa had told the Good Samaritan story often, and, of course, she'd been right.

Curt hugged Clara from behind. "Stay here. Daniel and I will return quickly. Pray for us. The task of tending to this animal won't be an easy one."

STILL HUDDLED with Mutti and her sisters in the grassy spot beyond the carriage house entrance, Clara exhaled the breath threatening to blow her heart apart. "If he's hurt badly, will the incident work in my favor?" She gently nudged Mutti's arm, then clasped her hands as if in prayer.

"Or would it increase the difficulties of your situation?" The missing sparkle in Mutti's eyes hinted at her sympathy for her daughter yet carried a strong warning. "Despite your feelings, you must do what is right."

"Ja. Now we must pray for him. How difficult." Clara was grateful that Curt and Daniel had followed her because Georg's blatant disrespect had been on full display. The people who cared about her had refused to trust him. "You know they came because they feared what he would do to me? They had good reason to believe he threatened me. He certainly took advantage of the opportunity—again—to make his usual untoward moves. I wish he were dead!"

"What a harsh statement." Mutti frowned. "I do believe your Vati instructed them to follow you. Nothing about this is easy. Let's pray while we wait for the three of them to return. The words of Psalm 16:11 is an excellent place to begin. *Thou wilt shew me the path of life: in thy presence is fulness of joy; at thy right hand there are pleasures for evermore.* Luke 8:50, when Jairus asked Jesus for his daughter's healing, is another good choice. *But when Jesus heard it, he answered him, saying, Fear not: believe only, and she shall be made whole."*

If Georg should recover, she wouldn't see her life filled with pleasures just because she loved Jesus, but she would be obedient to Mutti's lead.

Mutti and her daughters joined hands and quieted their spirits in His presence.

Mutti prayed. *Danke, Gott. You are an amazing, all-seeing God. Thank You for sending Curt and Daniel to protect Clara. Forgive me for saying this, but You know Georg isn't our favorite person. Still, the Bible says You made him in Your image just like us. Provide safety and healing, even as the boys tend to him*

We alerted his family, and we hope his injuries are minimal. Let them return quickly with Dr. Pfeiffer. Grant a speedy recovery. And then, O Lord, we pray for Your path to be revealed and for Clara's peace, joy, and pleasure in her life, however You have that planned. In Jesus' Name, Amen.

As they opened their eyes from prayer, Curt and Daniel pulled the wagon with Georg to a stop. Dr Pfeiffer's arrival was perfectly timed. He climbed down from his horse and strode toward the men. He climbed into the wagon and examined Georg. Clara and the others kept a quiet vigil. Clara hadn't wanted him in her life, but wishing harm on Georg would be as ugly as his untoward actions.

Gerwig Wolff dismounted his horse as Dr. Pfeiffer finished tending to his son.

"He took a harsh blow to his head and shoulder, Herr Wolff. Rubbing lineament will ease his shoulder pain. His hard head undoubtedly did more damage to the ground than the other way around. He'll have considerable discomfort for a few days, but I predict he'll be well shortly."

"You may rest and recover for a few days at home, but then I expect your full explanation." Veins stood out on Herr Wolff's neck.

Georg grunted and turned away from his Pa's staring eyes. "You enjoy humiliating me? Oh, but revenge is sweet."

"Are you a Kindergartener or a man, son? You perceive I have embarrassed you, but you take advantage of every opportunity to make me appear as an idiot." Herr Wolff's nostrils spread wide, and he snarled through his upraised lip.

Why would Clara be thinking this way at all? It would be the right thing to do, but would she speak before she abandoned the idea? She stood and moved toward the wagon. "Would you like me to visit while you recover?"

Georg grinned. He withdrew train tickets to Monte Carlo from his pocket and waved them in Clara's face. Her brows knit together. This is how he had responded to her kindness? She wished the ground beneath her would open wide and swallow her whole.

"Can't help but wonder what the flies flitting about Georg's horse witnessed when all this happened?" Dr. Pfeiffer shook his head and packed his bag.

"I look forward to your ministrations tomorrow, my sweets." Georg reached for her hand and placed a dank kiss on her palm.

With his Pa's and the Doktor's help, Georg climbed into his family's carriage.

Finally, they left for Gut Dinkelhof. Clara wiped her brow, shook the slobber from her hand, and gritted her teeth at the endearment she detested more each day.

"Gut Herrin, maybe a little stroll around the garden would help settle Clara. Would you allow me to do that with her?"

Clara kept her fingers crossed behind her back. His smile had always disarmed Mutti, and she loved Daniel as a son. She wouldn't be able to say no, would she?

Mutti rubbed her head and appeared in deep thought. "You know why I should deny your request. I may be suffering a loss of good sense at this moment, but a friendly conversation could be the medicine Clara needs right now. I'm trusting you both."

He helped Clara to her feet, and the two wandered down the cobbled walkway to the garden.

THE SOUND OF APPROACHING HORSES' hooves broke Curt's concentration as he paced a circular path around the cobblestoned area between their home and the carriage house. Family members and staff trudged down the back steps of the house joining Curt when they heard Vati coming.

Returning from a visit to the Backhaus, Vati's saddlebags bulged.

The fine people of Gut Apfelhof kept the Reinhold family supplied with bread and baked goods fit for the noble family. His family greeted him with nothing but somber expressions.

"Has someone died here? Why the dreary faces?"

"Daniel and I both witnessed it." Curt raked a hand through his hair.

"Witnessed what? I assume from the sharp tone of your voice that this involves Georg?" Kraig grasped Artax's reins and handed them to Daniel. "Be sure to cool him down and settle him in his stall. The rest of you, resume whatever you were doing before this news came to your attention. Curt, follow me to the pump house."

Tiny whispers buzzed in the air as the two men disappeared. Curt strained to make out the words swirling among family and staff. Vati's voice drowned the others.

"Curt, now!"

Behind the block walls of the pump house, Vati dipped himself a tankard of icy water and offered another to his son. "I want to hear this from you first. Alone. What happened today? I know Georg intended a surprise for Clara. It's clear that something took his plans in the wrong direction. I knew I could count on you and Daniel to protect her in the event it did."

Curt squirmed to find courage and perfect words. He had none and answered Vati's words with a simple, "Ja."

"Ja? I'm highly suspicious you're eager to divulge much more than that. What happened?"

"What do you know about the Tir aux Pigeons in Monaco?"

"A phony pretense by delusional men acting like they still need to hunt for their next meal. They take pop shots at dirty birds."

"And you gave Georg permission to raise these dirty birds on Gut Apfelhof land?"

"Nein. But what does this have to do with whatever happened today? You said I need to know. I'm listening."

"Georg called on Clara this morning. He invited her on a horseback ride to show her a surprise. I don't trust him close to Clara, and you did ask Daniel and me to be watchful. We followed them. Clara found no comfort in any part of the surprise."

"And how do you know this?"

"Daniel and I've spent enough time around Georg to know the man's habits. He mistreated Clara and Megs for years. Some folks overlook or even accept, ignoble actions like his. Those traits have never defined a Reinhold man or any of the Reinhold staff."

"How have you connected his behavior to pigeons?"

"The wall behind the old cottage. He lined it with advertising posters inviting travelers to the royal lifestyle of Monte Carlo. They displayed a wonderland far more lavish than Baden-Baden in the Schwarzwald and this new one is by the sea, too. A paradise of sorts."

"Posters? Pigeons? Paradise" Clara isn't safe?" Vati shook his head. "You weary me. What does one of these have to do with the other?"

"He discussed his plans with Clara to raise pigeons like the ones in Monte Carlo. She found the birds disgusting, but not as disgusting as Georg's wandering hands forcing their way up her body and his cigar-stench breath curling down her neck. We watched as she planted her fist on his jaw before we let them know we saw it all."

Vati squeezed his eyes shut and took a few steps back. "My daughter is a lady, but—hmm—apparently, she defends herself well."

"Curt kicked at the wall, sending a few loose pebbles flying. "I was proud of her, too, but please tell me you will retaliate."

"Give me the details." Vati's face flamed as red as one of their ripest apples.

"Georg dropped the indecent behavior as Daniel and I approached, and he feigned innocence. Our concern was to remove Clara from danger. Daniel helped her up on Landus with me, and he mounted his horse. When Georg hastily launched himself onto Quintus, he flipped over his saddle and fell on his head. We laughed, but Daniel jumped down to check on him and helped him up. Despite being hurt, he refused further assistance. This speaks for Daniel's kindness and integrity."

"And when I rode up?"

"Daniel, Willy, and I had gone back for him. Mamsell sent for the Doktor who arrived just as we did. He finished examining him. When you rode up, Doc and Gut Herr Wolff were leaving with Georg. Doktor Pfeiffer believes he'll be completely healed in a few days."

Vati clapped Curt on the back. "All's well then."

"Do you find relief in his imminent recovery or in the fact that we protected Clara from further fondling by the gadfly? Or because the creep is still around to court your daughter?"

With his coat sleeve, Vati wiped tears from his eyes. "I never granted permission to raise pigeons here."

CHRYSANTHEMUMS in full golden bloom lit up the garden like sunshine. Daniel and Clara meandered along the paths.

"I'm proud of your thoughtfulness, Clara, offering to spend time with Georg while he's recovering."

"And you saw how he responded to my suggestion. It was as though he expected it. I plan to send my regrets."

"But you'll bring real sunshine into his life whether he's aware of it or not."

"Where's the sunshine in our lives, Daniel?"

"These flowers represent the sunshine." Daniel let go of her hand to pluck one. "Do you know the meaning of these cheery flowers?"

"Georg certainly wouldn't! Do you?"

"Ja. They represent joy and optimism."

"Where did you learn that?"

"After Georg's big mistake, I asked your Oma." If only Daniel could tell her he had studied the language of the flowers and had pulled it from his deep wealth of knowledge. "I'd like us to focus on that meaning right now. Maybe add a couple of my Mutter's well-chosen Bible verses. It might improve both our attitudes toward our unfortunate position."

"I recall a couple Rosa would point out." Clara pulled her Bible from the pocket of her riding skirt.

"You have your Bible with you?"

"I counted on it being my shield today. I'm very thankful God used you and Curt to protect me."

What a beautiful, godly woman, and she loved him. He couldn't believe he deserved her. Georg certainly didn't. He swallowed hard, attempting to moisten his dry throat. "Have you already opened to Hebrews twelve?"

She nodded. "We're both thinking the same way." Clara handed the book to Daniel. He read the passage for them.

Wherefore seeing we also are compassed about with so great a cloud of witnesses, let us lay aside every weight, and the sin which doth so easily beset us, and let us run with patience the race that is set before us,

Looking unto Jesus the author and finisher of our faith; who for the joy that was set before him endured the cross, despising the shame, and is set down at the right hand of the throne of God.

For consider him that endured such contradiction of sinners against himself, lest ye be wearied and faint in your minds.

Ye have not yet resisted unto blood, striving against sin.

"We haven't suffered close to what Jesus did for us. We're not supposed to let our troubles weary us. Jesus endured death for the *joy* that was set before Him." Daniel spun the chrysanthemum between his fingers before offering the fluffy spot of joy to Clara.

"I'm so tired, though. What joys do you believe God has for us for enduring this agony? What lessons is He teaching us?"

Daniel wished he could see into the future and realize a much happier ending for them than what they both perceived. He brushed loose curls from her cheeks and gazed into her eyes.

"I wish I knew, Clara, but I'm going to trust God to bring us through in joyful victory over our sorrows. Please smile. I adore the sparkle in your eyes when you do."

"The strength of your faith lifts my spirits, Daniel Becker. Pray for me tomorrow when I visit with Georg. I'd like him to realize that Jesus lives in me. And that Jesus chases the darkness away."

"Now that's more optimistic! And your smile has returned." Daniel flipped back a few pages.

"But rejoice, inasmuch as ye are partakers of Christ's sufferings; that, when his glory shall be revealed, ye may be glad also with exceeding joy."

Someone whistled from the garden gate. "Daniel and Clara! Mutti says you've been out her by yourselves long enough."

Chapter Twenty-One

GUT APFELHOF, *Tuesday Morning, 13 September 1881*

CLARA PICKED at the apple designs embroidered on the tablecloth in bright reds and yellows. On any other day, the breakfast of oatmeal with applesauce, raisins, and fragrant cinnamon promised a tasty meal. Not today. "Why did I suggest I'd be kind and visit Georg while he recovers?" Despite her conversation with Daniel about joy and optimism, she needed another plan.

Sitting across the table, Curt poked his spoon toward her. "Come with me instead. We can ride back to the cottage. You may have been too distracted yesterday to notice, but the late sunflowers are still blooming, and they always make you smile."

"Should I expect another surprise?" Clara asked.

"Secrets and surprises everywhere." Curt tapped his chin and shrugged.

"I didn't sleep at all, and I'm not prepared for anyone to see me today. You're not planning for us to visit Gut Apfelhof neighbors again?"

"Nein, and I asked Daniel to have our horses ready now. We'll be back in time for you to keep your commitment to the Wolff. Besides, only the sunflowers will see you."

"I'd love to accompany you."

Excusing themselves, the twins thanked Dora for breakfast and scrambled off to the carriage house.

Clara covered her face, hiding the dark circles she saw in the mirror earlier this morning. How could she let Daniel see her like this?

A moment later, familiar hands tugged gently on hers.

"Your face is always the most beautiful one to me, my lovely lady." With his hands on her shoulders, Daniel looked into Clara's eyes.

"*Ahem*. All that lovey stuff. Daniel, did you say we only have two hours before you need the horses returned?"

"Ja. The farrier is coming today to check on all of the horses. Here, let me help." Daniel assisted Clara in mounting Lena.

She found her place in the sidesaddle. Did you check Lena and Landus? We've no need to worry about their hooves?"

"Not a bit."

"Still, I'll be sure Curt keeps his word about returning the horses."

Daniel chuckled. "And where will you be? Will he ride both of them back to the stable?"

"Maybe I'll come back too." She grinned and winked in his direction, then followed Curt as they trotted out of the stable yard and onto the trails around Gut Apfelhof. "If only my future happiness blew like this refreshing breeze on my face."

"Danke for coming. You can think about something besides your predicament for a little while."

"Look! A bunny! At least they'll only steal apples already on the ground." Clara pointed to the tree line and reined in her horse. She hopped down and picked a few apples, choosing the brightest and shiniest to offer to Lena. The horse munched eagerly.

Curt held one out for Landus, too. "Our time's short, and the workers out here will accuse us of stealing the crop they're harvesting." They rode on.

When the cottage came into view, Clara pressed a hand to her chest. "Goodness. What a spectacular display these posies provide this year. Maybe the most beautiful I've seen." Georg had led them in from another direction, or Clara would have noticed them yesterday.

They dismounted their steeds, threw the reins over a low stone fence, and wandered around the cottage's front yard. Weeds poked up between the walkway stones, and the faded red shutters hung askew. But the sunflowers towered toward the bright blue sky.

Both noticed it at the same time. Curt bent down to get a closer look. "Who buried a towel in the middle of the sunflowers, and why?"

"Nobody lives down here." Clara knelt beside him.

Together they pushed back loose earth, revealing a carefully folded cloth. Curt lifted the edges, exposing its contents, and covered them back up quickly.

Only an inch long, but tiny knees, elbows, fingers, and toes had begun to form. Eyes stared as if they pleaded with her.

Clara screamed. "Curt, you do know what this is?"

"I do, and the image is now etched in my mind forever."

"Who brought it way out here? We have a special place in the graveyard…"

Curt finished her sentence. "…unless this was intentional."

Clara shuddered. "I've heard it is not a baby until the woman feels movement in her body. If she had felt the baby move and miscarried, wouldn't she have buried the little one in the cemetery? Was there a husband or even a suitor or…? Now my heart breaks even more for the Mutter." Tears streamed down her cheeks.

"I know little about being with child, Clara. It's probably wise for us to rebury him, only deeper, where an animal won't find his tiny body."

Stunned by what she had seen, Clara managed to push herself upright. "I'll search for useful items in the cottage."

"I'll retrieve the rusty shovel lying by the back door. Tossed there years ago, but it'll come in handy today."

Clara returned with a piece of crockery. "I can arrange the bundle in this striped bowl while you dig a deeper hole."

"Should I dig in another spot so we don't disturb the flowers?"

"Rebury the remains where we found them. When the plants return each spring, they'll bloom on the grave."

Curt carefully replaced the soil. "The sun will set over a more respectable grave for this tiny one tonight."

Frown lines caught Clara's tears. "But we've uncovered another secret. Who and why? One of our neighbors is hurting. Should we report this to someone? I fear bringing more pain to a friend or neighbor. It could be one of the ladies from my Bible class. I'd want to comfort her."

Curt used his shirt sleeve to wipe sweat from his brow and catch his stray tears. "Men discuss their conquests. I'll listen for any bragging I hear among them. Are you ready to start back?"

"Danke for asking me to go, but ja, I'm ready to leave."

"Everything went so wrong. Not what I expected or hoped for."

"Perplexing and burdensome events define my life these days."

"Keep praying for answers and an unexpected reversal."

"Prayers. Nothing more than futile petitions." She grabbed Lena's rein. "Daniel awaits our return with the horses."

He pushed her chin up. "Pick a few flowers for Mutti before we go. Tomorrow you'll be with your friends in your Bible Class."

Flowers and the mention of her friends brought a hint of a smile. "My prayers remain unanswered."

"You have a special request for your friends from Megs." Curt shrugged. "She offered you hope?"

Chapter Twenty-Two

ST LUKE'S KIRCHE, *Gut Apfelhof, Wednesday morning, 14 September 1881*

COLORFUL SWATCHES in myriad patterns shimmered through the eastern-facing stained glass of the tower room where the ladies' Bible Class met. They danced across the faces of the five women and one tiny baby present. Aaron, Luisa's newborn, soaked up his admiration society's doting before settling snuggly in his Mutter's arms.

As they gathered in community around the polished oak table, each lady claimed her seat—the one with her favorite needlepoint angel cushion. Along with the angels, the winged oxen carved into the table's legs imparted perfect reminders of God's protection and sacrifice.

"Even after you married last year, you continued to join us unwed ladies." Clara stroked Aaron's wavy blonde hair. "What a delight to celebrate together with you for this new little life. And, Minna, what a lovely match between you and Michael."

Minna's grin was almost invisible behind the blood rushing up her face. Her happy reply mixed with a shaky voice. "It is true. Vater gave his permission last week. Our families have been friends as long as we can remember. The Weiners are poor farmers, but we pray there will be enough work for Michael and his Vater to support us marrying and beginning a new family next spring."

Clara rubbed Minna's shoulders. "I'll let Vati know."

"Danke."

"What about you, Clara?" Della tucked her face behind the pages of her Bible. "The baron arranged for Georg Wolff to court you, and there is talk of another wedding in the spring."

Clara grimaced, then crossed her arms on the table and pressed her forehead into them, taking a moment to compose a response. She focused on that joy in Hebrews but found no appropriate response. She lifted her head and simply nodded.

Luisa looked up from studying her baby's face. "Do you love him? I see sadness in your eyes. You do not."

"As the daughter of the nobleman, you have far more important things to do than spend your time with us, but we love that you do." Minna rubbed her fingers gently on the back of Clara's palm. "It's painful to see you hurting. Courting and marriage should bring great joy."

Joy. There was that word again. These ladies were commoners and she nobility. Social status meant so little to Clara. These ladies were her friends, but Vati had insisted she protect them from the troubles of their baron's family.

"Danke for your kindness, ladies." Clara opened her Bible. "We've been studying the Psalms, and we've reached number 139. Tilly, you've been very quiet. Would you read the first four verses for us, please?"

O LORD, thou hast searched me, and known me. Thou knowest my downsitting and mine uprising, thou understandest my thought afar off. Thou compassest my path and my lying down, and art acquainted with all my ways. For there is not a word in my tongue, but, lo, O LORD, thou knowest it altogether.

Minna tightened her lips while furrows slid across her brow. "Clara, do you hear what these verses say? God knows what's happening to you, even if you don't share details with us. He knows. He sees. He understands your sadness, and He knows every thought on your heart, whether you choose to speak them or not."

"More than once in the last few weeks, God's reminded me He sees me, and He sees my situation. Danke for the reminder. I'm expected to teach you, but all of you teach me too."

"From the next verse, we learn God not only sees us, but He's right behind us and right in front of us, and He has not only His hand but also His eye on us." Luisa caressed Aaron's head.

"I do love that our God is all around us everywhere." Clara smiled, hoping to shine a bit of joy.

"Verse six." Luisa's eyes lit up. "*Such knowledge is too wonderful for me; it is high, I cannot attain unto it.* I love what the Psalmist wrote here. It sounds like he doesn't understand this lofty way of God either. If King David struggled to comprehend, how do we even begin to fathom the reach of

God's love and care into our hearts and lives? Does anyone else find understanding the idea of His extravagant love for us a genuine struggle?"

Tilly pressed a finger to her cheek. "Is the answer by experiencing His love for ourselves?"

"A keen perception, Tilly. Next week, will each of you bring a testimony of experiencing how well God knows us and how He keeps His hand upon us?"

Without a warning knock, Vati stepped into the room. "Excuse me, ladies. I've been visiting the fine citizens of Gut Apfelhof today, and Luisa's Mutter sent Apfel pastries for you girls."

Thankful echoes came from the attendees.

"She also told me I'd meet our newest resident if I stopped by the church."

"Ja. This wiggly little guy here." Luisa grinned. "Would you like to hold him?"

He nodded. Luisa lifted him into the Gut Herr's hands.

"He reminds me of my babies when they were newborns. It will please me greatly to have grandchildren one day soon." He rocked the baby in his arms and cooed. Aaron delighted the baron with happy noises until the baby filled the room with a pungent stench. "I'll hand him back to his Mutter now."

"No pastries until this odor is eliminated." Luisa whisked Aaron off to another room to change him.

"Good day, ladies." As he turned to leave, Vati smiled and winked at Clara.

Dear God, he's already asking for grandchildren. Do You see this? Do You?

"Who's ready to indulge in these pastries?" Clara passed the plate while they waited for Luisa to return.

"I visited Megs in Paris last week. She asked about all of you and sent her love and a surprise."

"I wish she and Gus would move back to Germany. When she's in the room, her joy and enthusiasm make everyone happy." Tilly spoke, but everyone nodded in agreement.

"What did I miss?" Luisa returned with Aaron.

"If Megs came back to us, she wouldn't be able to make you this offer. Her successful custom dressmaker shop caters to wealthy society ladies in Chicago. While in Paris, we shopped for luxurious fabrics and trims for ensembles she'll create, but she needs fine reticules and accessories available for her clients to purchase. She remembered the needlework skills and creativity each of you possesses and invited you to be her supplier. She'll pay you handsomely."

"Our own cottage industry." Luisa all but shouted, then quickly covered her mouth. Her little one had fallen back to sleep. "I'd love for us to work on the pieces together. Turn our treasures and our fellowship into profits."

"How many will Megs expect at a time?" Minna raised an eyebrow. "Where would the supplies come from? They cost money."

"I'll gather pieces from Rosa's scrap stash, and we'll turn those finds into precious treasures. Your work will command high prices, enabling you to purchase the goods required to move forward. Megs' written proposal is forthcoming."

Claps of joy and hope for their families filled the air. They picked up their Bibles and wraps and headed down the cobbled walkway to their homes. The friends quickly joined their voices to Della's in a robust chorus of *All Creatures of Our God and King.*

Tilly lingered back from the group. Clara waited for her to catch up.

"I made an awful mistake a few weeks ago." Tilly spoke to the ground. "God is furious with me. I read the rest of the Psalm." She burst into tears and ran down a path through the woods behind the church.

Was she the one, God? I hear You saying, 'Wait and pray.' Our troubles draw us closer to You. I'm praying for Tilly and me.

"May I interrupt your deep thoughts?"

Daniel's voice was soft, and his shuffling feet marked his hesitancy. She gazed up at his handsome face. "You bring a smile to my weary heart. I'm not sure why you'd be here, but I'm happy to see you. You bring me a load of that joy we talked about."

"Jost and I delivered apples to the parsonage this morning. He returned home with the carriage. I decided to walk, hoping to meet you along the way, but I didn't expect you to be alone. My heart smiles too."

"You're headed back to the carriage house? The loop path around the orchards is a long way to walk by myself."

"Allow me to escort you." Daniel offered her his arm. She accepted and walked beside him, a spring in her step.

"Because Georg courts you, it's not fair for me to ask."

"Not fair to ask me what?" Clara's voice bubbled.

"You and I've always worked together decorating the harvest wagon for Erntedankfest. You arrange the harvest crops and offerings beautifully."

"Are you asking?"

"I am, my lovely lady."

"Oh, Daniel, I couldn't imagine you doing it without me."

"Ja. You agree then? It could create an ugly scene, though." Daniel grimaced.

"I'll invite Curt to join us, long-time friends working together and enjoying each other's company. There are no rules forbidding friendship." Clara's heart fluttered.

"We'll welcome his help if business doesn't take him elsewhere."

"I'll pray everyone is so consumed with their roles preparing for the festival, that no one at the house will miss us." Clara squeezed his arm. "Is my petition even a fair prayer? Sounds like I'm asking God's approval to break the commandment to honor my Vati, doesn't it?"

Daniel laughed. "It does, but I get the impression the fairness of it gives you brief pause for concern."

"We promised to love each other forever and always, no matter what. I choose to spend time with you."

"Clara Reinhold, I'll love you forever, too." Without a moment's hesitation, their lips met.

Daniel lingered in this sweet spot only a moment longer.

"You stopped." Clara pouted.

"Anyone can see us out here." Daniel smiled and tapped her nose. "We'll have many private moments while we decorate the wagon."

"We need a plan. Georg will be recovering for at least a couple more days. Vati requires your service today, or we could slip away now. Vati requested to hear your side of the story, too. If only it would make a difference for us." She was ecstatic about the time she and Daniel would have together and even more saddened because their fun would quickly end. Georg and the rules would always be there.

"If only it would, my lovely lady."

"As soon as he's well, Georg will send word of the times he intends for us to be together. I'll have your Mutter advise you of the best times for me to assist you, hoping those opportunities fit between Georg's plans and Mamsell's schedule for you to deliver family, apples, and supplies to their destinations in the next two weeks. Oh, this dreadful arrangement." Despite her attempts to resist it, growing resentment sank deeper into her soul.

"I've heard some rumblings. Expect Georg and an unwelcome surprise on Friday."

"He's unwelcome without any additional surprises."

Daniel lifted her chin and swiped his thumb gently below Clara's moist eyes. "No tears. I prefer your lovely smile. We'll be home in a couple of minutes. We should part now. Not give anyone reason for concern."

She stood on tiptoes and pecked her favorite driver on the cheek.

Clara's steps faltered down the remainder of the path to their home. What had he meant about expecting an unwelcome surprise on Friday?

Chapter Twenty-Three

GUT APFELHOF, *Friday, 16 September 1881*

The sound of snorting coming from below drew Clara to her window. What a strange sight. A donkey pulling a cart filled with cages trotted up their cobbled drive.

She rushed from her room and heard Fritz shouting at the bottom of the stairs. "Mamsell, do you know anything about a bird delivery today?"

As Clara descended the stairs, Mamsell joined Fritz. "What birds?"

"Cages full of nests. And adult birds in each cage."

"Nein. The only birds we need here are the chickens and turkeys Dora orders for dinner."

"Indeed." Fritz tapped his foot. "Fraulein Clara, you're expecting Georg today. Did he mention bringing birds?"

"I was warned he might arrive with another surprise. Docktor's orders prescribed bed rest for at least another day." She couldn't help but wonder why he was out visiting.

The cart, the donkey, and the driver came closer. Mamsell wiped her hands on her apron and made her way to the door. All three of them gaped at the sight of Georg crawling off the cart bench.

"It appears Georg arrived for a picnic with you and brought crates of squabs." Fritz covered his eyes as if doing so could make the creatures disappear.

"Call for the Gut Herr." Mamsell shouted the order.

"He left for the day." Fritz chewed his lower lip. "You arranged for Daniel to drive him and Curt to Stuttgart."

"I scheduled them to leave at 2. It is only 12:45."

"But Daniel and Jost hitched up the Landau, and Daniel drove away with Curt and the Gut Herr an hour ago, eager for an early start."

Curiosity battled her indifference until the first won. With halting steps, Clara made her way toward the cart. "What are those disgusting things? They look dead."

"Pigeon babies! Look, I brought the adults too. See them regurgitate pigeon milk for their offspring."

"*Ew.*" Clara grimaced, and her stomach lurched. "I believe they learned their manners from you. Regurgitated food? Explain how a dead creature eats."

"Clara, my sweets, they are not dead. Their little hearts will beat in a day or two, and their eyes will open the next."

The nickname rankled her. "You certainly recovered quickly. Weren't you ordered to rest for at least another day?"

"I hoped you'd be pleased to have your intended well and attentive again."

"Not after the warning of another surprise from you. I hardly expected stinky birds, though." Clara pinched her nose and gagged. "Now I understand Fritz's comment about you coming for a picnic. Are these the appetizers or the main course? Either way, your fowl fouled my appetite."

"Climb up, my sweets. The donkey and cart will deliver us to our special spot."

"You have a pigeon house set up by the cottage wall? And we don't have a special spot!" Clara jerked to look away from him.

"They'll live well in their cages for now. Unlike Apfels gathered from the trees in fall, the spelt harvest occurs in late July. Our workers need to be kept busy. My peasants will arrive here tomorrow morning."

"Curt and Daniel heard you yammering about pigeons on Monday." She spun back around to face him, her arms crossed over her chest. "Before they left this morning, Curt warned me of this possibility. What spy did you hire to advise you the moment they left?"

"You accuse me of snooping on the property of my future father-in-law? Hurtful, you would think of me in such a low way."

"It's the only way I think of you." Joy in her troubles had not found its way into her heart today. "You maneuvered and manipulated your way into our family from the beginning.

Vati granted his permission for courting. Doing what he's asked of me is all that holds this arrangement together. He doesn't approve of your pigeons."

"You'll help me convince him then?"

"Nein! Turn this cart around and trot your snorting donkey right back to Gut Dinkelhof. I dare the ole boy to roll around in your cut spelt. Might not be any harvested grain left to feed the cows or sell to the establishments in Monte Carlo."

"You wish financial ruin on our family?"

"Since Vati would never allow his daughter to be joined to a ruined family, I'd consider it a convenience." Leaning back on her heels, one hand on her heart, finger twisting a dangling curl, Clara pulled her lips into a hard smile.

"No need for your smug expression. I'm happy to visit the pastor with you. We'll get his opinion on the arrangement."

"His opinion covers pigeons?" Clara swallowed hard to soothe the fire in her throat. "Georg, leave. Now! I believe the courting candle burned out days ago. Seeing you again before Erntedank will be too soon."

"You owe me respect, my sweets. Your Vati will hear of your ungracious behavior. He'll see things my way. For now, I'll leave you, but you'll regret your attitude." Georg cursed, the donkey kicked up pebbles, and road dust flew.

Clara waved her hands as if doing so would make him vanish more quickly. Vati and Curt opposed the pigeons, and they'd warn Georg to stay away or change his mind about the creatures. Clara had hoped she and Daniel could decorate the harvest wagon down by the old cottage, where no one would see it until the festival day. Now she would worry about Georg showing up there despite her Vati's warning?

THE RATTLING of the gate stirred Clara from her slumped heap on the garden bench. "Who's there?"

Oma poked her head inside the gate. "Hello to my favorite granddaughter."

"We're all your favorite."

"Why so gloomy?" Oma sat beside her, leaned in, and held Clara in her arms.

Peace settled over her troubled spirit. Their embrace loosened.

"Your Vati created a tough sentence for you, my precious child."

"Thank you for noticing and for coming to find me. I've chosen not to burden you with my problems, but I wish the pain would go away and Georg with it. Am I just an unappreciative, spoiled child?"

"You are a most appreciative child, Clara."

"Appreciative then, but resentful. The two words don't go together at all, do they? I want to do the right thing, but I'm not sure what is right. Right, in whose eyes? Daniel and I talked about being joyful despite our circumstances, but I simply resent what's being required of me."

"I promised myself I would keep my opinions on this private, but as the family matriarch, I can't remain quiet any longer. Even though men ignore women's ideas, I shared mine with your Vati and Curt." Oma pinched a purple chrysanthemum blossom and rolled it between her fingers.

Just like Daniel had done the day before.

"Your Opa cared about them as neighbors, but he questioned the Wolffs' repeated trips to Baden-Baden."

"Can you tell me why?"

Oma's eyes followed a squirrel hopping between the chrysanthemums. "This sounds like gossip, and I shouldn't repeat it."

"You have piqued my curiosity now. It must be important. Tell me, or I'll pester you until you do."

"I'd expect no less from you." Oma giggled as she tugged on Clara's loose curl. It bounced back to her granddaughter's cheek.

"You've teased my curls as long as I can remember, and the gesture still tickles me." The tension of the moment was released.

"Back when the opulent Kurhaus operated in Baden-Baden, Gerwig and his Vater and later Georg too, frequently traveled there. The establishment hosted gambling, spas, and loose women. All three Wolff men earned reputations. I was never privy to the specifics, but Opa cheered when the notorious activities in the Black Forest fell to prohibition. He prayed the Wolff boys would find more admirable amusements, curtailing the threat of further shame on our local communities."

"What kind of shame?"

"People all over Württemberg discredited their reputation, and it reflected poorly on us since Gut Apfelhof sits adjacent to Gut Dinkelhof. Because of that proximity, your Vati and Opa often found it necessary to defend their honor in business deals. The church and state questioned our family's possible connection to the dishonest gains of the Wolff family."

"That helps me understand, but may I change the subject?"

"You're looking for more than one of my old lady opinions today?"

Clara nodded. "Did you know Georg treated Sarah poorly? Forgive me, because this sounds like gossip, too. But Megs saw him serve her drinks that made her sick. Sarah and the baby she carried died. No one spoke of the possibility, but as a member of the Wolff family, Megs was aware of things hidden from others."

"A story I've heard before. Perhaps it's true, or perhaps Sarah was ill and died. Georg lacks enough integrity. We won't discuss this part of his life."

"Are you aware he took advantage of my youth and naivety in despicable ways? He tried things with Megs, too—his own sister. He continues to be aggressive with me, and his unsavory attentions are most unwelcome."

Oma's head bobbed. Loose snowy curls brushed Clara's face. "As Mütter and Omas do, I see everything. Sadly, I believe you speak the truth."

"Would you tell Vati what you know? Have you already?"

"We've not discussed Georg's behavior toward you. Curt visited me at the beginning of this Georg matter. He believes your Vati has a deeper reason, maybe guilt, leading him to his decision."

"Do you agree?"

Oma scratched her head and gnawed her lower lip. "It grieves me to repeat gossip, and here I am doing what I would rather not. You're aware of the one ugly disagreement between your Mutti and Vati. There's no reason to repeat the story."

"Even if he still feels guilty about the incident, it's unlikely it contributes to his decision with the Wolffs, then?"

"Not directly. This old girl hears things, though. I reported to your Vati and Curt conversations I overheard at the Backhaus. The knots in this web are far from untangled, but I gave your Vati a few morsels to consider. Whether they prove enough to change his mind…" Oma shrugged.

"Danke. You have renewed my hope." She hugged Oma tight. "On another subject."

"A third subject in one day. You tire my old brain."

"It's about your visit with Tilly. After Bible Class, she needed to talk. She said that God was furious with her. Then she took off. I'd like to comfort her. Do you have any suggestions?"

"What part of the Bible were you studying?"

"Psalm 139. She read ahead of the rest of us. I know the end of the Psalm. It's beautiful, but she read a meaning into it I do not believe the psalmist intended. She believes God hates her. Did she…" Clara put a finger to her lips before she said more.

Oma clasped her granddaughter's hands in her own, shakiness traveling from them through Clara's arm. "We must protect Tilly."

"Curt and I found a tiny grave by the old cottage. Tilly was worried about something in that Psalm that speaks of the beauty of life hidden in a mother's womb. She started to tell me what upset her, but then she panicked and ran. Curt told me that when they found you with Tilly by the fire, you promised her the conversation between the two of you would be a well-kept secret. Is the grave we found part of Tilly's story?"

"A discussion for another day. I need to rest, meine Kinder. I'm going back to my cottage now."

Chapter Twenty-Four

SATURDAY, *17 September 1881*

CLARA RUMMAGED through a scrap bag Rosa had set aside for the Bible Class ladies. She drew out a treasured remnant and reminisced. Startled by a pinch to her elbow, she dropped the turquoise silk leftover from her favorite doll quilt. Curt stood at her side.

"Vati is meeting with Georg and Pastor Lange today about those pigeons. The meeting begins at the parsonage, but the conversation will undoubtedly move to the old cottage. Daniel and I'll be waiting nearby."

"What reason would there be for Pastor Lange to meet with them about pigeons?"

"Possibly to keep the peace, but I suspect a darker intent." Curt hurried off.

"I'll be there, too," Clara called after her brother and then stuffed the fabric pieces back in the bag. She took them to her room and set them with her Bible before heading down a side path to the old cottage.

A potting shed around a bend from the building provided shelter. As Curt predicted, the meeting had moved to the proposed location for the pigeons. Out of the corner of her eye, she caught a glimpse of Daniel and Curt spying on the exchange.

Clara shoved her hands under her arms and stood motionless. Her nerves jangled. Vati's voice clashed with Georg's in a commotion behind her.

She wore her narrowest skirt today, permitting her to duck behind a large oak tree. She heard Georg explain his scheme to Vati. She prayed their conversation would lead to the end of this entanglement. *O Lord. I pray only Your best awaits me. You tell us to ask without doubting. If I could be so bold, God, please include Daniel in Your best.*

Clara could hear their words, but her position made observing them, too, nearly impossible. She maneuvered until she could take in the whole exchange.

Vati pushed his hair back from his face and massaged his right ear before pointing a finger at Georg. "How is it you have Pastor Lange's support for your plan with these pigeons?"

"He's standing here. Ask him yourself."

"I have, and now I'm asking you."

"He expects they'll produce more income for both of us, the Reinholds and the Wolffs. More income and more taxes collected make church and state happy. Pretty simple." The smirk in his voice soured in Clara's throat.

"Only God knows why there is no church in Gut Dinkelhof, and why your family attends St. Luke's. After your pathetic answer to my first question, do I dare ask another? Is Pastor Lange involved in your pigeon business?"

"You question his integrity, too? Again, ask him yourself. You promised me your daughter's hand. You wouldn't have if I weren't a fine man from one of the finest noble families in our state."

"Your actions place you in a precarious position, Georg. I retain the right to rescind my decision at any moment I choose."

"But you won't. Pastor Lange, you promised to make Herr Reinhold realize the merits of my plan."

"The only place I know for you to sell those pigeons is Monte Carlo, a very long way to transport stinky fowl. Are you contriving another project you've not discussed with me?" Hesitation sounded in the pastor's voice.

Clara's twin asked his own question. "Georg, you and Pastor Lange have omitted important details. Monte Carlo forbids clergy members access to their grounds. What underhanded deals do you broker in Pastor Lange's stead?"

Laughter came from deep in Georg's belly. "Your Vati promised me the use of this piece of your property. He added no restrictions. I promised to make it profitable. See you this evening at dinner with both our families."

A knot tightened in Clara's stomach. Dinner? Mamsell had failed to mention this. Clara would not have forgotten.

Vati positioned his face two inches from Georg's and poked a finger into his chest. "Leave, and take those accursed pigeons with you!"

Georg shoved the finger away. "Pa and I will be back in two weeks. The pigeons will be delivered here and stay for now."

"And who will care for them?" Vati asked.

"I imagined Clara would."

Her throat constricted, and her heart throbbed. Hadn't he said their Gut Dinkelhof workers would tend to his smelly flock?

"You've permission to court her, but my daughter won't be feeding your birds. Ask Pastor Lange. I predict he'd find the task entertaining."

Georg stomped his foot and released a disgusted huff. "Good idea. How about it, Reverend?" Georg departed without his answer.

"My wife's waiting for me." Lange left too.

A sliver of hope. Clara had been thankful Vati had protected her, and for Curt's insights, but the birds were still there. Her faith in hoping anything would change had run out. Vati had not denied the dinner engagement. She would have loved to forget her way home today. Vati would expect her to entertain their guests on the piano again. One particular guest had no interest in the music. He liberally spread ingratitude and poor manners, yet harbored expectations far exceeding anyone's ability to meet them. And his demands of Vati? Why had Vati allowed himself to be treated with such contempt? This was not like the man Clara had known and loved all her life.

She waited until Vati and Curt were out of sight. Gathering her skirts, Clara pulled them with her as she stepped from behind the tree, coming nose to nose with Daniel. She ran her fingers through his blonde waves and melted into his kiss.

Bringing her hands down to his shoulders, she nudged a space between the two of them, pausing the tender moment. "Does any hope remain for us after hearing their conversation?"

"We'll keep our promises to one another. I love you, Clara."

"And I love you, Daniel. Forever."

Tears streaked her face again. She left her love, trudged home, and entered through the back door. She climbed the servants' stairs to her room.

~

DINNER WITH WOLFFS, *Gut Apfelhof, Saturday evening, 17 September 1881*

"MY LADY, you chose purple over black for your ride with Georg earlier this week because black was too drab. Now you want black. How about the gown with the pearl and rhinestone buttons and all the pretty lace?"

"The plain black one with a large bustle to provide extra distance between him and me will serve best. Black pointy jet buttons up to my neck and long puffed sleeves. Do we have black ribbons for my hair? Or a veil?"

"Are you in mourning? Who died?"

"You know I consider you a friend, and I rarely reprimand you. But remember, for today, you work for the Reinholds. And, ja, someone died."

"Black it is. As ugly black as lives in your wardrobe."

"An ugly duckling costume fits my mood today. Do I own web-footed black shoes to complete the ensemble? Forget the veil. Ribbons will be perfect."

Happy with her dark, drastic appearance, Clara tucked her feet into soft black slippers and padded a quiet path to the dinner table. Fine cut-glass goblets reflected the gas wall sconces' warm glow. Linen and lace napkins showed off a fancy embroidered R, and the Reinholds' finest china filled each place. Every piece of silver set in perfect order. Grateful that only Hannah had arrived so far, Clara took the seat next to her sister and sat quietly. The rest of the family and guests joined them.

Clara drew unwanted attention when she yanked and twisted a dangling curl. She quickly placed her hands in her lap and picked at her cuticles. Thoughts of the day's events bounced around in her head. Not even married to the fellow yet and the ever-presumptuous and never-loving Georg had seared her spirit.

Whose baby had they found? She mourned for the poor child and feared for the Mutter. And now the whole Wolff family gathered around their dinner table. She was tired of being a respectful and dutiful daughter. She was finished with the charade surrounding her.

Peeking through the lashes of her lowered lids created a perfect vantage point—an up-close view of everyone's horrified faces staring back at her.

Vati's face flushed scarlet. He remained quiet. Too quiet. A somber mood hung over the Reinhold dinner table.

"Join me in grace for the meal." Curt broke the silence.

After the prayer, Dora filled their plates. Sauerbraten marinated in her secret blend of spices served with potato dumplings and sweet and sour red cabbage on the side. Fritz poured the best of Gut Apfelhof's wine.

Their guests exclaimed over Dora's cooking before Georg took over the conversation, bragging, of course, about his pigeons.

"The squabs opened their eyes today. The adults have been collecting food and spitting it up for the little cherubs to feed. They'll be ready to make the pull before we know it."

Vati's and Curt's heads both jerked at the mention of the word pull. Clara had no idea what that meant. She realized they did, and that they didn't like what they'd heard. She hoped this moment might bring change, but hope becomes difficult when life only gets worse. She had prayed to count her trial a joy to endure because she believed in hope. Could she trust for a tiny glimmer of hope to poke through her shattered heart? She still intended to play Bach's music, 'Komm Susser Tod.' Come Sweet Death. Would their guests judge her harshly for her choice?

While Clara prayed silently, Vati folded his napkin. He set it on his plate and placed his hand on her elbow, encouraging her to stand. "Clara will entertain us once again."

Thankful he had requested no particular music piece, Clara took her seat at the piano. She tapped her palm on the bench, and Brigette joined her. "You're a great friend." With carefully placed fingers, Clara let the melancholic music flow. From her choice of music, would Georg realize she suggested he had killed his wife? She doubted it. Was it the music or something else that had turned Mutti's face green and set her body trembling?

Vati caught his wife before she fell from her chair. The others hurried to make room, bringing her cushions and a coverlet. Clara stopped playing and helped Vati tend to Mutti. Clara propped Mutti's head on the cushions and stroked her hair just as Mutti had often done for her. Her needs at this moment outweighed any worries Clara had about Georg's intentions toward her.

While the Wolffs were preparing to leave, Gerwig spoke way too loudly. Clara heard every word.

"What part have you played in this incident tonight, son?"

With his nose pointed high, eyes locked on his Pa's, and a scowl on his face, Georg answered. "Why would you even ask? I've no clue what this is about, none at all." He spun away, cutting his hands axe-like through the air. One last chop pounded his ample pouch, setting him off balance and tumbling to the floor.

"I don't believe you! Get up! We need to leave."

"Dora, bring some cool wet cloths." Vati held his wife's hand and swept a few stray strands of hair from her face.

Other staff members heard the commotion and came to offer assistance.

"Is she having the same problem Margaret did?" Rosa knelt beside Clara and whispered.

"I hope not, especially with Mutti's opinion on the subject."

When Dora applied the cool cloths, Mutti blinked a few times and rubbed her forehead. "Where am I? What happened?"

With a hand supporting her back, Vati helped her sit up. Clara propped the cushions behind her.

"Should I send for Doktor Pfeiffer?" Lottie asked.

"Don't intrude upon him. I'll be fine, but I would most appreciate a cup of tea."

Dora headed back to the kitchen and then reappeared with a cup in hand. "Chamomile and lavender soothe away stress."

"Danke, all of you. I'm much better now."

Did Mutti worry more than Clara about Georg and the Wolffs?

Chapter Twenty-Five

ST LUKE'S KIRCHE, *Gut Apfelhof, Sunday, 18 September 1881*

KRAIG AND CURT let the congregation move ahead of them in line as they made their way to the church door. "Did a mouse run up your leg?" Kraig shook Pastor Lange's hand. "You normally conceal your discomfort preaching on difficult Bible passages, but you have squirmed all morning. Is honesty a sensitive topic for you?"

"You're mistaken, my friend." Lange removed his alb and stole, shoved his hands in his pockets, and pinched his lips shut.

"Check the note glued inside the front cover of your Bible—the Bordeaux-leather one with the brass spine. *Lord, may I never believe anything I preach to Your people does not apply to me as well.*"

Lange fingered his pocket watch. "My wife expects me at home in five minutes. I must be going."

"Has she prepared extra Kuchen this week? Curt and I will be stopping by your home this afternoon. We're bringing questions, and we're expecting answers."

"Your questions can wait until morning."

"Nein. We leave in the morning and won't return until October first."

"At least give me a hint of what this is about."

"We already have. See you at three."

As Vati rejoined his family, Oma stood in a corner engaged in an intense conversation with Frau Lange. His Mutter knew more than she had been willing to share. Clara conversed with the young women from her Bible Class. Her eyes drifted to Daniel. He knew she loved him, but their family followed the rules. She despises Georg, but the stakes are too high to turn him away. Look at the way Daniel wraps his arm around his Mutter while she rubs the cameo at her neck—what a kind son. Georg or Daniel—neither made a suitable match for his Clara, but what choice did he have? He knew which one he would choose if it were not for the rules.

Lord, I'll trust Pastor Lange to provide answers. I believe his role in this conundrum is significant, but can he also help find a solution? Please encourage his honesty. In Jesus' name, Amen.

Curt tugged Vati's coat sleeve. "Pulling you from your thoughts. It's time to learn the truth about the pigeons."

"I'm becoming convinced Pastor Lange instigated this, and his intentions have much to do with the arrangement regarding Georg and Clara, the one you find so dismal."

Curt's eyes grew wide. "You admit it's dismal?"

"I do. Pastor Lange needed to preach his sermon to himself this morning more than the rest of his congregation."

"He believes in his innocence? Everyone else is at fault?"

Vati put a hand on Curt's shoulder. "I asked those questions. He fiddled with his watch. You heard his excuse to leave, but the Langes will expect us at three. I need you there as my witness."

"Shall we walk or have Daniel saddle the horses?"

"Neither. Have him hitch up the Landau. We'll pull up in noble style. Tell him to wear his very best driver's attire. Our visits to the parsonage most often tend to friendly business, but today our presence concerns serious matters. Pastor knows our family status, but we'll prod his memory in case he conveniently chooses to forget."

KRAIG STOOD in front of the fireplace in Lange's office. "Do you believe God doesn't require you to live according to the words of Scripture you preach to us? You delivered a sermon on honesty this morning. Have you been honest with me?" He lifted a finger toward the painting of Christ as judge. "Honest before God?"

"Again, Kraig—Baron Reinhold, Gut Herr of Apfelhof, and your heir here with you—I have no idea what you're asking. You present yourselves pretentiously for this visit. We're friends. Why so much ado?"

"A poorly disguised attempt to change the subject. You're speaking with your finest and most honest landowner in the area, while odorous whiffs of dishonesty accompany your words. Consider our stately appearance a regal reminder of our station."

"Continue."

"First, explain why I've been placed in a position of needing to defend my integrity over a vicious and long-buried rumor. Why does that defense require sacrificing my daughter and her future happiness?"

"Do you want me to answer with Curt standing here?"

"I do."

"You remember why. I find no reason to repeat the story."

"And we laid the rumor to rest years ago—an unfortunate misunderstanding. Enough damage ensued then. Why hurt my family more by threatening to resurrect it if Clara and Georg are not together?"

Curt fists clenched. "Respectfully, Pastor, you heard Georg yesterday, and you support him in this pigeon business on our property. Nothing adds up."

"The pigeons mean more revenue. More revenue means more taxes. You do understand that, correct?"

"Those were Georg's exact words yesterday. They don't explain this scheme any better today." Curt squawked like a wild bird. "Why on our Reinhold property?"

"And why promote the dishonest business dealings of the Wolff family at all?" Kraig asked. "Before you answer about the pigeons, answer my first question. It involves the pigeons, too?"

"Both of you lack respect for my position in God's church."

"You earn respect, and it's easily lost. You've lost much of ours, and what little remains dissolves quickly." Kraig pinched at his throat.

The pastor's confident stance slumped. "At lunch today, the grandchildren taught me their Sunday school lesson on honesty. I noted the irony. I have your daughter to thank for that lesson. What do you know or suspect already?"

"Everything's about money. What grim threats have you received from Gerwig and Georg?"

"I don't recall any threats. They've accrued hefty tax liabilities to the church, and therefore, to the state. They asked me to help them out."

"You're saying they've asked you to legally connect them to Reinhold money, to cover their debts? The audacity. They are relative newcomers to the area, only a few generations back, but you favor them over our family? They hold nobility status, perhaps, but they're not the upstanding citizens they'd have you believe. They tarnished their reputation long ago."

"Your family worries too much about maintaining a spotless reputation."

"Ja, we do keep the rules." Kraig thumped his fingers on Lange's desk. "No less is expected of you."

"What rule have I broken?"

"You tell me. We discussed my Mutter's observations. Seeing the conversation between her and your wife this morning, I believe she ratted on you."

"Gossiping?"

Curt's arms were pinned across his chest. "Gossip is not in my Oma's nature, but when she's dug to the bottom of a matter, she prays and follows the Holy Spirit's leading. She's careful to protect the people involved."

"I financed the pigeons. Now that you know, keep it between us." Lange fiddled with a wooden cross lying on his desk.

"Why? I asked you this yesterday, and I'm asking again." Curt stood tall. "Does the fact clergy are refused admittance to Monte Carlo have anything to do with your investment?"

"Er, I've never been to Monte Carlo." He shuffled about and slid the cross into his pocket.

Kraig jumped on his answer. "Of course not. They wouldn't permit you entrance. But Georg and Gerwig selling your trophy birds to 'The Pull' and waging your bets, benefits you and the Wolffs, correct?"

Flames of color scorched the pastor's neck, sprawled over his cheeks, and ears, and clear to his dusty brown hairline. "This must remain confidential, Kraig. You're my friends. Curt, you'll keep my secret? You and your Vati?"

Kraig responded first. "The church will defrock you when the state learns of your underhanded dealings. You expect us to keep your secrets, yet you mock my family for choosing to live by the rules. We're a well-respected and loved family. Honor does not fit Georg and Gerwig well, and they'll not hesitate to tell on you if you renege on your part in this." Kraig shook his balled-up fists.

"I still have your secret, if this one gets out."

"My wife knows the truth. I secured the item in the safe-keeping of my Aunt Caroline until I delivered it to Rosa. She read the note that accompanied it and will testify to my innocence for a second time. Will that be necessary?"

"Why would it? Even with your name cleared, the rules allow no opportunity for a marriage between Clara and Daniel."

Kraig shook his head. "One thing we agree upon. I'm giving you three weeks to fix this with the Wolffs. After that, I'll handle it my way. You have far more to lose than I do. Help them find another plan to pay their debts."

"They'll also be away on business the next two weeks, leaving me only one."

"We'll celebrate Erntedank the third week. How expedient will you be in your task?"

"In the meantime, Clara must allow Georg to court her," Lange insisted.

"I don't see a problem, since his plans take him away from here for most of that time. Clara won't even know we've talked."

"Curt, keep your mouth closed, too? I know how close you twins are."

"Ja, I promise." Hidden from Lange's view, Curt held crossed fingers at his side. The corners of Kraig's mouth edged up.

"Then all is well. Enjoy your travels." The pastor ushered them toward the door and closed it behind them.

"*Whew*!" Curt pounded one fist into the palm of his other hand. "Were you speaking in code? Your secrecy keeps me confused."

"While we travel this week, we'll ask for private seating on the train."

"You'll tell me what this is about then?" Curt widened his eyes.

"Not sure if I can. Gossip is an ugly thing, as Pastor Lange pointed out. More than one person suffers, especially when the story contains no element of truth and only casts unfounded suspicion."

"Which is exactly what has happened?"

Kraig nodded. "And it affected several members of our immediate family and our servants. Spend time with the family today. Important business takes us away from them for two weeks."

"Is this what you're saying? This rumor threatens to rise from its grave, affecting these same people and more. What problems are we likely to face before this is resolved?"

"Whether or not your Vati took liberties with another woman, and whether you and Daniel could be half-brothers."

Chapter Twenty-Six

CRAILSHEIM TO STUTTGART, *Monday, 19 September 1881*

KRAIG STARED BOLDLY at the conductor but never moved his tight lips. Glancing around, he nervously jingled a few coins.

"Give me a few minutes. I will arrange private seating for you." The conductor stepped away. True to his word, he returned a few minutes later and led them to their favorite seats on the luxury coach. Kraig slid the change to the conductor and porter, who stowed their bags. Their smiles brightened his morning. Always better to make the ethical choice. Why had he considered stooping to the low of bribery—exactly what he would have expected of those whose lack of integrity he detested.

The train's whistle blasted its excited note. Hefty puffs of steam billowed from the smokestack. Kraig pulled out *Der Brobachter* he purchased at the station and settled into the cadence of the train chugging down the tracks.

"Don't hide behind *The Observer*. You promised we would discuss yesterday's events. If I were your witness, what in particular did I witness?"

"The newspaper creates an extra barrier between us and other travelers."

"I'm waiting." Curt's foot wagged back and forth, tapping out an impatient beat against his Vati's boot.

"Is there a special lady you'd like to have in your life—one you haven't mentioned?"

"Vati!"

"I'm serious."

"I always had a crush on Megs, but she devoted her attention to Gus. Herr Wolff agreed to her choice, they married, and they left. It hurt as if my heart had been clawed to shreds."

"She and Gus have made a good life for themselves in America."

"From Clara's accounts, I agree."

"Are you ready to find someone new?"

"I could entertain the thought of a woman by my side."

"Viscount Denzler invited us to join him and his family at their estate on the Neckar. He has expressed interest in a courtship between you and his daughter, Lillian."

"How did this conversation go from dishonesty, rumors, and pigeons to me courting Lillian Denzler?"

"Tell me the prospect doesn't excite you at least a bit."

"I imagine Lillian has matured into a beautiful woman. I'll consider it. Now, please, placate my curiosity."

Kraig rocked his weight from one hip to the other and cleared his throat at least three times. "How do I begin? Many feelings accompany our disappointments and our joys. Sad and tragic events often carve unsightly scars on our hearts. Occasionally, our best intentions, offering help in a crisis, backfire in unexpected ways. Others greet them with misunderstanding. We find revenge by viciously assaulting those closest to us. I made a fool of myself in front of you a few weeks ago. I'm asking your forgiveness."

"The outburst was so unlike you, and it frightened me."

"I don't blame you for that. It scared me, too."

"We men are tough. We don't show our feelings as the women do. Will you tell me why you became so upset?"

"It arose from a misunderstanding over twenty-five years ago."

"When Clara and I were babies? Did we cause the problem?"

"Nein." Kraig rubbed away the tic poking at his eyelid. "My children, every one of you, are important and loved. Every day I grieve the two your Mutti and I lost. The part about turning our anger on those closest to us, I think you already figured it out."

"Mutti's hand?"

"She certainly didn't deserve that. Every day I'm reminded of my failure. I promised myself I'd never lose my temper again. And then the holy man we spoke to yesterday threatened to resurrect the past for an unexplained reason."

"If you refused Clara's hand to Georg?"

Kraig clenched the newspaper tighter, fighting the anger working its way to the surface. "Lange demands and expects a steep price to assure me he won't repeat the rumor. Clara's hand in marriage, even though we settled the untruth of it all so long ago."

"Would people remember if he brought it up again?"

Kraig shrugged. "I don't know the answer, and I'd rather not find out."

Curt shook his head. "I'm unclear on the matter, but I did witness you informing our pastor you're aware he's complicated matters with his questionable actions. The stakes for him are much higher if you expose him. Should I believe this involves comments made by businessmen we dealt with on our last trip to Stuttgart?"

"We went to purchase a gun, but I spoke with a few men who pledged to testify about the Wolffs' indiscretions, and Pastor's. Many have suffered because of their lack of integrity. I'm praying to secure private counsel these next two weeks. We'll visit with Barrister Ettinger while at your Aunt Caroline's home. Both she and Herr Ettinger will attest to the lack of truth in the rumor causing our problems.

"The arrangement with Georg has hurt you deeply and earned you a front-row seat to watch the agreement unravel. Clara must not know. At least not until we have firmly tied up each piece of the pigeon scandal."

"You'll make Pastor Lange responsible for convincing the Wolffs to confess?"

"They all have confessions to make. We'll be securing assurance they do, my son." Kraig winked. "And the part about Lillian—why, she'll add genuine beauty to our business these next couple of weeks and to our family for a very long time."

"Stop, Vati. You're making me blush, and men don't blush."

"She will when she lays eyes on you again."

"Will I ever hear the rest of the story?"

"Have patience. If I'm required to clear my name a second time, one more telling of the story will suffice. Afterward, forgotten forever."

Kraig lowered the Swabian newspaper. Vaguely familiar faces stared at them from seats across the way.

"Who are these men?" Curt whispered. "They look shifty, and my stomach's in a knot."

"Good morning!" A rugged-looking man with a shock of white hair barely hiding under his navy-banded straw sailor hat greeted them. The man stood to his full five-foot, two-inch stature and offered his hand.

"And to you, sir," Kraig replied. "Traveling to Stuttgart today, too?"

"Traveling back to Stuttgart. The city is home. And you?"

"Family business in Stuttgart. My son is traveling with me today. I'd introduce you, but you haven't shared your name."

"Nickel. Alfred Nickel."

"Pleasure to meet you, Alfred Nickel. Kraig Reinhold and my son, Curt."

Alfred spun on one foot and pulled his travel partner to his feet. The move placed Alfred face-to-face with the Reinholds again. "My brother, Ralph."

Stretching upward to his full height, Ralph towered above his brother by at least a foot—an interesting sight in his bright plaid trousers and golden waistcoat. With no additional room above his head, the man clutched his tall top hat, resting it at his waist.

"You boarded at Crailsheim. Do you make your home there?" Ralph leaned against the door of their compartment and tapped a thumb against his leg.

Kraig cupped his fingers around his chin. "The general area."

"Specifically, then?" Alfred asked.

"Gut Apfelhof." Curt nodded.

"We've heard of this place—heard they have a well-respected Gut Herr."

Curt filled his lungs and stood tall. "We like to believe so."

"Our adventures have taken us from home for two months now. A man we met on our travels claimed to hail from these parts. He bragged about this Gut Apfelhof fellow." Alfred poked his brother in the arm. "Did he say the Apfel guy was getting into the pigeon business too?"

"Indeed, he did. Is your Gut Herr the one raising those birds?" Ralph asked.

Kraig gritted his teeth and scrunched his eyes shut. His arm muscles quivered. "I am the Gut Herr—Baron Kraig Reinhold of Gut Apfelhof."

The brothers bowed. "Nobility in the pigeon business. Now I like that." Alfred grinned.

"Let me assure you, pigeons have no place in our community. Who exactly is this gentleman you met on your travels?"

"Gave his name as Wolff. Georg Wolff. Said this great Baron of Gut Apfelhof pledged his daughter to him in marriage,"

"Did he?" Beads of sweat trickled down Kraig's neck. "And he talked wildly about my daughter and his pigeons? Any pigeons in Georg's life reside at his home, Gut Dinkelhof, not ours. We grow Apfels and produce the finest Apfel wines in all of Europe."

Curt folded the newspaper Kraig had discarded on the seat and stuffed it in his case. "What was your business in Monte Carlo, Ralph? Alfred?"

"Monte Carlo?" Alfred ran his fingers through his unruly mane. "We never mentioned the place. It's a nice one, though, down on the French Riviera. Why do you ask?"

"Georg and his Pa play there." Kraig wagged a finger. "You've spent time around the Tir aux Pigeons?"

"Guilty as charged." Alfred hooted. "Join Georg on one of his trips. We'll all go and have a great time."

"We won't be visiting the place. The brakes are screeching, and we are pulling into Stuttgart. Perhaps we'll see you around the city."

The brothers extended their hands to Kraig and Curt.

"We're attorneys if you ever have need." Ralph tucked his calling card in Kraig's breast pocket.

Kraig and Curt stepped off the train and away from the solicitors. Tall white plumes waved from Tante Caroline's hat. She motioned for them from down the platform. Full of laughter, the Reinhold men headed to her outstretched arms.

"You're the most welcome sight today." Curt wrapped his Tante in a tight hug. "Do you know the long and the short of those two walking toward the baggage car?"

"The Nickel brothers? They are a colorful pair, but I wouldn't trust them with any business of mine. Did they talk the whole trip?"

"Only at the end." Kraig scratched his head. "They're rather well acquainted with our business. They may be more informed than we are and certainly know more than any stranger should."

"Their law offices occupy a storefront two doors beyond my neighbor's jewelry shop. They show excessive interest in everyone's business."

"Any reason to be alarmed that they met Georg in Monte Carlo and have become more than acquaintances?" Kraig studied her face for any hint of concern.

"They're rather harmless, but I don't trust them when they've tipped a few too many steins-full to their lips. Is there any way for you to undo this agreement you've made for Clara?"

Kraig looked around the crowd on the platform. "Too many ears, giving tongues cause to spread more gossip."

"Privacy awaits us at the house, and the cook's prepared for you two for a week. She'll feed you like barons. Well, one of you is a baron, and one will be one day." Tante Caroline motioned them toward her carriage.

"Don't promote him too quickly. I plan to see my grandchildren grow up."

"Your children need to be married first."

"I've heard Lillian Drexler is interested, and her Vater approves."

"Curt, do you approve?"

"It's been a couple of years since we've seen each other, but if she's as lovely and kind as she was then, I'll give a nod to the opportunity."

"You're blushing again, son."

With their bags tucked away, they settled into the carriage, and it rolled away from the station. "Angst about Georg and the pastor's pigeon business looms as heavy as twenty barrels of Gut Apfelhof wine." Kraig kneaded his shoulder. "Georg helped himself to our property for raising the birds. The Wolffs involved Pastor Lange, and he's connected it back to rumors surrounding the cameo all those years ago."

"The one Hermann Becker purchased for Rosa?"

"Ja. Please be ready in case I need your help putting the rumors to rest again. The Wolffs owe sizeable sums of back taxes, and they're holding Lange hostage over them. Curt pointed out that they don't admit clergy to the place. A betting man would put money on Georg placing wagers for Lange on the shooters at the Tir aux Pigeons in Monte Carlo."

"Good thing you're not betting men then." Tante Caroline wiped the grin from her face and pinched the pleats in her skirt. "How does Lange's illegal activity with Georg affect you?"

Kraig rubbed his ear, took a deep breath, and slowly exhaled. "Georg and Gerwig threatened to expose Pastor Lange's gambling habit should he turn them in for their tax indebtedness. They also convinced him the pigeons would prove a big moneymaker and secured his financial support."

"There's more?" Tante Caroline asked.

"Ja. A nightmare about raising pigeons at Gut Apfelhof."

Curt regurgitated the rest just like a mother pigeon feeding her squabs.

"Raising pigeons isn't a crime, is it?" Tante tilted her head and raised her eyebrows.

"Correct, but authorities would investigate. The industry the pigeons support became illegal in Germany when gambling was prohibited in 1872." Kraig smiled. "Unless, of course, they plan to serve them for dinner, a different matter altogether."

"I've recently heard people in boats along the shores of Monte Carlo gather the dropping birds for their supper." Tante Caroline's laughter turned contagious, and soon all three were holding their sides.

Seconds passed, and she grew serious again. "You groaned over the possibility of old rumors resurfacing? Pastor Lange brought Clara into this?"

"The Reverend Elmer Lange has long pitted Daniel and Clara's friendship against the rules of nobility. He used the dictates as the excuse he needed and hounded me to pledge Clara to Georg. At first, I believed he had no other motive, and it infuriated me when he suggested the arrangement. He counts on the Reinholds upholding the rules of nobility even to the detriment of our family."

"Remind me again how Pastor Lange heard the rumor. Spreading it wounded Lydia and Rosa and hurt their friendship for many years."

"As sure as my name's Kraig Reinhold, I never understood either. It's impossible to explain what I don't know."

"How does Clara feel about Georg courting her? He would never have been my choice for my great-niece. I find it difficult to believe he would've been my brother Otto's choice for his granddaughter either."

"After storming from the study when I first told her, Clara has shown me nothing but respect, but it's shattered her life. The threat to resurrect the old rumor will hurt Lydia all over again and hand another generation reason to question my honor. When Georg requested a piece of our property for a secret project, I thought he would build a new garden for his bride-to-be. What prompted me to entertain such an idea? Georg thinks of no one but himself."

"The understatement of the century." Curt pounded his fist on the carriage window.

"We're here this week, meeting with customers of our prized wines. I gave Lange three weeks to resolve his business with the Wolff men in an acceptable manner. Those two are traipsing somewhere over the next two weeks as well. Clara gets a reprieve. We return home the day before Erntedank. We'll get through the holiday, I pray, without incident. If the matter isn't resolved by then, I'll report Lange to the church and state. He has a lot more to lose than I do. Herr Ettinger's expertise and clout will go far. We plan to meet with him."

"If I'm correct, there's more than you've revealed."

"Ja. Gaping holes all over the story. From my knowledge, I'm able to fill in only a few of them." Curt shook his head and kicked a pebble from under his shoe.

"I'm surprised by Pastor Lange's involvement." Tante Caroline rubbed a finger on her chin. "I have always respected the man, but now, as you've said, he stands to lose much more than you do. I wish Clara understood your dilemma."

"I'll lay my life down to protect my family, but Clara must remain unaware of any of this. Curt knows in part because he was with me yesterday at the Langes' home. My witness."

"My eyes and ears follow Georg's every move. My sister deserves much better."

Curt was right, but Kraig had made a promise. Kraig grasped his Tante's hand but found it difficult to look her in the eyes. "We burdened you enough for one day. You and Onkel Knut are joining us for Erntedank, correct? If the meanness surfaces again, your presence will comfort Lydia."

"We wouldn't miss the celebration. I'll contact Barrister Ettinger first thing in the morning. Because of his expertise and experience, he'll impart great advice."

"Danke. We'll be here most evenings. Thank you in advance for arranging the meeting."

GUT APFELHOF, *Tuesday afternoon, 20 September 1881*

"DANKE, Georg, for the conversation and the flowers." Clara held the bouquet of sunflowers. She smiled as they wandered the path from the garden back toward the carriage house.

"I didn't blunder this time?" Georg took her empty hand in his.

"Sunflowers are a symbol of loyalty." Dread edged its way up her spine, but Clara allowed him the affection.

"And I'm loyal, you would agree?"

She sucked in a breath. Her gaze stretched upward. "Whose idea were these?"

"Mine, of course. A servant cut them from the field Ma had planted."

"You stole her sunflowers?" Clara pressed her teeth into her lower lip and shook her head. "Or did you have them cut from our patch by the old cottage?"

Georg shrugged and raised his eyebrows. "Does it matter? I brought them, and you love them."

"But your Ma suggested you bring them. She knows I love them. Wherever you grabbed the flowers, none of this afternoon was your idea."

"I chose Hamlet."

"Ja." An activity Clara would have enjoyed had he chosen something less morbid. "But a Tale of Royalty. Ghosts. Poison. Death. Loyalty to your wishes always." She pulled her hand from his and gave it a shake, ridding herself of his scum. "It's time for you to leave."

"Pa and I will be gone for almost two weeks. You'll miss me, and I promised Pa you'll feed the pigeons while we're gone."

"Nein. I won't feed your pigeons while you play games in Monte Carlo. Besides, you told me the Gut Dinkelhof workers need something to do now that your harvest is gathered in."

"Pa didn't keep them on, and someone must do it while we tend to our affairs. I invited you to accompany us." Georg's deep, shadowed dimples accompanied his deceptively sweet smile.

"And you knew I would have no part in your escapade."

"Escapade? This is business. Wolff fortunes will keep you in fine attire and allow us to travel the world in luxury."

"More of your delusions?"

Georg gripped her hand again and held tight. "You're coming with me to learn how to care for my birds. If we must cancel our plans because of it, you'll regret your refusal to cooperate."

She fought to be free of his grasp and dug her nails into Georg's palm. As they approached the carriage house, she grabbed for a lantern post along the path and held fast. Georg yanked hard, attempting to pull her toward his waiting carriage.

Pop. As she dropped to the ground, Georg released her hand. Clara clutched her shoulder and screamed. Within seconds, Daniel knelt at her side.

"Your shoulder. What happened? I heard the two of you arguing."

"That is not unusual for these two." Mamsell Lottie had joined them.

"Georg." Clara's voice barely rose above a whisper. "He hurt me."

Daniel poked her shoulder gently. Clara winced, and tears flooded down her face.

"This looks serious, Georg. Can we trust you to find Doktor Pfeiffer and bring him to Clara?"

"I don't trust you with my sweets, Daniel. Take your hands off her. I'll not leave her with you."

"Georg, I know better than to trust you alone with her. See what just happened."

Lottie gathered the strewn sunflowers and set them aside. "Jost, is there a horse saddled?"

"Ja," he answered from the doorway of the carriage house. "I'm on my way to get the Doktor."

Always prepared to handle emergencies at Gut Apfelhof, Mamsell Lottie took charge. "Daniel, bring me a quilt and a pillow from the house, please, and ask Dora for some winter-green. Herr Wolff, if you're staying, please sit in your carriage."

While they waited for the Doktor, Daniel returned with the requested items. Lottie applied the wintergreen liniment to Clara's shoulder. Daniel held her hand and prayed.

Clara wiped her eyes with a cloth Daniel offered her. "Danke. Did Georg leave?"

"Thankfully, he did. Not happily, judging by the ugly gestures made in our direction. I'm waiting right here until Doktor Pfeiffer arrives." Once again, Daniel had calmed her troubled heart and tended to her needs.

With Clara's back propped against Daniel's strong chest, Mamsell held Clara's hand, attempting to soothe the horrific pain. Clara struggled to get the words out. "Georg mentioned a cameo, threats to Vati…"

"Sh." Lottie touched her finger to her lips. "Rest, meine Kinder, until the Doktor comes. I have no idea about the cameo, but I'll let your Mutti know. If it's important, she'll pass the information to your Vati."

With a book and her puppets in hand, Emmaline burst through the door. "While you wait for the Doktor would you like me to read Heidi to you? And my puppets can act it out."

Mamsell Lottie scooted over, making room for Emmaline. "From Clara's pained expression, perhaps we should wait until after the Doktor has fixed her shoulder."

Clara nodded.

Emmaline, Daniel, and Lottie filled the time with a gentle chorus of *What a Friend We Have in Jesus.*

"We should pray for you, Clara." Emmaline pointed to Daniel. "Will you pray?"

Daniel rubbed his hand along Clara's good arm. *Heavenly Vater, You see Clara, and You see how she's been treated. She's hurt badly. Please bring Doktor Pfeiffer quickly. Give him wisdom to know how best to help her. In Jesus' name. Amen.*

Doktor Pfeiffer and Jost galloped up as the prayer ended. More family and servants gathered while the Doktor examined Clara's arm and prepared to push her shoulder back in place.

"It's going to hurt again. Hopefully, the liniment I'm smelling has numbed it some."

She screamed again, but it was fixed.

"Keep your arm in this sling. It'll help protect the muscles while they heal."

How would she and Daniel decorate the wagon for Erntedank? She imagined he had already concocted a plan. Clara smiled at him as everyone returned to their tasks.

"Danke, Doktor." Mutti waved to him as he rode off, then helped her daughter up and into the house.

"Please tell me what happened. I'll let your Vati know." Mutti propped Clara up on the white velveteen loveseat in the parlor and kissed her forehead. She took a seat in the wine-colored velvet chair next to Clara. "I'm an artist. I observe people's feelings from their expressions. Your furrowed forehead and scrunched brows tell a story of pain. In this case, more pain. I'm so sorry, meine Kinder."

Clara rubbed her eyes and relayed the events of the afternoon before Mutti had come outside. "You know the rest."

Propped up on the sofa, Clara motioned her little sister to her side. "Emmaline. About that book."

"*Heidi.* It's the new book by Johanna Spyri." Emmaline held it up for Clara to see.

Clara nodded. "I'd love for you to read it to Mutti and me."

With one little girl puppet on her finger, Emmaline moved her along the lines of the story.

"What did that say about a squawky hawk fussing at all the people making trouble for each other?" Clara's eyes squeezed closed. She chewed her lower lip and twirled that dangly curl. "Maybe some hawks would make good company for Georg and his pigeons. He and his birds certainly cause trouble for everyone."

Mutti covered her mouth as if that would hold her giggles in.

Emmaline finished the last pages of the chapter.

"Let's let Clara rest now," Mutti motioned Emmaline to her side for a hug. "You can read more to us another time."

"You're safe now." Mutti brushed her hand over Clara's cheek. "Lottie instructed Daniel to post guards until they're sure Georg and his Pa have left on their trip."

"If they leave on their trip."

~

STUTTGART, *Baden-Baden, Germany, Tuesday evening, 20 September 1881*

KRAIG PULLED his spectacles from his face and lifted his eyes from his journal. He stared at Curt sitting across Tante Caroline's dining room table. Lights from two oil lamps flickered behind his son's head. The shadows wove eerie patterns as scary as the pact holding him captive. He shook the impression loose and focused on Gut Apfelhof's business and happier thoughts. He tapped his monogrammed fountain pen on the pages. "I expect the newest addition to our Gut Apfelhof wine collection to win big accolades and garner big orders from our customers this week, but Friday's entry excites me the most."

Curt stepped around the table, stopping behind Vati's chair. "Who is Wilhelm Fein? You have not mentioned him before now."

"Wilhelm Fein is a man we must get to know." Kraig chuckled. "A businessman with great creativity and sharp intellect. Wilhelm and his brother invented the first medical inductors that advanced treatments in the medical field. Their latest ingenious technology brings substantial improvements to the fledgling telephone. Their model is receiving lofty commendations."

"Better than the one Alexander Bell invented and has Americans applauding?" Curt held one fist to his ear and one to his mouth.

"That's the news I've heard. The talking box will change life as we know it. Fein agreed to meet us here. Your keen mind must have many questions. Bringing this new invention to our community will place us on the forward edge of a new trend for communicating."

"A promising concept, but do you trust people will gravitate to this new device? I've read about Bell's invention and already have more than a million questions for Herr Fein."

"That is a lot of questions. Ask him all of them. Rumors circulate at the Backhaus, and a few folks there expound upon the criticisms of everything new." Kraig rubbed his temple. "They are skeptical that sound can come through a hunk of metal, and they're certain they'll need to shout for someone to hear them on the other end."

"Critics of progress always believe it safer to stay with what's known and trusted."

"We will watch the interest grow after we talk to Fein and have more information to share back home. This could also be an opportunity for employment for our residents. I imagine the Feins will need many hands to install the wires and boxes and all the other pieces."

"Clara mentioned Michael Weiner needs work so he and Minna can get married. Could we help them this way?"

"Excellent idea, son. We'll pay attention when we're back home about others who need help for their families."

"A question on another subject—or the same one as before." Curt leaned back, crossing his arms. "You used the word rumor again. You never fully explained the first time, and you left me with more questions than answers. Will I need to ask Tante Caroline for the details?"

"When we return to Gut Apfelhof will be soon enough."

Curt shook his head. "I'll not persuade you before then?"

"Nein. Anyway, a story about a box in the house that allows you to talk to someone down the street or across town without leaving home? Let's focus on the possibility because I see many benefits the sooner the telephone comes to our community. As other towns and cities are linked in, we'll be able to do some of our business without leaving home."

"Progress interests me greatly, and so does your rumor. Tante Caroline will tell me."

"Next week we'll spend two days with the Denzlers and two more with Tante Caroline. She'll ask lots of questions about your young lady."

"She's not my young lady, and must we even tell Tante?"

"Too late. The invitation came through her, and she has joyously regaled Fraulein Lillian with stories of your childhood."

Curt rubbed his face in his palms and moaned. "Tante Caroline describes bigger and more embarrassing stories than Mutti. Is it too late to decline this invitation?"

"Lillian's a delightful young lady, and I need grandchildren before I go to heaven."

"Vati, slow down. Let Lillian and me get reacquainted, please."

"Sure, just hurry up." Vati winked.

"In our haste to be away from the Nickels, we left the sample cases of wine at the train station. Do you think they're still sitting on the platform?"

"Thankfully, the porter and baggage handlers noticed, and Onkel Knut takes excellent care of us. He already sent a cart to retrieve the wine. Without allowing them to taste, our clientele would hesitate to place an order."

"A toast to our customers." Curt raised an imaginary goblet, then hesitated before moving from the table. "Meeting the Nickel brothers deeply troubled me. What mischief lurks under those hats of theirs? Do you think Georg's schemes involve them to help entrap us?"

Kraig shrugged off the anxiety that plagued him as well. "Tante Caroline confirmed they are nosy fellows, but I don't plan to lie awake worrying. See you at breakfast."

"Clara and I have a twin connection. Urgent nudges keep pricking me in the gut."

"If there had been trouble, your Mutti or Mamsell would have sent Fritz to dispatch a telegram." Kraig stood and pulled out his pocket linings. "Empty. I don't have any messages tucked away. No one here has brought bad news to our attention. Sleep well, my son."

"Clara's in danger!"

Chapter Twenty-Seven

STUTTGART, *Baden-Baden, Germany, Wednesday Morning, 21 September 1881*

"IT'S MUCH TOO EARLY for such a commotion." Kraig stood in the dining room doorway, rubbing sleep from his eyes.

"The loud knock and the whirring doorbell awakened you. I'm very sorry." Tante Caroline's cook, up early, pointed to the home's entryway. "Someone pounded the door with urgency. He must've carried critical news. I placed the telegram at your place at the table."

"Danke." He waited for her to return to the kitchen before opening it.

Dearest Kraig, Clara received note from Georg yesterday. Threatened harm. G came. Refused to leave without C. Hurt her. Doc was called. C recovering well. G talks: pigeons, nickels, cameo, threats. C scared. I'm scared. Daniel helped her and posted guards. Finish your business in Stuttgart. See you next week. Love, Lydia

The handrail on the stairs squawked as Curt's palm slid down the length of it. "Vati, please, send a wire. I've not slept a wink."

Eyes downcast and swallowing the growing lump in his throat, Kraig rattled the paper and shoved it at Curt. "You heard the early commotion too? Read this."

He scanned it, his face going as grey as the ash on the hearth. Curt had known. "How do we help? Pigeons we understand. Nickels? Do you think it is the two we met? And the cameo? I know very little about said cameo, but Rosa wears one every day. Is it the one?"

"It is."

"What stories has Lange divulged to Georg?" Curt tousled the hair on his sleepy head. "Help me resolve my perplexities. What has Georg repeated to the Nickel brothers? Are others besides my sister in danger?"

"Probably."

"Probably? Which question does that answer? We should return home now."

"We scheduled ample time for each client today. Tante invited Ettinger here tomorrow evening, but we can meet with him sooner. We'll cut a few meetings short and squeeze in a visit with the barrister today. We've always counted on him to take excellent care of our family, and he knows the story from the start. He'll head to Gut Apfelhof immediately and protect the family until our return."

"And keep us informed?"

"I'd wager my life on it."

"Wager? A little joke, Vati?"

STUTTGART, *Germany, Wednesday morning, 21 September 1881*

"WHEN THE KUNZ family rebuilt and restored Krueger's Gasthaus to its former glory, it gained renewed prestige in Stuttgart. Its guests enjoy the best cuisine during their stays. Gut Apfelhof wines have long been a part of their reputation." Kraig's hand rested on his son's shoulder. "Think they're ready for our visit today?"

Curt and Vati stepped through the door. "Peter Kunz! Great to see you, old friend." Vati extended his hand.

"Greetings, Reinholds. The pleasure is mine, as always. Come in." Herr Kunz summoned his grandson. "Petey, take our guests' coats."

Two men sat in the dining room with their backs to Vati and Curt.

As the boy reached for his cloak, Vati wobbled. He gripped a nearby chair but slid to the floor.

"Petey, quick. Ask the cook for a wet cloth." Herr Kunz knelt at his friend's side. "Should I summon a Doktor?"

"Nein. My pride's wounded, but I'm not hurt. No need for the wet rag unless it's for washing away the fuzzy memory that just filled my head."

"What memory?" Curt rubbed his brow.

Vati swiped a hand in front of his face. With help from Curt and his friend, Vati sat up.

The cook entered carrying a tray with steaming cups of coffee. "Where did Alfred and Ralph go? They ordered coffee and kuchen."

"They left while I've been tending to Herr Reinhold."

"Thank goodness." Vati rubbed the back of his neck.

"Vati, you're sure you're not hurt?"

"I'm quite alright, son. Alfred and Ralph? I remember now. Years ago, early morning. The day before the fire broke out, two much younger men sat in the very spot the Nickel brothers just occupied."

"And the wire this morning?" Did Vati suspect a connection to the Nickels? "Will we see Tante Caroline again before meeting with Barrister Ettinger?"

Vati gestured Curt's questions away. "Later. Right now, bring out a bottle of our newest vintage."

"It's still morning, but not a more perfect moment than the present to sample the Reinholds' *Rotes Paradies.*" Curt handed the wine to Vati

With a flourish, Vati uncorked the bottle. "Peter, for you and your guests—the added touch of cherry and hazelnut coupled with our famous sweet-tart apples."

Herr Kunz turned Petey by the shoulders and sent him to the kitchen. "Bring goblets, and have Cook serve the crackers and cheese."

With the first sip, Herr Kunz's face gleamed. "I request an exclusive on this one! In Stuttgart, they'll only find this glass of perfection at the historic Krueger Gasthaus."

"The one and only, owned and operated by the respectable Herr and Frau Peter Kunz." Vati used his knuckles to polish the lapel of his waistcoat and beamed. "An exclusive will cost you, my friend."

"You're a fair and reasonable businessman. Whatever price you decide, I'll pay it. It's that special."

"Curt and I will deliver our proposal before Erntedank."

"Take all the time you need, but promise me it'll be our Krueger Gasthaus' specialty here in Stuttgart."

"When we've all agreed to the terms, you'll have it."

"Danke."

The inn's morning guests had finished their meals and left.

Vati tapped his fingers on the table. "Peter, you worked here when the Kruegers owned the place. Did the Nickel brothers frequent the inn then, too?"

"Because of their penchant for nosiness or curiosity—call it whichever you choose—they meddle in all the businesses in Stuttgart. They always have, and they've never been the most welcome guests. You mentioned a memory of them. The way you reacted, did something about these men haunt you?"

Vati worried his right earlobe. "It did, but I'm not sure why. Were all the guest records from the time of the fire lost? I don't remember what we salvaged."

"One guest book remains—the one from the week of the fire. We found it in a metal box in an outbuilding behind the inn. Whether Lenard carried it out with him or threw it to Rosa before he went back to rescue more guests, we can only guess."

"May I see it?"

"I keep it here on the side table. People enjoy pursuing memorabilia."

Vati studied the pages and pointed to the spot. "When we encountered them on the train on Monday, I knew I had seen those two somewhere before. A much older version now—their straw-colored hair has turned all white. But it's them. Seeing them today sparked a deeply buried memory. Curt and I need to leave. I'll explain when we return."

"So, you'll give me an exclusive on the wine?"

TANTE CAROLINE'S KITCHEN, *Later Wednesday, 21 September 1881*

THEY COULD HEAR A RUSTLING sound inside the entryway. Tante Caroline must've already stood at the door. Curt twisted the key to the doorbell anyway. This one delivered special whirring and clicking sounds of the gears spinning, and they brought a smile to his heart every time.

"Tante Caroline, you're here."

"I am. If you smiled any wider, your grin would reach the sea. And so much fidgeting. What happened today?"

"We collected new puzzle pieces at the Gasthaus this morning, and Vati needs your help."

Pointing to her rustic kitchen table, Caroline invited Curt and Vati to sit and summoned her cook to serve lunch. She rubbed the finish on the treasured neoclassic antique table while she listened. "I know most of the story, but are you telling me the Nickels spread the rumor about the cameo? How? This sounds preposterous even for them."

Vati traced imaginary designs on the table. "I'm piecing it together. When I caught a glimpse of them in the dining room at the Gasthaus today, a memory surfaced. A vision flashed in my mind of two younger men I didn't recognize. They sat on a bench in the yard of the burned-out inn.

"The scene took place the exact moment I delivered the cameo to Rosa that day. It all began to make better sense. They were the Nickel brothers. The moment I explained to Rosa that the cameo was a gift from the Vater of her baby, the two disappeared."

Curt's heart thumped in his chest. Was Rosa the woman Vati had referred to? He kept his questions to himself. Vati, with Caroline's help, would divulge the whole story one piece at a time.

"Hardly grounds for suspicion. Reviewing what we know, and if I understand you correctly, Georg has knowledge of the cameo?"

Vati traced a bigger design on the table. "We know he met the Nickels, and the Nickels and the Wolffs discussed pigeons."

"How does that prove the Nickels were the men sitting on the bench that day?" Tante Caroline propped an elbow on the table, her chin resting on her hand. "You're certain Pastor Lange didn't tell Gerwig or Georg about the cameo? We kept the family business private, but the rumors about Lydia's hand spread around the community and beyond. And while the Nickels poke around in other folks' business, it doesn't mean they heard your conversation. What other proof do you have?"

"The telegram this morning, plus the fact the Nickels seem to know about everything. There must be a connection." Curt flipped his pocket watch open.

"I learned about Lydia's telegram after the two of you left this morning. Did she send bad news?"

Curt flipped the watch closed, then open, again and again. He slipped it in his pocket, drew out a paper, and handed it to his great aunt. "Here's the telegram. Read it yourself. Vati scheduled a meeting with the barrister today instead of tomorrow. Have you spoken to him again?"

"I have, but this new information will be of significant interest to him. I'll pray for Clara's safety." Caroline smiled. We know, despite the rules, her safety will be Daniel's primary concern until you return to Gut Apfelhof."

"I trust Rosa's son like he's my own." Vati patted Curt's hand. "Knowing he protects Clara comforts me until we return."

Chapter Twenty-Eight

GUT APFELHOF, *Friday morning, 23 September 1881*

"YOU HAVEN'T FINISHED READING *Heidi* without me, have you?" Clara used her good hand to ruffle Emmaline's caramel curls as she joined her at the breakfast table.

"I'm impatient to do that, but I waited for you. Would you like me to read while we enjoy our Kuchen and sausage?"

Clara glanced around the room. "The rest of the family's here. We can wait and not spoil the story for anyone who hasn't read it yet."

"Don't read any girly story to me." Wilhelm squinted and scrunched his nose.

"But you're helping Daniel with the Erntedank wagon today." Emmaline's lower lip protruded. "There won't be time later."

"Would you like to help Daniel and me?"

"You mean it?" Emmaline's pout vanished.

"It'll be a while before I can be much assistance with the work, but I can make suggestions. You could help Daniel carry them out. It'll be the prettiest Erntedank wagon yet."

"Ja. I'd love to help. What will we make today?"

"You can be my extra hand to braid ribbons and wheat. Daniel will need help too, attaching our work to the wagon."

"And when we're finished for today, I'll read more of *Heidi* to you."

Clara closed her eyes and sighed. Heidi had prayed for God to give her his blessings and the desires of her heart. She was ready to find out if He had. If so, Clara would hold more hope that He would bless her prayers, too.

"I'd rather not douse your enthusiasm, but you cannot miss your Klassen." Mutti passed the Kuchen to Emmaline.

"You gave Lehrer next week off to be with his family for Erntedank, and he's leaving today. Since there won't be lessons this afternoon, wouldn't reading to Clara be a wonderful idea, Mutti?"

"You're right, Emmaline. I needed a reminder." Mutti lifted her palms.

"I'm eager to hear the rest of the story." Clara sipped her coffee.

"I can't wait either." Emmaline bounced in her chair. "Hurry and finish breakfast so we can begin."

"Emmaline, slow down. The way you shovel the sausage in your mouth, you'll have a stomachache and be unable to help them at all." Mutti slowly shook her head. Her grin made it obvious she was delighted her daughters would enjoy their morning together. And then her brow furrowed.

"Where's Hannah?" Mutti bit her lip and glanced toward the foyer. "She never misses breakfast unless she's not feeling well."

"I overheard her and Rosa talking in the sewing room while on my way." Clara shrugged her free shoulder. "I caught the words list and garden. Perhaps they had an inspiration about flower seeds they planned to plant out there. I didn't give any more thought to it."

Mutti held her hand over her cup when Dora attempted to refill her coffee. "Someone check on Hannah, please."

"They mentioned the garden. She loves that place like I do." Clara folded her napkin and set it on the table. "Emmaline, we'll stop there before we help Daniel. Mutti, may we be excused?"

"Run on, but let me know you've found her before you play with decorations."

Emmaline tucked *Heidi* into her pocket along with her puppet friends and took Clara's arm.

When they entered the garden, Clara pointed to Hannah seated in a patch of cockscomb flowers. "Wonder what she's scribbling on those pages?" Clara whispered to Emmaline. "She hasn't even heard us."

They tiptoed toward her and peered over Hannah's shoulder.

Hannah jumped and then covered her papers.

"Mutti's worried about you." With her unhurt arm, Clara held onto a limb of a nearby shrub and lowered herself next to Hannah. "What're you writing so early this morning?"

She hid her face behind her pad. "Nothing I can share."

"Maybe she'll be the next Johanna Spyri and write a novel for us." Emmaline giggled.

"It's not funny at all, Emmaline. The truth is, I was writing a list for Clara."

"For me. Please, may I see?" Clara reached for the pad.

"It's embarrassing. And Rosa caught me. She promised to tell Mutti if I didn't scratch through everything on my list and write Matthew 5:44 beside each one."

"Is that the verse that says, *But I say unto you, Love your enemies, bless them that curse you, do good to them that hate you, and pray for them which despitefully use you, and persecute you?"* Clara barely whispered.

"Ja. That's the one." Tears welled in Hannah's eyes. "Over and over, King David asked God to punish his enemies. I read through the Psalms, made a list of some of those Bible verses for you, and inserted Georg's name in them as the enemy. I wanted you to be able to pray them to get rid of that awful man."

"Oh, Hannah, however wrong Rosa found your idea, I treasure your intention. Now I must see."

She kept her head down and passed the pages to Clara.

Break thou the arm of the wicked and the evil man (Georg)*; seek out his wickedness till thou find none* (Psalm 10:15).

Arise, O Lord! Deliver me, O my God! For you have struck all my enemies (Georg*) on the jaw; you have broken the teeth of the wicked* (Georg) (Psalm 3:7).

Arise, O Lord, in your anger; rise up against the rage of my enemies (Georg); *Awake, my God; decree justice* (Psalm 7:6).

Let the extortioner catch all that he (Georg) hath; and let the strangers spoil his (Georg's) labour. (Psalm 109:11)

Several more verses lined the page with the Matthew verse beside them all, but Clara couldn't read on. Tears rolled down her cheeks. "These descriptions of wicked men do sound just like Georg. Just this week, he spoke to me of loyalty and then hurt me so badly."

"Is it so wrong to pray as David did in the Psalms?" Hannah clutched her knees and rocked.

"We all wish he'd go away, especially me. But Rosa's right. We need to pray for Georg and let God take care of the outcome."

"Where's my helper?" Daniel called out.

"Both your helpers." Emmaline jumped to her feet and hugged him.

"Tears and smiles all mingled together. What've I walked into?"

Clara extended her arm, and Daniel helped her to her feet. "Emmaline will be assisting us today."

"And Hannah?" Daniel nodded toward the sister who was still sitting on the ground. "Could you add some harvest Bible verses to the ribbons on the wagon?"

"I'd love that."

"Are you happy to have all the Reinhold sisters working with you?" Clara traced the smile on his lips. Because they were in the company of her sisters, she fought off the urge to kiss them instead,

Clara turned to Hannah. "We'll wait for you, but please inform Mutti you're with us and you're not hurt or in trouble."

~

STUTTGART, *Württemberg, Germany, Friday, 23 September 1881*

CURT WAVED to a man standing on the third-floor balcony of the Krueger Gasthaus. He whistled a few measures of a merry tune as he and Vati disembarked from the hired carriage. "I can't believe we're meeting Wilhelm Fein today, the man with the patent to the telephone that is even better than the one Alexander Bell invented."

"You are giddy as a young lad." Vati burst into laughter. "Not only are we meeting the man, but I'd also like to invest in Fein's company."

"You're convinced he'll bring the telephone to Gut Apfelhof, and you're ready to sign the contract? And add jobs for our neighbors?"

"I'm eager to meet the man—ask him a few questions first. Have your questions ready, too."

Curt followed Vati inside the Gasthaus for the second time this week.

Wilhelm Fein rose from a striped settee. "You must be the Reinholds."

"Kraig Reinhold. My son, Curt."

Without hesitation, Curt spoke up. "Your telephone uses a horseshoe magnet, correct? I've heard it's even better than Alexander Graham Bell's device. It's creating a stir in America."

"It is proving to be a better concept." Fein smiled at the compliment.

"Where's your company installing its telephone networks? At least a couple of them must be here in Stuttgart. How much time is required to install a network? Can they be installed anywhere? How many people does it take to do the work?"

"My, but you have a barrel of questions, young man. The current news at our company is that we'll cover the city of Barcelona with a network starting next year."

Curt bounced from the balls of his feet. "Having Gut Apfelhof all connected by a telephone network would make us the envy of every community around. Vati, imagine calling the doctor instead of having to ride to the Medizin office to get him. Or we could speak to a friend on the other side of the Gut without leaving home."

"I eagerly anticipate telephone service in our community. It would make my residents' lives much easier. Let's sit down and discuss the possibility and the details. But first, is anyone else ready for lunch?"

Herr Kunz came from his office. "Would you like to hear the day's menu, gentlemen?"

Fein rubbed his stomach. "I understand the noon meal includes the Gasthaus' famous Sauerbraten and Kartoffelklöße. Your roast and potato dumplings come recommended as fine as any the Kruegers ever served. I'll have that."

"Thank you. Herr Fein. It is our tradition at lunch to fill our guests' steins with robust German beer, but today, we have a special treat. The Reinholds brought their newest vintage, Gut Apfelhof's *Rotes Paradies* wine." Herr Kunz handed a corkscrew to Vati.

Vati poured the wine.

Curt beamed. "Herr Kunz asked for an exclusive on it here in Stuttgart. Shall we make a toast to progress?" They all lifted their goblets. "To Fein Company's telephone networks connecting us all."

Vati bowed to the inventor.

"Thank you, my new friends." The pewter goblets clanged.

"And, Kraig, I hope this means…"

"Ja, Peter, I have a contract for you in my case. We'll settle before Curt and I leave."

"You make me a happy man."

Vati lifted his eyebrows and widened his eyes. "Give me a reasonable date for your company to bring a network to us."

"I'll need to visit and make an assessment of your land holdings, homes, and businesses."

"When's the soonest you can come?"

"Will mid-October be soon enough?"

"Mid-October. Excellent. I'll have it added to the family calendar when we arrive back home tomorrow. Expect a telegram no later than Monday with details for your visit

Bring your family and enjoy the countryside."

"Danke." Fein pushed back from the table. "Herr Kunz, your famous Sauerbraten and Kartoffelklöße did not disappoint."

Vati patted his stomach. "We'll all need to stretch our legs and help it settle before we leave."

Herr Kunz handled business with Herr Fein, then reappeared at the Reinholds' table. "Kraig, Curt, what is your best offer for the exclusive?"

Fifteen minutes later, they signed the contracts as the sun gleamed through the etched glass parlor windows.

Petey shoved the parlor door open and bolted through. "Herr Reinhold, your Tante's driver delivered this just now and said to waste no time giving it to you, sir." He placed it in Vati's hand.

Wolffs arrived home early. G sent C a kidnap threat. Protecting your interests. Daniel.

Chapter Twenty-Nine

STUTTGART TO CRAILSHEIM, *Saturday, 24 September 1881*

"THE TELEGRAM your driver delivered to us at the Gasthaus assured Ettinger is attending to matters with efficiency, but Vati is eager to get home." Curt tapped a gold-sealed linen envelope in his palm. "He insisted I place this formal invitation in your hand and entrust you with its safe delivery to Viscount Adam Denzler. Train tickets included." He slid it across the breakfast table to Tante Caroline.

"We're counting on your powers of persuasion to convince the Denzlers to travel with you next week." Vati flashed her a charming smile. "We secured tickets for Tante Adeline and Onkel Martin too, all of you traveling on the same train to Crailsheim."

Tante frowned and patted Curt's hand. "You're both anxious about your sister. She's well protected, but I'm relieved you've rearranged your travel plans. You'll have more peace, seeing for yourselves."

Her frown turned to a smile. "I'll deliver your invitation today. Your Onkel Knut and I enjoy traveling together. See you next weekend. We'll begin the party on the train. Will you be jealous?"

Vati's blue-green eyes reflected more of the grassy hue. "Definitely, but following our meeting with the barrister, I resolved to confront the situation at home as soon as possible. He left for Gut Apfelhof immediately after our meeting. His presence there comforts my anxious thoughts, but arriving there in person will ease my worries and relieve Daniel of the responsibility to protect my daughter."

Tante Caroline shook her head and rubbed her temple. "I believe the part about confronting the threat in Daniel's telegram. As for Clara, I suspect you'd like to protect her from Daniel, more because of the rules, but—"

Vati thumped his fist on the table. "Putting a stop to Georg's threats and squelching the rumor again promises to be no simple task. I agree with Pastor Lange. Clara and Daniel as a couple isn't possible. But where he first learned the rumor about the cameo and the current threats connected to it remains a mystery."

"What does one have to do with the other?" Curt rubbed his head, hoping an answer woud pop out. None did.

Tante Caroline and Onkel Knut's driver pulled their carriage to the front door. She handed them a basket of fresh Kirschkuchen before sending them on their way to the train.

The two climbed into the carriage, and the driver headed to the station. Vati sank against the seat. His head shook back and forth. "Do you believe our family can be happy again, Curt? Recurring memories about our peaceful and loving home before this arrangement plague me day and night."

"You're a praying man, Vati. The Bible says, *'Confess your faults one to another, and pray one for another, that ye may be healed. The effectual fervent prayer of a righteous man availeth much.'*"

"My prayers are fervent, and I confessed my fault in this years ago."

"And what was your fault in this? You've only hinted at things. My imagination runs wild."

"I asked God's forgiveness for any action on my part that has created confusion and for the pain I've caused your Mutti."

"The pain about her hand or another woman?" Curt had hoped Vati would confess to him, too, but that hadn't happened—only cryptic answers.

"Witnesses cleared my name before, and I pray it remains without blemish."

"I trust it will. Jesus covers your sins and mine with His righteousness." Sweat formed under Curt's collar.

"I find it tough to allow myself to accept His grace."

"We're still missing pieces of this puzzle. I'm praying for revelation of the remaining secrets, and I promised myself I'd uncover them." With his arm across Vati's shoulder, Curt asked, "Will that help you find God's grace?"

"Ja. Nein. I don't know. Maybe. I'm tasked with the challenge of breaking a promise and righting wrongs, while so much is so wrong with me." Vati raked a hand through his hair. "And son, I'm sorry we canceled our visit with the Denzlers."

"I'm disappointed too." Curt lay his head back. "I do hope Lillian and her family accept our invitation." He would rest on the way home, but visions of the grown-up version of a sweet childhood friend filled his head.

"They will. So much to give thanks for this Erntedank."

Curt popped back up. "I heard you tell Pastor Lange he had a full week after Erntedank to come to a new arrangement with the Wolffs. A solution to satisfy all their conflicted problems and one not involving Clara or any other member of our family. A dismal cloud is hanging over the festival this year."

"Since Georg rearranged his plans to be home this past week, I pray Lange completed that confrontation."

"Do you believe Georg will give up so easily?" Curt harumphed.

"I prayed and analyzed, prayed and analyzed, and then prayed and analyzed again."

"Analyzing." Curt chuckled. "One thing you are very good at. Did you reach a conclusion or make a plan?"

"I'm uncertain what to believe. One thing I've become more convinced of, though, the Nickel brothers share responsibility for this. All those years ago and now again. The sinner in me wants to retaliate. If only I knew their specific involvement."

"'For it is written, '*Vengeance is mine; I will repay, saith the Lord.*' You know the verse. Clara knows Romans 12:19, too. But now that Georg injured her, I would not blame her if she exacted revenge."

"What do you mean? What has she said to you?"

"She loathes the man. Clara shared with me how the idea of living with him scares her. She also fears being alone without a husband, too. Clara wants to believe you love her more than this, but she's confused and conflicted. My feelings defy explanation—you call it 'the twin thing.' It causes me to presume her kind, tenderhearted self is capable of less kind or tenderhearted actions. She believes she's lost you, and you won't be happy with anything she does short of marrying Georg."

"Would she hurt herself, Curt?" He blotted his eyes with his palms.

"Doubtful, but Georg stands to lose much—his pride and a little of his flesh at the hands of a beautiful but heartbroken and angry woman. Can we stop discussing this until we get home?" Curt lay his head back again. Minutes later, he dozed off and danced with Lillian on the pages of a picture book.

"WHERE'S OUR DRIVER?" Kraig stood on tiptoe as he searched for Daniel in the crowd.

Jonas Ettinger scouted in every direction until he spotted them. "Welcome home, Reinholds. It took a little persuasion, but Daniel allowed me to drive the fancy carriage and bring you the rest of the way. He prefers guard duty at Gut Apfelhof."

Curt had hoped Daniel would continue to be there for Clara and continue checking around on his own. He appreciated Daniel's determination to help him and Clara.

"Problems continue at the Gut?" Vati rubbed his eyebrow.

"Georg's being Georg, but I believe he's behaving—for now. Your driver handles him well. Considering the contrast in their positions and their conflicting desires for the same woman, it's admirable that Daniel's been able to keep things peaceful. The real reason I came is that I need private time with the two of you. I left instructions with the baggage handlers. They transferred your things to the inn. Early tomorrow morning, we'll climb into the Landau, and I'll drive you along the old Roman stone-paved roadways leading to Gut Apfelhof."

"Herr Ettinger! Herren Reinhold! Welcome!" The friendly doorman pointed to the desk attendant. "Your rooms are ready. Make Charles aware of anything more you require."

"Charles, you heard the man. We require a table where the door is visible to us but not too close, and three dinner menus. All these mingling aromas increase my appetite by the second." Herr Ettinger stroked his broad, thick handlebar mustache. Charles led them to their table.

"Thank you for having everything in perfect order for us."

"Your table request is always the same, Barrister. Doubted it changed, and I'm always prepared for my best guests." Charles handed them menus.

They each claimed their place around the three-inch thick table, diamond carvings embellishing the edge. Charles returned with their drinks and took their orders. "Three Wiener Schnitzel. Excellent choice." He left them to take the orders to the cook.

Vati drummed his fingers on the table. "I trust you received fine treatment at Gut Apfelhof and you've spoken with the parties in question. You met us here with arrangements to spend the night. You have important updates?"

"First, what does Curt know? Findings from my investigation

will reveal facts you may prefer your son hear first from you."

Sparks of hope flickered around Curt's brain. Would he finally learn the truth?

With his hand on Curt's balled fist, Vati leaned toward his son. He cleared his throat. "It's all a nasty rumor. I prayed it would never resurface. Since it has, I promised to share the details with you, but your sisters and brother, your Mutti, Rosa, and Daniel all need to be with us. Then it would only be necessary for me to tell it one more time. We need the Wolffs and Pastor Lange present, too."

"My thoughts—the possibilities surrounding this unfortunate situation grow the longer you delay."

Herr Ettinger cocked his head toward Kraig and then Curt. "Worry about the others later. Tell him now."

Their Schnitzel arrived. As Vati took his first bite, his face turned green. Would his meal reappear just like the old rumor?

Vati fidgeted with the utensils. "You guessed correctly about the cameo Mutti mentioned in her telegram. Oma told you about the fire at the Kruegers' Gasthaus. Rosa's Vater and husband lost their lives rescuing guests. Hermann Becker, Rosa's husband, had purchased a cameo for Rosa from Tante Caroline's friend's jewelry shop. She promised him fancy wrappings, but her shop bustled with customers at the time. He needed to go and asked if she would deliver it to Caroline. He requested that your Opa and I bring it to the Gasthaus that evening."

Curt rubbed the stubble on his chin. "I don't see anything

unseemly about his request. I expected a more fascinating story."

Vati paused Curt's comments. "Rosa wailed as she and I stood in the yard after the fire. Daniel tugged at her skirts. In my humble effort to console her, I held Rosa and Daniel in my arms. I excused myself a moment to reach into my pocket and pulled out the gift-wrapped cameo. I told her it was a special gift from the Vater of her baby boy."

"I'm still not understanding." Curt stared at Vati.

"Go on." Ettinger nudged Vati's elbow. "Curt needs to hear the rest."

"A meddling individual twisted the story until it reached your Mutti's ears. She heard I gave the cameo to Rosa, and I was the Vater of Rosa's baby—Daniel's Vater." Vati froze.

Curt's vision clouded. His heartbeat pounded in his ears. "Are you?"

"I deserve your accusing tone. Rosa's a very special lady, one I've always cared about. But your Mutti is the only woman I've ever loved. I am not Daniel's Vater."

Curt nodded. "There's more, though?"

"Following the fire, Opa and I invited Rosa and Daniel to live at Gut Apfelhof. Your Oma and your Mutti welcomed Rosa as a trusted member of our household staff. Then the twisted version of the story reached your Mutti's ears."

A pent-up breath whooshed from Curt's lungs. "That's why you and Mutti argued and why her hand is crippled?"

"She learned the truth. She forgave me, but I haven't forgiven myself for my rage in that moment. Your Mutti and I consider

Daniel as close to a son as you and Wilhelm. She and Rosa have a special kinship now, but it took time."

"Who told Mutti the vicious rumor?"

"Until this week, I didn't know." Vati pointed to Ettinger. "I'm praying our barrister friend learned details of what I now suspect. I almost passed out at the Gasthaus earlier this week because the old memory flashed through my mind. When I caught sight of the Nickel brothers sitting in the parlor, I recognized them as the two much younger men sitting on a bench in the yard of the burned-down inn. They sat there while I offered Hermann's gift to Rosa."

"I smell bird dung, but the pieces still don't add up. How do you connect them to create a courtship and marriage agreement for Georg and Clara?" Curt pressed his lips together in a straight line. He shifted his gaze between Vati and Herr Ettinger. "I suspect there's still more to this tale."

"Take it from here, please, Jonas." Vati sighed and lowered his head to his chest.

"*Whew*. I believe the game will play itself out before the end of the week. A hint of mischief crinkled in the barrister's eyes. The Wolffs, Nickels, and Pastor Lange will each publicly expose their hands.

"We'll watch the gamblers' cards fall. A few pigeons, too."

Chapter Thirty

ST LUKE'S KIRCHE, *Sunday, 25 September 1881*

THE LADIES in Clara's Bible Class spread their creations across the table in the room where they met. Clara selected an ivy and ivory striped drawstring reticule fastened with a carved ivory button clasp from those displayed. She laid it down, picked up the next and the next until she had perused the details of each of the bags with equal awe.

"What charming pieces you created for Megs—and so quickly! Danke for bringing them today. Plan for us to prepare the packages on Wednesday and send them on their way to America. I will wire Megs to expect their delivery."

"Time to feed my little man and tuck him in for a nap." Luisa blew a kiss to her friends. "Della's tending to her ailing Oma today. I'll give her the good news that our first items are ready for Megs' Designs."

Michael awaited Minna outside the door. She hugged each of them before joining her beau. "See you girls on Wednesday."

Tilly helped her injured friend, slipping her hand inside Clara's elbow. The two ladies strolled along the path from the church. "Your family would say my concern is unnecessary, but you're my friend. I worry about you with Georg. Be careful, sweet Clara. His noble birthright means little. He's a skunk!"

"Or a Big Bad Wolff." Clara slapped a hand over her mouth. "I'm concerned, but I find comfort in knowing another man protects me well, especially from the likes of Georg."

"Your favorite man. Ja, Daniel cares about you and your safety. If only a fairy godmother waved her wand for the two of you."

Whatever fantastical story Tilly was envisioning, Clara imagined it as a wonderful tale. Clara hugged herself and twirled about. "Splendid idea, Tilly, but fairy godmothers only live on the pages of fables and folk tales." Her joy sputtered and fizzled like a sputtering firework.

They came to a fork in the path where they would go their separate ways. As they were saying their goodbyes, Georg and his driver clopped up behind them with a pair of horses pulling a small carriage. "Greetings, ladies! Ah. A double helping of luscious sweets this fine day."

His dimpled cheeks failed to impress Clara. Her tummy filled with the same unpleasant stir present when Vati announced the courting arrangement. But she'd made a promise to Vati, and it prodded her civil reply. "Greetings, Georg."

"I knew we'd find you dawdling. My parents scurried off

after church, and I engaged another of our drivers for myself and my sweets. Allow me to see you home."

Tilly slid her hand from Clara's elbow and laced her fingers with her friend's. "Can you walk fast despite your injury?"

"No reason to be scared." Georg's low cackle and beguiling smile said otherwise. "A two-minute ride, and you're home." He stepped from the carriage to help them in.

Her eyes glazed over as Tilly pushed Georg's hand off of theirs. "It's a quick walk, too."

"And an unnecessary one."

"I'll allow you to escort me home. And you'll see that Tilly arrives home safely as well." The lumpy knot in Clara's stomach grew.

Georg guided them close to the carriage and boosted them inside. "Promise me you won't jump. You'll not get far if you do."

"You find joy in inflicting pain. After the confrontation earlier this week, I'm more afraid you'll push us out." *O Lord, how do I find joy in this trial?*

"Harold, you know the way. Lead on." Georg shouted to his driver.

"The way to where? You promised to take us home." Clara glued her gaze on Georg, wary of his intentions.

"I have a special stop in mind first."

"No more pigeons."

"No pigeons today, my sweets. But it is my birthday."

"I've received no invitation to a party in your honor."

"I planned my own, just me and you, and now Tilly too. Our cook prepared exquisite birthday treats."

"My Vati's men watch me. They'll find us if you take us somewhere you shouldn't. I only agreed to come with you because Tilly's with me."

"Maybe your Vati's men should watch more closely. They allowed you to stay at the church after your family left. Besides, you're mine, Clara, and I've been waiting a long time. I expect your cooperation. I would hate to hurt more than your arm."

"Like you hurt Megs, and like you hurt me?" Tilly leaned in front of Clara as if she could protect her. "You've hurt Clara so many times. Nobody treats their friends like you do!"

"Friends? Tilly, you're a commoner. Unlike the Reinholds, the Wolffs shun friendships with commoners."

"Not the sentiment I heard from you when you wanted something." Tilly stared intently at him and pressed herself deep into the corner of the carriage.

"I'd like something now. You two will bestow a few birthday gifts on me at my carefully chosen party destination."

"Too close for Monte Carlo then. I'm not interested in going there at all." Clara kicked her foot across the carriage, landing it on Georg's ankle bone.

He moved his foot back and kept talking. "This place is much closer than the luxurious seaside resort, but I welcome your gifts to me at either place. While we're on our way, I'd like to play charades. You enjoy the game, my sweets. And as memory serves me, Tilly, you are an exceptional player."

"My family will search until they find me. They don't like you, Herr Wolff." Tilly gritted her teeth and twisted her mouth into a frightful visage, one that should even scare a wolf, but Georg never flinched.

"Song title. Two words. First word,

Turned around, pushed aside, failed

All the best intentions derailed."

Tilly wagged her finger at him. "Good idea! We'll derail all your intentions."

"But Tilly, Lehrer Frederick bragged about your way with words. He claimed the riddles come easily for you."

"He never bragged about yours, though, did he?" Clara sneered. "If your clues are even possible, give us a good reason to solve them."

"Your Vati demands you respect me. I'll tell him."

"What will you tell him? He expects you to be loving toward me. He disapproves of the way you pull me away from others. And what did you say about hurting more than my arm? Do you believe hurting me again will make him happy?" Clara rubbed her arm where the tenderness from the injury lingered.

"Back to the clue."

Clara huffed before answering. "Perturbed."

"I am, but that's not the word."

"Disturbed, then." Tilly sighed. Her body shook frantically.

"Not it either."

"But you are disturbed in the head, Georg." A vein throbbed in Clara's neck. "I promise my Vati will hear of your shenanigans. How about annoyed? I am annoyed with you and this game."

"By my recollection, you loved playing charades with another man. Now you're playing with me, and your answer is still incorrect. How long will this take?"

"It'll stop now." Tilly slowly shook her head. "We don't want to guess your stupid clues."

"You disappoint me. You know the answer, so make me happy. Shout it out."

"I have no desire to make you happy." Tilly grimaced.

"So, you don't know the answer? I win either way."

"Thwarted. I knew it the whole time." With an emphasized harumph, Tilly crossed her arms upon her bodice.

"See how easy that was."

"What is your purpose in this?" Clara tapped her feet together. Fear hammered in her heart.

"Do you know the rest of the song's title? I'll help you out. Here is the second clue:

Swinging around in playful measures

Landing the tastiest of treasures."

"'Thwarted Happiness.'" Clara scowled her answer. "I have played Schubert's song. In the lyrics, the poor man loses every time. He misses out on the kisses because of the dog, her Vater, or unfortunate happenings. So, Brigette, or Vati, or a broken ladder, or your broken head, or any other distraction will thwart your goals. Someone will find us, thwart your intentions, and inform my Vati of your foolish behavior."

"You've memorized the lyrics to the song, but we are here in the forest. No one will find us, and I'll have my way. Nothing will thwart my plan today."

Was there no end to Georg's mean-spirited behavior? His cruelty and insensitivity poisoned Clara's being. She swallowed down the bile threatening to spew all over them.

"If you're going to vomit, please do it outside." Georg exited the carriage, then grabbed both girls, tugging them from the conveyance.

Tilly whimpered quietly. Georg set her down with a thrust. She lost her footing and landed at the feet of a gnome, greeting them at the door of his forest home.

Holding her achy arm to her body, Clara side-stepped Georg to tend to her friend. "Are you hurt?"

"I'll be fine except for a slight bruise from bumping my head." Tilly rubbed her arms and the spot on her head. She sobbed quietly as she sat up. She pointed to the gnome. Her eyes blinked rapidly.

"Is this place familiar to you? You've experienced a torment here in the past?"

Tilly lowered her head. Clara stood between her and Georg. Intense pain pounded in Clara's chest.

"Georg, you expect this imp chiseled from a tree trunk to bring you better luck today than all the other times your song speaks of? What is this little house burrowed into the side of the hill between these two ancient trees?"

"The gnome's home will host the perfect party. After you." Georg opened the door and swept the girls, gowns and all, through the four-foot entrance. "It's bigger on the inside than it looks from the outside."

Savory aromas of Zimf-Streuselkuchen and cocoa invaded Clara's senses. "It's no surprise you provided refreshment, but I'm surprised you went to the trouble way out here."

"The better to entice you, my sweets."

"You sure are cocky, you Big Bad Wolff." Clara spat the words at him. The warm, homey cinnamon scent she inhaled contradicted the icy chill running through her veins.

"You call him the Big Bad Wolff, but a black coat with a white stripe down the back suits him perfectly. He oozes the stench of a skunk—and the meanness." Tilly stepped outside the open door. "Georg! Your driver just left with the carriage."

Grabbing the sash on the back of her dress, Georg yanked Tilly back inside. "He's hiding it, as I instructed him. Now I'm ready for your kisses." He turned her to face him and lowered his mouth to hers. "I hoped for Clara's first, but since you're in my arms, Tilly…"

"No!" Tilly pinched his cheeks and shoved him away.

While turned away from Georg's view, Clara snatched one of the fifty-seven gnomes gathering dust around the cottage and conked him on the head. "You'll receive nothing from me either unless the pastor pronounces us man and wife. That'll never happen."

Georg thumped the bump on his head. "Didn't hurt a bit. Of course, our marriage will happen, my sweets, and it could be sooner than spring. Pastor Lange agreed to officiate any day —even today."

"Never! Curt will stop you."

"Do you see him here to protect you? And my agreement is with your Vati."

"Take us home. Now! No marriage!. And you won't hurt Tilly."

"I'll teach you to respect me!" Georg stepped to the corner of the room. He pulled a rope from a cabinet. He shoved the girls onto back-to-back stools. He secured Clara's sling to her body with the rope. After wrapping it all around them, Georg knotted the cords between their backs. He cinched their three remaining hands tightly.

Clara winced. Pain wracked her whole body. Her limbs trembled. She bit back the nasty words on her tongue. If only Daniel would come, he would rescue him.

"I'll be back soon with the Pastor. No one will find you here. You'll not find your way out either." He turned to the door. "Harold!"

The carriage and driver failed to appear. Georg stomped off.

Tilly scootched in her seat. "Can we untangle these ropes?"

"Can we even loosen our fingers? If we can, then what? He's bigger than us. I'm injured."

Clara and Tilly unsuccessfully wiggled and jiggled to free themselves from the ropes holding them captive to each other and to the gnome's little stools.

"We're stuck here." She attempted to kick them loose, but Clara's legs felt like they weighed a ton.

A few moments later, Harold pushed his way through the door. Clara's breath hitched. Had he come to help?

Harold inspected the bindings. "Young Herr Wolff bumbles many things, but he mastered knot tying." Harold snorted. "He'll have me fired if I untie you."

"We thought you drove Georg to get the Pastor." Clara gritted her teeth.

"Not wanting you to escape, he went by himself. He left me on guard." Harold's eyebrows inched toward his hairline. "So, you're ready to marry the man today?"

"Nein!" Would Harold help them stop this madness?

"Our families will search until they find us." Tilly shook. The girls' stools rattled, but the ropes remained secure.

Harold pried himself from the doorway and took a few steps outside. "No one's here." He dropped to his knees and frowned at them through the doorway. "Good luck. I'm not free to help you. No one remembers this place is back here. They'll never find you."

"I'll never forget." Tilly's elbow nudged Clara's back.

"That won't matter to anyone else." Harold's head dropped to his hands.

"How many scratches did the carriage collect from bushes and debris poking at it as we traveled here? Branches snapped all along the narrow lane, leaving a trail."

"I doubt that. Your fear has made you delirious, Tilly. Try to calm yourself," Harold suggested.

"They may upset my queasy tummy, but could we nibble on treats while we wait?" The request bought time for Clara to concoct an escape plan. They needed a map.

Crawling back inside, Harold snatched a piece of the kuchen and held it out to Clara.

"We've read far too many fairy tales." Tilly cleared her throat. "Suggest something besides the Kuchen, Clara, because I would rather not risk poisoning."

"*Ew*, I didn't think of that." Clara bit his hand.

Howling in pain, Harold shoved his way through the doorway and back outside.

Clara begged her brain to create an escape plan. "Tilly, do you think the gnome keeps a map?"

"What? How? Where?"

"I don't know! You're as panicked as I am. We're stuck in an impossible situation."

"Gnomes bringing good luck—an old superstition. Georg trusts the one I bumped my head on to help him today. It won't. Someone must have seen the carriage veer off the road. They'll come to rescue us."

"Tilly. Harold's too afraid for his own interests to help us. I can't blame him. Even if someone saw the carriage veer off the road, no one knows Georg snatched us. Any minute, the Wolff will return with Pastor."

Tilly had no further response. An eerie stillness seeped into the cottage. The ropes between them snugged as Tilly trembled.

"Tilly, are you reliving a nightmare?"

"I can't talk about it."

"Then talk about getting out." Clara struggled for her next breath.

"There's no way by our strength."

"Then whose?" Clara's chest tightened.

"I know Who waits to help His children. He's not a folktale or an imaginary spirit. God's plan is better than any man's or a gnome's map."

"We claim we believe that, but do we?"

Tilly rocked gently, the motion rubbing comfort along Clara's back.

"I do have a better suggestion. Prayer."

"What was that I said about you girls all teaching me? *With God nothing shall be impossible.* And another verse, too. *Be careful for nothing; but in everything by prayer and supplication with thanksgiving let your requests be made known unto God."*

Clara looked up at the low ceiling and cried out to the God high above them. *God, Your word instructs us to pray for our enemies. We don't want to pray for Georg or thank You for him. We do thank You that You see us and know where we are. Thank You that You can and will bring our families to rescue us. Please keep them from being delayed three weeks like the angel on his way to Daniel, the prophet."*

Tilly concluded her friend's prayer. "In Jesus' name, Amen!"

Horses whinnied outside their jailhouse. They heard voices.

Pastor and the Wolff.

DANIEL TAPPED his fingers staccato-style on the bench in front of him. "I think better here in the carriage house, and I'm certain this involves Georg."

With his elbow on the bench, Fritz leaned toward Daniel. "But you fear saying it out loud casts you in a jealous green haze."

"I stay in a green haze concerning the Gut Herr's arrangement between the Wolff and his daughter, but the baron asked me to protect Clara until he returns—especially from Georg. We have looked everywhere, Fritz. She's gone. On my watch."

"The lady follows her whims, making your job more difficult." Fritz sucked in his lips.

"Most often I adore that about her, but if her whims caught her in a trap today, ja, they have added extra difficulty to my assignment." Picking up binoculars, Daniel stepped outdoors and scanned the estate again. Nothing. Nothing except Mamsell standing nose to his spyglasses.

Lottie took a step back, pushed the binoculars aside, and looked Daniel in the eyes instead. "Have you checked with her Bible Class ladies? Hannah mentioned Clara talking with them before the family left the church."

"Nein. I haven't spoken to any of them. I didn't see Della today. That leaves Minna, Luisa, and Tilly." Daniel motioned for Jost, standing nearby. "Grab a horse, make a circle of the Gut, and call on the ladies from Clara's Bible Class. Maybe she walked one of them home."

"Would she visit a friend with the Gut Herr expected home today? He'll call his family together, and Dora'll be serving dinner a short time later." Jost shrugged.

"You're right, but I'm out of ideas where to look. Go quickly."

Jost mounted a fast dapple horse and tore down the path.

If fisting his hands could have drained all the worry out, Daniel's fears would have been depleted. "Mamsell, you saw Georg near the pump house earlier. What do you think he was doing there?"

"He had a couple of horses pulling one of the Wolff's carriages. He and the driver engaged in a spirited conversation and then left. Anymore, when I see that man, I see pigeons, whether they're real or imagined. In my opinion, they had a feisty debate about the birds again. Since they took off, I gave it no further thought."

"He was here before the church service ended?"

"Ja. Hours ago."

"Most of us have lived here our whole lives. We know every inch of the estate. We've searched every corner. Where could he hide her?" Daniel bounced on his heels. A tick spasmed his eyelid.

Hannah poked her head around the corner of the garden wall. "Besides this garden, think of a place you stumbled upon even once. What place stirred your imagination as a spot to sit alone with your thoughts, or dare I say it, with Clara?"

"The old cottage, a place Clara loves. We checked there three times already. I'm dumbfounded, and the whole situation reeks of Georg's antics."

"Where would he take her, knowing Vati's expected home soon?" With her arms hanging limp at her sides, Hannah sulked back toward the garden.

If Georg was responsible for her disappearance, he threatened his agreement. Daniel fooled only himself. He plopped down on a weathered crate by the carriage house—his shoulders slumped. He imagined he would lose the job he loved, near the girl he loved. He had done a lousy job keeping his promise to her and her Vati.

A mere fifteen minutes passed like hours since Jost took off to inquire among Clara's friends.

Finally, a thunder of galloping horses jolted him from his grim ponderings. The dapple flew toward him. Tilly's brother, Rudi, was right behind Jost on the second horse.

Scrambling toward the duo, Daniel caught up with them halfway up the drive. "What's the news?"

Jost sucked in a deep breath and pointed to Rudi. "I'm boiling with anger. Tilly's brother can tell you."

"Do you know of a place called the Gnome's House set deep in a forested area? Tilly's missing too. I suspect Georg has both of them. He took them there."

"Some elders around here tell stories about the place. It was abandoned ages ago, and the only entrance is buried in a hill-side. It would be covered in dense brush and overgrown vines after all these years. Did Tilly tell you about it? Why? Can you find it?"

"No time to explain." Rudi's feet bounced in his stirrups. "I pulled her patchwork story together from the snippets she shared. I plotted a map from her descriptions."

"Are there enough details to locate the place, Rudi?"

"I hope so. They may be in grave danger."

"Does this story have anything to do with Georg?"

Rudi nodded. "My heart gallops as fast as this horse did to get here."

"I have a horse ready to go."

Daniel, Rudi, and Jost turned their steeds off the cobbled roads around Gut Apfelhof. Rudi led them onto a dirt path and into an overgrown forest area. Only a trickle of sunshine made it through the leafy canopy. Evergreens reached scratchy arms across their path. Moss and ferns poked up indiscriminately along the way. Distant whipping sounds cracked the air.

"MY SWEETS, come out. Your wish is granted. Here's your pastor."

I hate you! Would going along with Georg's charade buy them more time? She extended her fingers claw-like. Her heart thudded like a bass drum. "You'll free your precious sweets then?" Her lilting soprano carried her request out the cottage door and to the men's ears.

Pastor followed Georg inside and stared incredulously at the ladies. "You tied them up!" Pastor Lange knelt beside the girls and began untangling the ropes. "How do you plan to explain this to Gut Herr Reinhold?"

"She's mine, Reverend. And I want her now, not next spring."

Pastor Lange grimaced. "Why the rush?"

"Clara doesn't want this marriage. She may try to escape from this arrangement, but you're here now. You can marry us before anyone interferes or she gets away. Hurry up with those cords." Georg marched on shaky legs in circles around the ladies and the one who came to their aid.

"You make no sense. She's shown you more respect than I expected about the agreement. Since you dragged me out here, I'll take all the time I wish. I don't see you helping."

Under the pastor's skillful hands, the ropes fell. A rush of relief. They wiggled their fingers and massaged their palms. They had no remedy available for the rash the ropes had left on their wrists.

"Ladies, step outside and breathe some fresh air. You too, Georg, so I can keep my eye on you."

When they stretched their stiff limbs and stepped out the door, Clara gasped at the chill hanging there. "I saw quilts lying on the hearth. They would keep us warm."

While Harold gathered the quilts, Georg pressed her against his wide chest and slid his sweaty palms down her arms. "I'll keep you warm instead, my sweets."

"Ouch! Careful of my arm—the one you hurt. Besides, there's time for touchy stuff later. Much later. Let go of my hands!" She shook them loose despite the pain. "If you and Pastor insist on making this my wedding day, we need to make the setting pretty. Brightly colored autumn leaves line the hillside above us."

Tilly gazed up and all around. "Looks like a perfect place up there to stand—up on that hill between two pine trees. Could you men find some logs and build a small altar?"

"A perfect idea." Harold scurried to collect logs.

"This isn't how I planned to spend my afternoon. My normal wedding responsibilities don't include decorating." Pastor Lange cleared his throat. "Then again, the details of her wedding are important to a bride. You should've had things ready before I arrived, Georg."

Cocking his head sharply, Georg stared at the preacher. "You're helping me, not them, remember? Forget the fancy stuff. Just get Clara and me married."

"I don't like this, but head up the hill. Do as Clara has asked. The bride deserves a say about her wedding." Pastor shook his head.

"I need a veil." She reached into her dress pocket, fumbling with its contents.

"My handkerchief could work, but here's a much better idea. Tilly, please untie the back of my overskirt. We can fashion it into a headpiece. It's tasteless as wedding attire, but we'll create a veil from what we have."

Georg stuffed his fists in his pockets. "Well, hurry up."

As Tilly maneuvered the skirt around, affixing it to Clara's locks, a small box fell from Clara's pocket to her feet. Tilly recovered it quickly and pushed it under the cuff of her gown.

Clara's eyes slowly widened as the corners of her mouth lifted. Tilly's eyes smiled back. Clara had worn this overskirt in Paris. Tilly had the matchbox.

"What a beautiful bride, Georg." Tilly turned Clara to face her groom.

"Lovely." No kindness flowed from his dour face. "This means you're ready now?"

"Did you also bring my Vati or brother to walk me down the aisle?" Clara fluttered her eyelashes in Georg's direction.

"My sweets, we have the pastor."

"I only said we could not get married without a pastor. I need my Vati and my family."

"I'm your family now. Harold has the altar ready."

"I'll walk with you, Clara." Tilly took her friend's shaky hand and shooed the rest of the party up the hill.

Outnumbered and lost, not one escape plan would get them out of there. *Please, Lord, answer our prayer.*

Georg held his head high, his chin jutted forward. His face boasted the smirk she expected. Clara clasped Tilly's arm tighter. Her legs wobbled beneath her skirt, and her foot caught in its hem, plunking both girls in a heap at Georg's feet.

"Your shoulder. Did you hurt it again?" Tilly cradled her friend.

Clara winced. "Just a little."

Expletives flew. Georg ranted. With his arms swinging wildly, he pranced all around, shouting more disgruntled words.

"I'm not moving. I'll sit here and be your witness." Tilly pushed the bride to her feet. While everyone took their positions, she pulled the little box from her cuff.

"Clara and Georg, can we begin now?" Pastor Lange asked.

Silence.

"We are gathered here to join this man and this woman in the bonds of Holy Matrimony. Should anyone present know of any reason that this couple should not be joined together, speak now or forever hold your peace."

A column of smoke drifted up between the bride and groom.

Flames traveled from the lower edge of Clara's veil and climbed up Georg's pants legs.

While he fell to the ground rolling about like a crazed dog, Tilly jumped to her feet, swept Clara off to the side, and pulled the burning fabric from her head.

"We object!" Two male voices broke into the panicked moment.

Lange froze in place. "It's not what you think."

"Then exactly what is it, Pastor?" Rudi aimed his rifle toward Georg's head. "I've come for my sister."

"And what've you come for, Daniel? You can't have Clara." Georg's nostrils flared.

"You have made that point clear, but the Gut Herr expects me to protect her. As if you haven't already given everyone at Gut Apfelhof enough reasons to be concerned about you, my friend here brings his own grudges. You may call them rumors, but we both know better. You deserve that sooty charred leg.

Harold had used the quilts to beat out the flames. A lightness filled Clara's head. She and Tilly clung to one another. They prayed aloud that the other four men would not come to blows.

"Everyone, take a breath and act peacefully." Harold rolled the charred logs away.

Georg pouted and hollered at the reverend. "This is all your fault. You agreed to her whims."

Daniel ambled toward Clara and Tilly. He pressed a hand to his chest and let out a sigh. "We found you! Everyone in the Gut is frantic with worry."

Tears ran down her cheeks. Before he could say more, Clara ran into his arms and kissed him like no one was looking. "Tilly and I prayed angels would arrive before the Wolff returned with Pastor Lange. We thought God forgot us."

"What do you mean 'before the Wolff returned?' Georg dumped you here and left?" Rudi asked.

Tilly hugged her brother. "That's exactly what the skunk did. He demanded we play games with him, because he claimed it's his birthday. When we didn't fulfill his birthday wishes, he went for reinforcement."

"He left you a chance to escape, but you had no idea which way to go to get out?" Daniel looked around the area.

"We would have run until we found our way out, but he left no chance for us to break free. He tangled us together with the tightest knots. We feared death or worse."

Clara pointed at Georg sulking off. "Isn't your birthday in February?"

"No matter what month he was born, he missed out on any gift he expected. He got what he deserved instead." Tilly clapped her hands together with Clara's.

"A Wolff with angels, gnomes, prayers, games, birthday treats, Pastor Lange, and a wedding—perfect fodder for an interesting tale. With all parties accounted for, I'm ready to hear Georg's warped version of this story." Daniel stood beside Clara.

"I heard that!" A few giant steps brought Georg face-to-face with Daniel. "Get away from her! She's mine."

"Not yet, she's not."

"She won't ever be yours. I saw that kiss. I warn you. She's promised to me."

"She deflects your kisses."

Rudi came from behind all of them with his fists raised, ready to connect with Georg's jaw.

"Daniel's holding his temper in check. Please do likewise." Pastor Lange caught Rudi's arm in his grip and held it tight.

"But I can't let it happen again." Rudi glared at the pastor. "Explain why you didn't help them escape."

"I'm under no obligation to answer you, Rudi Feldt. To be sure, though, I questioned Georg about it and reminded him that a bride has expectations about her wedding."

"But you didn't stop it." The veins in Rudi's neck stood out.

"This wedding became much more complicated than I expected when Georg came for me."

Deeply furrowed lines spread across Tilly's brow as she shook her head, silencing Rudi.

"There is no solution here that will meet with Kraig Reinhold's approval." Pastor Lange addressed the group. "If Georg shared his version of what happened, he'd lie. The rest of you all have your tales. I recommend you keep them to yourselves."

"Respectfully, Pastor, what about you? I know it's not my place, but I must ask. Can you keep your mouth shut?" Daniel stared at the preacher.

"You're right! No servant should speak to a reverend the way you have, but I'll not tell. You won't either."

Daniel's laugh sounded more like a pig snort.

"Clara, your Vati and brother will be home when we arrive." Pastor smiled. "Georg, here's my version of the story, the one we'll use. All of us left the church as a group of jolly friends out enjoying ourselves this pleasant autumn afternoon." Pastor Lange cut his eyes toward Georg.

Georg nodded.

"And you're only in charge of protecting Clara. Do you understand my meaning?" The reverend pointed his finger, dagger-like, into Daniel's chest.

Clara could not imagine Daniel agreeing to these terms. Vati needed to know.

Daniel pinched his own Adam's apple and looked him in the eye. "You have wearied Curt and the Gut Herr with lies, Pastor. You expect me to keep another? I understand your meaning, but as her assigned protector, she's riding on the horse with me." He squeezed Clara's hand. "I'll take whatever precautions I deem necessary to honor her Vati's trust. Don't rely on any of us to repeat your lies. Integrity matters."

Clara beamed on the inside.

Taking her in his arms, Rudi lifted Tilly onto his horse. She sat sideways in the saddle and sighed. Clara leaned into Daniel's strong back.

Leaning against the backside of her fairytale dream, Clara headed deeper into the reality of her Wolffish nightmare.

Chapter Thirty-One

GUT APFELHOF, *Later Sunday afternoon, 25 September 1881*

"Finally." Kraig sighed with relief as the weary party came up the drive. Would Clara be with them? What explanation would they have?

The horses and their riders cantered closer to the carriage house. Behind them, Pastor Lange arrived with Georg in the Wolffs' carriage.

"Look at the beating their buggy endured." Curt scratched his head. "I'm curious. Someone explain this misadventure."

The pastor bounced out of the carriage and extended his hand to Kraig, while Kraig kept his to himself.

"What a wonderful afternoon, and all's well. Georg planned a splendid outing. We left from the church, a group of friends out enjoying ourselves on this beautiful autumn day."

"You're quick to speak for him. Why? And why should we believe you?" With their hair and clothes so unkempt, some members of this group have been out for more than a Sunday drive. "I would say Clara and Tilly found little joy in this outing."

"Trustworthiness isn't necessarily a strength of Pastor Lange's." Curt sneered. "I'm concerned about whether the Wolff harmed my sister and her friend."

"No one's hurt. Nothing happened." Georg pointed toward Clara while Daniel helped her from the horse. "See for yourself! Your daughter is well, Herr Reinhold. But she's riding with the rascal you forbid her to see."

"Whoa, Georg! You twist my words."

"You promised her to me."

"Stop reminding me. Are you suggesting I made a mistake? Have Harold take you and Pastor home."

Curt and Rudi gathered their sisters into their arms. Kraig stood next to them rubbing his ear again. "The family shared their side of the story. Pastor, I don't believe your account. I'd like to hear from these two Frauleins."

With two fingers between his lips, Curt whistled for quiet. "Allow Clara and Tilly to tell us, please."

The girls took turns recounting the tale of their dismally long afternoon filled with tears and fears.

"Nein! It can't be true!" His hands already covering his ears, Vati inched them toward his hairline and raked through his tangled waves.

"Rudi, how did you know where to find them?"

"Mein Gut Herr, it's more than I can say, and still protect my sister."

"We're home, Vati." Clara's voice wavered. "And we're safe."

"Pastor and Georg, I believe I'm being duped, but I'm hungry and happy to see my family. Rudi, I'll not prod you for details, but I'm sending Curt and Daniel to visit with you tomorrow."

Vati signaled Mamsell. "Ask Dora if she has enough food prepared for guests."

"I'll not need to ask. She's made enough for three families."

"Daniel, take the carriage and bring the rest of Tilly and Rudi's family to dinner."

"Gut Herr, Danke. Dinner, our family, and much-needed rest await Tilly and me at home."

"I understand. Another time, perhaps. Daniel and Rosa, join us tonight. Mamsell, gather the staff. Curt and I feared the worst, and all's well. Let's celebrate."

Kraig followed them all inside. He excused Clara to clean up for dinner. A muffled conversation at the door drew his attention.

"Who's calling uninvited?"

Curt opened the door to the one person he did not want to see. "Vati sent you home. He did not invite you to dinner."

"I'm courting your sister."

"And I'm her brother." Curt shoved a fist toward the bloke's chest, curtailing his rage just short of impact. "News traveled fast to Stuttgart. Vati and I know how you treated Clara while we were away. And what foolishness you engaged in earlier today, making up more lies with Pastor Lange. I'll learn the true intent of your mischief."

Georg kept his nose up in the air, as though held by a taut wire. "But today is my birthday."

"It is not! No one cares if it is! We're having peace in our home today. Leave as my Vati asked."

"I did nothing wrong."

"You never do. I heard your Pa ask you about another problem. You were unaware I was listening, and it's doubtful you'll admit to that conversation either?"

Words sputtered from his mouth. "I, I, I have no idea—what do you mean?"

"Your tongue twists and trips. An argument with your pa in your barn. I waited outside, planning to return this." Curt drew the official paper from his pocket and taunted Georg with it. "Reacting to your vague answer to your Pa's question, I left. I kept the document. I'm not letting go of it now either."

"Georg!" Vati hollered after him from the stairs. "Leave now! Be in my office in the morning at ten."

Georg kicked and stomped to his carriage. Without glancing back, he, Harold, and Lange drove away.

"He's gone." Did you overhear our conversation?"

"Ja. Every word. Jonas and I both did."

Ettinger chuckled. "If I were to give Georg his best piece of advice, it'd be wise for him to keep his cards close to his chest." He slapped Curt on the shoulder. "Did I imagine it, or do you have another piece of information?"

"That's a possibility. I am not a gambling man, but with an analogy to the games, I expect to grab the last trick."

~

MONDAY MORNING, *26 September 1881*

CURT RUBBED his horse's nose, smoothed his mane, and handed him an apple from the saddlebag. It's time to head to the Feldts' home. The horse chomped while Curt mounted his friend. Daniel rode beside him on the dappled steed.

"Friend. That is who you are, Landus, and we'll practice asking our questions by confiding in you. It'll prove difficult for Rudi to share what he knows."

"Perhaps not so much." Daniel stroked his horse's mane. "I've overheard some things, too. With what you've already learned, and what happened yesterday, he'll be ready to divulge everything."

"I pray you're correct. Our barrister depends on me to bring the trick I promised. If Rudi confirms my suspicions, we have an even more tangled mess."

Landus lowered his head, ears pointing forward. He nickered, deep and soft.

"You understand." He patted the horse's neck. "Let's circle the orchards and check on the harvesting. Daniel, we'll pray that inhaling the fruity aromas out here brings inspiration falling from heaven. I'd like for us to handle this well. *God, please help us learn the truth and put all our clues together."*

Deep in conversation about the many puzzle pieces they had gathered—often painful ones—they almost rode past the Feldt's home.

Rudi tended his Mutter's veggies in their small front yard as the duo rode up. "Welcome, friends." Rudi's voice jarred them back to the moment. "Tie your horses to the fence post."

"Instead of talking here let's go where Tilly won't hear us.? How about behind that old cottage?"

"For an abandoned place, it's received a lot of attention recently." Daniel rubbed his neck. "Rudi, do you think the cottage is a good choice?"

Rudi's shoulders twitched, and beads of sweat trickled from his hairline. He glanced about as if looking for a better location. "Memories." He muttered almost imperceptibly. "It'll be fine though."

Curt lifted a silent prayer and motioned to Rudi and Daniel. "Follow me. That huge oak tree and the fence will provide privacy."

Despite the vulnerable position his family faced, Rudi recounted recent incidents. "Georg shamed my sister badly. We've been silent until now. My family will cooperate. Whatever you need us to do. We have the privilege to live under the protection of the best Gut Herr anywhere."

"Very kind words. Danke."

"That's also what makes all this so strange." Rudi paused, peering around the tree. "This may not have been such a great place after all."

Curt stepped out from behind the wide trunk. "Why are you here, Herr Wolff?" Curt snatched a shovel from Georg's hand.

"And I might ask, what does your friend mean by 'makes all this so strange?' All what?"

"None of your business, Georg! You lack permission to dig here. You've overstayed your welcome everywhere."

"And you're in the company of Daniel and Rudi. If you welcome a Feldt, you're a fool. It should be beneath you to make friends with stinky commoners."

Rudi circled Georg, sniffing the air several times before he stood in front of him, nose to nose. "Be careful who you call stinky." He almost growled the words.

Georg exhaled a lengthy string of vulgarities. Daniel must have read Curt's silent hint. He stepped into action. The two grabbed the offensive lout. They threw him to the ground and held him down.

"We've collected many dirty facts about you! I'll play my best move when it hurts you most. For now, get back to Gut Dinkelhof. Stay there this time."

Rudi and Daniel jerked Georg to his feet. Curt kicked him in the rear. "Get moving."

As he skulked off, Georg shook his fist at Curt.

"Did he hear our conversation?" Rudi flinched.

"If he had, Georg would've come out swinging." Daniel tugged at his collar.

Curt looked Rudi in the eye. "Your secret's safe until we need it."

Chapter Thirty-Two

GUT APFELHOF, *Thursday morning, 29 September 1881*

Crisp autumn air with a stirring of chimney smoke greeted Curt as he strode to the stable. "Daniel, three horses ready so early?"

"At your Vati's request. He said you two and Herr Ettinger have business to attend to early today."

"Mine will be earlier than theirs. Thank you for all your help." Curt jumped on Landus. "This day promises to be an interesting one." With a high wave, he sped away.

Ten minutes later, he and his horse thundered up to the Backhaus. How fortunate that Georg had already arrived and was still outside. Curt tipped his hat to him. "Meeting your accomplices this morning? We need to talk before you join them."

"Talk about what?"

"Let's begin with why you avoided my Vati's request to see you. He asked three days ago."

"What request?"

"You had already left our property, I'm aware. But Vati had the message delivered to you. Don't deny it."

Georg shrugged. "I have nothing to say. Your pastor explained everything."

"Truly? You'd jeopardize your courting agreement? I'm asking my questions before Vati talks to you. He's on his way."

"I don't need to answer your questions!"

"You're getting loud. Walk with me. I'm asking, and you will answer—with words or the lack of them. I'll learn the truth." Curt pushed the reluctant fellow to a spot behind the bakery. Their discussion would be unheard by other Backhaus guests.

KRAIG CLOBBERED the breakfast table with his fist. His coffee cup jumped in its saucer, scattering blooms of dark liquid onto the lace cloth covering the Reinholds' dining table. "It's been three days since I requested Georg's presence in my study."

"I've visited with the other players this week. They've all anted up." Jonas' eyes widened.

"But one has not, and he's hiding behind those birds." Kraig lifted an eyebrow.

"It is time to raise the stakes and call the hand." Jonas clapped.

"What's your plan?"

"You've impressed me with how well you brought your community together, planning for the success of the celebration. With Erntedank just three days away and everyone scurrying about in preparation, no one'll miss us if we disappear for a while."

"Because they love me." Kraig smiled while he blotted up the mess he had made.

"Ja, ja." Jonas guffawed. "There'll be a fine party here in a few days. Danke for inviting my wife and family too. But for the party to be a happy event, the trouble must be resolved. Talking to Georg before Sunday is urgently necessary."

"I prefer an enjoyable party to an uneasy weekend, while many hunches remain on the table. I prioritized finding Georg above all else today and asked Daniel to ready my horse and Curt's for a ride this morning. He prepared another horse for you."

"And where will we find the Wolff?"

Kraig shrugged. "I'll take a wild guess—at the Backhaus. We'll check there first. Besides, it's a fine morning to claim another cup of coffee and the latest gossip."

"You're expecting to learn more?"

"I'm not sure what I'm expecting, Jonas. I doubt Georg ran off, but he's avoided me. The same people who talked years ago probably steered him away from our scent, but the Wolffs rarely miss a morning at the Backhaus."

"Would any other scent get past those pungent cigars?"

"Agreed. Clara complains about them often. Follow the stinky cigar trail. Let's go."

"It is our lucky day," Kraig shouted as they reached their destination. If it weren't such a childish thing to do, Kraig would have jumped up and down at his excitement upon entering the establishment. All the players sat around the Backhaus table, deep in conversation. Kraig's heart froze. All except Georg.

"Ahh, the aromas of Apfelkuchen!" Kraig inhaled deeply. "Pastor, Nickel brothers, Gerwig, your raucous voices suggest you added a unique ingredient to the coffee."

"May we join you?" Jonas scraped two chairs across the floor.

The Frankens, owners of the Backhaus, provided two more mugs of hot brew and plates of fresh Kuchen.

The door swung wide, and Curt pushed Georg toward Vati. "I asked the man my questions. Now ask yours."

"You arrived for a party, but you ignored my request to show up three days ago."

"I forgot."

"Have you forgotten Clara, too?" Kraig closed his mouth before his words damaged their defense. Jonas' cold, hard glare was warning enough.

Curt grabbed a chair for himself. Georg took a seat beside the others. Jonas and Kraig stood.

"While you're all here, tax collections begin next week." Money and profits had always been Pastor Lange's first concern. "With the harvest gathered, be sure you bring the state their share."

"You bring this up at an awkward time." Kraig pointed a finger toward the preacher. "What benefit do you hope to gain? We've not celebrated Erntedank yet, and you're already worried about taxes."

"All for the state, my friend."

"You've no reason to worry about the Reinholds' account. We pay on time." Kraig brushed a hand through the air as if to erase the conversation, then turned to the man making his daughter's life miserable. "Georg, you squirm like a young lad with chiggers in your Lederhosen. Are you Wolffs low on funds?"

"You insult me. A Wolff has never donned the peasant wear."

"Forgive me." He laughed, hoping to snap the tension. "But wasn't a wolf seen in Oma's night clothes once? I hear your nerves jangling."

Jonas nodded one at a time to the men sitting around the table, hoping to divert the flying barbs. "I spoke with each of you privately this week, except for Georg. Have you filled him in and divulged your little secrets to each other? It amazed me how easily each of you ratted out your friends. You even gave up your secret roles."

A brewing storm hung in the air, thick as fresh-mixed concrete. Kraig motioned to Georg. "You're coming with us now."

"We'll refrain from embarrassing the rest of you at the moment." Jonas helped heft the man to his feet from the tight corner seat where he cowered. "When we finish questioning him, we'll decide if we return Georg to you here or meet in a less public location."

"You bluff. You know nothing." Alfred Nickel answered for the group.

Ralph punched his brother's shoulder. "We know that, but they don't. Let them have their fun. The tables will turn."

"Ah ha! Then there is a bluff to call." Jonas' eyebrows rose and fell a few times.

Kraig pulled a generous sum from his pocket and handed it to Frau Franken. "To cover their tab and ours."

Outside the Backhaus, Kraig stood face-to-face with Georg, only a nose width between them. "The truth. It's time. Begin with what happened to Sarah."

Huffing, Georg jerked back from Kraig. His nose jutted into the air.

"I'd like to know why Gut Dinkelhof finds itself in tax arrears. And what is the real purpose of the pigeons you brought to Gut Apfelhof?" Jonas grilled him. "What's your real interest in Clara Reinhold?"

"I expect those brothers played their nickels right into your palm. Your explanation?" Kraig pressed him.

"Sarah was sick. She died. It wearied me with grief. How does information about my deceased wife matter now? She is gone." A smile twitched across his lips. "But Clara's here."

"And treated poorly by you. You say Sarah was sick? Did you cause her illness? I'm waiting for your answers." Kraig stood his ground.

"Do you want an apology from me?" Georg eked his infamous, haughty sneer. "An apology for Sarah? I had nothing to do with her death. Ask Dr. Pfeiffer."

"I believe we will. Here he comes now." Jonas walked toward the Doktor as he dismounted his horse.

"Ja. An apology, or better, a confession. Your attitude speaks for itself." Kraig continued to thump him for answers while holding Georg by both arms, ready to pounce. He desired to strike him or shake him until Gerog's last breath left him. He prayed he wouldn't. "My strength is in the Lord, Georg. His strength surpasses your devious intentions."

He motioned to the barrister. "Jonas, if you finished questioning him, have Doc invite the party out here."

"Here they come now." Jonas patted his pocket. "I have a summons for each of them. We'll hold court at your home shortly." He handed the papers to the men.

With all the characters accounted for, Kraig addressed Pastor Lange. "You've had the week to work this out. With all due respect to your title, Reverend, you failed." He then turned to the motley assembly. "Our urgency in this matter increased when we walked in on your gathering this morning."

"What urgency in what matter?" Pastor yawned.

"Jonas will reveal the whole matter shortly." Kraig instructed the men to ride out to his estate. "You have your summons. Jonas will present our case, and he has the alerted authorities to be available. We hope no one will be arrested today, but consider this your official warning. Your presence is required. The law has been informed to follow any of you attempting to get away.

"Others need to learn of your foolhardy deceptions. Each of them is at the estate today preparing for Erntedank—for Sunday's Thanksgiving festivities. Saying the word 'Thanksgiving' makes me shudder. Will God get any glory from our celebration this year? If no one starts an argument, maybe we can keep our friendships intact and please the Lord with our Erntedank offerings."

"Finished preaching your sermon, Kraig?" Pastor Lange laughed cynically, further framing the moment.

Leaving Curt and the barrister in command of leading the group to the estate, Kraig took off on Artax at a full gallop. He patted his steed on the shoulder. "Home, Artax!"

When they arrived at the stable, Kraig handed the horse off to Jost. "Cool him down with a little extra care. I rode her hard."

"You had a good reason to push this fellow. I'll take care of him."

Like a well-aimed dart, Fritz launched himself away from the door, narrowly averting a full-body encounter with the Gut Herr. Kraig flew past him, then turned to look over his shoulder. "Where is everyone?"

"Who are you including in everyone?" Fritz asked.

"Lydia, Clara, Curt, Emmaline, Hannah, Wilhelm, Rosa, Daniel, my Mutter. Where are they?"

"By my account, the big celebration is only three days away. Your family insists on taking part in the preparations. I'll get Mamsell. She knows where to find them." Fritz headed to the kitchen.

"Here she is now." As he entered the kitchen, Mamsell was helping Dora place pies in the pie safe.

Kraig entered the kitchen on Fritz's heels. "Mamsell, gather my family, Rosa, and Daniel. Others will join us shortly. Have them assemble in the large parlor. Hurry, please."

Kraig disappeared to his study. With the door bolted securely behind him, he knelt beside the soft leather chair, the same one he had collapsed in a month ago. The argument with Curt had stoked his will to uncover the truth about Georg

Wolff—whatever he missed or had been misled to dismiss. He knew only one place to go now and only One capable of unraveling this mess.

Heavenly Father, it's me, Kraig. I've desired to be a Vati to my children like the one You are to me and a good husband to Lydia. Maybe I haven't followed Your example as well as I'd like. My anger deeply afflicted Lydia. She came to recognize the misunderstanding and fully forgave me. I prayed for Your forgiveness, too. You forgave me. Why am I forced to relive it again?

This time, Clara suffers the repercussions of the unfounded story. The guilty parties depend on each other's ongoing lies. Please help me to keep quiet while Jonas exacts their string of untruths and reveals all their dirty tricks. Forgive me for allowing myself to be influenced to involve Clara in such an unfortunate way. Give my children grace to forgive me, too.

Curt keeps some information to himself right now. Whatever it is, I pray it is huge. I'm grateful for whatever help Daniel provided him. They have both fought for Clara. I desire for Clara to always be my little girl and to trust me that I do have her best interests at heart.

Doors slammed, and feet pounded across the wooden floors below. *Come with me, Lord. Let us face this together. In Jesus' name. Amen.*

Chapter Thirty-Three

LATER THURSDAY MORNING, *29 September 1881*

WITH ALL THE parties and the audience assembled, Kraig stood before them in the same formal parlor where he had announced the courtship agreement just over a month ago. "Half of you know exactly why we're here. The other half of you will learn of the drama played out in front of us for the last twenty-six years. The characters acted their parts so well, no one recognized the malice they intended."

Lydia stared down. She picked at the cuticles of her fingers. That and the rippling of her skirt alerted Kraig. *It's time to whisper a little reassurance to the love of my life.* He stepped to her side. He brushed loose tendrils away from her ear and leaned in close. "Lydia, you've always been and you always will be the only lady for me." He kissed her forehead.

Kraig stood in front of the group again. "Long-time counsel to our family, Barrister Jonas Ettinger, spent countless hours this week with several of you. He possesses an uncanny knack for exacting truth. I've asked him to speak to you together. He'll ask questions, and I expect your truthful answers." Kraig nodded toward him. "Jonas, please begin."

"The story surrounding the cameo and the implied guilt heaped on Gut Herr Reinhold took place over twenty-five years ago. It was a rumor then, and it's a rumor now. Kraig enlisted my help in discovering how it resurfaced and why. I intend to keep order here because Oma Dorthea, Gut Herrin Lydia, the Reinhold children, along with Rosa and Daniel, deserve your honesty and respect.

"Georg Wolff, Herr Reinhold promised his daughter to you. A few of those present with us today have witnessed the untoward attention you paid to her at a very young age. The stories have met the Gut Herr's ears, and he finds them troubling."

"Indulgences any young man would take in the presence of a beautiful young woman."

"You admit no respect for women? Not even innocent young girls?"

"I admit I'm a man with needs. Nothing more."

Low groans turned to growls. The odors of the Wolff's filthy deeds overpowered the room.

"He also asked you what happened to your first wife. Sarah, I believe? I assume she disappointed you as a wife?"

"She died."

"I hear little grief in your words. Did you play a role in her death?"

Gerwig bolted to his feet. “What do you accuse my son of?”

“He’s misdirected us on the answer to this question, but Doktor Pfeiffer keeps excellent records. He told us the sad details. Sarah required a midwife in her hour of need far more than pennyroyal tea and a Doktor willing to take other chances with her life.”

Georg spun around to Dr. Pfeiffer. “You didn’t tell them!”

“I count the Reinholds among my dearest friends. My fear for Clara outweighed any promise to keep your secret any longer. You made it clear to Clara you have no interest in having children?” Doktor Pfeiffer dabbed at his eyes.

“Where did you hear that!” Gerog bellowed.

“Georg, your outburst is unnecessary.” Jonas cut him off. “Clara described to me in great detail incidents that recently occurred in Paris.”

Gasps drowned out Georg’s sputters. No matter. Only nonsense came out.

Jonas addressed the Doktor. “Other than the secret you kept so well for years, we found you had no other part in this.”

Clara’s chest expanded with each deep breath. She twisted the dangly curl around and around. Rosa rubbed circles over the cameo.

“Is it possible to rub the face off a brooch?” Kraig had to ask.

The mention of the brooch served as the perfect transition for Jonas’ attention to another character. “Pastor Lange, you were the first to repeat the story of the cameo. As the spiritual leader in the community, you still found reason to spread news of others’ presumed sins. Is that correct?”

"All parties concerned should have an opportunity to forgive one another."

"But you handled the gossip by going straight to Lydia. If you believed the story, you should've followed the advice you preach from your pulpit."

"What advice would that be?"

"Matthew 15:18. You're familiar with the verse?"

"Could you enlighten me, please?"

"Of course. It is the verse about taking the grievance to your brother first, between you and him alone." Jonas kept his eyes fixed on Pastor Lange.

"But her husband wronged her, then invited the woman and her child into their home. I consider it my responsibility to help families through a crisis."

"Instead, your shared hearsay that created the crisis and led to Lydia's injury."

Pastor Lange gritted his teeth. His hands were planted on the arms of his chair. The chair wobbled despite his apparent efforts to hide his shakiness.

"One more question, Pastor. How did you hear the story, and did you seek the truth of it?"

"I tried." Lange dug for a handkerchief and mopped his damp brow. "No, that's a lie. I repeated it to Lydia as fact. I heard it from those two sitting to my left."

"None other than the Nickel brothers. I will come back to you, Pastor." Jonas shifted his eyes to the pair.

"Nickel brothers, you followed Kraig and Curt last week after spying on them on the train. When they encountered you later at the old Krueger Gasthaus, Kraig had an unpleasant impression vex him. You're many years older than you were then, but with your fuzzy hair poking from your straw hat, and the tall and short of you both, that sparked the memory. Why, do you think?"

"We're charming and unforgettable characters. Why your curiosity?" Alfred lifted his hat to the barrister.

"I understand you disappeared while Kraig was being tended to after the encounter. With Peter Kunz's help, they confirmed your presence at the Gasthaus on another occasion over twenty-five years earlier. They found your names written in the guest registry from the week the Gasthaus burned. By what I call divine providence, that particular volume survived the fire."

Alfred's fingers twitched, and Ralph slithered about in his seat like bugs had taken over his britches.

"Kraig recalled the much younger version of you two seated on a nearby bench outside the inn when he delivered the cameo to Rosa."

Ralph cleared his throat. "We were there. What does that prove?"

"You repeated what you thought you heard and made it into a slimy accusation. Your long-standing reputation around Stuttgart continues—two nosy meddlers who help themselves to others' business every opportunity. True?"

Alfred faced his brother. "I believe they caught us, Ralph." He poked a stubby finger into Ralph's lean chest.

They both snorted.

"Next question. Pastor, Ralph, Alfred, any of you may answer. How do you know each other?"

"Why would that matter? Pastors meet many people." The Pastor's knees bounced.

"Too late to concern yourself about it now." Alfred snickered. "You know Gerwig introduced us. We play bookmaker for you, and you count on us to know the odds."

As Jonas eyed all those in the room, a few yelped. His audience, with faces agape, stared back at him.

"Am I understanding all of this correctly?" He directed his comments to the Nickel brothers. "You relayed a half-truth to Lange, and he told Lydia. The rumor left the Reinhold family nearly torn asunder, but you wouldn't tell Lange's little secret if he spread your gossip."

"Sums it up." Ralph smirked and nodded.

Jonas studied Kraig, who rubbed his earlobe. "Would you like to pick up the cards and put the deck in order?"

Slowly rising to his feet, Kraig hung on to his earlobe like his life depended on it. "I promised Curt I would tell the story only once. We have an eccentric cast of characters telling it for me. Georg nearly made a fool of me. I invite him to explain why he used this evil to manipulate me into making a most regrettable arrangement. Georg, speak loudly enough for everyone to hear. Use your braggadocio voice, and don't omit one detail."

Clara stared at her knees and gripped her elbows. Kraig understood her gesture. *She's listening intently.* He studied his girls—all of them. He observed the puppets on Emmaline's fingers. Romeo and Juliet! My adventurous daughter tells the mocking tale from her spot in the audience. Would Georg understand the connection?

"My sweets, your Vati and brother question my wisdom and my intentions. I only seek to increase the assets of your Vati's land holdings and of the Gut Apfelhof community. In the hands of the Nickel brothers and myself, expect the pigeon enterprise to boost the revenue of your Vati's business and spread his name to Monte Carlo and beyond."

Before the braggart could utter another word, Kraig snapped his fingers in Georg's face. "What nerve you have addressing your lies directly to my daughter as though you love her and are doing this all for the sake of that love."

Clara's head rose just enough to peer upward at Georg.

All warmth was missing from his girl's dark chocolate eyes. "Georg, you have no poker face. Clara sees your true intentions. We all do. The Big Bad Wolff plays poker with marked cards and an arsenal of pigeons. What are you trying to pull?"

"This is the truth, Herr Reinhold. You and your daughter need me."

Jonas pressed himself right up to Georg's gut and grabbed a clump of the scoundrel's hair, giving it a jerk or two. "I'll tell them what you've done. Sit down and listen.

"Gerwig and Georg Wolff manipulated everyone. They suffered huge gambling losses over the years, beginning in the luxurious Kurhaus casino and spa. When our government passed laws prohibiting the gaming industry, men with substantial financial resources quickly moved their businesses to Monte Carlo. The Wolffs' addiction to the games grew.

They traveled to Monte Carlo. Their wagers grew and so did their losses."

The Wolffs' complexions turned as red as Riding Hood's cape. Visible beads of sweat covered their foreheads.

"You recently lost an even larger portion of your land, Gerwig. As a barrister, I am privileged to all legal records. They include the proof. You've fallen behind in submitting tax revenues. You had the Nickels place bets for Pastor Lange. He lost, too. What a pity for the pastor's sins to be exposed because the four of you schemed this sorry plan." Jonas twisted one point of his mustache and stared at the Wolffs. "Admit it. What a perfect setup."

"Sounds like pigeon poop is about to be slung." Curt settled back in his chair.

"Poop of their own making," Jonas addressed the Wolffs again. "We counted on your help shoveling out the mess. You didn't disappoint."

Georg attempted to bolt from the room but met with a barricade just outside the door. The Gut Apfelhof staff stood ready to serve him with justice of their own.

With a shove, Fritz and Jost turned Georg around to once again face those he had wronged.

Jonas cleared his throat. "You concocted your plan. Pastor Lange would forgive your huge debt and cover for you with the state. If he delivered Gut Herr Reinhold's daughter, Clara, as your wife, you'd keep his secret. You'd move closer to the Reinholds' fortune, and Clara would be the lovely ornament on your arm when convenient. Clara and Daniel love each other, despite their forbidden union. You counted it the ace Pastor Lange would play to win Clara's hand for you. The old rumor would resurface if Clara's castle-in-the-air romance with the carriage driver did not come to an end. Clara knows the rules for her class, making a marriage to the man she loves impossible. You threatened to expose the old cameo story and a juicy tale about Kraig being Daniel's Vater. Pressure grew for the arrangement binding your two families, and the lies spun like a roulette wheel with not one ounce of truth to any of them. The mis-told tale has caused enough pain already, and yet you only add more. You're disgusting."

Kraig stared at Georg's bright blue eyes. Tears gathering in Georg's eyes had entwined with the pompous lowlife's pride.

Jonas' oversized mustache twitched as he rubbed his chin. "Georg? Gerwig? Your next plan required raising pigeons for Monte Carlo on the Reinhold property and involving them in an industry they avoid. You sell the birds to the Tir aux Pigeons and keep the Nickels placing the pastor's wagers. After all, good clergy people don't take part in such activities. If they tried, the casino wouldn't grant them entrance."

A pin dropping from Rosa's sachet would be enough to break the eerie silence, but no one even took a breath.

"There's more." Curt signaled to Jonas that he needed a private conversation.

Jonas addressed the group. "Excuse us, please. No one is to leave. I believe Curt holds the last card."

His handkerchief soaked from wiping his sweaty brow, Curt tossed it to a maid as he walked outside with Jonas. "This information will embarrass more people than Georg. At least

I hope it embarrasses him. It angers me more than all we've already divulged."

"After what we've heard today, it's difficult imagining anything worse." Jonas twisted both ends of his mustache before reaching up to scratch his head.

"Clara and I recently discovered a fresh grave near the abandoned cottage. How ironic we call it abandoned. It's been the setting for several scenes in the past weeks." Curt divulged the ugly truth.

As his eyes widened to the size of the full moon, Jonas clasped his head. "What are you saying? Who? Why?"

"The baby was a fully formed human being, one too tiny to live outside of the womb."

"You know who the Mutter is?"

"I do. And the one who humiliated her and put her in such a compromised and embarrassing position."

Realization filled Jonas' eyes. "Georg."

"Daniel suspected something from a conversation he overheard. After the debacle Clara and her friend, Tilly, faced in the woods with Georg, Daniel and I pressed Rudi—Tilly's brother—for the truth. He's enraged with Georg. He promised his complete cooperation. He's counting on us for protection and justice for his family."

"We can promise him that. Tell me the rest."

"Georg forced himself on her at the gnome's cottage some months ago and threatened her when she became pregnant. If she didn't do what it took to restore her monthly time, he would blame Daniel publicly. Daniel's position as driver for our family would have been destroyed. And the repercussions for Tilly's family…" Curt could only conjecture the potential outcome for Tilly and her family. He would rather not entertain those thoughts. "Georg knew she wouldn't shame her family since it would draw horrible attention to herself. When Daniel and I spoke with her brother on Monday morning, he admitted their family would like Gerog dead." Curt kicked at the cobblestones. "Vati needs to know, but how do I reveal the facts without exposing the Mutter?"

"Does the grave remain as you found it?"

"It remains in the same location, but Clara and I reburied the baby more respectably."

"Do you need to say who? You've already spoken to Georg about this."

"Indeed, I have. He acted outraged I would accuse him of such, but he didn't deny it. The Mutter of the baby privately confessed all the details to my Oma. Oma is well-acquainted with my determination in this matter. I set out to prove to Vati that Georg is unsuitable for any woman, especially my sister. Oma suggested I make Georg talk."

"Go back in there. Ask him the right questions. Force him to admit to his heinous wrong. There was a penal code for rape established ten years ago."

"And there's a punishment?"

Jonas nodded. "Absolutely. If found guilty, he faces up to two years in prison."

"It would be difficult for a nobleman to be found at fault in a case with a commoner, I assume."

"Correct, but with the testimonies we heard today, a court will convict him."

"That's the best news I've heard today."

"Is Clara's friend nearby? Seeing Georg face consequences for his actions will bring her a measure of peace."

"She and her brother wait with Daniel in the carriage house. Give me a few moments to speak with them. I'm praying that when he sees them, Georg will buckle under the strain and confess."

"I'll inform the others you'll return shortly."

CURT AND RUDI entered the room, Tilly grasping their arms. Daniel guarded them from behind. Georg stared straight at them. He held a fist in front of his chest, cocked his head, and sneered. When Tilly's arm squeezed his tighter, Curt laid a reassuring hand on hers.

"Vati, I told you I would prove Georg's rancorous behavior to you. One of his indiscretions looms close to home. Tilly knows everyone in this room well, since she and Clara have been friends since childhood. She confided in Oma, and she bravely agreed for me to question Georg in front of all of you. See his jitters as I speak?"

Tilly covered her eyes. She left just enough space between her fingers to observe through the cracks. Tears burst from behind her hands, flooded her cheeks, and dripped down her cuffs. Rudi wrapped her in his arms.

"Is there proof of what I think you're saying?" Kraig bounced his knee and kneaded his earlobe.

"Clara and I found a tiny grave by the abandoned cottage. The place that has recently hosted several of Georg's foolish actions. Had it been the sad event of a miscarriage by a married woman, we have a special place in our cemetery for those little ones."

Gerwig jumped up and addressed his son. "You told me you took care of the problem! Not well enough!" Gerwig turned to face Kraig again. "My son embarrasses me further. He and I will be leaving."

"Whoa, Gerwig!" Jonas pushed him back down in his seat. "Your son forced himself on this poor girl and added additional threats. When she conceived, he planned to tell another lie if she didn't drink the pennyroyal tea. He would blame the baby on Daniel, compromising two of Clara's dearest friends. Georg, are you aware that by law you face up to two years of imprisonment for this?"

"No one will convict me. I have a name."

Jonas glared at the man. "Do you answer to the name Arrogance? You're so filled with it. *Pride goeth before destruction, and an haughty spirit before a fall.* In this case, it's your fall. With the testimonies we've heard today, I'll easily convince the courts of your guilt. We have already notified state authorities, and they're here now."

The uniformed officials had arrived just as Curt and Jonas spoke outside. Jonas had asked them to wait until he signaled he was ready for them.

Jonas moved to where he could speak with Daniel privately.

Moments later, Daniel showed the authorities in. They led Georg away in handcuffs.

~

Leaning toward her Vati, Clara held her breath as his hesitant steps brought him to her side. She floated in a strange place between disbelief and hopefulness.

Vati held her hand and drew circles on her thumbnail. "The Grimms' fairytales meet Shakespeare's tragedies. Even with Georg arrested, you and Daniel remain star-crossed lovers. Our social status and the rules are firm, but you are both very much alive and free to pursue future happiness." He bent on one knee and dug in his pocket, pulling out his handkerchief. He laid it in his hand. With the other hand, he carefully unfolded the cloth, revealing its treasure.

Holding a lemon drop up to Clara, he asked, "Will you forgive your foolish old Vati?"

"Does this mean?"

"Ja, Clara, it does. You're free of Georg."

"Then I'll forgive you. Of course, a whole handful of lemon drops..." Her radiant smile broke through weeks of accumulated pain.

Vati held her in his arms. "My wish is for you to stay right here forever with no lousy man ruining my little girl's life and happiness."

She dropped her right arm from around Vati and motioned the other family members and Tilly into a tight circle.

"Rosa, you're a faithful servant and friend to this family. Please join us too." Vati grabbed for her hand. "And where's Daniel?"

Herr Ettinger stood by the door. "He went with the other staff to watch the authorities haul Georg away. I'm joining them."

Vati nodded to his friend.

"Rosa, Daniel has always been like a son to me, a brother to my children. It has always grieved me that he hardly knew his own Vater. Your son is a good man. Like Curt and Wilhelm, like a son, he protects my interests."

Clara folded her hands under her chin and fixed what she hoped was her best pleading look at Vati. "What is it, Clara?"

"I beg to be excused, please. I have a message of my own that needs to be delivered to Georg before he leaves. I'll return quickly for all these hugs."

"Go on. I trust you'll be well protected."

"I will. While I'm gone, I trust all of you will assure Tilly God doesn't hate her, and neither do any of us in Gut Apfelhof."

WHEN THE AUTHORITIES thrust Georg into their wagon, he kicked like a girl, unsuccessfully fighting their brawn.

Clara approached the wagon just as it was about to pull away. Clara had come out here with an ugly message in mind. Could she forgive Georg instead? She had pondered Hannah's intention with the rewritten verses and Rosa's rebuke. She considered her conversation with Daniel about joy and endurance. If she didn't forgive, would she ever truly be free?

Clara's hand rested on Georg's arm. "Because of your behavior, I've learned to pray for my enemies. Thank you, Georg." *And thank you, God, Your way is far better than mine.*

As they drove out of sight, Clara slowly turned toward the most handsome face on earth and fell into Daniel's outstretched arms.

He lifted her chin and caught her gaze. "I followed you to be sure you were safe from him, like I promised you long ago. I wish this counted as more than a brotherly hug."

With her hands pressed gently against his cheeks, Clara touched her smile to his lips.

As she drew away, she spotted Vati. She unlaced her fingers from Daniel's.

"We're celebrating Erntedank this weekend. You two have responsibilities to tend to. Go on about them. Stop dallying in the road." Vati kissed her on the cheek.

THE HEAVINESS of their discovery settled over Clara's heart like an albatross. "Daniel, could we hold a real funeral for Tilly's baby?"

"Here she comes with Curt and Rudi. We'll ask her."

"I'd like that very much." A rosy hue colored Tilly's throat.

"We'll use this to mark the grave." Daniel pulled a small, intricately carved wooden cross from his pocket.

"Marcus?" Clara asked.

"Oma learned a few things around that fire." Curt shrugged.

"And we learned a lot from Rudi, too." Daniel handed the cross to Tilly. "Curt carved it. I added the name. Marcus is his name, right?"

Tilly beamed. "The name Marcus implies honor, courage, bravery, and strength—qualities far different from Georg's."

"I love that, Tilly." Clara hugged her friend.

Tilly, Clara, Daniel, Curt, and Rudi strolled the path to the old cottage. Autumn wildflowers had sprung up between the now sleepy sunflowers. Tilly pressed the cross into the earth between them. Daniel gently cradled Clara's hand while Curt prayed.

"Most loving and Heavenly Father, You bade the little children to come unto You. You laid Your hands on them and blessed them. We thank You that You welcomed Tilly's precious Marcus to Your side. We trust You to take the very best care of him until the day comes when You reunite him with his Mutter. We look forward to the heavenly home You prepare for us. Comfort Tilly with Your peace and assurance of Your love. Amen."

Clara glanced up as Curt said Amen. Why would Curt have ended the prayer with a squeeze to Tilly's shoulder? He had confided in Clara about anticipating Lillian's visit and courting her. It wouldn't be the same wound, but Tilly had endured enough. She prayed Tilly considered the gesture as only an expression of friendship. "I'm happy we buried your baby properly, my friend."

"You've all been like angels to me today. Danke."

"If you experienced God's love for you today, then I am grateful to have been like an angel." Curt smiled.

With two fingers, Tilly pressed her shy smile. "I love the cross."

"Carving it supplied a balm to my saddened heart, too." Curt moved aside and stood with the others, giving Tilly a few moments alone.

Daniel plucked a wildflower and tucked it in Clara's curls, then kissed her cheek.

The men headed back, leaving Clara to linger alone with Tilly.

"When you feel the devil's lies that you're unworthy in God's eyes, read Romans 8." Clara squeezed Tilly's hand.

"The words of that chapter are treasures. I'm memorizing all thirty-nine verses. Your Oma suggested it."

Clara and Tilly recited the first verses together. *"There is therefore now no condemnation to them which are in Christ Jesus, who walk not after the flesh, but after the Spirit. For the law of the Spirit of life in Christ Jesus hath made me free from the law of sin and death."*

Until they reached the path leading to Tilly's home, she and Clara walked arm in arm. "Thank you for suggesting this little service. I've embarrassed myself and my family, but sharing the burden lightened the boulder in my chest."

"Tilly, don't feel ashamed or embarrassed. You're not responsible for Georg's actions. Did he force the tea on you, too?"

She nodded. "It was awful. He found me. He took me back by the cottage and held me down, forcing the liquid down my throat. He punched me in the stomach, too. Then he left."

Flames licked at Clara's insides. Her stomach was scorched by the knowledge of Georg's ever more vile conduct. "An hour ago, I forgave him for all my family and I had endured at his hands."

"It was the right thing to do, Clara."

"A brave thing for you to say. We need another verse to ponder." Clara picked up a stone along their path. "I am hearing this one from the deep reservoir of those Rosa shares. It's from Ezekiel. *A new heart also will I give you, and a new spirit will I put within you: and I will take away the stony heart out of your flesh, and I will give you an heart of flesh."*

"Even though I realize the impossibility, I pray for you and Daniel. He loves you too, you know."

Clara smiled. "See you Sunday at church. We do have much to be thankful for."

Chapter Thirty-Four

SATURDAY, *1 October 1881*

"I've always loved Erntedank." Clara gazed upon the autumn-colored flowers and ribbons decorating their wagon. "Residents adding the first fruits of their harvests always holds me spellbound. Pride for our community swells within me."

"Your smile and enthusiasm melt my heart." Choosing one last cheery yellow chrysanthemum, Daniel handed it to Clara. "Add this one to the wagon, and we're ready for all the joys Erntedank brings. With all that's transpired over the past month, I feared to dream we could do this together again."

"And I feared looking back on our lifelong dream of doing much more than a Thanksgiving cart together. Star-crossed lovers we are, Daniel. Our love and nobility's rules reign equally, but the tie breaks in favor of the rules."

"You know my heart aches over our troubles." Daniel took her into his arms and turned their faces toward the cottage. "We make a great team, you and me. What if we fix up the cottage?"

"You mean a special hideaway of our own?"

"Exactly what I mean, my lovely lady." He held her from behind with his hands around her waist and laid his cheek to hers. "You're very quiet."

"May I linger in the joy and contentment of this moment before I must remind myself again there's no future for us. I keep asking God why. He created everyone equal in His eyes."

With a finger pressed to her lips, Daniel quieted her doubts. "Not now, my lovely lady." He hummed a sprightly tune. Clara added her lilting soprano, singing the words to "Frühlingsstimmen."

Daniel turned her to face him. "One, two, three, and one, two, three." He led them through the waltz's slides and turns. With a spin, he brought them closer. His lips rested against her cheek. He whispered, "This moment belongs to us. Strauss' *Voices of Spring* ignites a joyous spark."

"Sadly, position and circumstance douse this delightful glow." Her arms drooped at her sides. "Before I weep again…" She pointed to the wagon.

"It'll be my pleasure to wipe your tears away any time." Daniel ran his palm across her cheek, drawing out her smile.

"Danke for the dance, and danke for inviting me to work with you on the Erntedank preparations."

"The wagon looks wonderful because of your touches. Everyone will love the turquoise and rust accents on the horses' leather accessories. This wagon's my favorite of all we've decorated."

"I believed Vati's decision would tarnish my memories of this Erntedank forever, and in many ways it will."

"Cherish this part. Our special moment."

"Every day married to him would've held a painful reminder of our dance and the joy I wished for you and me. Vati and the law stopped Georg's games, but I hurt so much for Tilly, and our situation remains unchanged."

"Run away with me. Bring Tilly with us."

"And where would we go? Vati has eyes everywhere? The state watches every move he and his noble family make. They scrutinize every action we take. No life exists for you and me anywhere in Germany."

"We can join Megs and Gus in Chicago."

"Vati loves you like his own son. I've heard him say it many times—even today. He takes great care of you and your Mutter. But he'd never pay your way to America, especially with me." Clara smiled but shook her head. "Impossible."

"Make a plan to go alone. Visit Megs. I'll join you later."

"You'd give me so much hope? Megs suggested the same solution. Moving across the ocean without respect for our parents leaves us without the opportunity to return, even for a visit. Vati would disown me, and I'd miss my family so much."

"Promise me you'll think about it."

"I promise, but I can't imagine making the move. We're out of time today." She leaned into his side. "We need to move the cart to the carriage house. I'll sit on the seat beside you for the short trip and keep the love glowing and fresh for a few lingering moments. Our lives return to ordinary days on Monday, and Vati will have plans to keep you busy."

"Shh. Let's not borrow tomorrow's troubles."

Clara's heart suddenly felt hollow, and flutters filled her tummy. Could she give up her family for love? Romeo and Juliet had died for theirs. Could she go across the ocean if she knew Daniel would follow? She chewed her lower lip until words finally formed. "I agree!"

"Agree to what?" Daniel reined in the horses. His cheeks puffed out with his next inhale. He blew out the breath and stared at Clara.

"We have played this game way too long, my love. The old cottage or America. Either one is fine with me as long as we're together."

"You mean it?"

"I do, with all my heart."

He cupped her face and laced his fingers into her curls. Their hearts beat in unison, and their lips met. Their mouths softened, and she melted into his deepening kiss. The reverberations of love throbbed through her whole being. Even her curls tingled.

Chapter Thirty-Five

GUT APFELHOF, *Erntedank Sunday, 2 October 1881*

"GERWIG. GUTEN MORGEN." Kraig scowled at his neighbor. "At least it promised to be a good morning, a splendid start to a beautiful day until you showed up with a wagon filled with pigeons."

"Our two families agreed over a month ago to celebrate Erntedank together." Gerwig bounced off the cart seat and flashed a wide smile.

"Our agreement preceded Thursday's public revelation of your son's and your misdeeds. You have nerve. I assumed you understood you're no longer welcome in our home."

"How will our family celebrate Erntedank? Our staff helped yours with the preparations."

"Did you apprise your wife of what happened here a few days ago? Or did you feed her a tall tale about Georg's new residence? And our Mamsell sent your staff in another direction about Erntedank plans."

Gerwig's face reddened.

"You've no respect for your wife either. Whatever you choose to tell her, your time has run out. Erntedank begins in a few hours. I anticipate you'll tell her more lies. Regardless of how you handle the situation, you Wolffs are not welcome to join us for any festivities."

"I'm not easily discouraged."

"Really? Barrister Ettinger spent the week here. I'll call him out here now, and I'll send another of my men to bring the authorities again. Would you like to join your son in jail? Take your birds and get off my property."

"I'll be delivering these pigeons to the church as our contribution."

"Of course. Bring your offerings to the church. Has Dinkelhof suffered a dismal harvest this year, giving you an excuse to bring pigeons?" Kraig clenched his teeth. "Take them to church, but your family isn't welcome at the Reinholds' party."

~

Erntedank Parade, *Sunday, 2 October 1881*

A fluttery sensation swirled in Clara's middle as she observed the crowds arriving. Tongues wagged oohs and ahs in praise of the festive job on the wagon. Daniel took her hand in his and raised them high. The masters of the creation took a bow.

Baskets filled with the bounty of the land—apples, pumpkins, potatoes, grains, and more—were handed up to Daniel and the other coachmen standing on the wagon. They placed them with Clara's directions. The presentation gleamed.

Those with their own smaller donkey carts lined up behind the fancy one. Clara waved to the ladies from her Bible Class group carrying Erntekrone. Excitement and chatter about the poles bearing braided grains and decorated with ribbons and paper flowers filled the air. The parade moved slowly. A few walked before and behind.

The crowd lifted their voices in praise all the way to the church. *"Nun danket alle Gott mit Herzen, Mund und Händen."* Now thank we all our God with heart and hand and voices.

Clara hugged her sisters. "My heart grows and my spirit soars every time I hear that hymn, a perfect tribute to the God of the harvest and of our lives. One of my favorite parts of this day."

Huge Erntekranze, garlands of grain woven into fancy shapes, adorned the heavy bronze doors of the church and beckoned the grateful worshippers inside.

Clara beamed as children from her Sunday school Class led their parents to the altar bearing the harvest fare. Many of these families had barely enough for themselves, yet they had come with food to share with those who had even less. She prayed a blessing on each one who came and each gift they'd brought. She asked for blessings over those who would benefit from their generosity. A few inside this church today had proven less than friends, but Clara blessed them anyway. "Bless everyone in Gut Apfelhof."

The ingathering complete, Pastor Lange welcomed the congregants now settled in the pews. "We gather to celebrate this special day of thanksgiving to God. Each of you contributed generously. Your baskets of vegetables and grains promise meals for hungry souls."

Dancing reflections from the stained glass created sparkles on the harvest. Acolytes lit the candles, and Pastor Lange began the service. "In the name of the Father and of the Son and of the Holy Ghost."

And the people said, "Amen."

More singing and more liturgy followed. Pastor Lange climbed the seven steps to the high pulpit from which he would bring the sermon. "This has been an unusual week for me. I'm grateful today to begin the new week with thanksgiving.

"Our text for today is Colossians 3:17. *And whatsoever ye do in word or deed, do all in the name of the Lord Jesus, giving thanks to God and the Father by him.* When our actions deviate from loving deeds done in the name of the Lord Jesus, they're not behavior to be proud of but behavior often accompanied by dire consequences."

Would he admit to the consequences of his own behavior? She would need help to forgive him for the pain his actions caused Mutti, Vati, and Rosa. Was it fair for her to complain to the Lord about the pain they caused her, too? She thanked God for leading Pastor to preach from this Scripture today. She thanked Him that by His Spirit she had freedom to speak and do every word and every deed in the name of His Son, Jesus. She thanked Him, especially for forgiveness and salvation. Her behaviors over these past months had not always been a good example either. Clara continued her personal meditation on the Scripture of the day. She considered its impact on all that had transpired in her twenty-six years of life.

When the pastor said, "Amen," she stood and gratefully acknowledged his next words. *The peace of God, which passeth all understanding, keep your hearts and minds through Christ Jesus.*

Communion was distributed, and the service ended with organ music and voices lifting the notes and words of the doxology high into the rafters and the heavens.

When her Vati shook Pastor Lange's hand, a strange look passed between them. Vati stepped to the side and waited.

"Mutti, see the questioning look on Vati's face? What is happening?"

"Things your Vati will handle."

"Another secret story?" Clara whispered her question. "It only took me twenty-six years to learn the one about your hand."

Lydia pressed a finger to her lips. "Shh. Many ears surround us, meine Kind."

"HEAD BACK HOME. Welcome our guests. Assure them I'm coming right behind you." Without any care for who saw them, Kraig kissed his wife on the lips, then faced Pastor Lange.

The pastor looked around. "The congregation has headed to the party. So, what's troubling you, Kraig?"

"Pastor, you seem too jovial for a man whose tricky hand got caught."

"There's a party to attend, right? Good reason to be happy."

"What about the consequences of your actions? Thursday's revelations placed a lot of guilt on you. Your devious behavior sets a pathetic example for our community."

Pastor Lange shrugged. "We're all sinners saved by God's grace."

"You aimed darting glances in my direction during your sermon. The text you chose, your quivery hands, and your cracking voice while you spoke confirmed what God clearly showed me this morning. You directed Gerwig to deliver those pigeons to my home."

"Kraig, my friend, God welcomes his pigeon offerings."

"I trusted we put the past behind us this week. Those pigeons belong in the past. You'll take them to the poor for dinner, and we'll not mention them again."

"Ja, I plan to."

"I'm grateful people will benefit from them after all the trouble they brought on my family and on your reputation. If you and the Wolffs plot another stunt like it, I'll have Jonas report everything."

"You mean you haven't?"

"Nein. Except for Georg's crime against Tilly, we confined our knowledge of the many evil deeds done to the people present. I won't be sharing the details with anyone else unless I'm given cause. And they would be the truth—not rumors."

Lange's eyes moved upward. "A prayer of thanks in my heart then."

"Be sure to remind those Nickel brothers we know about their shenanigans and won't tolerate more from them either."

"You'll be thankful I decided to cease all communication with them—in person or through others."

"I'm not sure why I should, but I'll trust your word, Pastor."

"Danke. Trusting my word couldn't be easy considering my contribution to your family's troubles."

"I forgive you, but I admit I wanted to shame you publicly."

"It's what I deserve. Again, danke, Kraig. You're the more honorable man. What do you require of me to make amends?"

Kraig handed Pastor Lange an envelope. "Open it."

Staring at its contents, Pastor flinched and turned away. He shook his head slowly and pivoted back toward Kraig. His pensive eyes studied the man's face. "Did you discuss this with Gerwig?"

"Nein. I'm allowing you the honor of presenting him with the good news. The Wolffs' tax worries are over. Dinkelhof now belongs to Gut Apfelhof. Ettinger did his due diligence. It is legal and binding."

"Bearing this news to him is asking much of me."

"You'll concoct the perfect plan."

A sheepish grin crept up the pastor's face. "Anything else?"

Jonas joined them and motioned to the church officials he had invited to accompany him. "As a matter of fact, your superior here has more to say."

Reverend Biedermann's brow furrowed. He eyed Lange narrowly and drove out a disgruntled sigh. "Elmer Lange, word has reached us in Stuttgart." He tugged the stole from the pastor's shoulders. "I have been sent to defrock you."

"But you said you didn't tell anyone?" Lange's face blazed. "Kraig..."

"Kraig didn't tell on you. Jonas alerted us a few days ago. We allowed the Erntedank parade and service to go on as planned for the community's sake. You won't be joining the party, however. You'll be coming with us."

"And I'll take this." Jonas retrieved the contract. "It should only take me an extra half hour to deliver this to Gerwig personally. Save me some food."

"It'll prove difficult now, Pastor, but your apology to Clara would mean much to me. She has looked up to you since she was a child, and she's hurting. Maybe you could find it in your heart to send her a kind note." Kraig waited patiently.

Lang swallowed hard. "Apologies to women do not come easily for men, but Jesus always treated them well. I'll do it." A winsome smile and a handshake sealed the agreement. "I'll pray you find a husband for Clara. One who'll make everyone happy. Especially Clara."

Kraig's breath hitched in his throat. "I like that idea."

Chapter Thirty-Six

GUT APFELHOF, *Sunday afternoon, 2 October 1881*

"I'M DROOLING over this spread of tasty dishes." Clara studied her fingers. "If soiled gloves wouldn't give me away, I'd snitch a bite of Dora's Rouladen now."

When the partiers returned from church, the aromas of the feast rose to meet them. Dora and Henry missed the Erntedank service again, but they spread a fancy feast across the tables. Apfelkuchen, cherry quarks, and Black Forest cakes prepared by the women of their happy little community surrounded the main dishes and delectable sides.

"I'm happy for the Bratkartoffeln, those fried potatoes Dora promised to serve with the roasted goose and the spicy applesauce. Yummy!" Emmaline inhaled deeply of all the flavorful scents surrounding them.

"I love the bread, and what a treat to have several varieties with the main meal." Hannah reached over to snatch one of the Wecken. "I hope I don't get caught savoring this dinner roll before Vati says grace."

"Leave enough to go with the Kurbissuppe." With a tsk of her finger toward Hannah, Emmaline licked her lips. "It gladdens me someone had the idea to bring pumpkins to Germany. It would be sad for only Americans to enjoy this scrumptious soup."

Clara took a step back and crossed her arms, then lifted a finger to her chin. "Do you think Megs and Gus celebrate Erntedank in Chicago?"

"You could visit her and find out." Emmaline winked.

Clara's heart smiled on the inside. Would they be surprised when that happened—maybe sooner than anyone had thought?

Vati whistled for the partiers' attention. "Danke to all of you Gut Apfelhof residents for your kindnesses and loyalty. I'm the luckiest baron in all of Germany."

When the thunderous applause died down, Vati continued. "We offer the common table prayer together. *Komm, Herr Jesu."*

The thankful community joined in. *Be our guest and bless what You have given us.*

"My family and I are grateful our Heavenly Father walks among us today and every day."

Curt led Lillian to the food table.

"Dare I believe I'll have grandchildren one day?" Vati glanced across the crowd gathered in his yard.

"I heard that." Clara lay her head on Vati's shoulder. "Don't expect them from me, not for a very long time. Maybe from Curt."

"Maybe, but I'm not counting any of my children out for this blessing."

Everyone ate heartily. The musicians tuned their instruments, and rollicking polkas and tender waltzes bolstered the party spirit to the sky. Vati twirled his wife and his daughters. He then reached out to his Mutter to discover her in step with the viscount's widowed Vater. He had accompanied the Denzlers to Gut Apfelhof.

Clara winked at her Oma. Her face glowed with pleasure.

Brigitte bounced between the guests, gathering tummy rubs from all. Clara scooped her up and spun their way to a corner of the yard where Daniel stood surveying the merriment.

"My happy tail-wagger would like to ask you for the next dance."

"With or without my lovely lady?"

Clara fluttered her eyelashes.

"You enchant me with your teasing. And right where your Vati can spot us? You wish me to lose my position as his trusted driver."

"Duck behind the garden wall then. Michael and Minna, and Luisa and her husband happily waltz and join in the high-stepping polka rounds. While I am so very happy for their joyous unions, I'm also jealous of their happiness."

Daniel guided Clara behind the wall. With her head resting on his chest, they swayed to the music. "How long until they miss us?"

"If Brigitte's happy arffs don't betray us, we have one dance at least."

"Like a fairytale, my lovely lady, we'll write our story with a happy ending." Daniel lifted a wooden object from its hiding place behind a perky holly bush and presented it to Clara. "My gift to you—a special box to save our coins until we accumulate enough for fare to America for both of us."

"You carved the sunflowers." She traced the intricate lines in the wood. "They're beautiful." She swallowed hard. "Danke. I would love for us to make the trip together."

He smiled like the expanse of it could reach clear to America's shore. "It's still a few days away, but will you meet me at the cottage Thursday afternoon?"

"How do I know Vati won't be here and see us?"

"Your Vati and Curt have a meeting in Stuttgart keeping them away from Gut Apfelhof for at least a week. I drive them to the train in the morning. Thursday afternoons are still my time."

"Does Vati and Curt's business involve a certain blonde-haired lady—the Honorable Lillian Denzler?"

"Why do you ask? And you didn't answer my question."

"Ja, I'll meet you there, and I'll bring Emmaline's finger puppets and a volume of Brothers Grimm for inspiration."

"We've been compared to a couple from a Shakespeare tragedy. You're bringing the Grimms' book. Are you sure? Georg lives in one of their stories."

"We'll find a happier example. How about *The Frog Prince*?"

"Ribbet! You see me as a frog? Less dangerous than a wolf, I suppose."

"I see you as my prince."

"Remember when the princess reconsidered her promise, her Vater encouraged her to keep her word to the frog."

"Vati would disown me before he pushed me to keep my promise to you. Think of which different story we could choose."

"A different story for what?" Curt poked his head around the corner.

Startled, Clara jumped out of Daniel's arms.

Daniel pulled her back to himself. "We're tired of tales about Red Riding Hood and the Big Bad *Wolff*. We need a new one."

Curt took a step toward his friend and whispered in Daniel's ear.

"Danke! I knew we could count on you."

Clara shifted her eyes between Daniel and her twin.

Curt pressed a finger to his lips. "Shh. Ja. I heard the whole thing. All you need is a government official." He leaned out from their hiding spot just long enough to signal Onkel Martin to join them.

"All that's required for a legal union is a civil ceremony." Onkel Martin's eyes crinkled as he smiled at Clara and Daniel. "Shall we?"

She hadn't expected this. What would it mean to really be married to Daniel? If she agreed, her world would tip upside down. Was this the right thing to do? Her heart raced to keep up with her thoughts. "Onkel Martin, you can do that?"

He nodded and sprang a grin.

Then, ja." Clara beamed at Daniel.

"That's the best news of a lifetime." Daniel shook Onkel Martin's hand.

Promises made. Blessings pronounced. Without another wasted moment, "and now, Daniel, you may kiss your bride."

Curt reached deep into his jacket pocket and dropped a few golden marks into Clara's box. "May it add up quickly but not too quickly. Your absence will leave a big, empty, impossible-to-fill hole at Gut Apfelhof."

"Danke, Curt. Always like a brother to me." Daniel hugged his best friend. "And where is Lillian? A special lady to have at your side, my friend."

"Emmaline and Hannah whisked her away for a few minutes. Probably tending to womanly things."

The three friends locked arms just as they had done when they were little Kinder. Brigitte ran in circles around them as they rejoined the partiers.

Chapter Thirty-Seven

GUT APFELHOF, *Thursday, 6 October 1881*

DANIEL PACED the floor of the once-abandoned cottage. She had promised to meet him today.

Clara bounded through the wide-open door and ran straight into his arms. "I love you, Daniel Becker."

"And I love you, Clara Becker." He led her to the sofa at the back of the cottage. Sunlight streamed in the window where they sat. "I have more news. I'm eager to see your face when I share it."

"I love surprises as long as they're good ones."

With a teasing smile on his face, Daniel brushed the ever-stray curl from Clara's. "First things first. I need a kiss."

"I'll never argue with you about those."

His lips found hers easily—tenderly at first, then ever deeper.

Daniel broke the lock between them. "Did you bring the sunflower box?"

"I hid it here in the cottage while you drove Vati and Curt to the train." She wandered to the kitchen cabinet where she'd placed it on Monday. "I couldn't risk someone finding it and asking questions."

"We'll travel to America in spring, the perfect season for love and new beginnings."

"Will we have enough saved by then? We must keep our wonderful news a secret from everyone. We can't ask for help from Vati, and he'd never agree."

Daniel shrugged, then opened the sunflower box. He added the twenty marks he'd saved to the twenty marks Curt contributed. "We have forty marks already."

"And we need sixty just for third-class ship fare. And that's just the beginning. We'll have so many expenses along the way and in establishing our new home."

"Don't worry, my lovely lady. I have orders for several sunflower boxes already."

"Who ordered them?"

"Lillian did, for all her friends. Twenty in all at three marks each."

Clara's eyes flew wide. Staccato-like gasps hitched in her breath. "She did?" She pressed her teeth over her lower lip.

"She promised to gather orders from members of her book circle, too. And one more thing." Daniel held up an official-looking, neatly folded piece of paper. "Remember when Curt pulled me aside Sunday?"

"He was whispering secrets to you. I hope it's another good surprise."

They unfolded the parchment together.

"Our marriage certificate." The paper crinkled in her shaky hand. "I'm so nervous, fearing I'll wake up and discover this is all a dream rather than a miraculous answer to our prayers."

"It's God's miraculous answer, my lovely lady. A dream to last a lifetime."

Daniel caressed her shoulders before allowing his hands to move tenderly to her cheeks. He traced his thumbs across her brows. Their lips met again, igniting the fireworks of their love.

The End

Author's Notes

My grandmother shared a few vague facts about her life. Regretfully, I was much too young and naïve to know the questions to ask to learn more. I know she would have happily answered them. She's been gone over five decades now. What I've pieced together from a few family members and a little research, her mother (my great-grandmother) was the daughter of a wealthy baron in Southwest Germany. She despised the man he had chosen for her, and she was in love with the carriage driver. One of her grandsons confirmed that much to be true. Over the last twenty-plus years, a few additional details have emerged—enough to inspire this series. Inspire is the keyword. The story is my imagining of what might have been.

Except as noted below, resemblances to people and places are unintentional. The series is a work of fiction.

First crafted in 1875, Romeo y Julieta cigars went on to earn many gold medals a few years later. In the story, Georg would have traveled to Cuba or known someone who did and brought them to him. By 1885, the company's owner traveled extensively throughout Europe and the Americas, and his cigars became highly sought after by the very wealthy. Some of the gold medal awards are still depicted on the bands of the brand's cigars today. Churchill's iconic cigar was often a Romeo y Julieta. The cigar was named for Shakespeare's characters.

Breuninger Department Store was among the first and most successful department stores in Europe. It opened in Stuttgart on March 1, 1881, and currently has eleven stores across Germany.

Hotel Westminster remains open in Paris today. It may or may not have had fireplaces in its rooms. For the sake of the story, I included them.

Fashion designer Charles Frederick Worth's showroom, Maison Worth, was located in the fashion district near the Hotel Westminster. Sarah Bernhardt was an important client of Worth's. I have no knowledge of either of their personalities or specific situations. That Sarah visited a fine dressmaker in Chicago and encouraged Worth's attention to her designs is highly unlikely but a fictional tidbit that fits the story.

Pierre Sajou's haberdashery, Maison Sajou, remained open in Paris' Sentier District for decades. It has an interesting history. As with many businesses during the last few years, the main store has now been closed.

The Tuileries Gardens, the statue of Renommée riding a horse, Pegasus, the Louvre, and the churches mentioned in Paris were part of the Parisian landscape at the time this story is set. The Palais Garnier's inaugural performance was on January 15, 1875. A soprano fell ill, and selections from Faust and Hamlet were omitted from the performance.

Fein Company has long been known for its high-quality power tools. In addition, Wilhelm Fein incorporated the horseshoe magnet into the design for the telephone. His concept was the one used in telephones for years. Fein Company installed the phone system in Barcelona between 1882 and 1885.

Schinderhannes, a notorious outlaw in Germany, masterminded one of the biggest crime sprees in the country's history. The legends conjured fear for many travelers long after his death.

Francois Blanc, referred to as The Magician of Monte Carlo, successfully operated many casinos in the area, including Monte Carlo on the French Riviera. The luxurious Kurhaus in Baden-Baden in the Black Forest was closed during a time when gambling was outlawed in Germany. The money and the clientele moved to other locations, primarily Monte Carlo. Monte Carlo's opulence was said to have far exceeded that of the Kurhaus.

Good luck pig figurines, gnomes, the Bleigessen game, and birthday parties are a part of German culture. Germans were the first to introduce birthday cakes. Among the games played at parties, Charades was played as a game with spoken clues such as rhymes long before it became an acting game.

Jack-in-the-box toys were invented in Germany in the 1500s.

Apfelhof is a fictitious community. Crailsheim had a train station in the 1880s, and I envisioned it as the nearest railway station to Gut Apfelhof. There may have been an inn by the station, but it is a fictional one in the story.

The reasons women throughout history have chosen abortion are the same as today. Inconvenience. Too many children already. Financial hardships. Rape. The belief was held for centuries that until a woman felt the baby move (quickening), a baby was not considered to be alive. Beliefs about this were in transition at the time of this story, but to "bring back menses" up until quickening was still an acceptable practice. It was accomplished by several means, some safer than others. Pennyroyal tea was one of them.

Discussion Questions

1. A theme of forgiveness runs through this story. How did forgiving those who wronged them bring freedom to the ones wronged?
2. Not only did Georg treat Clara terribly time and time again since she was a young teen, but he was also in on the schemes manipulating Vati to promise him Clara's hand in marriage. After learning the truth and receiving Vati's apology, Clara thanked Georg for helping her learn to pray for her enemies. Would you have done the same?
3. Reverend Lange, the Nickel Brothers, and the Wolffs all had excuses for the gossip, blackmail, and lies that wounded the Reinhold family. Why did they each believe they were justified in their actions? In what ways have you experienced similar reckonings either in your personal life or in someone else's actions toward you?
4. God's Word clearly shows us that all are created equal in His eyes. How do you believe Jesus would have reacted toward the nobility and their rules? Why? Are

you tempted in your own life to see some as more worthy than others? In what ways?

5. Family is very important to the Reinholds, Rosa, and Daniel. Clara and Daniel decide to act against the rules in the end, knowing their marriage could be easily annulled, or one or both of them could be sent away and never see each other or their families again. Did they make the best decision? Why or why not?
6. As much as she was committed to Daniel, agreeing to marry him was a difficult decision for Clara. What would you have done in her shoes? Keep in mind the time period and prevailing attitudes toward women.

Acknowledgments

As a child, I dreamed of flying around on a magic carpet, collecting stories to write. The culmination of that dream stretched beyond my grasp for decades. But our amazing God knows our deepest desires, He remembers, and He equips us for them in His perfect timing. I have felt His presence, His guidance, and His love throughout the writing of *Tangled Promises* and in visions for the sequels. Just like God always does, He showed up in some of the most unexpected ways. My highest thanksgiving and praise to Him for the precious gift of His Son, for salvation, for the Holy Spirit that encourages and inspires us, and for every beautiful gift that comes from Him.

Many of His blessings along the journey came through family and friends. Thank you to my husband, Steve. For years he's teased (encouraged) me in his own special way to write my novel. And here it is. You'll find his creative genius when you visit my website. Thank you to our children and grandchildren for your constant love and encouragement. Rachel and Paul, David and Amy, Mikah, Emerson, Isaac, Mary, and Mel, your lives are a testimony to God's love and faithfulness.

Johnnie Alexander, Patricia Bradley, Candace West, and Shannon Vannatter. You were among the first who saw beyond my fledgling attempts. This book would not have happened without your encouragement and expertise.

American Christian Fiction Writers (ACFW) Memphis Chapter, you trusted me as your president for two years while I was a newbie to fiction writing. I am so grateful our group is a safe place to share, grow, and celebrate together.

Ladies of Hope, New Hope Women's Class, and my Huddle Up Writers (My Book Therapy), you have all held me and this project in your prayers. Becky Yauger, your daily prayers for each of us in our huddle are an amazing source of strength.

Writing means research trips for an author, right? I was eager to visit the community where my great-grandmother lived. A friend here in the States grew up in a nearby community in Germany. She knew and lived the culture and the language. What a blessing. We planned the trip. And then COVID-19. With plans canceled, I will be forever grateful for the hours she spent helping me learn about the area, the customs, the history, and more, including switching her computer's keyboard to a German one so we could learn more about my great-grandmother's specific community. She even found a photo of what we believe to be the family home. The name of the community will remain anonymous. Gut Apfelhof and Gut Dinkelhof are fictional. I've done my best to portray the people and the culture accurately. Thank you, Tanja Hodges, for your time, interest, and the long lunches.

Gladys Strickland, virtual assistant extraordinaire. I miss your creativity and dedication but wish you all the best with your own writing journey.

Shannon and Liz, your editing made the story sparkle. Thank you.

About the Author

Lynn is the great-great granddaughter of a real-life baron from southwest Germany. Snippets of her family's story inspire her fiction writing.

Following in her grandmother's footsteps, Lynn sewed for the public—everything from adorable children's outfits to bridal and formal wear. She and her artist husband, Steve, created The Lynn'n Butterfly Collection of counted-cross-stitch leaflets.

In 2007, Lynn became a certified reflexologist, and *Footsteps in Eden* was born. Lynn's touch-therapy skills bring relaxation to her clients one pair of feet at a time.

Jasmine, the resident feline, runs the place, while Lynn combines her passions and her heritage –

Stepping through Time, Stitching Stories of Faith

Your reviews are the best way to support authors. Have you enjoyed Tangled Promises? I would be forever grateful if you take a few minutes to share your thoughts. Even a sentence or two make a world of difference.

Here are a few places where you can leave reviews:

Goodreads

Bookbub

Amazon

Come along with me as I continue on this writing adventure.

My website: https://lynnuwatson.com

Subscribe to my newsletter – Inklings from My Pen

https://lynnuwatson.com/subscribe

Join my Facebook readers' group – Coffee, Kuchen, & Good Books

https://www.facebook.com/groups/1108709330081009

Follow me

Facebook: https://www.facebook.com/lynnuwatsonwriter

Goodreads: https://www.goodreads.com/author/show/16289814.Lynn_U_Watson

Instagram: https://www.instagram.com/lynnuwatson/

Book Bub: https://www.bookbub.com/profile/lynn-u-watson

I would love to hear from you. I can be reached by email: Lynn@LynnUWatson.com

facebook.com/lynnuwatsonwiter

x.com/lynnuwatson

instagram.com/lynnuwatson

bookbub.com/profile/lynn-u-watson

pinterest.com/lynnuwatson

amazon.com/stores/Lynn-U.-Watson/author/B01N4N-H1OA?b

Books by Lynn U. Watson

COFFEE COTTAGE INSPIRATIONAL COLLECTION FOR WOMEN

The Essence of Courage: Cultivating the Fruit of the Spirit in Solomon's Locked Garden and in Your Heart (Book 1)

The Essence of Joy: Filling Your Heart with the Aromas of Jesus' Nativity (Book 2)

The Essence of Humility: Live and Love Like Jesus (Book 3)

PROMISED DESTINY SERIES

Tangled Promises (Book 1)

Frayed Promises (Book 2) – 2025

Planted Promises (Book 3) – Date to be announced

Tangled Promises Prologue

Tangled Promises Prologue

TANGLED PROMISES BONUS SHORT STORY

LYNN U. WATSON

GUT APFELHOF, Reinhold Estate, *Württemberg, Germany, May 12, 1871*

Their three-story half-timber house and surrounding gardens provided the perfect backdrop for the twins' party. "Time for Charades!" Clara jumped to her feet with the first clue.

"Song title. Two words.

First word:

Let me tell you a pretty story

About painting a morning glory."

"Morning glories are blue!" Tilly shouted from the blanket spread beneath the giant oak tree where she was seated with the other girls.

"You guessed correctly, Tilly. Perhaps my clues need to be more difficult?"

"The rest of us may not be as clever as Tilly," Curt, Clara's twin, replied. It's my birthday, too. I'd like a chance to prove I am learned."

"Boys against girls." Hands planted on her waist Clara swiveled her hips setting her hooped skirt swinging. "I'm happy my girlfriends are smart."

Tilly twirled one of her long raven braids in the boys' direction. "We pay more attention in Lehrer Frederick's classes than you boys do."

The boys huffed their indignation.

Clara clapped her hands. "Let's see how smart you are with the clue for the second word:

"It runs with abandon to the sea

Meandering swift and free."

None of the girls deciphered the riddle, but one of the boys spoke up.

"If I may, a wild guess. The song title is *Blue Danube*?" Daniel, the family's carriage driver, winked at her. "Looks like the boys win this one, Clara."

You won my heart long ago, Daniel. What a perfect response that would be. Oh, but the rules. "Do you have your clue ready?" She fluttered her eyelashes in his direction.

"Oh, I do, Fraulein." A sly smile teased on his lips. Daniel nodded to each guest one by one. "My friends, we're all here —simple commoners—neighbors to the noble family we serve. We celebrate our friends' sixteenth birthday. Thank you for including us all, Gut Herr Reinhold."

Kraig touched his brow, followed by fingers drawing curlicues in the air. He bowed toward Daniel—the silly salute attested to the friendly camaraderie among them. "You have a clue for us, Daniel?"

"Ja. Ja. A play. Two words, or three."

"Which is it?" Georg Wolff snarled.

Daniel ignored him.

"First word

"Gallant lad wooing young lovebird

With charm and wit holds her enraptured."

Her blue eyes grew to the size of saucers. Tilly's gaze met Daniel's. Her mouth formed into a perfect "o". A giggle escaped. "Daniel, I do believe you refer to Romeo."

"Do we even need the second clue?" Curt asked.

"Tilly answered correctly. Even if the second is unnecessary, I took the time to compose it.

"Angel lass, the face of his sweetheart

Alas, naught on earth shall rip them apart."

"The answer is Juliet." Megs, Clara's best friend since childhood and baby sister to Georg, chimed in. "But Daniel and Clara fit if there was a play by that name.

Clara's cheeks burned from the glow of Megs' smile and the implications of her answer. While the teens chuckled, the adults' smiles turned upside down.

Georg's expression grew smug. "Daniel and Clara? Star-crossed, same as the Shakespeare couple." He erupted into a fit of laughter. "It can't happen. Lucky for me, she'll be mine one day."

Lucky in love. Memories of Georg's repulsive behavior three years earlier flooded Clara's mind. Her heart and her head sank. Her little sisters pulled at her skirts. Seven-year-old Hannah reached up for a hug.

Emmaline's head danced side-to-side. "Cake will make you smile, Clara. Is it time for cake?"

Curt joined his sisters. He drew a handkerchief from his pocket and blotted the tears working their way down Clara's cheeks. "Emmaline is right. Treats will make it all better. Mamsell received the delivery of our birthday cake from the Backhaus this morning, and it's ready to serve."

"We like to pass out napkins." Hannah took the neat linen stack and handed a few to Emmaline.

"What a perfect idea, girls." Curt nudged them on their way.

The two skipped among the guests. Emmaline chanted, "It's time to sing the birthday song."

"My turn to hug my favorite twins." Their Vati, the Baron of Gut Apfelhof, kissed his daughter on the cheek and extended a hand to his son. "You're so grown up now. A fatherly reminder is in order. We always welcome all our friends and neighbors, but we follow the rules of nobility when we choose a husband or wife."

Clara stood on tiptoes and returned a peck to his cheek. "Oh Vati, we are sixteen, not twenty-two!"

"I was among the partiers while you and your friends played the games today. Daniel's a fine man, but… "

"…but he is the carriage driver." Clara singsonged the remainder of Vati's sentence.

"Ja. And our neighbors, the Wolffs, are nobility. Gut Dinkelhof's boundaries lie just across the road. You'd live near us always. I'd like that. Think about it, Clara. I hear your Mutti calling for me."

"Is he suggesting what I think he is?" Curt pulled at his hair. "Oh, Clara, I'll protect your honor."

Daniel rubbed Clara's back. "I apologize, Clara. Not for my clues. Only for the embarrassment to you."

"You didn't embarrass me, Georg did. You impressed me with your clever clues."

"Georg is correct—at least strictly by the rules he is, but I'll not allow those to stand in the way. We've done everything together our whole life. I never want that to change."

"Nor do I." Clara rested her head against Daniel's shoulder.

With Curt as our witness, Clara Reinhold, I pledge to you that no matter our stations, I will always protect you from every threat to your happiness. Ja, that includes Georg. And I promise you my love forever."

"Thank you! And I promise you my heart belongs to you forever, Daniel Becker."

"That is a breach of the rules I stand behind. A promised union of my twin and my best friend." Curt moved behind the pair, allowing them a moment's privacy to seal their promises.

* * *

You may not have recognized the game Clara and her friends played as Charades.

During the 1880s instead of acting out the clues, the clues were spoken phrases or sentences with tricky wording—quite a contrast to the "no speaking" rule we follow today. And the lines of the clues were meant to rhyme!

You can learn more in Let's Talk Charades, a blog post on my website: https://lynnuwatson.com/lets-talk-charades/

Your turn: (NOTE: Only main words have clues. Answer may also include articles, prepositions and/or contractions that are not part of the clue. For example: the, and, of, etc.)

Song – 2 words:

1st clue: Shh. Not a sound

To be heard all around_________________

2nd clue: A drape of black

Dots of white may crack_________________

Movie – 2 words:

1st clue:Sweetly floats the sound of a bird

While a kitten softly purred________________

2nd clue: Written in dots and lines

And a myriad of signs________________

Book – 2 words:

1st clue:Rubbing it oh how smooth

Wrapped in it may soothe________________

2nd clue: A soft brown lump

Watch it jump__________________

Book – 2 words:

1st clue:Red, blue, green they come

And smallish as your thumb________________

2nd clue: Beat 'em up; knock 'em down

Unto a raging showdown__________________

Book & Movie – 2 words

1st clue:Underside painted red

And twigs for a bed__________________

2nd clue: A not so nice place to stay

Your head may tarry beneath all day__________________

CHALLENGE: Make up your own clues—**ONLY** titles of **clean** books, movies, & songs, please. Email them to me: lynn@lynnuwatson.com.

I'll share them to Coffee, Kuchen, and Good Books*—my Facebook Readers Group; We'll see if the group members can solve your riddles.

*Coffee Kuchen and Good Books readers group: https://www.facebook.com/groups/1108709330081009

Song—2 words:

Silent Night

Movie—2 words

Sound of Music

Book—2 words

Velveteen Rabbit

Book—2words

Grapes of Wrath

Book and Movie—2 words

Robin Hood

www.ingramcontent.com/pod-product-compliance
Lightning Source LLC
Chambersburg PA
CBHW072337020726
47506CB00004B/912

* 9 7 8 1 7 3 2 9 2 8 1 4 5 *